A STRANGE ATTRACTION

As Terri stared at the rolling landscape below, she saw no trace of modern life anywhere—only the endless hills and trees and grass. The only sign of civilization was Dun Cath, and in the world she knew, such things existed only as ancient ruins.

"My world is gone," she said. There could be no doubt of it now. She was truly in a different time, a different world.

Conaire walked up behind her and placed his hands on her shoulders. The warmth and strength in them flooded through her. "If your world is gone," he said gently, "then stay in this one."

She turned to him, focusing no longer on the wide expanse around her but only on this man. "I will stay," she answered. "And King Conaire, even if I had the choice to return—which I don't see that I do—I would still want to stay here. This is the most beautiful, exciting, adventurous place I have ever known, and I am drawn to it in ways I can't begin to describe to you."

Carefully he drew her close to him, stroking her long dark hair. "I would hope that you would be drawn to me, Teresa Maeve, as well as to the land I live on."

She hesitated, content to lean against that broad chest and feel the slow, strong beat of his heart. Finally she pulled back from him a step. "I stay here because I choose to stay here, Conaire. But I must earn my way and find my place here."

A pleased smile appeared. "I have no doubt of your place. You belong at my side, as my wife. As my queen."

Her eyes narrowed. "I will stay here on my own terms. I have just stated them. And they do not include being anyone's wife, or anyone's queen!"

QUEEN of THE SUN

Janeen O'Kerry

LOVE SPELL BOOKS   ⬦   NEW YORK CITY

For Chuck . . .
and all of his boys.

LOVE SPELL®

July 1998

Published by

Dorchester Publishing Co., Inc.
276 Fifth Avenue
New York, NY 10001

ISBN 0-505-52269-1

PRONUNCIATION GUIDE

Conaire—*CON-ah-ree*
Treise Maeve—*TRIH-sa MAYVE*
Firelair—*feer-ah-leer*
Dary—*DAH-ree*
Sean—*shawn*
Daoine Sidhe—*THEE-na SHEE*
ban sidhe—*ban shee*
banrion—*ban reeon*
ri—*ree*

QUEEN of The SUN

Chapter One

"Midsummer Eve is no time for a woman to ride out alone! And you are a stranger here!"

Old Sean set down the pony's foot, and glared at Terri as he picked up a heavy steel rasp. Without another word he lifted the hoof again and began smoothing and shaping it with the rasp. The black pony stood quietly, dozing in the cool aisleway of the old stone barn, and paid no attention whatever to Sean or Terri or the spectacular beauty of the Irish summer afternoon.

Terri MacEgan stood in the sunlit courtyard in front of the barn, dressed in a man's white shirt, smooth gray breeches, and high black boots. She had her hands on her hips and her temper in a boil.

No one back home—no *man* especially, not even one old enough to be her grandfather—would ever talk to her like that without getting a retort they wouldn't soon forget!

Terri wasn't sure just what she expected from this vacation, except maybe a little freedom. She wanted to gallop through the spectacular countryside on her own, not just ride across it at a walk with a group of tourists content to do slow single-file pony trekking. But though she'd only just arrived this morning, it seemed that everybody, from the tour guides to old Sean the stable man, was trying to tell her what to do.

She took a deep breath. All right, so County Tipperary,

Janeen O'Kerry

Ireland, was a bit different from Washington, D.C. Wasn't that what she had come to Ireland for? To experience something new and different for a while, and get out of the same old routine that had taken her nowhere?

Terri stepped into the cool darkness of the high-ceilinged barn. "So tell me," she said, walking around behind the pony. "Why shouldn't a woman ride alone on Midsummer Eve? What's so special about today?"

Sean peered up at her, frowning beneath thick silvery-gray brows. "'Tis the shortest night of the year," he growled. "A favorite night of the little people. They come out in numbers like no other time."

Terri snorted. "Little people? You mean leprechauns? I thought they give you a pot of gold if you catch them at the end of the rainbow, or something like that. Doesn't sound very dangerous to me."

Sean set down the pony's hoof and straightened up again. "I am not talking about silly stories meant to enchant the tourists and charm the money out of their pockets. I'm speaking of the *Daoine Sidhe*."

Terri frowned. *"Theena shee,"* she repeated. "I swear I'll never learn a word of Gaelic. It's got to be the most confusing language on Earth! Now, what does *theena shee* mean?"

"It means . . . the people of the hills. The fair folk. It's one of the old names for them in the Irish."

Now her curiosity was getting the better of her. All traces of her earlier annoyance faded away. "'Fair folk.' You mean fairies? Sure, I know about fairy tales and fairies. But *theena*—what was that word again? I've never heard fairies called by that name before."

"Daoine Sidhe," he said again. "The Host of the Unforgiven Dead. The ghosts of the pagan ancestors who do yet live in these hills and caves."

His voice was dead-serious. He certainly wasn't talking about leprechauns. A slight shiver ran through her and she

10

turned away, walking back out into the sunlight of the courtyard to gaze at the beautiful view.

The old stone barn sat high on a hill, overlooking some spectacular white limestone cliffs. A short distance away beside the cliffs stood a quaint old white brick house, at least one hundred years old, which now served as an inn for tourists come to Ireland for a riding vacation. But at Terri's feet lay the rolling hills and beautiful forests of County Tipperary.

The unspoiled land stretched on around her for as far as she could see; green and lush with grass and cloaked in the ancient majesty of towering oaks and silvery birches. She breathed deep, and the gentle breeze brought to her the sweetest of scents: grass and flowers basking in the warmth of the summer sun.

Trails led into those cool shadowed forests and through those grassy fields. She wanted nothing more than to get back on one of the ponies and finish what the brief riding tour this morning had begun. She wanted to explore this new and lovely land! It called to her, it drew her in, as no place ever had before.

Here was a place she could lose herself in—here was a place of adventure! It held new experiences, things she had never seen or heard of. Her heart beat faster at the mere thought of riding down those trails and into those secretive woods. What might she find out there?

Then a movement caught her eye. She looked closer, and for just a moment another shiver ran through her.

The ghosts of the pagan ancestors . . . who do yet live in these hills and caves.

"Well, somebody lives out there," she said as casually as she could. "Look—that way, on the highest hill. A fire's burning."

Sean stepped quickly out of the barn to stand beside her. His eyes widened slightly, and his fist clenched around the steel rasp.

11

Far in the distance, on the highest of the grass-covered hills, a slender column of wispy black smoke rose straight up into the blue summer sky. "Every year, it burns," Sean whispered. "The fire burns on Midsummer Eve."

"Only on Midsummer Eve? Who lights it? I don't see any roads or houses. They'd have to hike a ways to get there."

"No one knows who lights it. No one ever goes near that place. It is a fairy fort, and not to be disturbed—by *anyone*." He looked pointedly at her.

Terri's chin rose, and she grinned. "Now, what could be the harm in riding out to such a beautiful place—especially if no one else ever goes near it? This is just the sort of thing I came to Ireland to see!"

But his scowl became even fiercer, if that were possible. "It is a fairy fort," he said again. "It is their domain and not to be trespassed upon. Mortals can be drawn into such a place—and in the land of the fair folk, a century can seem like an hour. Such mortals are never seen again."

Terri could only stare at him. He was serious. He truly believed what he was saying. And before she could think of an answer, he had untied the shaggy black pony and begun leading him back to his stall.

Suddenly she hurried after him. "Sean! Wait!"

He stopped. She reached for the pony's lead rope. "I won't be any trouble. I'll just take Ri. *Ri* means king, doesn't it? That's what the tour guide said. They assigned me to Ri because he's the tallest of the trekking ponies and the others really didn't suit me—I'm so tall, practically six feet."

He looked at her, his head cocked slightly, as though he were seeing her for the first time. "So you are," he said. "And you have something of the old coloring about you . . . the dark hair, and the eyes clear and light as glass. . . ."

His voice trailed away. Again, Terri was surprised. What was he talking about? And why was he staring at her? But she plunged on ahead. "Anyway, Ri and I got along just fine on the trekking tour this morning, so you know I'll be all right with him. I'll saddle him myself. I don't want to cause you any more work."

But Sean only studied her closely, his old gaze so hard and unwavering that she felt certain he would never agree to let her take the pony out.

Terri set her jaw. "Please! I cannot stay in on such a glorious evening! I didn't come all the way to Ireland to stay inside and play cards as if I were still back home in my own apartment! I'll go out on foot if I have to. I'll walk until—"

"Wait here," he said.

He left her standing there with Ri. As she watched, he took a fine leather halter and lead shank from the tack room and then opened the door to another stall.

In a moment he led out another horse, and Terri breathed a sigh of admiration. This was no shaggy, plodding pony for the trekking tourists. Beside Sean walked a powerful, silver-gray mare, so tall her back was as high as Terri's head.

The mare's steel shoes rang on the stone floor of the barn. Her long silvery tail swept the surface of the stones. Her liquid brown eyes and aristocratic face held a calm intelligence as she walked up to Terri.

"Now, this is something else I came here hoping to see," Terri murmured, reaching out to touch the lovely mare. Its short slick coat was warm and smooth beneath her fingers. "An Irish hunter. No other horse like them in the world."

"And no horse like Firelair, either," Sean said. "Do you know the story of the true mare?"

"True mare," Terri said. "No, I don't think so."

"Well, now. The true mare, being the seventh filly foal in an unbroken line of filly foals, keeps any who ride her safe from all harm. No evil can ever touch such a mare . . . and in a race, she will never be bested."

13

Terri raised an eyebrow at the story, but smiled instead of saying anything as the mare touched its gentle nose to her hand.

"If you must ride out tonight," Sean said, "I'll have you ride none but the true mare."

Terri gathered the black leather reins and swung up on the silver-gray mare. From high above the ground she looked out at the wide Irish countryside, at the beautiful dusky sunlight and the shadows just beginning to lengthen.

Firelair walked with long strides down the narrow paved road away from the inn. Terri glanced at her wristwatch. Just past seven-thirty; plenty of time to ride to the highest hill and back. It didn't get completely dark until nearly ten o'clock this time of year. Besides, she felt that she could ride to the moon and back on this fabulous Irish horse!

She turned off the road and onto a worn path leading through the field, always keeping the high hill with the bonfire in sight. Firelair went willingly, and began to trot through the fragrant grass.

At that moment, Terri forgot all of the fatigue and small irritations of her long trip. She was here in the most beautiful, inviting land she had ever imagined, riding the finest horse it had ever been her privilege to sit. Faster and faster they went, trotting on, now cantering, now galloping, now jumping over the low drystone wall that divided the field of sweet grass.

At this moment, it seemed possible that she would never want to go back to her life in Washington, D.C. The farther she rode, and the more the sun-warmed breeze caressed her face, the more unbearable the very thought became.

What did she have to go back to? A high-powered advertising job that kept her locked in a tower of glass and steel day after day after day. If she looked out a window, all she would see was the thousands of other people in their own high-pressure jobs in the other cold steel towers.

And at the end of the day, when she finally did get back to her own small apartment inside yet another tower of glass and steel, what waited for her there? Only emptiness.

She had thought that that life would lead to money and success, and so it had. But she had never thought it would also lead to loneliness. Everyone, it seemed, had fallen into the same trap she had—the trap of endless commutes, relentless pressure, and meaningless work that was never, ever finished and left her with no time for a life of her own—a personal life.

Terri closed her eyes. This last relationship, she swore, had been the end—the end of men who were such a poor match for her own strength, her own sense of adventure, her own lust for life. The men she encountered seemed only to want her for what she could do for them—not for what the two of them could do together. Such relationships might be good enough for other women, but not for her.

But she could not forget the loneliness, the despair that sometimes caught up with her in the dark silence of the nights. Would she always be alone? Was that the price of her freedom?

Or was she asking too much? Most people—men and women both—seemed happy enough to have a mate who was nice-looking and well educated and gainfully employed. And most of all, predictable and safe. Why couldn't it be enough for her, too?

The mare halted. Terri looked up through the haze of her thoughts. She found herself in the shadows at the foot of the highest hill, from the very top of which a thin black column of smoke rose into a twilight sky.

She quickly forgot her worries. They were here!

For a moment she hesitated—the sun had set and the light was beginning to fade—but the top of the hill and that mysterious fire drew her like a magnet.

The chance to see this place might never come again. She leaned forward and touched her heels to Firelair's sides, and the mare instantly launched herself into a canter up the grassy side of the hill.

The powerful mare took only a few moments to reach the top. Terri halted her to let her catch her breath—and to try to catch her own at the sights that lay before them.

Crowning the hill beneath the pale white half-moon was a huge, circular, crumbling earthen wall. The rain and winds of many centuries had worn it down and even collapsed it in spots, leaving it towering ten feet tall in some places and dipping to only a foot or two in others. The whole thing enclosed an area at least two hundred yards across. And in the very center of that vast circle, beside a tall and timeworn tree, was a smoking, snapping bonfire.

Terri rode straight to the wall and began to walk the mare around it. She was so close that she could reach out and touch the ancient structure with her left hand. The wall seemed to have been made of dirt and small stones heaped over a framework of heavy timbers, most of which were now broken and rotted and sticking out through the old earth and stone. Bright tufts of grass grew all over the earthen heap, as if trying to cover and heal the damage done by the relentless years.

She continued to circle, the horse walking the first time around, trotting the next, and then cantering the next. Terri caught tantalizing glimpses of the bonfire inside as she rode past the low spots in the wall. Finally she found just the right place and turned Firelair away, moved off several feet, turned her around again, and aimed her straight at a two-foot-high section of the crumbling wall.

The mare cleared it with a small hop, and cantered over the lush grass within the ancient circle. Terri slowed her to a walk and approached the bonfire.

Within the crackling red and orange flames she could see precisely stacked wood. Surrounding the pyre was a wide area of ash and bare soil ringed with heavy stones. Clearly, this fire had been carefully built and deliberately set.

How strange it was to find a man-made blaze in this utterly deserted place! Yet it seemed to Terri entirely right that these flames should burn, no matter who had set them. This fire was an offering, a reflection of heat and light to the very powers that kindled and fed every fire—the winds and the trees and the ever-burning sun.

If ever there was a place of magic, of power, where great and wonderful things had happened in ages past, this walled enclosure was that place.

She started to turn away, but a sudden bright gleam in the grass caught her eye. Curious, Terri dismounted and led Firelair toward the flames.

Yes, there was something there, lying almost hidden in the long lush grass near the firestones: a bit of metal, bright and softly glinting in the fading evening light. She reached for it and picked it up.

A ring. A lovely gold ring, looking clean and new as though someone had dropped it there only moments before.

She examined it closely. It was heavy and wide, but small in size, as if made to fit a woman's hand rather than a man's. Yet she could see that this was no store-bought bit of costume jewelry. It had an old-fashioned, handmade look, and its surface was covered with the most delicately carved designs—beautiful designs like nothing she had ever seen before. She had to hold the ring up to make out what they were, turning it in the last light of the sun.

Flames. The gold ring was covered with engraved flames, an unbroken circle of them.

As far as she could tell, there were no initials or inscriptions on the ring's inner surface that might identify it. She would just have to take it back with her to the inn and leave it with the staff; no doubt whoever had lost it would be very happy to regain such a beautiful piece.

Terri started to tuck the ring in her shirt pocket—but found she simply couldn't resist. She slipped it on her right finger, and it rested there as though it had been made for her.

So much for Sean's insistence that no one ever comes up here! Terri set her foot in the stirrup and swung back up on the mare. As she settled herself in the saddle, she found herself hoping that no one would claim the ring. A lovelier remembrance of her trip to Ireland would be hard to imagine.

A safe distance from the bonfire stood a solitary tree. She turned away from the blaze and walked the mare to the tree, wondering how it had come to be the only growing thing on this hill besides the grass.

The tree was huge. It towered over her head and over the ancient walls. Terri guessed that it must be forty feet tall. The light gray bark was cracked with age, yet the tree was still covered with fresh new leaves of dark green. Its lacy white flowers gave off a strong perfume in the warm evening breeze.

Far in the distance, against the blue-black sky, she could just see the striking white cliffs of the hill beside the inn. A few signs of modern civilization were readily apparent— the twinkling lights of the inn, the tiny moving headlights of a car on a distant winding road. Yet they hardly seemed real, hardly a part of this strange and wonderful place that she had found.

In the limestone rocks at the foot of the tree was a spring of clear water, just a small pool a few feet across. As the mare lowered her head to drink, Terri's thoughts drifted back to old Sean and his warnings about this particular hilltop.

Why had Sean seemed so convinced that this was a dangerous place? It was so peaceful, so unimaginably beautiful. Surely, Terri thought, if there was anything threatening or dangerous here, the horse would be the first to sense it. But Firelair stood calmly by the tree and drank from the pool, her only movement an occasional swish of her tail.

Terri felt as though she were standing at the center of the universe. All around her was the great circle of the horizon, the twilight sky a deepening blue that became a red glow where the sun was setting.

At last she looked up into the sky. The stars had begun to appear. There, not far above the setting sun, hung a group of three stars—one red, one silver, and one gold.

She caught her breath. The planets had come together this night in a rare and special way. Now, what could be more appropriate to such a place than this beautiful conjunction gleaming far above it? She could only wonder how long it had been since the world had last seen this particular grouping of planets—a hundred years, five hundred, a thousand?

Terri sighed. Probably as long as it had been since the men she dreamed of walked these lands—the powerful, noble men who once climbed these very hills and looked at these same stars.

Men had not always been the tame, drab, work-obsessed creatures of the city that she dealt with in the present. In another age, another time, things had been very different. Men had been as wild and as strong and as full of life as this land they had once commanded, willing to lay down their lives for the women they loved.

Chapter Two

In the heavy blue twilight just before the set of the sun, King Conaire and two of his men rode their weary horses to the very top of the hill and walked them to the grove of elder trees. The deep green leaves of the trees were already blending in with the night, but their flat wide flowers gleamed out of the darkness like stars.

Conaire halted his horse and breathed deep of the flowers' heavy fragrance. Before him lay his land, his world, shadowed and peaceful in the fading light.

"Is it still light enough to see where we are?" asked Ros, hurrying up alongside him.

"Can you see our fire?" asked Sivney, making a rather precarious halt beside Ros. He guided his horse with one hand, and kept the other placed firmly on the small young stag draped in front of him over his horse's shoulders.

"There," Conaire said. All three were silent for a moment, their attention held by a small bright spot on a distant, smaller hill.

"It'll take us half this night, at least, to get there," said Sivney. "We'll only be walking, what with the darkness and this load I'm carrying."

"Then half a night it will be," said Conaire. He walked his horse a short way into the grove, where a spring bubbled up out of the ground and formed a small pool among

20

the rocks. He dismounted and knelt down to drink, even as his red stallion reached down to the pool.

The other two soon joined him, and men and horses drank deep of the sweet cold water. Conaire led his horse out of the trees and looked again at the small point of brightness on the faraway hilltop.

"The solstice fire," said Ros, standing on the grass beside him with his quiet bay horse. "The people are not going to be pleased that their king is late."

Conaire glanced at him. "I think they would be even less pleased to know that their king—and his two most trusted friends—caught a glimpse of a broken-legged stag and simply rode on past. It was important to track the creature down and finish it at once, not leave it to die in pain days from now. And I think they'll be happy enough to have the venison."

Sivney walked up to join them, his stag-laden horse dropping its head down to graze on the lush grass. "I believe they'd be even happier to have you bring them a queen," he said. "They were hoping that this time—"

"This time was just like all the other times," Conaire said. "That woman would never make a queen. She was quiet and polite and pretty enough, and in truth, Sivney, I think *you* ought to marry her"—Sivney grinned, and quickly reached up to steady the stag as his grazing horse took a step forward—"but she was not a queen."

"Can you be so certain?" asked Ros. "You merely sat and spoke to her. All the others had to pass at least one of your tests. Why not her?"

Conaire shook his head. "There was no need for any of the tests. She was not a queen, and never will be."

"Are you sure you're not frightening the women away with these tests of yours, Conaire?" Ros went on. "It's not the usual way to—"

"Nothing will frighten away my queen. Nothing in this world or any other."

21

The sun disappeared beneath the horizon. In the blue-black sky above it gleamed three bright stars nearly together—one red, one silver, and one gold.

"Now, there is a rare sight," said Ros.

"Almost as rare as a clear sky at sunset in Eire," added Sivney.

Conaire took a step forward. "We'll have no trouble finding our way back to Dun Cath tonight with such a guide," he whispered.

"Maybe it's a good sign," said Ros. "If something like this can appear in the sky, then maybe Conaire's queen can be found, too."

Conaire turned and swung up on his horse's bare back. The other two men quickly pulled their horses' heads up from the grass and did the same.

"I make no apologies," Conaire said. "I have said many times that I will have no ordinary queen and neither will my people. A bad queen is as harmful as a bad king. If she is timid, or barren, or shrewish, or petty—"

He shook his head. "A woman like that can poison a kingdom and destroy a king. I swear that I will have a queen worthy of our people and our land, a woman strong and noble, beautiful and brave. A woman worth dying for!"

His voice echoed from the distant hills. As if in answer to his shouted oath the wind suddenly stirred, blowing the high thin clouds beneath the shining stars of the conjunction.

The wind picked up, lifting Terri's hair just as the sun dropped below the horizon. Night was descending, but she was unconcerned; she could still see the twinkling lights of the inn and the pale white cliffs beside it. The shining half-moon and the red-orange glow of the bonfire would light her way down the hill.

She really should be going . . . but it was difficult to leave this peaceful, magical place.

At last she took up the reins to turn Firelair around. But as she did, a sudden gust of wind whirled and whipped around them, sending the smoke and sparks of the bonfire rolling over them both in a thick, stinging, choking black cloud.

The land and sky and bright stars of the conjunction all vanished in the swirling blackness. Terri struggled for breath, and the mare snorted and danced beneath her, clearly as disoriented as her rider.

Terri rubbed her stinging eyes on her white shirt sleeve, and then kicked Firelair with both heels to drive her out of the smoke. The mare made a tremendous leap forward, and Terri grabbed her mane with both hands to stay with her.

For a long, long moment, Terri rode Firelair through air and darkness. The earth seemed to have vanished. There was only black silence and the sensation of floating.

At last, after what seemed like an eternity, the mare came back to solid ground and stepped gingerly over the grass. Terri took a deep breath of the fresh night air and felt better—they were out of the smoke. She twisted in the saddle to glance back at the bonfire. That had been a strong gust of wind; she hoped it had not scattered any sparks.

But where the fire had burned a moment before, there was nothing. Nothing but darkness, and lush grass rippling in the gentle night breeze.

She turned around to face forward again. Yes, there were the three stars of the conjunction, red and silver and gold, just where they had been before. She was certain that the fire had been behind her.

Terri looked the other way, towards the spring and the towering tree. But in that spot now was an entire grove of trees, smaller trees not quite ten feet tall, with dark green leaves and flat white flowers. They surrounded the spring where she had let Firelair drink just a few minutes ago.

What was happening here? She had not imagined the bonfire. There had been no grove of trees, just one very large tree. And Firelair had not been nervous about being up here, as she was now, still dancing and snorting and trying to turn around to face the way they had come.

Terri decided that she'd had enough, too. She let the mare turn around, intending to jump the low spot in the wall and get out, but now the grove of trees was in the way.

The mare galloped around to the other side of the grove—and then skidded to a violent stop. Terri threw her arms around the mare's neck to keep from bouncing off, and looked up to see what had frightened the horse.

She caught her breath. Not twenty yards away were three men on horseback, just standing there in the grass, gazing out at the stars.

She couldn't believe her eyes. No one had been up here a few moments ago. Had they followed her? Who were they?

Their horses suddenly jumped and started. All three swung around to look at her. But Terri was not about to wait around and find out who these men were—Firelair wanted out of there, and so did she.

Terri began searching for the wall—it was hard to see in the darkness, without the bonfire's light.

But the mare galloped on, and began making her way down the side of the hill. There had been no sign of the crumbling wall. There was nothing on that hilltop but grass and a grove of trees—and three strange men who hadn't been there a moment before.

Firelair reached the bottom of the hill and galloped on into the starlit, moonlit night. She needed no guidance, and was intent on going in just one direction—towards home! Terri knew she could trust the horse to return to her own barn, so she just leaned forward over the flying silver mane and let the mare take whatever path she wanted.

But as they raced through the shadowy darkness, Terri began to feel a growing uncertainty. On the trip towards the bonfire they had followed a paved road for a time, but there was no trace of it now. They had jumped at least one low stone wall and passed a couple of small farmhouses, but now she could not make out any walls or houses anywhere in the darkened fields.

The disappearance of the landmarks left her cold with fear and confusion. She was alone in a strange and deserted country—and there was nothing to do but stay with Firelair and hope the mare could find their way home.

Were those hoofbeats she heard behind her? No—it couldn't be—she must be hearing the echoes of Firelair's pounding strides as she raced between the hills, and the sound of her own swiftly beating heart.

At last they came in sight of the high white cliffs. Terri was certain that they were the same cliffs that stood beside the resort inn—she'd never seen anything like them before. But there was no sign of the inn or its lights.

Firelair galloped straight to the top of the hill beside the cliffs, the spot where the old stone barn had stood. She stopped beside a tree, fretting, and Terri flinched as she suddenly whinnied loud and long into the night.

There was no barn here now. Like the other hilltop where the bonfire had burned, there was nothing in this place but grass and stars and windy darkness.

Terri froze as a sound came out of that darkness—the ringing, answering neigh of a stallion.

Hoofbeats rose up from the bottom of the hill. And before she could move or react, three men on horseback galloped up out of the darkness and quickly blocked any path she might take to escape them.

For a moment she kept still and tried to think. Firelair, too, stood motionless, her ears flicking back and forth as she watched the men in front and behind and alongside her. But the mare did not seem frightened. Was it possible that she knew these men and their horses?

Terri looked closely at them. They did not resemble any

25

of the men she had seen at the resort. These three rode bareback on small powerful horses with proud arching necks. Their clothing was of a type she'd never seen before, not even in Ireland—soft boots with laces wrapped up the calf to the knee, and wool cloaks pinned over their shoulders with heavy gleaming brooches.

As they stood silhouetted in the light of the half-moon, she could see their long hair blowing wild and free in the night breeze. One of them, the tall one with the broad shoulders who sat his horse as if he owned the world, had a soft curling beard as well. She could not see his face, but his gaze was burning through her, she could feel it. . . .

"What do you want?" she demanded in her strongest voice.

The bearded man nudged his horse forward. Terri tensed and lifted the reins, and instantly the mare raised her head and flicked her ears back.

But the man came no closer. Instead, he began to speak to her.

His face was in shadow and she could see nothing of what he looked like. All she could hear was his voice, a soft, calm voice that nonetheless carried the weight of authority. That voice told her that he was not young, but not old either, and strong, and accustomed to being heeded when he spoke.

For a moment she simply listened to him in fascination. He was speaking in Gaelic, she was certain; the native language of Ireland sounded like nothing else.

But she could not understand the words. He spoke and then paused, spoke and then paused again, clearly asking her a question and waiting for her to answer.

"I'm sorry," she said. "I don't speak Gaelic. I don't understand you."

The man glanced at his two companions and then said something to them, pointing at Terri's hands.

Puzzled, she looked down at her hands—and froze.

26

There, gleaming in the moonlight, were her gold ring and diamond-trimmed wristwatch.

She could have kicked herself. Here she was, Ms. Street-Smart Terri MacEgan, caught alone in the middle of nowhere with her best and most expensive jewelry displayed for all the world—and every robber in it—to see.

Well, there was nothing to do now but brave it out. "I must be going," she said, beginning to back Firelair away from the little group. "My friends are waiting for me. I—"

But the bearded man spoke quickly to the other two, who answered him in turn. Terri braced herself, and the mare pinned her ears flat against her head, as all three men pressed their horses forward and surrounded her.

"No!" Terri shouted. Firelair lunged forward, shoving the smaller horses out of her way, and as she snorted and plunged, Terri tore off the wristwatch.

Turning in the saddle, she flung it at the men. "There! Take it! It's all I've got! I don't have anything else to give you! Now leave me alone!" And with that she kicked the mare into a gallop and went plunging down the side of the hill into the darkness, hoping that the watch would be enough to satisfy them and send them looking elsewhere if they wanted more loot.

She wasn't about to give them the gold ring. They'd just have to be content with a watch worth a mere few hundred dollars.

After a perilous, sliding descent down the dark slippery slope, she reached the silhouetted trees at the foot of the hill. Terri turned the mare and sent her into a gallop along the trees, searching in the blackness for a place to enter the forest and hide from her pursuers. Firelair's silvery coat would be too easily seen in this moonlight—they would have to find some cover, a clearing in the woods—anyplace would do if it would keep her out of sight.

In the next instant she had thrown herself forward and was clutching desperately at Firelair's mane as the mare stood up to her full height on her hind legs. Her eyes wide with sudden fright, Terri caught a glimpse of a man standing directly beneath the silver mare's wildly pawing steel-shod hooves—a bearded man with long hair and the gleam of gold upon his broad chest.

Firelair dropped back hard to the earth. And stood perfectly still as the man closed one hand over her reins and reached up to Terri with the other.

He opened that hand, and held out her diamond wristwatch.

Terri could only stare at him as her heart pounded. Then he spoke, and she knew the voice. This was the same man who had tried to talk to her on the top of the hill. The man with the soft, authoritative voice.

He took a step forward, and now she could begin to see his face more clearly, though it was still shadowed. He did indeed have a beard, soft and curling, and windblown hair down to his shoulders. His eyes glinted beneath thick dark brows, his gaze level and unwavering. His age was hard to guess; not so young as she might have guessed at first, but not old, either, perhaps not much older than she was.

Again he spoke, in the soft hypnotic Gaelic that sounded as sweet as birdsong. His hand was still open and he raised it toward her, clearly urging her to take the watch.

Keeping a wary eye on him, Terri reached out and lifted her watch from his palm. She was careful not to touch him. He smiled broadly as she tucked it in her shirt pocket.

Then he reached out and placed his hand on her knee.

Shocked at that warm touch, feeling such strength in the iron hand that it seemed he must be a giant instead of an ordinary man, Terri's nerve broke and she snapped into action. *"Ha! Run!"* she shouted, and swung Firelair away from the man to send her galloping back down the tree line the way she had come.

Terri was not going to wait for anything else to appear out of the night. She turned the mare straight into the dark woods, crashing through the brush until the trees surrounded her. At last she stopped and cautiously turned around, peering through the forest until she could catch a glimpse of the hillside.

Something was moving out there. Black shadows—two, or perhaps three, she was too far away to tell—moved silently down the grass-covered slope of the hill. They were men on horseback. As Terri watched, they cantered off back the way they had come and vanished into the night.

She breathed a great sigh of relief. Now she and Firelair could take shelter within these woods until dawn, when she could get her bearings and decide what to do next.

It was frightening, being out here alone in this silent, empty darkness, lost in a strange and baffling country. But she had no other choice that she could see; she would have to stay in this place and care for herself and Firelair as best she could, and try to find her way home in the morning.

Right now they needed both water and shelter. Down the back of the hill, behind the place where the old stone barn had stood, she remembered seeing a brook. Cautiously she rode out of the forest, careful to stay in the shadows, but saw no sign of any men or horses. She followed the line of trees around the foot of hill until she heard a clear trickling sound and saw a bright glimmer in the moonlight.

Yes, there was a brook here, winding among the trees. She resolved not to think about whether or not it was the same brook that had wound behind the same barn she remembered—a barn that was now alarmingly absent.

She dismounted and looked up at the great silver mare, amazed at just how tall Firelair really was, and then quickly unsaddled her. Looking in one of the saddlebags, Terri found a black leather halter and lead, which she slipped on the mare's head in place of the bridle.

Firelair was damp all over, and had patches of sweat on her back and head from the equipment, but there was nothing to rub her down with. So Terri used her hands to groom the mare, who responded by gratefully rubbing her itchy head hard against Terri's hand.

She let Firelair drink from the brook, and then led her into the deepest shadows of the trees to tie her securely. At last they were safe—or so she hoped. The men on the hilltop seemed to have lost interest in her, and at any rate hadn't seemed bent on harm. Maybe they were just curious about her, a foreigner out riding alone after dark.

They must have been gypsies, she decided. She'd read about the Irish gypsies, traveling famiies with horse-drawn wagons who went from town to town in search of work. Most likely those three had just been heading back to their camp after a long day's work.

After all, she told herself, this was quiet, rural Ireland— not the downtown streets of a U.S. city. It hardly seemed likely that she would encounter roving bands of criminals out here. Those men had not even wanted the watch she'd tried to give them.

Well, whoever they were, they were long gone by now. She sat down wearily in the grass and reached into her shirt pocket for her watch. Once it was back on her wrist, she dragged the saddle over and began rummaging in the other saddlebag.

She found a hoof pick and a silver flask, and smiled. Sean had thought of both the mare's feet and Terri's comfort. Silently thanking the old stableman for his consideration, she lifted the silver flask to drink—and froze.

Rising from the very top of the hill, clearly visible against the moonlit night sky and lit from below by the orange glow of a campfire, was a thin black column of smoke.

Chapter Three

Her heart pounded. It would seem that the men had not left after all. Was it safe for her to stay here? Maybe she should go—leave this deserted place and just keep going until she found some sign of civilization, of modern life.

Terri picked up the flask, lifted the saddle, and started to go to Firelair—and nearly collided with a tall bearded man.

She gasped, but made no other sound—just hugged the saddle tight and stared at him in shock.

It was him! The same man who had followed her and returned her wristwatch. But how had he gotten here? She had heard no sound from within the forest, seen no one moving across the rippling grass. Firelair stood calmly beneath the trees, watching with interest and not alarmed in the least. How had he managed to creep up on them?

"What do you want from me?" she demanded. "Go away! Leave me alone!"

Smiling politely, the man offered her what looked like a small package wrapped loosely in a piece of fabric. When she simply looked at him wide-eyed, he set the package in the grass at her feet and vanished back into the darkness of the trees.

Terri stood motionless for a moment, listening. There was no sound except the singing of the brook and the soft breeze in the trees. Then curiosity got the better of her, and she set down the saddle and reached for the package.

It was a small bundle of coarse plain fabric that she recognized as linen. She unwrapped the linen and found two pieces of flat bread, with a layer of what seemed to be butter and honey between them. On top of the bread was a thick slice of cheese.

She could hardly believe her eyes. Her first thought had been that he had come to do her some harm. But he had only brought her food, and then politely gone away.

Well, she was not one to waste an opportunity when it came along. Cautiously tasting the honey with one finger, she found it delicious—and quickly devoured the rest of the meal he had brought her, walking back beneath the trees to share a piece with Firelair.

"I suppose if I have to be lost and alone in a foreign country, it's nice to be lost and alone in one that thoughtfully provides a midnight snack," she murmured as the mare took the bread and honey from her hand.

Walking back to the saddle, she wondered again who this strange man was—this man who seemed so concerned about her. She might never know, and the thought brought with it a strange feeling of disappointment. There was something about him . . . he was certainly not like any man she had ever encountered back home. Such strength, such fearlessness . . . the soft deep voice, the piercing gaze she could feel even in the darkness . . .

Terri sat down and closed her eyes, bone-weary from the long, bizarre day she had just endured. She pulled the saddle close and, with a soft groan, laid her head down on it. In a moment she was asleep.

The soft night wind brushed her cheek. Terri rolled over, seeking to get more comfortable, but still it moved with gentle insistence across her face . . . touching her, caressing her. . . .

Her eyes flew open and she was on her feet in an instant. "What are *you* doing here?" she cried.

The bearded man sat cross-legged on the ground, looking up at her with a mild expression. The golden brooch at his shoulder gleamed in the darkness, as did the heavy gold neck-piece at his throat. "How long have you been sitting here next to me?" she demanded, pushing her dark tangled hair out of her face. "How long did you sit there touching me?"

She could not be sure how long she had been asleep. The moon had risen well above the trees, and she felt chilled and damp. It must have been hours.

He made no answer. He merely smiled, gently, reassuringly, and then got slowly to his feet.

He stepped into the moonlight and allowed it to shine down directly on him, deliberately showing himself to her. As before, she saw the soft beard and long hair and shining eyes. Now she could also see smooth skin and strong features, and an expression of kindness and amusement on a fine and noble face.

But now, standing so close to him, she could also feel the very essence of power, of protectiveness, flowing over and around her.

The man before her was no sneaking thief or cowardly criminal. This man stood as though he owned the land and everything on it, bold and hiding nothing, practically inviting her to study him. And study him she did.

His cloak, heavy with fringe, was thrown back over his right shoulder. Beneath it he wore a sleeveless shirt of some kind, and she saw for the first time how powerfully muscled his arms were. The right arm bore a slender twisted armband, resembling a gold serpent, wrapped around the thick muscles just below his shoulders. A similar curved piece of heavy gold rested around his neck. His chest was so broad that she wondered if her arms could reach around it. And even more than his physical power was the sheer boldness, the fearlessness, that she could sense from him.

"We don't have anything like you back home in D.C.,"

she whispered. "Who *are* you?" But he did not answer. Instead, he reached up and took her hand, smiling into her eyes.

She should have pulled away . . . but his eyes, shining with the reflected light of the moon, held her fast, as did his infinitely gentle touch and the boundless strength that pulsed beneath it.

Terri felt no fear of him. It seemed plain that since she could not understand his language, he was trying to communicate with her as best he could. He seemed to want to comfort her, to reassure her.

"I really am glad to see you," she began. There was no way to know if he could understand the English words or not, but she had to try! "I seem to be lost . . . and I could really use some help."

He smiled, and his expression became almost playful. It was a strange combination, this power and playfulness. But she forgot about that as his fingers began caressing hers. He touched her ring, running his strong finger delicately over the finely wrought gold, and then he lifted her hand so that the moon could shine down on the ring.

"Beautiful, isn't it?" she said. "I found it while I was riding out today. I'm hoping no one will claim it. I have to admit, I'd love to keep it." He glanced at her, but made no reply. "It would certainly make a wonderful souvenir of my trip to Ireland," she went on, glad to have something to talk about. It made her feel more comfortable to hear the sound of conversation, even if it was rather one-sided.

She cocked her head to study the ring. The delicate flames seemed to dance along its surface in the moonlight. "It's very special. Almost certainly one of a kind. I feel sorry for whoever lost it."

He gazed at her again, and it was clear that he did not understand a word she said. Terri sighed, and started to withdraw her hand.

But before she could do so, the man took hold of the

ring and slipped it from her finger. Without so much as a backward glance he turned away and began walking back up the hill, out in the open in the moonlight, heading straight for the fire that burned at the very top.

"Hey!"

Shock and indignation shot through Terri. Just when she'd thought he was actually looking out for her—that he was such a kind man!

She hurried after him, up the steep slope slippery with long grass. "I thought you came to return my watch, not steal my ring. I want that ring back, and I want it *now*!"

He paid her absolutely no attention. He climbed to the top of the hill—the hill where the black smoke from the campfire still rose into the starry sky—and stood calmly beneath the glowing half-moon, holding her ring up high to examine it.

Terri reached the top of the hill, and paused. Beside the red-orange glow of the fire sat the two other men who had ridden after her. One of them roasted chunks of meat on sticks propped over the flames, while the other worked diligently with a knife on something spread out on the ground in front of him—a deer, she saw, recoiling slightly: the body of a slaughtered deer. Glancing at the shadowed trees, she saw the dark silhouettes of three small horses.

The two men looked up at her and stared long and hard, but made no move to get up. The bearded man walked close beside the fire and held out her ring in the flat of his hand.

For a moment Terri feared he would drop the ring into the flames. But instead, he looked up into the sky, up where the three shining planets of the conjunction looked back down at him. He raised his hands high, palms up, as though inviting the light of the planets to shine down on the ring—shine down red and silver and gold.

Then he crouched beside the fire and gazed down at the ring, closely, intently, seeming to speak directly to it. Finally he tossed it from hand to hand through the crackling flames, once, twice, three times.

Terri stalked over to the men and stopped beside the fire. She stood with her feet braced and her hands on her hips, glaring at all three of them, shaking with anger. "That is *my* ring! *My* property! It belongs to *me,* and I *demand* that you return it!"

The bearded man looked up and smiled, and handed the ring to Terri as though it were a gift he had brought especially for her. With a cold glare she snatched the gleaming ring from his palm and slipped it back on her finger.

The gold felt hot and alive after its passes through the flames; it tingled, almost electric, as if it had been struck by lightning. Terri rubbed her finger and gazed down haughtily at the bearded man. "If you expect me to thank you, you're going to be waiting a long time." She raised her chin and turned her back on him, intending to return to her little camp at the foot of the hill.

"I have already been waiting a long time for you," came the soft low voice from behind her. "A long time. And now you are here."

Terri whirled around. Her indignation rose even more, though she would not have thought it possible. "You didn't tell me you could speak English!"

"You did not tell me you could speak Gaelic," he answered.

"I can't speak Gaelic—!" In frustration, she let the matter drop. There were more important things to worry about just now.

The bearded man got to his feet and stood close, nearly eye to eye with her. For the first time, she noticed that she was almost as tall as he was. But by now she didn't care how tall or short he was—she had had quite enough of his bizarre actions! Terri started to turn away, but the man caught hold of her hand and began to caress the tender skin beneath her wrist. His eyes never left hers.

"Strange and wonderful things do happen on Midsummer Eve, beneath such strange and beautiful stars." His voice was even more arresting now that she could understand the words.

Terri held still, listening, looking up into his shadowed face. Her breath caught as she waited for him to speak again. But he looked away into the starry night sky, beyond the glare of the flames and into the clear darkness. With some reluctance her gaze followed his.

Again she saw the beautiful conjunction, three planets gleaming red and silver and gold against the blackness. It was the only remnant of the world she had thought of as her own, the only thing she recognized from before . . . before she had gone off alone to investigate that mysterious bonfire out there on the highest hill.

He looked at her again and smiled, reaching down to take her other hand. "And strangest of all, I have found my queen at last," he said.

She frowned, and tried to step back from him, even though he still held both her hands. "What are you talking about? No, never mind that. I want to know who you are!"

He stood tall in the moonlight as the fire glowed behind him. She could see now that his fringed cloak was a dark plaid, shades of gray and red and white woven together. Its heavy gold brooch shone bright against his chest. "I am Conaire, the king of Dun Cath."

Well, she could almost believe he was a king. His bearing, and his gleaming gold, and the way the other two men obviously deferred to him—it was clear that he was no ordinary man. "Pleased to meet you, King Conn-ah-ree." At least his name was something she could pronounce. "It isn't every day that a lady meets a king. You are, I take it, king of the gypsies?"

He gazed down at her, a question on his face. "I do not know what a 'gypsies' is. I am king of the people who live at Dun Cath, half a night's ride from here." He smiled, and

37

took a step closer to her. "I am also a king in need of a queen—or rather, I was. But now you are here, and I have found that queen."

Terri almost laughed. "Ah—well, that's very flattering, I'm sure, but I'm really not in the market for a new job—"

Again he took a slow step forward, and she found herself in his arms.

He had not pulled or forced her. It was as if she had moved into his embrace of her own accord, as though it were the most natural thing in the world. That soft voice, and tremendous feeling of power, had drawn her in before she realized what was happening. Somehow he had read her thoughts and feelings, and then simply given her what she would have asked for, if she'd only felt the freedom to do so.

And now that she was here, so close that she could feel the wool of his cloak through her light cotton shirt, she found that she had no wish to pull away.

Terri blinked and looked up into his face, amazed at her reaction to all of this. She was lost and he was a stranger. She should be desperate to get back to a place she knew and find some help—but she was not. No matter who Conaire actually was, it was clear he meant her no harm. With a sigh, she admitted to herself that it was good to stand here in his powerful embrace—the embrace of a friend, a protector.

He ran a gentle finger down the side of her face, and she closed her eyes. Never had she felt such strength from any man. He was as solid as a tree rooted in the earth, as irresistible as any force of nature. How right it seemed that she should stand here with him beneath the beautiful night sky.

At last she looked up at him again, and noticed how the branches of the trees behind him framed his head and wind-blown hair. For a moment he looked like an antlered stag, a horned pagan creature, like the very devil himself.

Then he moved and the illusion was gone. Conaire gazed down at her, as calm as she was flustered. "I am pleased that you and I are able to speak to one another now," he said. "Tell me—"

But she quickly interrupted him. "Yes. Now! But what about before? You did something to the ring—even I could see that. What did you do? Or were you just playing a trick on me by pretending you didn't understand English?"

"It was not a joke," he answered, and something of seriousness came into his gleaming eyes. "The druids taught me well. I studied with them for many years, and would have become one of their number had I not been chosen king. On a rare occasion—rare as a Midsummer night with stars lined up red and silver and gold—a little of the power is mine. But I do not think we will see the like of this night again."

The smile returned, and briefly he tightened his hold on her hands. "Now—tell me your name, and where you are from, and how it is you are riding out here alone on that enormous mare. Never have I seen the like of her."

Terri made herself let go of him and move back a step. Even in the darkness, she felt as though she were stepping into the shade after standing in the hot light of the sun. She took a deep breath and pushed her tangled hair back from her face.

"My name is Teresa Maeve Deirdre MacEgan, and I'm from Washington, D.C., in the United States of America. I came here on a vacation. Earlier this evening I rode out on Firelair, the big gray mare you saw, and I got lost. I was sure I could find my way back, but I must have gotten completely turned around because I didn't recognize a thing. I let Firelair have her head and she seemed to know where she was going, but . . . when she stopped, everything was gone."

Conaire nodded slowly, thoughtfully. "You are here now, Teresa Maeve Deirdre, and you are safe with me."

He paused, considering. "I have never heard of 'Merrica'; I do not know the laws and customs there. You will have to tell me about them. But I give you my word as king that no harm will come to you so long as you remain in my lands."

She gave him a small smile. "Well . . . thank you." If he said he was a king, who was she to doubt him? And she did feel safe with him. She could almost believe that he was what he said he was.

"I'm sorry I thought you were a thief," she went on. "I do appreciate your bringing my jewelry back to me, though you didn't have to risk your life to do it! I thought Firelair was going to knock your head off when you walked out of the woods and stood under her like that."

"Ah, but are you not worth the risk? My queen will be a woman worth risking my life for . . . a woman worth dying for." He touched her cheek again. "I am so happy that you are here. So glad that I have found you at last."

"Found me at last? What do you mean?"

"I believe that you are the one meant to be my queen, Teresa Maeve Deirdre, the queen of Dun Cath. I have looked for you for a very long time. Perhaps it is these stars that have led me to you."

Terri raised her eyebrows, and stared at him for a moment. "You said something about that a minute ago, didn't you? I must have thought I was hearing things." She cocked her head and tried to study his face in the darkness. "I'm certainly not a queen, and you could hardly have been looking for me. You don't even know me! I already told you, I'm just a tourist—a visitor here."

He took a step toward her. "Queen or no, all visitors are welcome in Dun Cath, and you more than any who have ever come before," he said. That voice, that low soft voice coming from the shadowed face, vibrated all the way through her. "Will you come back with me? You must have shelter and care. You cannot remain out here alone. I assure you, the hospitality of my home will be yours to command.''

She sighed. He was sincere; he really was trying to help her. ''Well, that's certainly very nice of you. I thank you very much for offering me a place to stay. But I must get back to the resort. I have to get Firelair back to her barn. If you would be so kind as to show me the way, I would greatly appreciate it.''

After a long moment, he nodded, and his voice was quiet. ''When the sun rises, I will show you where you are now and try to show you where you want to go. If you still wish to ride on by yourself, then so you shall—but I hope you will stay with us. With me.''

Relief swept over her. ''Thank you.'' Then, as she drew a deep breath, curiosity began to replace the anxiety of the last hours. ''Now, what did you really mean when you said you wanted me to be your queen? Queen of what? The gypsies?''

''As I said to you, I have never heard of 'gypsies.' I am looking for the queen of Dun Cath, and after searching nearly the whole of Eire I believe that I have found her.'' He reached out and stroked her long hair, so lightly that Terri could hardly tell if it was the night breeze or his fingers that she felt.

''What makes you so certain I'm the one?''

He grinned, and his voice became playful. ''Well, I am *nearly* certain, Teresa Maeve. Of course, I will have to find you worthy first.''

''Oh? Find me worthy?'' Terri laughed. ''I see. And just how do you plan on doing that?''

Conaire shrugged. ''You will have to come to Dun Cath to find out. But for now—'' He raised his hand and stopped her before she could speak again, and as he did a long, plaintive whinny rose out of the night. ''For now, let me help you bring that mare up here. She is alone in the darkness at the foot of the hill, and would no doubt rather be

41

among her own kind—as I believe you would, also.''

"I don't need—'' She stopped herself. Maybe *she* would be willing to camp out here by herself, but she was not the only one to be considered. It was clear that Firelair did not want to stay tied to a tree alone in the middle of a dark and frightening forest. "All right. I'll stay up here tonight, and so will Firelair.''

"Good.'' He sounded very pleased. "I will go with you.''

Together they started down the hill, but after a few steps Terri hesitated. She had grown accustomed to the fire's glare, and found it difficult to see on the steep shadowed slope. But Conaire took her arm and pulled her close, and she put all her trust in him as she allowed him to lead her down into the darkness.

Chapter Four

At the bottom of the hill, the air turned cold and damp and the ground became wet. A mist had formed and it hung just above the grass, weaving its way through the trees. Terri heard Firelair whinny again. Finally, as she and Conaire pushed their way down the tangle of brush within the forest, the mare's silvery form took shape.

Her coat was damp and she was shivering, more from fear than from cold. Terri's heart sank as she reached up to untie her. "No horse wants to be tied up alone at night," Conaire said, patting the mare's neck. "There are wolves about."

Terri froze for a second, then pulled the rope down from the tree. "I should never have left her."

Conaire placed his hand over Terri's, over the halter rope. "No one should be alone in this forest, Teresa Maeve. You should not be alone—and you do not have to be."

His hand closed tight over hers. The other hand touched her shoulder as he stepped close in the blackness.

She turned to him, but could see nothing at all. There was only a great and powerful force surrounding her, an overwhelming sense of masculinity, the feeling of strong arms around her and a great heart beating beneath the broad chest. For a moment the world faded away as she stood within that warm, protective embrace, thinking of how good it would feel to surrender to that strength.

Abruptly she pulled away from him and turned back to the mare. Never had she surrendered to the control of any man, and she was not about to start now! *She* had always directed such situations. Nothing ever happened without her inviting it first, and any man who showed any sign of grabbing or pushing or taking over was instantly set straight and shown the door.

Yet Conaire had not pushed her at all. As before, she had come to him of her own accord, and he had been there waiting, offering what he knew she wanted, what she had always wanted . . . what her body craved, what her heart desired. . . .

What she had never had before.

Terri started through the brush, leading Firelair out of the misty forest. Conaire picked up the saddle and bags and followed at her side. His warmth and strength continued to envelop her even as they walked, as if he still held her in his arms, as if at any moment he would reach for her again. Terri's heart began to beat faster, though not from the exertion of the walk.

At last they reached the foot of the moonlit hillside. Together they led Firelair to the top, to Conaire's camp, where the fire glowed beneath the bright half-moon and shining stars.

The other two men were already asleep beside the fire, just two unmoving forms beneath their wool cloaks. Terri led Firelair to a tree a short way from the other horses and tied her there.

Conaire brought the saddle and set it down in the grass. Terri smiled up at him, and it was with some disappointment that she watched him walk away and lie down near the fire, near his companions.

With a sigh, she unfolded the thick woolen saddle pad and curled up on it, dragging the saddlebags close to use as a pillow. Settling down on her makeshift bed, she gazed at the brightly burning fire and the still forms of Conaire and his men. She listened to the snapping of the flames and the soft sounds of the horses as they moved beneath the trees.

Conaire had been right. She was very glad to be up here now, instead of alone in the cold wet darkness at the bottom of the hill. No one should be alone in this forest, he had said. No one should be alone . . . no one. . . .

The stars shown down from the clear night sky, red and silver and gold.

Terri took a long, slow breath. The air was suddenly warm and close and she felt hot. She opened her eyes, blinking in the brightness, and slowly raised herself up on one elbow.

The morning sun, warm and bright beneath the silvery sky, shone directly into her face. She found that she was covered with a heavy wool blanket, a thick fringed plaid of gray and white and deep red. No wonder she was hot! Terri threw back the blanket and sat up—and for a moment sat unmoving, simply staring at the scene before her.

"Oh . . ."

The sun had raised the curtain of the night, and now lit up a whole new world for her to see. Lost she might be, but at the same time she had found a place that was more beautiful than any she had ever imagined.

All around was a vast panorama of gently rolling hills, all shining with a silvery coating of dew. Some were still touched by mist. The trees spread their branches and pale green leaves over the fresh new grass and up to the early-morning sun. Birds called and sang, high in the trees and down in the valleys. The morning breeze was fresh and cool with mist, and sweet with the scent of grass and flowers.

The Ireland she had known was certainly a beautiful place, but nothing she had seen the day before compared to this. It was as if the world had somehow been renewed, become whole and fresh and new once more, as it had been in the beginning . . . and Terri realized that she felt the same way. For whatever reason, she, too, had been renewed, reborn in this place, given a fresh start in a new and pristine world.

The old one seemed hardly a memory.

Slowly she got to her feet. Conaire and the two other men were nowhere in sight, but their horses were still tied beneath the trees. Cloaks and other belongings still lay heaped in the grass beside the smoldering fire. Firelair stood waiting beneath the tree where she had been tied last night, head high and ears up, watching Terri closely.

Terri returned to the little makeshift bed and began to gather up her things. Breathing deep of the sweet cool air, she was amazed at how good she felt. Oh, she'd been camping out once or twice before, but only in a nice dry modern tent equipped with a floor and a cot and a heavy nylon sleeping bag.

She had expected to wake up cold and stiff and uncomfortable after sleeping out on the ground all night. But the thick wool saddle pad had kept her dry and protected her from the dampness of the ground. The smooth leather saddlebags had served perfectly well as a pillow. And the plaid blanket had kept her quite warm all night.

That blanket, red and gray and white and heavy with fringe, looked handwoven—and familiar, she realized, lifting it up to examine it.

This was the cloak Conaire had worn last night. He must have placed it over her as she slept.

Her blood stirred at the thought. He had stood over her in the darkness, laid the cloak over her sleeping form, and then gone away and left her untouched as if he had no interest in her at all.

But she knew that was not true. He had been more than interested in her last night. The memory of it all came as bright and clear as the morning sun into her mind.

Last evening she had left the barn and ridden into the twilight, searching for adventure—and it would seem that she had found it. She had also found Conaire, a strange and powerful man, so very different from any man she had ever met before. He was almost enough to make her believe that she had indeed left her own world and come to another—but which one? And where?

Terri sighed. Right at this moment it hardly seemed to matter, as she examined her own feelings and was amazed at what she found.

She ought to be afraid. She was lost in a foreign country. She ought to be looking for the stone barn, for the comfortable white-painted inn, for a road or a car or any sign of safe, modern life. Yet this land, and this perfect morning, enveloped her like a sweet dream. Nothing in the busy, frantic modern world seemed half so attractive as staying here in this sunlit countryside . . . here with this wonderful mare, and most of all with the mysterious man who had come to her aid when she'd needed him most.

She folded the heavy cloak, setting it down just as Firelair began nickering and pawing. Terri went to her and gave her a quick pat to quiet her. The men would certainly hear, and Terri wanted at least a moment of privacy in the trees before they all returned. "Hold on now for just a minute, and then I promise you I'll take you down for some water."

When Terri came back out from behind the trees, Conaire stood with Firelair, stroking her neck. The mare stood calmly, ears up, watching Terri but clearly enjoying Conaire's attention.

His back was to her as Terri approached. Hearing her footsteps, he turned around, and at last she could see him in the bright clear light of the day.

Yes, he was tall, as she remembered, and broadshouldered, with the broadest chest she'd ever seen. The gold serpentine bracelet that wrapped itself above his elbow seemed scarcely able to contain the power of that heavily muscled arm, which rippled as he stroked the mare's silver coat.

His hair was a soft red-brown, as was his beard and mustache, and it glinted in the sun. He wore a tunic of dark green with a brown belt of carved leather, brown leather pants, and soft boots wrapped with leather laces to the knee.

The clothes were most assuredly like none she had seen before, but they were fine and new and well made. There was some sort of intricate blue-and-white embroidery on the cuffs and neckline of the tunic. Heavy gold gleamed at his neck and arms and even on his fingers.

The whole impression was one of strength, of command, of power and position. But her gaze was drawn to his face.

He had a smooth brow, with skin touched by the sun, and thick eyebrows, red-brown like the hair and the soft curling beard. The nose was slightly curved, giving an impression of strong will. But it was the eyes that held Terri's attention, gleaming, intense, dark-brown eyes with dark heavy lashes. Narrow lines creased the skin beneath them, lines made by the sun and by laughter.

The face of a king if ever she'd seen one.

He smiled, his teeth white and straight beneath the neat curving mustache. "And how did you sleep this first night in my kingdom, Teresa Maeve?"

"Better than I expected," Terri said, walking to Firelair's head. She stood for a moment basking in the warmth of the sun, and then took another deep breath and smiled up at him. "Thank you for lending me your cloak."

"You are most welcome. This place seems to suit you quite well, by the look of you." He was studying her now, in the light of the sun, just as she had studied him. Her face warming, she turned away and reached up to untie Firelair.

"Tell me about this mare, Teresa Maeve," Conaire said.

"She is a beauty—magnificent, one of a kind. As her rider is."

Terri glanced at him. He said no more, just stood waiting for her to answer, his dark eyes gleaming. "She's not mine," Terri answered, starting to lead her away. "She belongs to the stable at the resort—at the place where I'm staying."

"Do you still wish to search for that place?"

She stopped. "Of course, I—" But then she found it difficult to answer. Did she still want to go back? What did she have to return to?

"What will you do if you cannot find that place again?" Conaire asked quietly.

She felt as though a cloud had passed in front of the sun. The mention of the present day, and of an inn and a barn that should have been here but were not, broke the spell. Despite the beauty of the morning, the strangeness of it all began to intrude.

It was one thing for her to choose to leave her old life behind. It was quite another to be pulled out of it by force and left with no choice.

She looked around again, out in to the distance, all around the top of the hill. This had to be the same hill where the stone barn had stood, just above the inn. There were the white cliffs, and there was the path between the hills where the paved road was—or should have been.

What will you do if you cannot find that place again?

She looked up at Conaire, and at his strangely dressed men and their little shaggy horses. With a sudden chill she realized that she had not seen them use one bit of modern equipment at this camp—not a canteen or a duffel bag or even so much as a match.

All she could do was stare up at Conaire, wide-eyed. She wasn't just lost. She was more than lost. Something very, very strange had happened here, but she could not begin to imagine what—and wasn't sure she wanted to.

"I hope you will like my world, Teresa Maeve."

Terri could not answer him. At that moment Firelair nudged her arm. Quickly she turned and led the mare away, trying to force her thoughts to more immediate matters. She had a horse to care for and her own needs to tend. Minor things like what world she was in, and when, and where, would simply have to wait.

Terri walked Firelair back down the side of the hill, back to the brook where she had made her little camp the night before. She walked a few steps upstream, holding the lead rope as the mare lowered her head to drink.

Terri knelt down on the bank and used her hand to drink the clear running water. It was so cool, so sweet, so pure, unlike the water she was used to back in her own piped and treated and chlorinated world. This water was as sweet and invigorating as the life-giving sun and the grass-scented wind.

Finally, after splashing her face, she got to her feet—and found herself eye to eye with Conaire, beneath the shade of the tree-lined bank. He said nothing, waiting with her while she tried to collect her thoughts here in this beautiful, peaceful place.

But Terri only grew more tense as the moments passed. She wanted desperately to talk to him about where she was, and what she would do, but did not know how to begin. What could she say? "I think I've somehow been transported to a completely different place and time, and I don't know how it happened"? He would think she was out of her mind.

"You wanted me to tell you about Firelair," she said at last, to break the silence.

He sat down on the soft grass of the bank as the mare began to graze. "I would like that very much," he said. "She and I are friends already."

Terri smiled. It had certainly seemed that way each time

she'd seen the two of them together, now that she thought about it. "Well," she began, "Firelair is what's known as a 'true mare.' "

"True mare," he repeated.

"Yes. She's the seventh filly foal in an unbroken line of filly foals." She searched her memory, trying to recall what Sean had said before she rode out to the hill. Had it really been yesterday evening?

"In a race, a true mare will never be bested," Terri went on, "and her rider will never come to harm." She looked at Conaire, who watched her closely, listening to her every word. "But I suppose you know all that. It's an old Irish story, I'm sure."

He got slowly to his feet. "It is a new story to me, Teresa Maeve," he said, "and I have heard too many stories to count. But I will be watching with the greatest interest to see if your story is true."

Terri rested her hand on the mare's lowered neck, watching her as she eagerly grazed the lush green grass. "I will have to find some grain for her, and soon," she said. "This grass is lovely but it will not be enough to keep her fit."

Conaire grinned at her. "So, you are staying, then? I am glad to hear it."

She shrugged her shoulders. "I don't see where I have much choice. Right now, my first concern is caring for Firelair. And for myself. The rest of it will have to wait."

"Teresa Maeve, your mare will have everything you want her to have, just as you will have everything that Dun Cath can provide. Not only are you my guest, you are the one meant to be my queen—and you will surely have the best that I can offer."

Terri raised her chin and stared down her nose at him. She'd nearly forgotten what he'd said last night, about him wanting her to be his queen. She still couldn't decide if he was serious, or a bit mad, or just playing a colossal joke on a lost tourist.

"Queen," she repeated, staring straight into those gleaming dark eyes. "And what makes you think I'd accept?"

His eyebrows rose, and his smile faded. For a moment he simply stood gazing back at her. Clearly this was the one response he had not expected! Then the mischievous sparkle returned to his eyes. "Come now," he said lightly. "What woman would refuse such an offer? What woman would not want to be a queen?"

"The one standing in front of you, for starters," she snapped. "For one thing, I hardly know you! And even if I did, I will tell you right now, King Conaire, I will never be any man's queen."

She paced back and forth, even as the mare continued grazing. "What kind of life does a queen have? She merely sits at the side of the king, a grown-up fairy-tale princess, a prisoner in the fairy-tale castle. There is no happily ever after for a queen. She belongs to the king! What kind of life is that? It might be all right for some women, but not for me. Never for me!"

Terri stopped, surprised by her own sudden outburst. What had sent her off like that? She'd never spent any time contemplating the life of a queen before. But even as she looked at Conaire, and the expression of amazement on his face, she realized what had triggered it.

The life she had led up until now had been distressingly similar to that of a fairy-tale princess. Groomed for success from her earliest days, sent to the finest schools and dressed in the most perfect clothes, she'd been handed over to the very best of companies like a prize—and then spent the rest of her days in that lonely castle of glass and steel.

"Never for me, King Conaire," she whispered.

He walked around the mare to stand in front of Terri, and reached out to play with the curling ends of her long dark hair. "You have so much to learn about kings and queens," he said. "But you do demonstrate an important trait."

"Oh? And what would that be?"

"Wisdom."

"I see." She turned away from him, following the silver mare as she walked slowly down the bank of the sparkling stream. "Is that something you look for in a woman?"

"It is not. There is no need for me to look for it. All women are wise, Teresa Maeve. Men need only the wisdom to listen to them from time to time."

Terri grinned, in spite of herself. She pulled up on the lead rope, dragging Firelair's nose out of the lush grass, and started leading her back up the hill. "All right then, King Conaire. I will accept your hospitality, and I will go with you to this place you call Dun Cath. And I thank you."

"You are most welcome." He followed her up the hill, and the sun grew brighter by the moment.

53

Chapter Five

An hour later, Terri rode beside Conaire through the sunlit countryside. His red stallion, small but powerful, occasionally broke into a jog to keep up with the silver mare's long strides. Some distance behind them were Sivney and Ros, their venison-laden horses holding to a steady walk.

Last night Terri had been too confused by the darkness, and unnerved by Conaire and his men, to be certain of where she was or how she had gotten there. Now, traveling at a leisurely pace in the light of the day, she had plenty of opportunity to study her surroundings.

The hill where Conaire had made his camp last night was the same hill where the barn and the inn had stood. Everything was there except the buildings and the paved road. And now, as they rode out into the open country, she saw not one sign of modern life—no roads, no telephone lines, no fences, not a single house or barn. Only the rolling, forested hills beneath the bright blue sky.

This was indeed Ireland, but an Ireland far different from the one she had known.

She turned to Conaire as her heart began to pound. "You have never heard of the United States of America?"

"I know of no place with that name," he answered as his stallion tossed its head.

"You've never seen a car? Or a telephone?"

"I am certain that if I had seen such things, I would remember them."

"What about a fifty-story tower of glass and steel?"

Conaire stopped his horse and stared hard at her. "Teresa Maeve Deirdre, I have ridden from one end of Eire to the other, on her every track, every path, every mountain, every valley. I know every animal that lives in her forests and fields, every fish that swims in her waters, every bird that flies in her skies. And I say to you, never have I seen such places or such things as those you ask me about. They may well be a part of the Otherworld, where it is clear that you have dwelt; but here in Eire, we do not have any such things."

Her first response was a slow smile aimed at the puzzled Conaire. Then, as they continued on their way, she began to think.

Eire, he had said. Air-eh. Yes! *Eire* was the Gaelic name for Ireland, the old name. Very old. How old? Years— centuries.

It was possible that the modern world was still out there somewhere. But she did not know where or how to find it—and much to her amazement, she realized she had little desire to try.

She looked out again at those misty, untouched forests. Could she really have somehow traveled back to the past, back to the ancient days of this old and magical country? Could it be that all those quaint stories of fairies and forts and ghosts and lost travelers had stayed alive so long for just one reason—because they were true?

Perhaps they *were* true. Perhaps she had just become one of the fortunate few to actually know the truth.

The idea filled her with shock, and with a kind of wild joy. It was all true. All of it. She had discovered the ultimate adventure. This was her world now, and it would take all of her strength and resourcefulness to find her place in it. And she could hardly wait to begin.

Terri gave a whoop of joy and kicked the startled Firelair into a wild gallop. "I am free! In the most beautiful place in the world, I am free! With a whole new world to conquer!"

A few hours later, the little company rode up the side of yet another tree-covered hill. They stopped their horses at the top, beside a wide burnt-out circle of ash, and lined up side by side in the shade. Conaire steadied his horse and then pointed out into the distance.

"There is our home," he said, looking out at it. "There is Dun Cath."

Terri followed his gaze, and then cocked her head. "Well," she began, not wanting to be impolite, "it doesn't look like any castle I ever saw." Then she grinned. "But whatever it is, it's spectacular!"

Conaire's "castle" crowned a flat grassy plain nestled within the hills. It was a vast circle at least a hundred yards across, maybe more, and entirely enclosed by a solid wooden wall at least ten or twelve feet high. No, it was a double wall, she saw, standing in her stirrups to get a better look, and filled in with something—brush or branches, she could not tell from where she sat.

"Thorns," Conaire said.

"What?"

"The walls are filled in with thorns."

"Oh . . . is there some kind of danger here? Do you have enemies?"

"Everyone has enemies, Teresa Maeve. The danger lies in not recognizing them."

He would say no more, and after a brief moment Terri turned back to studying Dun Cath. It was filled with buildings, large and small, their roofs shining, golden in the sun. What made them look as though they were made of gold? Could they really be—

"All right, King Conaire. Show me this golden-roofed castle of yours!"

Heart pounding, the blood racing in her veins, Terri sat up tall and proud and rode beside Conaire toward the massive gates of Dun Cath. She actually looked down on him as they rode, so tall was Firelair beside his small shaggy mount; but he seemed not to notice, and rode as proudly on his compact prancing stallion as she did upon her long-striding mare.

A wooden bridge stretched above the entrance like a cat-walk. On it stood a huge bearded warrior in a knee-length yellow tunic. The man wore his hair long, with the rough yellow ends blowing in the breeze, and he held a tall spear pointed up to the sky. His expression was stern and his face unmoving, but as Terri rode beneath the bridge she noted how he kept his eyes on her—staring at her in fascination and in awe.

Within the gate, stretching out before her in a great wide circle of green and completely surrounded by the solid wooden wall, lay Dun Cath. To the left and right of her were sheds and buildings up against the wall. One of the larger sheds was partly fenced off into a paddock and some pens, which held a few head of cattle and several more of the tough little horses like the ones that Conaire and Ros and Sivney rode.

Scattered across the center of the fortress were a dozen or so small round houses. These were made of something smooth and white, like clay or plaster, and topped with roofs of thatched straw.

Terri smiled. Those straw roofs gleamed like gold in the bright afternoon sun. Here in this land, in Conaire's land, Conaire's kingdom, even plain and ordinary objects were transformed into things of beauty.

Her spirits rose even more as she thought of what other new things, exciting and beautiful things, she might find here. She had wandered into a great adventure, perhaps the greatest of all. . . . She really had been drawn into another place, another time, courtesy of a few old legends that had turned out not to be legends at all.

They halted their horses in the center of the grassy open space. Slowly, the people of Dun Cath walked out of the buildings and sheds and houses and gathered around to greet them.

They were ancient and wild, these strange men and women, and children, too, all tall and strong with fair skin and long thick hair ranging in color from light brown to red to blond. She saw eyes of deep brown and clear blue gazing up at her from those faces, their expressions like those of the watchman above the gate—curiosity, and amazement, and a boldness and fearlessness she had never felt from any modern folk.

These were not gypsies. These were Celts: the ancient, pagan, wild Irish Celts. They could be nothing else.

Terri glanced round at the serious faces and offered them a small smile, but no one in the crowd changed expression in the slightest. At last she turned away and looked to Conaire.

He slid down from his horse and left its reins dangling for a boy in the crowd to catch. He went to Ros and then to Sivney, taking the bundled venison from them. Wading into the crowd, Conaire allowed several women—they looked like servants, perhaps, with their plain worn dresses and dull iron brooches—to take the meat from him. The women disappeared back into the crowd. Conaire turned away and began speaking quietly with two other men.

Terri dismounted and stood beside Firelair's shoulder. Now she was eye to eye with these people, and saw that many of the women were as tall as she was. Never again would she find herself apologizing for her height! Again she tried to smile at them, but at the moment it seemed that all their attention was on the great silver mare.

Well, that was understandable. Firelair stood at least a foot taller at the shoulders than any of their own horses; her coat was slick and smooth, her legs slender, her mane and tail long and silky. The horses of Dun Cath were small and shaggy, rough-coated and strong, much like the native ponies she had seen used for the trekking tours. Yet Terri knew that they were the fine mare's ancestors; it was from them that Firelair had inherited much of her great strength and courage.

But right now, Firelair was just a tired horse in need of care. Terri took a few steps toward Conaire and cleared her throat.

Instantly he looked up at her. "King Conaire, my horse needs water and grain and a place to rest. I seem to remember a promise you made to me—that Firelair would have whatever she needs."

Immediately Conaire walked over to the boy holding his horse and leaned down to speak to him. The boy hurried away with the red stallion, leading him through the crowd and toward the sheds and paddocks.

Conaire turned back to Terri, and as he did the two men who had been speaking to him approached him once more. They stood beside their king, but Terri could see that they had eyes only for her and for Firelair.

These two, she judged, must be persons of some importance. They wore fine clothes in bright shades of blue and green and brown, and nearly as much heavy gold jewelry as Conaire. One was tall and blond, the other shorter, with soft brown hair. Both stood a little apart from the other people of the crowd, clearly enjoying the favor of the king and having no interest in the doings of the commoners.

Conaire placed his hand on the shoulder of the taller one, the one with the blond hair and young face and cold, intense expression—though he could not hide his equally intense curiosity in her and the mare.

"This is my cousin Lonan," said Conaire. "And beside

him stands his foster-brother and my chief druid, Brann.'' The shorter man's face was like a mask, but he never took his eyes off of Terri.

"Before you is Teresa Maeve Deirdre. She is a guest at Dun Cath, my guest. She is welcome here and will be shown every courtesy our house can visit upon her.''

"May I ask you, Teresa Maeve Deirdre, where you are from?'' It was Brann who spoke, the druid. Somehow she'd had the idea that druids were all ancient longbeards dressed in flowing white robes. But Brann had a young face—not much older than thirty, she guessed—and he wore a bright blue tunic and several fine pieces of heavy gold.

Terri looked up at him. She started to answer, then stopped. What could she tell them? Conaire had not asked her where she was from—she had told him only that she had gotten lost, and he had inquired no further.

"She hesitates,'' Lonan said. His voice was cold as ice. "Do you not know where you are from, Teresa Maeve Deirdre? Or do you simply wish to keep your origins a secret?''

"The Otherworld,'' murmured Brann.

Conaire glanced at him. "Why do you believe this?''

"Believe what?'' Terri broke in. "What do you mean, the 'other' world?'' She had heard that reference before. Conaire had said something about it as they rode together earlier that afternoon.

Conaire paused, and then answered her without taking his eyes off of Brann. "The world that lies beyond this one, yet beside it. The world in which mortals may reside for a time, in pleasure and comfort, among the gods and goddesses and great heroes—unless they somehow find their way out of that world and back into this one.''

A chill ran through Terri, though she stood in the bright sun. "I rode out last night and got lost. The only world I'm from is the modern world.'' When they gave her only stares, she went on. "America. I'm from America. Washington, D.C., to be exact."

"Merrica?" Lonan took a step forward, his eyes flicking up and down her body. "Never have I heard of any place called Merrica." He laughed, but it was cold, derisive. "She is telling you a tale, Conaire. A lie. No doubt she is some servant driven out of her own dun in disgrace—a thief, a liar—"

Conaire glared hard at him. Lonan fell silent. Conaire turned to face the crowd, raising his voice for all to hear.

"I say to you as your king that Teresa Maeve Deirdre is a guest here, that she is my guest, and that it does not matter where she came from." His voice was ringing and clear. "It matters only that she is here."

Terri relaxed a bit. Brave though she was, she was alone among strangers in a very strange land, and she had no objection to hearing Conaire stand up for her and proclaim her to be his guest in front of them all.

"Besides," Conaire went on, "Merrica is no doubt some small and isolated tribe, of no importance. She has expressed no wish to return."

Terri blinked, and almost laughed. Well, it was true, wasn't it? In this time, the place she knew as America did still belong to its native tribes, and was most certainly isolated. She'd never told Conaire she wanted to return—just that she didn't know where she was. And now that she did know . . .

Lonan's manner instantly changed. "Of course," he said, smiling. "She is an honored guest at Dun Cath, and she is welcome here."

At that moment, the stable boy whom Conaire had sent away returned, pushing his way through the crowd while struggling to carry two heavy wooden buckets. He set them down in front of Terri. One bucket was brimming with clear water and the other was full of oats—clean, dry oats.

Firelair reached eagerly for the offerings. Terri let her

drink, but pulled away the bucket of oats. "I must let her rest a bit first," she said, glancing from Conaire to the boy. "She should have hay before the oats, and I must make sure she is cool and dry before I let her eat."

"She is in good hands, I see, with you to care for her," Conaire murmured. Terri merely looked at him, and then reached into the bucket to sift a handful of oats through her fingers—yes, the grain was sweet and crisp, as good as anything Firelair would have had back in her own barn.

"I must ask about that animal," Lonan said. "Has anyone ever seen the like of it before?"

"No," Terri said quickly. "She is one of a kind." Well, it was true! Even in her own time, she had never seen any horse like Firelair.

"I am told she is a 'true mare,' " said Conaire. "The seventh filly foal in an unbroken line of filly foals."

Lonan almost laughed. "And what difference would that make?"

"A great deal of difference, it would seem," Conaire answered.

"Hmmph." Lonan turned his attention back to Terri. But before he could say anything more, Conaire touched the stable boy's shoulder. "Take the mare to the barn. Make enough room for her and give her the best care the dun has to offer."

The boy reached for the reins. Instinctively Terri held tight to them. She could happily place herself in the care of these people, but handing over Firelair was another story.

Conaire smiled gently at her. "Please. You can go to see her whenever you wish. Evin is the boy who cares for my own horses."

She remembered the powerful, tireless red stallion Conaire rode. "Well, yours do seem to be in good shape." Terri sighed. "All right, then. Thank you," she remembered to say. She gave Firelair a final pat on her damp neck, and watched as she was led away.

"Teresa Maeve, will you come with me and accept the hospitality of my house?"

She turned to Conaire, who stood politely waiting for her answer. Terri pushed her hair back from her face. She was tired, and hungry, and in need of a bath. "Thank you, yes. I will."

She walked with him as he strode away, and a few of Conaire's men and a half-dozen servants moved quickly to follow them. Dun Cath may not have been the castle she had pictured, but its people certainly seemed devoted to their king.

The men and women dispersed, moving back to their work in the bake-house and armory and barn, but Lonan made no move to go with them. He stood motionless, his eyes fixed on the backs of Conaire and that strange other-worldly creature he had brought with him to Dun Cath.

"Does he think he's found his queen at last?" Lonan whispered.

Brann took a step forward to stand close to his side. "An Otherworld woman for a queen—now, that would be a prize. A queen even Conaire would accept."

Lonan clenched his fists. "Conaire deserves no queen at all," he growled. "He is not—he should not be—"

Brann silenced him with a glance. "Your feelings are well known to me, but you must keep them between us. Conaire was chosen king and there is nothing anyone can do to change that."

"It should have been me," Lonan said. "It should be me. I will never feel otherwise."

"Some of us will never feel otherwise, either. Your father was a good king. But the law allows the free men of the tribe to choose, and no one knows the law better than I do. They chose your cousin. They need not give their reasons."

"There was only one reason!" His voice rose. Brann

took him by the arm and walked with him across the wide green lawn of the dun, towards the main gate where no one would hear them.

"Conaire is king only because of his lies," Lonan hissed, through clenched teeth. "Lies the rest of them believed!" Even now he was surprised at the strength of his anger, at how it flared in an instant, at how he had held on to his rage for all of the long, cold year since Conaire had been chosen king.

"It's nothing but talk."

"Talk that cost me the kingship! And I cannot disprove what he has said!"

"Not all the men believe him."

"Enough of them believed to choose him over me. To this day he tells that I ran—turned my back and hid—during that battle with the men of the bog. Five years ago, and still he lies to every man in Dun Cath."

They kept walking, following the high wooden wall until they were near the barn. "I thought it was at the cattle raid on Dun Gleas—three years ago."

Lonan turned on him, trembling, glaring fiercely, feeling that his rage would flare like a torch at any moment. "All of it is lies! All of it! He cannot even keep his stories straight! He would do anything to discredit me and grab the kingship for himself! And so he has!"

Brann paused, blinking. He stared at Lonan, his face blank. Finally he said, "My only interest is in the law. Conaire was lawfully elected king and we must all recognize him as such."

"I am your foster-brother! Is the law more important than that?"

"The law says only that—"

"The law says nothing to me! I only care about what is fair!"

Brann merely stood silent, staring. Lonan slammed his

fist on the paddock fence and looked away from him in disgust—and then he saw it.

The huge silver mare stood a short distance away in the paddock. A stable boy waited at her head, watching closely as she dipped her nose into a bucket of oats.

"What is fair," Lonan repeated, and then looked at Brann again. "Conaire stole the kingship, which should have been mine. He might have that, but he deserves nothing else. He does not deserve a queen like this Teresa Maeve Deirdre with her strange mare. I may not be able to take his crown, but I can take his woman. She will be mine, never his. Mine!"

The sun seemed to have brightened. He slapped Brann on the arm and walked away.

Chapter Six

Terri and Conaire walked together through the scattered grouping of houses, and then came upon a sight that made Terri stop and catch her breath.

Stretching almost all the way across the rear of the circle was a long rectangular building, one made of dark heavy timber. Its enormous corner posts were beautifully carved into flowing, intertwined lines and birds and animals, and the straw roof gleamed golden in the sun. Two huge doors, one near each end of the long side of the building, were equally ornate.

"Now, this could *almost* be a castle," she said.

"It is the Great Hall," Conaire said, escorting her inside through the door nearest them. "This is where the people of the dun can gather for the feasts and celebrations, where I speak with my druids and fighting men, where the women sometimes do their weaving and spinning and sewing."

He led her inside, and she moved slowly into the dimness of the cavernous hall. It was a full two stories high. The center of the thatched straw roof was open to the sky, directly above a circular stone-walled firepit ten feet wide. Bright shafts of sunlight streamed into the pit, as if the fire were being fed directly from the sun itself and needed no earthly fuel to make it burn.

What was this on the floor? She seemed to be walking through stacks of thick dried grass, strewn over the entire

66

floor to make a thick carpet. "The rushes here are always fresh," Conaire said. "I require that my hall be kept clean at all times. It's not like some kingdoms' halls, where bones and scraps are left to rot for months at a time."

"Glad to hear it," Terri said faintly. She looked up again. The hall held a partial second story; it reached over on the long side exactly like a balcony. There seemed to be rooms up there; she could see doors set into the wall, and a wide walkway running along in front of the rooms.

"The *grianan*," Conaire said. "The sunroom. I had it built especially for the women. It is their own place, where they may work or rest or gossip, as they choose. Rooms for our guests are just beyond it. One of them shall be for your use alone."

He glanced over his shoulder at the small crowd of men and servants who stood waiting at the doorway, and then turned back to her. "Dorren will care for you and bring you anything you require. You have only to ask her. Please, make yourself comfortable here, and I will come and see how you are later in the day."

"Thank you, King Conaire." She ran her fingers through her hair and smiled at him as he walked out the door, his men following him. The other serving women hurried away, and only Dorren was left.

Terri turned to Dorren and offered her a polite smile. But the woman only stared. She was old and bent, her hair gray and tattered, with wisps and pieces of it sticking out from its tightly pinned twists. Her clothes were worn and stained, and the only jewelry she wore—a brooch pinning her shawl and a solid, open-ended necklet—were made of dull and somewhat rusted iron.

"Hello, Dorren," she began. "My name is Teresa—but everyone calls me Terri."

There was no response. The woman only stood still and stared even harder, her widening eyes flicking over Terri's clothes.

67

"Oh," Terri said, looking down at her smooth gray breeches and high black boots, "I must look very strange to you—but I was just out riding, and I got lost—"

"Come with me," the woman whispered, and turned to walk across the rush-strewn floor of the hall. After a brief hesitation, Terri followed, craning her neck as she walked to catch a glimpse of the bright blue sky through the hole in the roof.

At the far end of the hall, just below the overhanging balcony, were a set of steep stairs made of narrow planks. Terri followed Dorren up the stairs, and in a moment stood on the wide balcony overhanging the hall. Benches and stools and a couple of wide wooden looms stood against the solid wooden wall of the balcony.

Some half-dozen doors were set into the wall. Dorren led her to the very last one, at the far end of the balcony.

The heavy wooden door made no sound as the old woman pulled it open. She stopped just inside the door, holding it open, waiting for Terri to come inside.

Slowly, Terri walked in, trying to take it all in at once. The room was perhaps ten feet square, about the size of the average apartment bedroom. It had two heavy bordered windows, one in the long wall and one in the end wall. Shutters of heavy wood by the windows were presently pulled back against the inside walls, letting the sweet warm air fill the room.

"I will bring food," Dorren said, "and some decent clothes." She quickly turned and slammed the door behind her. Terri blinked, suddenly alone as the gentle breeze played over her hair and brought with it the scent of sun-warmed grass.

The floor was of smooth wood, shining as if it had been waxed and polished. She almost felt guilty for walking on it with her damp and dirt-stained boots. Just inside the door was a wide bed which would probably be called "queen-size" back home in America—or "Merrica," that small settlement of no importance, she thought to herself with a grin. The bed looked like a large wooden box sitting directly on the floor. The box was filled with clean bright straw, and on top of that, like a giant pillow, was the mattress itself: a big linen case filled with the softest of feathers and down. Completing the fine bed were a stack of fine wool blankets, beautifully woven in bright fringed plaids of red and blue and green and yellow and white.

Against another wall was a narrow table that held a bronze pitcher and basin, and a delicately carved wooden comb. In front of the table was a small bench, and beneath it on the floor was a plain clay pot. Well, she could guess what that was for. This might be a lovely and exciting place, but one thing it could not be expected to have was indoor plumbing.

It was a little crude by modern standards, perhaps, but still quite inviting, and obviously was considered very fine accommodations. Yes, she would be quite comfortable here.

She walked to the window at the back of the room and looked out. Just below, in the space between the Great Hall and the curving rear walls of Dun Cath, were a few more of the small round houses like those she had seen in the center of the dun.

One of the dwellings, though, was much larger than the others. It was beautifully decorated with the same tall wooden posts and graceful carving as the Hall. She had seen no others like it. It was a curious place, obviously meant for someone or something important, and she wondered who lived there.

Well, it was just one more mystery awaiting her. Terri turned away from the window and went back to the feather-filled bed. She sat down on one soft corner of it and pulled off her high leather boots—first one, then the other, dropping them to the polished wooden floor.

She sighed and lay back on the delightfully soft mattress.

How wonderful it would feel to walk barefoot through that thick green grass . . . the flower-scented breeze blowing over her face . . . and Conaire beside her, close beside her in the warm summer sun. . . .

The door swung open. Terri quickly sat up. Dorren pushed her way into the room with a wide wooden tray holding dishes. Behind her came four other servants, each pair carrying an enormous wooden chest between them.

The servants placed their heavy burdens against the long wall, beneath the open window. "Oh," Terri breathed, getting up and walking over to the nearest chest. She ran her fingers over the beautiful carving and glanced up at Dorren. "They're like treasure chests! May I look inside?"

Dorren only frowned, ever so slightly, and then made a little move with one hand as though waving Terri on to do whatever she wished.

Terri reached for the lid. As with the door, it was silent as she raised it. Inside were stacks of fine fabrics—linens, and wools, and something that appeared to be a blend of the two woven together. The colors were soft and warm, some solid, some gloriously combined in plaids. She saw red, green, gray, blue, dark gold, cream, brown, and black. Shaking her head in wonder, she lifted out the fabric on the top of the stack—soft folds of silvery gray in the lightest and most delicate of wools—and draped it carefully over her arm.

Quickly she moved to the other chest, and there she found riches she could only have dreamed of. Golden ornaments, some set with jewels, gleamed and sparkled from within the shadows of the chest. There were brooches, rings, necklets, bracelets, things whose use she could only imagine. Gingerly she lifted out one shining piece. It was a bracelet, flat and wide, open on one side. Its surface was covered with beautifully wrought figures in beaten gold—intertwining vines and leaves, and trotting horses at each end.

She could only imagine what such work would be worth in the modern world. Very carefully she laid the bracelet back on top of the gleaming stack.

In one corner of the chest, kept back by a wooden divider, were things made of leather. Terri lifted out long slender belts in black and brown, some smooth and some carved with the same graceful animals and leaves and flowers as those she had seen on the jewelry.

She shook her head. "It's incredible," she said, still staring at the gleaming hoard. "Thank you so much. I'll be very careful—" But when she turned back to the servants, they were gone. She was speaking to an empty room.

Well, perhaps this was just the way they did things around here. Maybe they would like her better, feel more comfortable around her, if she dressed the way the other women did. She turned back to the chests.

A few minutes later, she stood in the center of the room, arms outstretched, trying to see herself in this most unfamiliar garb. She had selected a creamy linen undergown, and on top of that was the silvery-gray gown of light and airy wool.

The gowns were ever so simple in cut; it was like wearing a long loose nightgown with modest rounded neckline, the skirts cut wide for freedom of movement. Terri took up the waist with a black leather belt. It had no buckle, so she tied it instead, and slipped her feet into the soft black leather boots, ankle-high with leather string laces to pull them snug.

It did feel strange. She was not accustomed to going around in ankle-length gowns as everyday wear. But she would fit in now, she would be dressed like the other women here, and that was what counted.

Except for one thing. She noticed the shine of her modern diamond wristwatch just beneath the handmade woven gown. Quickly she unfastened the watch and lay it down on the narrow table, beneath the flaring edge of the bronze basin. *Now* she was properly dressed for Dun Cath!

Terri sighed, and looked around in contentment. She had a fine room, and beautiful clothes, and a treasure chest filled with gold, and Firelair was well taken care of—what else could she want?

As a rich savory scent drifted to her nostrils, she quickly realized what she could want. Food! It had been hours since her quick meal with Conaire out at the hilltop camp. But there on the small table was the tray Dorren had left, and it held lunch.

There was a kind of bread, hot and flat and slathered with a mixture of butter and honey. And on the large gold plate beside the bread was a stack of thick-sliced roast beef, still steaming and juicy, with a little dish of salt beside it. And a tall golden goblet of sweet cold water.

Famished, she pulled out the bench and dragged it over to the window, and then set the tray right on the windowsill. There did not seem to be a fork, but no matter. There was a small knife for slicing the beef into long strips and that suited her just fine.

Terri had stayed in some of the world's finest hotels and been served the very best room service, but never had she enjoyed a meal as much as this one. She sat in silent contentment at the windowsill, eating her hot honey bread and salted roast beef and gazing out at the summer afternoon.

Just as Terri drained the last of the water from the goblet, she heard a knock at the door. She set the goblet down beside the empty plates and rose to walk to the door.

When she opened it, she saw nothing—until she stepped out onto the balcony. Conaire stood alone on the *grianan,* leaning on the railing and gazing down into the hall. Then he turned to face her, and Terri found that she was no longer looking at the simple kindly stranger who had taken her in when she was lost.

Before her stood a king.

He wore a linen tunic of the deepest red, shining with lines of gold thread embroidery at the neckline and the cuffs. A heavy gold circle lay around his neck. His trousers were also of linen, dyed a soft gray like her gown, and crossed with laces to hold them tight from ankle to knee. His boots, too, were like hers, soft black leather folded and laced to fit. At his shining black belt were both a dagger and a long, heavy sword.

His red-brown hair had been combed out until it rested on his shoulders, curling at the ends. Yes, he was indeed a king; she could sense the strength and power in him even from where she stood. But as she studied him, her eyes were drawn irresistibly to his face.

Again, the eyes, soft and brown, returning her steady gaze, studying her, acknowledging her changed appearance with a small gleam. Beneath the smooth soft beard and mustache his firm mouth twitched ever so slightly.

So, it seemed that her appearance pleased the king. She raised her chin, but not before he spoke.

"Now we see each other as we truly are," Conaire said. "I told you the truth when I said I was a king, and when I told you that you were a queen."

"I am no queen, Conaire." She walked back into the room. "I am merely your guest—an honored guest," she added firmly, turning and looking him straight in the eye. "I thank you for all of these beautiful things you have sent. As I tried to tell Dorren, I will be very careful with all of it."

He followed her into the room, seeming to fill it with his presence. "I am glad that you liked the clothes and the ornaments. And your room? Would you prefer some other room, or one of the houses, perhaps? You have only to ask."

Even with the distance between them, Terri could sense the restrained power of his body. If she had been uncertain before about where she was, Conaire proved beyond a

73

doubt that she was far from her own world—for never had she known any man with the sheer, overwhelming masculinity of this one. "No, no. This—this room is fine. Better than fine. It's perfect."

"Good. A queen must have the best of everything her king has to offer." He stood straight and tall in the center of the room, arms crossed, grinning, as though inviting a retort.

She drew a deep breath and refused to rise to the bait. "My horse is what concerns me now. I was just about to go and see her. Would you go with me so that we may both be sure she is properly cared for?" She cocked her head and waited for his response, wondering how the king would react to her request.

But he only nodded, his grin wider than ever, and stepped back a pace to allow her to go through the door. She looked over her shoulder at him as she swept out of the room, still a bit off balance and uncertain at suddenly encountering Conaire the king, after having only known Conaire the man, the lonely traveler like herself.

The barn was a low wooden structure, small and close, really just an oversized shed. Firelair stood tied in a far corner. She raised her head and nickered as Terri approached, and Terri's heart sank as she saw the mare's ears brush the rough beams of the ceiling.

Quickly Terri went to her. The mare was dry and cool, her coat rubbed smooth and clean, and she stood on dry ground. Even her mane and tail had been meticulously combed out. A wooden pail of clean water hung from the wall.

But Terri shook her head. "She cannot stay in here, Conaire. This roof is too low for her. Look, she cannot even raise her head! If something scares her she will hurt herself badly."

She could feel the tense silence around her. The stable men all seemed to be holding their breath. Who was she to talk this way, to make such demands of the king! "Of course, I know your men have given Firelair the best of care. I can see that. It's just that she's so tall. It's not their fault."

But Conaire only nodded in agreement. "She'll take the roof off with her head." He turned to the young stable boy. "Evin—the weather is fine today. Lead the mare outside and give her a paddock of her own. We will see about making her a shed were she can stretch her neck like any other horse."

Terri smiled in relief. "Thank you. Although I don't want to make any extra work for—"

"Do not worry about it. If I have to build her a new barn with my own hands, I will do it."

Terri's spirits rose. "I doubt it will come to that!" She reached out and touched Firelair's smooth coat as the boy led her out, and she and Conaire followed them outside into the warm sunlight.

Terri ran her hand over the smooth worn wood of the paddock fence. "What can I show you now, Teresa Maeve?" Conaire asked. "The bakehouse? The armory? The gardens?"

She gazed up, away from the confines of the Dun, her eyes scanning the horizon. "There," she said, and pointed to the nearest hill. "Isn't that where we rode in this morning? Where we saw the remains of the fire?"

He glanced up. "Yes. The very same."

"I would like to go there."

Conaire's eyebrows raised a bit in surprise, but he kept his smile. "Why do you wish to go there?"

"Because I want to see where I am. I want to walk outside these walls and stand on that hill and see exactly what this world is like."

"So you shall. Come with me, Teresa Maeve Deirdre, and I will show you this world—my world."

* * *

They walked out through the open gates of the Dun, and set out through the ankle-deep grass for the neighboring hill. The first thing Terri did was to reach down and pull off the folded leather boots. She kept up easily with Conaire's powerful strides, and quickly learned to pick up the hems of her long skirts or kick them out of the way as she walked.

Now the summer sun began to warm her skin, on this the longest day of the year. The freedom of half-walking, half-running through the grass set her blood to racing, and the freshness of the sun-scented breeze made her feel intoxicated.

By the time they reached the top of the hill, Terri's heart pounded—but not from exertion. She had never felt so alive, never known what it meant to have her blood sing. It seemed that she had never known what freedom really was until she had come here, to this place, with this man.

They walked out of the trees to the clear side of the hill, the side closest to Dun Cath, and stood beside the large ashen circle. Now Terri took one final look at this world. It was the only one she would ever know again, the one she would have to accept as her own if she wanted to have a future.

As before, there was no trace of modern life anywhere—only the endless hills and trees and grass. The only sign of civilization was Dun Cath, and in the world she knew, such things existed only as ancient ruins.

"My world is gone," she said.

There could be no doubt of it now. She was truly in a different time, a different world. And one that suited her surprisingly well.

She could only believe that all the old stories were true—that she had been one human who had discovered the truth and vanished within it forever.

Conaire walked up behind her and placed his hands on her shoulders. The warmth and strength in them flooded through her. "If your world is gone," he said gently, "then stay in this one."

She turned to him, focusing no longer on the wide expanse around her, but only on this man. "I will stay," she answered. "And King Conaire, I can tell you in all honesty that even if I had the choice to return—which I don't see that I do—I would still want to stay here. This is the most beautiful, exciting, adventurous place I have ever known, and I am drawn to it in ways I can't begin to describe to you."

Carefully he drew her close to him, stroking her long dark hair. "I would hope that you would be drawn to me, Teresa Maeve, as well as to the land I live on."

She hesitated, content to lean against that broad chest and feel the slow strong beat of his heart. Finally she pulled back from him a step. "I stay here because I choose to stay here, Conaire. I want to be a part of this life, of this place. I want to find out what I can do to earn my way and find my place here."

A pleased smile appeared. "I have no doubt of your place. You belong at my side, as my wife. As my queen."

Her eyes narrowed. "I will stay here on my own terms. I have just stated them. And they do not include being anyone's wife, or anyone's queen."

Chapter Seven

Conaire frowned, and turned away from Terri. "Would you tell me, please, just what it is you find so repellent about being a queen? Every other woman that I have ever known would leap at the chance to be a queen, whether she thought highly of the king or not." He shook his head. "You would never want for anything. The treasures you found in your room would only be the beginning. The finest clothes, and furnishings, and food, and jewelry, and horses . . . all that was mine to give you would be yours."

Terri placed her hands on her hips. "Is that what you want for a queen? Someone who can be bought with dinner and nice clothes?"

He actually stepped back a pace, looking as if she'd slapped him. Terri pressed on. "You say I would have horses. But when would I have any time to ride those horses, King Conaire? Would you care to explain just what is required of the queen in return for all those lovely things?"

He gave her a small smile. "You are quite right. The people of Dun Cath will need their queen as much as they need their king."

"Oh, I'm sure they will. Almost as much as the king will need her."

"The king will have the greatest need for her of all."

"Of course he will. Now, don't tell me, let me guess.

The queen stays in each day and works among the women. She might advise the king if he should happen to ask her a question. But most important, she's expected to produce a baby every year. Am I right?"

"Hardly every year, Teresa Maeve. That would be a strain even for someone of your stamina. Every two years would be quite adequate."

"Just as I thought." Her fists tightened. "So tell me. Where does all of that leave the queen enough time for so much as an afternoon's ride through the countryside— much less anything else she might want to do on her own?"

He shrugged, but his face remained serious. "I do not know what else a queen might want to do on her own. I cannot imagine that being queen would not be challenge enough, even for you."

Terri sighed, and turned away from him. She looked again at the distant hills and trees and pushed back her hair from her eyes. "I still don't understand why you've decided you want *me* for your queen. You don't even know me. Don't you already have a wife? Or at least a girlfriend?"

She could not imagine that a man like Conaire didn't have several of either. Certainly the women here must find him as desirable as she did.

But he only laughed. "I do not have a wife. My wife will be queen. That is why I am searching for her so carefully."

"Well, I'm still just trying to figure out why you *don't* already have a wife. Or do you have to prove yourself in a test or something, like in the old stories where the hero has to do some brave deed to win the lady?"

"Ha!" he said. She jumped, then turned to face him again, annoyed by his sudden outburst. "As I said before, my queen will have to prove herself to me. And for someone who does not care to be queen, you seem very interested in who that queen might be."

She raised her chin. "I'm not interested. And if I were, I can assure you that it would be just the opposite. If I were queen, the king would have to prove himself to me!"

Conaire cocked his head, eyebrows raised, and grinned even more broadly. "Oh! Now I understand. You do have an interest—you just don't care to say so."

"No, I don't have *any* interest! I just cannot imagine why you would want me to be your queen—your wife—when we know nothing about each other."

At last his face grew serious, and he reached out to her. "Oh, but you're wrong, Teresa Maeve. I know that I have never encountered a woman of your spirit. Of your very strong, let us say, individuality. And surely a horse like the 'true mare' would only be found in the company of a very special woman—perhaps even a queen."

Terri stared up at him, becoming lost in those gleaming brown eyes. He stared back as if she were the only thing of any importance in the world, and at last she made herself look away.

"I believe I am here because the old stories and legends really are true. A person *can* be drawn into another world, and for some reason—whatever reason—it happened to me." She paused, and gave him a sharp look. "But that doesn't mean I'm going to marry you just because you seem to be in need of a queen."

All he did was laugh. And the more he laughed, the more her temper rose. She turned and made as if to stalk off down the hillside, but Conaire caught her by the arm and gently turned her around.

"Let me tell you what I am searching for," he said. "I will never take an ordinary woman as my wife, for an ordinary woman would never make a queen. She would wither and fail in the attempt, and drain the life and strength from her people as she did.

"Mind you, I am not looking just for 'my' queen. I am looking for the queen of Dun Cath, of my family, of the people who follow where I lead and depend upon me to protect them. No, I am quite serious when I tell you that I will have nothing less than a woman worth dying for as the queen of Dun Cath.''

''I can understand that,'' Terri said, after a moment. ''But why are you so sure I'm the one?''

''Oh, I'm not sure. I'm not sure at all.''

Her temper flared. ''Not sure! When you've been telling me all this time that I've been sent here just for you? To be your wife, to be your—''

''I *believe* you should be my queen. But you will have to be tested first.''

She put her hands on her hips, not believing what she was hearing. ''Tested.''

''Of course.'' He sat down against a lone young tree, the sun shining on his face, and grinned up at her, locking his fingers behind his head.

''Do you want to tell me what these tests are?''

''Since you are so interested—and I'm so pleased that you are—I will tell you.'' He unclasped his hands and sat up before Terri could say a word.

''There are three things that I require in a queen.'' He began counting on his fingers. ''One—beauty. Two—humility. Three—courage.''

''That's all?''

''That's everything.''

''And you're telling me that you have found no woman here who is beautiful and humble and brave?''

He shrugged. ''Oh, many women have exhibited one of those traits, and a few have shown me two, but not one has ever shown all three. Only when I see all three displayed in one woman will I know that I have found my queen.''

Terri stood right over him, looking down at his smooth bearded face with the coldest glare she could muster. ''King Conaire, if you believe that I will go through some kind of test for you—when I don't even want to be queen

81

in the first place—you are wrong. *You* will have to prove those things to *me*—and I may not stop with just three things!''

She continued to stare him down. With increasing irritation she waited for his response. But he only grinned up at her, practically beaming, all but laughing, and at last she turned away and marched to the very edge of the hilltop.

Terri tried to look out at the view and forget about Conaire, but her temper would not allow it. Pacing, she began muttering under breath. ''*Test* me! Test *me*? I'll show you a test, you king of all conceited men!''

Suddenly she stopped, and tugged at the neck of the gray gown. Light as the fabric was, she was not accustomed to wearing long wool gowns in the middle of the summer. Finally, exasperated, she untied the black leather belt, pulled the overgown off over her head, and threw it down to the soft grass.

She stretched out her arms and faced the soft breeze, letting the wind stir the light linen gown and clear away the heat and anger. She closed her eyes, enjoying the cool breeze on her body and the warm sun on her face.

Conaire came up behind her. She tensed, then held very still as strong hands rested on her shoulders, clasping the linen of the gown and caressing the smooth skin of her arms.

She ought to move away from him—let him know in no uncertain terms that she would be the one to say when he might touch her, caress her, hold her . . . but her body felt so heavy and warm, she could not will herself to take a single step.

''So, you would not stop with just three tests?'' he murmured. The hair of his soft beard touched her ear. ''Where would you stop, Teresa Maeve?''

Terri closed her eyes and leaned back, just enough to

feel the rise of his chest as he drew breath. "I may not ever stop," she murmured. "Not ever . . ."

She shook her head slightly, still unable—or unwilling—to move. "I am here, in this magical place . . . the stories are true, they're true, and this place seems to have been made for me . . . for me and . . ."

At last she turned to him, and he drew her close. "For you," he whispered, his mouth against her forehead. Then the fine hair of his mustache pressed against her lips. It was soft and smooth, like the locks that fell to his shoulders and brushed gently against her neck.

She reached up to his face and ran her fingers down his cheek. Never had she known a man who wore a beard. Certainly none of the men she had worked beside in the city would ever dream of it. Yet she found that she was drawn to this male emblem, to this unmistakable proof of Conaire's masculinity. She brushed her mouth across its softness, searching out his lips beneath the softly curling hair.

The hot sun shone down, and Terri felt as though she would melt from its heat. But no, it was not the sun's heat burning her; it was the overwhelming presence of Conaire, enfolding and enveloping her, pulling her closer, closer, the heat of his mouth melting into her, his body pressing hard against hers as all that warmth flooded through her and her knees began to weaken.

She ought to stop. She ought to pull away. He was a stranger; she had known him less than a day; she was not in the habit of falling into the arms of men she had only just met. But every beat of her heart was saying to her *yes, it's your choice, take this man, such desire, you are free, you are here, you are free, you are free—*

Yes, she was free now, free of her old restrictive life, that cold and gray and empty life lived out in sterile fortresses of steel and glass and concrete. Gone were the tentative, hesitant, modern men who did their dating by the book and were oh, so cautious of where and when to touch, and who would pay for what, and when to make a move— and how many times would his pager go off and how many calls would he make on his cellular phone before their little evening was over?

No, here was life, and warmth, and the heat of the sun, and another heart as strong and vital as her own . . . powerful arms to pull her close and a hard male body to crush against her until she softened and felt as though he was sinking into her, flowing over and through her, even as they stood on the grass on the side of the hill.

She could no more turn away from him than a young flowering tree could turn away from the sun.

Her body began to yield, and she gave herself over to the strength of his rock-hard arms. He kissed her as though all the vitality of the air and sun themselves were in his lips, and she opened herself up to his energy even as she opened her lips to his kiss. It was like stepping into a bright hot summer day after a lifetime of cold grayness.

She lay back in his embrace, feeling as though she were floating within the day's shimmering summer heat. She found herself resting gently on the grass, still on the hillside, out in the open in the brightness of the day.

Yet the openness did not matter. They were here, alone, on their very own hilltop, and the sun shone only for them. All that mattered was this virile male presence, pinning her to the sun-warmed grass, one hand grasping her shoulder and the other pulling away her skirts, his bare knee pushing against the inside of her thigh.

He slid his arms beneath her and held her shoulders tight, and she opened herself to him and pulled him close, closer, until she found what she sought and his hard male body found and filled her feminine softness. She arched her back and returned his ardent, powerful embrace, moving with him, drawing him ever deeper within her, feeling that now, at last, in this time and place, she had found what she had searched for all her life, and that she would never feel empty again.

Later that day, as the slow-moving sun began to approach the horizon, Terri sat on the hillside with Conaire's head resting on her lap. Gently, almost absently, she stroked his hair and beard.

Neither of them spoke as they watched the evening begin. Slowly, a single gray rain cloud drifted across the hazy sky to hover above the swollen red-orange sun, and after a time a narrow curtain of rain began to fall from the cloud—a silvery veil cast down over the face of the enormous red sun.

"I've always thought of the colors of summer as being green, for the grass, and maybe blue, for the sky," Terri said softly, gazing at the strangely veiled sun. "But now . . . now I will always think of them as being red and silver."

Conaire's head moved slightly on her lap. "Red for the burning sun, and silver for the life-giving rain," he murmured. "Those are the colors that create all that green."

"I see that now." Looking down, she saw how the crimson of Conaire's tunic lay against the soft gray of her gown, and smiled.

After a time, they got to their feet and began making their way back to Dun Cath beneath the heavy, silvery skies. Terri kept her fingers placed lightly on Conaire's massive arm. So alive was every nerve, every sense in her body, that she felt as if she were floating down the hillside.

Never had she known that it was possible to find such satisfaction in the arms of a man. And now that she did know, she was almost afraid to imagine how her life would change.

As if it had not changed enough already.

But right now, she wanted only to walk with Conaire back to the dun. She could think only of the comfort and privacy of her delightful corner room in the Great Hall, and of what it would be like to be there alone with him.

As they walked in the fading light across the open green lawn of the dun, Terri was distantly aware of Conaire speaking to the servants who came to greet them. She kept walking, almost pulling him—*come on, come on! Come with me to my room, so we can be alone together once more!*

At last they entered the Hall, went up the steps, and walked into the dimness of the corner room. Terri hurried in before him to stand beside the bed. But Conaire only waited by the open door, looking down the hallway.

She was confused, and impatient, and more than a little disappointed. She was amazed at how eager she was to hold him again, to draw him close, to make him a part of her once again as she had done out on the sunlit hillside.

But he paid her no attention at all. She wanted to reach for him, but was suddenly unsure of herself—what could she do, what could she say? She was not quite bold enough to grab him and drag him back to bed when he was standing in an open hallway.

Terri almost laughed to herself—she did not recall ever reading anything in the etiquette books to cover quite this situation!

Before she could decide just what she wanted to do, Conaire stepped back into the room to make way for two servants. One carried a small bench, which he set down beside the table, and the other one brought in a tray bearing food. Finally, after arranging everything to the king's satisfaction, the two servants left and closed the door behind them.

At last! Now she had him all to herself. But he only walked past her to the center of the room as if she were not even there.

With a sigh, Terri turned to face him. Scattered candles cast a wavering, flickering glow over the polished wooden walls and floor, making the room even more inviting, more romantic, than it had been before. Conaire stood beside the small table, which now had a bench on either side of it. On the table rested two gold plates laden with hot food. He pulled out one of the benches and looked up at her, clearly inviting her to sit down.

But instead of approaching the table, she sat down on the big soft bed and leaned back on her elbows, gazing up at Conaire through lowered lashes.

A long moment passed. Finally, he walked toward her and her heart leaped. Now she would have the chance to hold him again—she could hardly wait to lose herself in that strong embrace, as she had done out on the hillside. . . .

But to her astonishment he simply stood waiting, looking down at her. "You are not hungry, Teresa Maeve?"

She could hardly believe it. "Hungry?" Her fingers tightened in the heavy wool cover on the bed. "Yes," she said. "Yes. I am hungry. I'm—"

"Good." He reached out for her. "Your evening meal is ready for you. Please, come and join me."

Terri sat up on the edge of the bed and took his hand. "It's not food that I'm hungry for." She looked straight into his brown eyes, which gleamed in the candlelight, and refused to be embarrassed.

"Ah. I see." He sat down on the bed beside her, but before Terri could move he gave her hand a gentle pat. "And I am so pleased to find that you have a good appetite. Another admirable trait in a woman."

Terri's indignation flared. What was that supposed to mean? Was he joking about her feelings for him? Her temper began to rise. "Is that all I'm going to hear from you, King Conaire? Judgments and pronouncements?"

He looked surprised. "Of course not. Only until you become my queen, when no more judgments will be necessary."

She started to snap back at him, but he closed his hand

firmly around hers. "For right now, I have need of your counsel."

She blinked. "Beg your pardon?"

"I would like to ask you your opinion of something." He leaned over, slowly, drawing close to her face. "But don't worry—I never allow my guests to go hungry." Then, just before his lips could touch hers, he got briskly to his feet.

Terri frowned, turning a fierce glare on him. "Is this another one of your tests?"

He shook his head. "It is not. As I said, I already know that you are wise. Right now, I have need of some of that wisdom. Will you help me?"

Her face began to burn, but not with anger. "You mean—you brought me here to talk?"

He cocked his head, seeming to be genuinely puzzled. "Of course," he said. "I am not interested in a woman simply for her skill and enthusiasm in lovemaking. I want a queen who will share her wisdom with me—who will speak to me with the voice of the women of Dun Cath, when all I usually hear is the shouting of the men. Will you do this for me, Teresa Maeve?"

Her face burned even hotter, but now it was from humiliation. She could scarcely bring herself to look at him.

How many times had she insisted, often quite loudly, that she wanted a man who was interested in her for her mind, not just her body—a man who would talk with her and listen to her and have some interest in what she said and thought. And now that she had found exactly such a man— and one who was handsome and powerful and desirable beyond her dreams—she was actually annoyed because he wanted to talk to her instead of ravish her.

She cleared her throat, and settled herself primly on the bed—ankles crossed, hands folded in her lap. "Why, of course, King Conaire. I would be happy to discuss with you—ah, whatever it is you want to discuss.''

"Good." He caught one of the benches and dragged it over. "Now, listen, and I will tell you. . . ."

Chapter Eight

Conaire settled himself on the bench and looked straight at Terri. "There is a fierce animosity brewing between two of my fighting men," he began, leaning forward with his elbows on his knees. "I fear it may end in the death of one of them if something is not done."

Terri frowned. "What's their problem?"

Conaire shrugged. "A boyhood rivalry that continues to fester. Usually such things are worked out in a good honest knockdown fight or two, and then everyone forgets the slights and spends a long night drinking honey wine. But this one has never been resolved. Some of the old, deep feuds can only be resolved by blood—by death."

"Death?" A slight chill passed through her. This place seemed so lovely, so magical, but if what Conaire said was true, it was far from perfect. "Surely you wouldn't let it go that far."

"If they choose to fight, I cannot stop them. I cannot always be there looking over their shoulders as if they were small children."

"But you are the king! Don't they have to do what you say? If you tell them to leave each other alone, isn't that enough?"

He smiled, gently, patiently. "Teresa Maeve—these are free men. Warriors. They know as well as anyone that they may keep the company of any man they wish. They also know that the king's will is not greater than the law.''

When she looked puzzled at this, he paused for a moment, and then went on. "The law is for everyone. No one is above it, not even the king. I cannot simply order my fighting men to do this or do that, according to my wishes. They are free men and would not suffer a tyrant for a king.''

"Not even to save their lives?''

"Not even then.'' He smiled again, his eyes shining this time. "I will have to find a better way.''

Terri nodded, thinking to herself that this was not the response she had expected. "I'm surprised. And impressed. I thought a king was an absolute ruler whose word was law.''

Conaire shook his head, gazing down at the polished floor. "That has never been the way of things in Eire. And certainly not in Dun Cath. A king serves always at the will of his people, and it is at his peril that he forgets that fact.''

She considered. "Maybe you could remind them that since you cannot force them to end their feud, they should put loyalty first—loyalty to you, as their leader, and loyalty to Dun Cath itself. Isn't that more important than any disagreement they may have between them?''

He looked up at her with a thoughtful gaze, and then a slow smile. "That is good advice,'' he said. "You do understand where true loyalty lies. But sooner or later the druids will have to hear their grievances. They may well decide that I must choose between these two men. If I do, then one of them will be pleased and the other outraged.''

Terri raised an eyebrow. "But the one who would be outraged would not have made a loyal warrior anyway— would he?''

Conaire grinned. "You may be right. And if you are, then I would be better off without him, because I will have none but the very best to follow me. Just as I will have none but the most worthy to be my queen.''

"Well, in that case, you've still got a ways to look."
She waited for his response, but he only smiled at her and
then waved his hand toward the golden dishes.

"I am sure you must be very hungry by now," he said.
"Will you join me at the table?"

Terri glanced at the fine hot meal which waited for them.
"Well . . . I suppose it will do for now," she said, looking
pointedly at him.

She took her place on the bench as Conaire sat down
across from her, and wasted no time sampling the dinner
they had been served.

There were thick pieces of a roasted, strong-flavored
meat; boiled vegetables, white and pale yellow, of a kind
she had never seen before; and, as always, flat hot bread
with dark yellow butter and golden honey. Tall golden goblets of cool clear water finished off the meal.

"What kind of meat is this?" she asked, dipping a long
strip of it in its own juice and lifting it to her mouth.

"Venison. From the young buck we found on our journey."

"Oh." She paused before taking a bite. "Then you must
have—"

"I killed it myself. It was injured. I would never leave
an injured animal to die."

"I see." She took a small piece of the meat, and then
set it down on the gold plate. "I don't think I've ever had
venison before . . . but this is very good."

Terri yawned, hugely, suddenly aware of how long the
day had been. "Very good," she added softly, shaking her
head and taking a deep breath to clear her head. *Wake up!
This day isn't over yet. The night has not yet even begun!*

"It would seem there are many things here that you have
not had before," he said. Terri glanced up at him, but he
merely looked at her with a gleam in his eye and went on
eating.

She yawned again, and then made herself sit up straight

and finish her dinner. It was all very good and she had been very hungry; but the room was so warm, and so softly lit, and she was so sated after the fine meal, that fatigue began to steal over her like a soft curtain.

But she did not want the night to end without once again holding Conaire close. Terri was conscious of moving from the table and sitting down on the bed to remove her boots and belt and soft gray overgown. She lay back on the softness of the bed and gazed up at him, closing her eyes as he gently ran his fingers down her cheek.

Such a beautiful place . . . such a magnificent man . . . she could hardly wait for tomorrow to arrive so that it could all begin again. This place seemed to be made for her, almost perfect, almost too good to be true . . . too good . . .

In a moment she was fast asleep.

Conaire closed the door, leaving Teresa Maeve alone in the soft bed in the dark and quiet of the Great Hall's finest room. He descended the stairs into the shadowy torchlit hall, empty now except for the few men gathered around the softly glowing central hearth.

He walked over to join them. Brann and Lonan and Sivney and Ros all stood silently in the ankle-deep rushes, watching him expectantly. "Please sit down," Conaire said. They did, slowly, Lonan on the edge of the hearth and all the rest on furs thrown down upon the rushes.

Not one of them said a word. They all stared up at him, waiting for him to speak. Conaire could feel the tension and the questions hanging in the warm air of the hall.

He paced a few steps, and then turned to look at them. He almost smiled at their anxiety, but kept his face somber. None of them would say a word until he broke the silence.

"I believe I have found my queen," he said.

"Have you?" Lonan said, almost interrupting.

Conaire glanced at him. "She affects me as no other woman ever has. Never have I met the like of her."

93

Lonan attempted a smile, but it was more like a sneer. "You are smitten like a boy, King Conaire. Just because a woman is attractive hardly means she's worth marrying."

"I will not let my feelings cloud my judgment," Conaire said, pacing again. "I know well that I must choose not only a wife, but a queen—a queen that will be loved and accepted by her people, even as I love her. That is why I want to know what you think. I trust you all. I value your judgment."

"We know nothing about her," said Lonan.

"Yet she is beautiful and strong," said Ros.

"She could be from the Otherworld," Brann reminded them.

"And the tallest woman I've ever seen!" added Sivney.

Conaire almost laughed at their comments. "Do those things make her a queen?"

"A queen is born to the role," Lonan said. "This 'Teresa Maeve' will not even tell us where she is from."

Sivney broke in, scowling at Lonan. "If Conaire marries a servant, that makes her queen!"

"Only the people can make a woman queen, just as only they can make a man king," Brann said.

"Brann is right." Conaire looked at the four grim faces. "When I learned that the free men of Dun Cath had chosen me as their king, I felt the weight of it—and knew that they had not had an easy choice." He looked directly at Lonan, who raised his chin and stared right back.

Sivney glowered. "If Conaire marries her," he repeated, growling, "the people will have no choice but to accept her."

Brann looked at Conaire. "The people always have a choice. They have the choice of whether or not to follow you as their king."

Conaire matched his gaze, and nodded slowly.

Lonan stood up. "She is an enigma and a mystery. She has no past. She could be anything—except a queen."

Conaire's mouth tightened. "I have never seen such strong will—"

"Such strangeness!"

"Such furious self-reliance—"

"Such clothes! That monstrous mare!"

"And such remarkable strength of spirit." Conaire stared them all down. "I have always said that I would take no ordinary queen—and now, I have found, at last, a woman who is anything but ordinary.

"Just as the land needs a whole and powerful king, a king needs a whole and powerful queen. I can think of no better way to serve my people than to give them a worthy queen. And I assure you"—he glanced up at the *grianan*, at the last door—"I will make sure that she is worthy."

The dawn entered Terri's room, a sweet cool breeze smelling of wet green grass and fresh leaves. She stirred beneath the heavy wool cover and stretched luxuriously, breathing deep of the fresh air, and then lay blinking in the pale gray light.

She had not dreamed it. She was still here, still in this beautiful land that seemed like heaven—still here in this place with the man known to her as King Conaire.

Terri roused herself from the soft warm bed and swung her bare feet down to the hard polished wood floor. Ah, yes, another day of discovery and adventure and exploration—she and Firelair could go out and explore the surrounding countryside, and she would spend time learning all she could about Dun Cath and its people.

She would find a place here. There could be no doubt of it. And she would not object if the place she found was very near to King Conaire—though not as his queen, of course. As she had so plainly told him, she was not about to become anybody's queen.

Some man's wife, some man's property, his handmaid and symbol? No, she had spent all of her life fighting for her freedom—to be independent and strong—and now she had finally come to a place where her strength might truly mean something, where her independence would bring her freedom and adventure instead of loneliness and isolation. No, she would never give it up.

Yesterday she had gone to Conaire out of choice, out of genuine desire, and it had been the most wonderful experience of her life. She was more determined than ever that she would never, ever have it any other way.

As she washed in the basin—there was still water in the bronze pitcher from last night—her mind turned to one piece of hard reality. Just last week she had been to her doctor's office for another injection. She would not have to worry about becoming pregnant for at least a few months. After that—well, she had no idea what her situation would be this very afternoon, let alone weeks or months from now. As eager as she was to jump in and experience everything this world had to offer, she knew that some things could only be done one careful step at a time.

Terri went to the nearest chest beneath the window, the one that held the fine handmade gowns of linen and wool. Her hand rested on the beautifully carved surface of the chest as she crouched down before it, lost in pleasant thought.

Which of the gowns would she wear today? She planned to do a lot of walking and exploring within the dun. She would want something light and comfortable, definitely the linen, not the wool, in some bright cheerful color—perhaps one of the brilliant reds, or golds, or the green and blue plaid she had noticed.

Terri raised the lid. The carved chest was empty.

She drew in her breath. What had happened to all the fine clothes? Even her own white cotton shirt and gray breeches were gone. She leaned in to look closer—there was something in the very bottom of the chest. She reached in and lifted out a length of rough, heavy linen fabric, plain and dull and undyed. A gown? No, a skirt and a long tunic, and a rectangular shawl. The crude garments seemed to be clean, but were old and worn and stained with use.

She let the clothes drop back into the chest and looked up, frowning. Quickly she moved to the other chest—the divided one that had held the beautiful ornaments and belts and accessories—all that gold, all that priceless work. . . .

Gone.

The leather items had vanished, too, right down to her own black belt and tall black riding boots. All she found was an ancient pair of worn brown boots, cracked and stiff, on one side of the chest. Where the gold had gleamed lay only a rusted iron brooch and a heavy neck-ring. Even her wristwatch had disappeared from beside the bronze basin on the table.

What could have happened? Was this someone's idea of a joke? Or could someone have stolen those treasures while she slept?

She had slept so well, so deeply, after yesterday. She would not have heard a stampede of horses running through the room last night, much less a quiet thief.

She would have to tell Conaire. He would have to know that there was a criminal among his people. She sighed. Well, nothing was perfect—not even this place. But, in some ways, that imperfection only made it that much more interesting.

With some distaste she lifted out the pieces of coarse linen. Just rags, really; even the servants had not worn clothes in such bad condition. Maybe she could put them on over the top of the gown she wore now—but no, she might want that one later. It was made of smooth, fine linen, bleached almost white, nothing like these other awful things.

Terri sighed. Well, there was nothing to do but wear them. She stripped off the fine gown, rolled it up, and hid it under the mattress. If there were thieves about, she was not about to let them have her last best gown.

The stained tunic hung nearly to her knees, and had no sleeves. The ragged skirt wrapped around her waist and was tied with knotted strings. The boots were hard and uncomfortable; no doubt she'd have blisters if she had to wear them for long.

But she doubted it would come to that. She'd only have to wear these things long enough to get downstairs and tell Conaire what had happened.

She found the mantle, a long rectangle of ragged linen, and wrapped it around her shoulders. She picked up the dull iron brooch, cold and heavy and edged with rust, and managed to fasten the mantle with it—pushing the straight iron pin in and out through a spot in the fabric not already torn, and then turning the half-circle of iron so that the end of the pin rested against the curve.

Terri wiped the cold rust from her fingers and caught sight of her shining gold ring. Well, that was one thing the thieves hadn't dared to take. Glancing back into chest, she saw that it was empty except for the heavy iron neck-ring.

She slammed the lid and headed for the door. Never, she told herself, would she wear a thing like that.

Clad in rags, the hideous boots flapping on her feet, Terri left her room and walked down the *grianan*. The hall below was filled with servants preparing food, some of them eating breakfast.

She made her way carefully down the narrow wooden stairs, struggling with the long ragged skirt and ill-fitting boots. Finally, she stepped down into the rushes and stood there as the servants gaped at her. She kept her chin high, though she knew she must look a fright—she had not even taken the time to comb her hair.

She glanced around the hall. There seemed to be only servants here; she could see no sign of Conaire or any of his men. Terri pushed her tangled hair away from her face and cleared her throat.

"I must see the king," she said.

No one moved. Finally she saw a familiar face. "Dorren!" she cried, her voice rising in desperation. "I must see the king. I must see him now! If no one here will go and get him, I'll go find him myself."

Dorren made a quick gesture to one of the men, who set down the basket of wool he carried and walked quickly out the door.

Most of the people in the hall were sitting on scattered benches, eating from wooden plates. Terri saw slices of cold meat and chunks of bread with dark yellow butter, and small cups filled with fresh milk.

"Breakfast," Terri said, trying to smile. She made another attempt to smooth back her hair. "Do you mind if I join you?"

Dorren pulled out a small bench and dragged it over to Terri. Terri sat down on it, and after a moment the old woman came back with a wooden plate and cup.

"Thank you," Terri said, accepting the plate. "I'm starved—" She stopped, looking down at the plate.

She had expected to see sliced meat and buttered bread. Her plate held only a few pieces of dry bread. Reaching up, she took the wooden cup. It held only water.

"What is this?" she said, standing up. "I thought I was a guest. First my clothes are gone, and now this?"

She set the plate and cup down on the bench and faced the cowering servants, her hands on her hips. "Something is terribly wrong here! I'm going to see the king and I'm going to see him *now*!"

The servants scattered as she started across the room— but she stopped halfway as a shadow appeared in the doorway. A moment later, a smiling King Conaire entered the Great Hall.

At any other time she would have felt a great surge of

happiness at seeing him. It would have been so wonderful to know that this tall and rugged man, arms rippling with muscle, chest powerful and broad, had come here just to see her—just to be her companion in this place of beauty and adventure.

Again he looked every inch a king in his dark green linen tunic and bright gold ornaments. Again he gazed at her with admiration and amusement, as though he did not see her tangled hair and did not notice her rags.

"Good morning to you, Teresa Maeve! I am told you asked to see me."

"Yes, I did." She held her temper, not wanting to alarm the servants any more than she already had. "I am sorry to tell you, but all the things you sent to me last night—the gowns and the belts and all that beautiful jewelry—it's all gone. And so are my own clothes and riding boots. I'm afraid you have a thief in your castle, King Conaire."

"There are no thieves here," he said, still smiling. He walked closer to her, close enough to touch.

Terri frowned. "But I just told you—it's gone. All of it! It was gone when I woke up this morning!"

"I know it was," he said. "I ordered it taken away."

Chapter Nine

"You?" Now Terri was truly bewildered. "*You* took all of my things? Why?"

He looked surprised, as though she ought to understand. "Why, it's part of the test, of course. Part of what I must do to determine whether or not you will someday be my queen."

She stared at him, unbelieving. "You mean—you took my riding clothes and my boots? Because that's what you mean by 'testing' me?" Her voice rose and she could feel her face flushing.

Conaire folded his arms across his chest and grinned even more broadly, seeming to enjoy her outrage. "You are exactly right. I am testing you."

"How is stealing somebody's clothes going to show you whether or not they should be queen?"

"Taking away your treasures is the first of my tests, the test of humility. That is a very important trait in a queen."

"Humility!" She was shouting now. "What right have you to humiliate me! Steal from me! Who are you to do this?"

He waved his arm toward the servants. They all immediately got up and hurried to the far end of the hall. Conaire took Terri by the elbow. She stiffened, glaring at him, but he took no notice and walked her down to the other side of the hall, away from the agitated servants.

"I am the king," he said to her, his face serious now. "And it is the king who does this."

She wrenched away from him. "King!" she cried. "Thief is more like it. You took my riding clothes and my boots—all the clothes I came with. I thought you told me the king was not above the law. Don't you have any laws against stealing?"

"Of course we do," Conaire answered. "And your clothes have not been stolen. Merely—put away for a time." Then, before she could get a word in, he went on. "You must remember, your own clothes are very special. They set you apart almost as much as your fabulous mare. Is that what you wish? To be set apart, different and special, above all the other people of the dun?"

"Of course not. I want to fit in. I want to find a place here—and yesterday," she said, looking pointedly at him, "I thought I had found that place."

"I believe your place is at my side, as queen of Dun Cath."

"Oh, yes, so you've told me. Well, if you're king, can't you choose whoever you want? Why don't you just marry a princess like all the other kings?"

His eyes narrowed. "The queen is the queen of all the people. She is not the property of the king, as you seem to think, nor is she his servant. But if she will not serve the people, as the king does, they will not accept her, and both they and their land will suffer. That is why I must be sure, and that is why I will test you."

"You can test me all you want, King Conaire, but it will be for nothing. Any woman who is married ends up living her life for that man. That's reason enough never to marry—but a queen?"

Terri shook her head, her matted hair falling into her face. "Being queen means belonging body and soul to whoever is king. And I will never 'belong' to you or any other man. This land offers me the freedom and challenge

I could never find back in my own world. I will not throw that away the minute I arrive by attaching myself to a man—not even you! I am not your queen. I am no man's queen!''

He made no reply. She turned away from the esoteric questions of kings and queens, and back to the practicalities of the moment.

''You told me I was a guest,'' she said, still angry and bewildered over his treatment of her. ''I thought I was *your* guest. You most certainly do not have to give me gold and jewels, but surely you do offer your guests food—and allow them to keep their own clothes!''

''Were you offered food this morning, Teresa Maeve?''

''If you can call it that! Dry bread and water!''

''And were you not provided with clothes?''

''Rags! Even your servants would refuse to wear this. My own clothes were stolen from me, you took back everything you gave me, and there was nothing else to wear!''

''So, I see what this is really about. You require gold and carved leather and bright clothes to maintain your pride and self-respect. My queen will have no need for such decoration, such ornamentation. My queen could wear mud and rags and still be known for a queen from a hundred paces off.''

He grinned, and Terri's blood boiled. ''Do you want your decorations back? I will give them to you. You have only to ask.''

''I want nothing from you! I just want back what is rightfully mine!''

''No, Teresa Maeve. You want what will make you look like a pampered and lovely and spoiled queen—whether you actually are a queen or not.''

She drew herself up. ''I want nothing from you, and I will take nothing from you. I would rather starve and go naked than take anything from you. And I don't care whether you or anybody else thinks I'm a queen, because

103

I'm not! Queens belong to kings—and I belong to no one!''

Terri turned her back on him. She walked to her bench, reached for the wooden cup, and drank down the water. Grabbing the bread, she turned and stalked toward the servants, all of whom were busy doing nothing at the far end of the hall. ''All right, then! I'm one of you now. If I am not to be a guest, I will earn my own way! Show me what there is to do!''

In that moment, Terri plunged into the job of being a servant with all the determination she had once reserved for her career as a highly paid marketing executive. She looked up to see Dorren standing in front of her, staring. ''Well, you heard me! I'm here to work. Where do I start?''

The woman held up another wooden bucket. As she accepted it, Terri's nose quickly told her what this battered bucket was used for. She squared her shoulders, looked up toward the *grianan,* and headed for the steps.

Well, it was a job that had to be done daily in this place, a job like any other, and Terri was determined to turn away from nothing they might ask of her. She went down the *grianan* and emptied the chamber pots in each room into the battered old bucket.

At last she was done. She started to go back down the steps—but suddenly remembered something. Terri set the bucket down and went back to her corner room.

Raising the lid of one of the wooden chests, she reached in and took out the rusted iron neck-ring. Grimacing, she worked the cold heavy thing around her neck, and left the room with a slam of the door behind her.

Finally she worked her way down the stairs with the heavy bucket hanging from the crook of her arm. As she stepped down, she found the servants standing and staring at her again.

''Look,'' she said, trying to keep the exasperation from her voice, ''I'm going to be helping you out for a while, so you may as well start showing me what to do.'' She lifted up the bucket. "Now, where does this go?"

They looked at each other, and then Dorren waved her toward the door. The rest of them scattered and fell back to their tasks like so many worker ants.

As Terri followed Dorren across the hall, weaving her way around the busy servants, she looked up to see Conaire standing in the doorway.

She headed straight toward him. He stood waiting, watching, clearly expecting that she would stop and speak to him.

"Teresa Maeve," he began. His smile was polite, but his eyes sparkled with amusement, even when his gaze flicked over the iron neck-ring she now wore. "I want you to understand that I will return your things to you if you wish. All of them. I—"

But she made a point of pushing past him, lifting up the bucket as she did. His nose wrinkled and he stepped quickly out of the way, much to her satisfaction. "I am sorry. I can speak with no one now. I have work to do." She walked out the door of the hall with her head held high, carrying that awful bucket as proudly as if it held all the gold in County Tipperary.

For the rest of that morning, Terri followed Dorren and helped with every task the old woman performed—which proved to be some of the hardest and dirtiest work to be found in the dun.

After her trip to the refuse pit with the slop bucket, Terri moved on to the job of picking up the bones and scraps of everyone else's breakfast and collecting them in another battered wooden bucket. When the bucket was full, she set out again for the pit.

She wiped her face on her rough linen sleeve and shifted the heavy bucket from one hand to the other, trying not to think too hard about this sudden twist of fate.

She had come to Dun Cath literally riding high. On the

magnificent Firelair she had towered over everyone, even the king. After that she had spent the afternoon looking down upon the rooftops of the dun from the magical hillside, and had remained high above it all night in her fine lofty room in the *grianan*.

It was as if she had seen nothing but the tops of silvery clouds.

Now she had fallen hard to earth. Now, it seemed, as she walked to the edge of the pit and dumped the breakfast scraps into it, she would learn this place from the ground up—or maybe even lower.

Dorren went into a storage shed beside the bake-house, and handed out clean buckets to Terri and four other women. The little group trudged out through the gates, into the sunny, hazy morning, and walked a short distance to the woods. Terri breathed deep of the fresh damp air as she walked along, swinging a bucket from each hand. She was glad to be outside, even if it was only a few yards from walls of the dun.

Just on the other side of the trees ran a clear brook, its water sweet and cold. Following the lead of Dorren and the others, Terri set down one bucket and lowered the other into the brook. She dragged it through the shallow water and hauled it out when it was full, and then did the same with the other.

When all the buckets were full, the group started back toward the dun. Terri tightened her fists and raised her forearms in an attempt to lug the heavy, sloshing buckets all the way back without dropping or spilling them.

"I can make it," she said to Dorren, gritting her teeth. "It's not too far—only one trip."

"Three trips," Dorren told her.

Terri raised the buckets higher. "Three trips." She struggled on, clenching her fists around the handles and fixing her gaze firmly on the gates of Dun Cath.

*   *   *

For the rest of the morning, as the sun rose and the cool fresh morning began to give way to close summer warmth, Terri put all thoughts of Conaire out of her mind and concentrated on the heavy, unaccustomed labor that Dorren and the others assigned her. On one hand, it was drudge work of the worst kind; on the other, it was a fascinating, behind-the-scenes look at the daily life of the dun.

Three times, Terri hauled brimming wooden buckets of clear water from the stream all the way to the Great Hall. Well, where did she think that goblet of water had come from last night? From a faucet? She could only imagine what the people here would think of having water pour out of their walls.

Crossing the open grounds of the dun after her final trip to the stream, the buckets ready to drag her arms out of their sockets, she managed to glance over towards the paddocks. Firelair stood there with her head over the top rail, ears up, head turning as she followed Terri's movements across the wide lawn. Terri could have sworn the mare wore a look of amusement on her aristocratic face, and even swung her fine silver head up and down as though laughing at the sight of Terri working harder than the lovely mare had ever had to do.

Hours later, when the sun began to approach the horizon, the servants gathered around the hearth. Terri stood up from where she was spreading an armload of fresh rushes and wiped her hands on her ragged skirts.

Food! It was time for dinner. Somehow she had missed lunch entirely. Her appetite had gnawed at her all day long, but she'd steadfastly ignored it, taking long draughts of water from the stream and concentrating on her work.

But now, after only bread and water and several hours of very hard work, she had to have something to eat. She could stand the work, and the dirt, and the ragged old clothes, but not on an empty stomach.

Terri hurried up to her room and poured some clean water into the basin, then scrubbed her hands with the little pebble of soap. It stung her scratched and blistered hands, and she quickly rinsed them in the cool water of the basin.

Back downstairs, she approached the hearth with some hesitation. She had come here as an honored guest, but now that Conaire was subjecting her to this ridiculous test, she no longer held the status she had so briefly enjoyed.

The servants clearly did not know what to make of her. None of them would speak to her unless absolutely necessary. Terri knew that to them she was a bizarre curiosity, an outsider in every way, and a small creeping dread began to come over her.

She could stand up to Conaire. She could gladly relinquish her role as his pampered guest, his playacting queen, and insist that he treat her as an independent woman who belonged to no man. She could show him that her freedom was the most important thing to her, that she would sleep with servants and dress in rags if that was what it took to convince him—but she had not thought that perhaps she would not find a place among the ordinary people of the dun.

But it seemed that she need not have worried. Dorren turned to her and handed her a bowlful of what she was ladling out from the cauldron—boiled meat and some sort of white vegetable, with a generous chunk of flat bread thick with dark yellow butter. "Thank you," Terri whispered, and the old woman actually gave her a small smile before turning back to her work.

As Terri sat down with the savory food, she felt a great sense of relief. If the humblest of these people accepted her, she need never be afraid of not finding a place.

That night, all but a few of the servants retired to their modest houses in the far corners of the dun. But Terri returned to her room just long enough to wash up, and then went back down the steps to the quiet hall. After making a deep bed in one corner with the cleanest and softest of the rushes, she curled up in it and covered herself as best she could with the ragged mantle. With a sigh, she closed her eyes and fell into the deep sleep of complete exhaustion.

For the next two days, Terri continued to work alongside the other servants at the very lowest tasks to be done in Conaire's castle. She hauled water; she brought in wood for the fire; she dug the garbage out of the rushes and hauled the slops to the refuse pit.

It seemed that everywhere she turned she saw Conaire, or Ros, or Sivney, watching her with a mixture of curiosity and amazement. Yet her only response was to lift her chin high and go about her work. If Conaire thought she was not strong enough to earn her place, or that she would beg for her things to be given back, she would show him what she was really made of!

In the evening, Terri had the job of banking the fire, keeping the coals covered and glowing so they would not go out. As she finished the task and got awkwardly to her feet, all she could think about was pulling off those awful boots and washing her blistered feet in cool water. She could haul one more bucketful of water to her room—it was not quite dark yet, the gates of the dun would not be closed for another half hour or so—

She nearly bumped into Conaire.

Instantly her fatigue vanished and in its place was a flaring disdain. "Yes, King Conaire? How may I serve you?"

He smiled gently, but his face was very still. "Have you truly found your place, Teresa Maeve? Here, among the servants? I cannot believe you would be content to do this for the rest of your days."

She gave him a cold stare. "I will be content to work and earn my way as long as I must. I don't go where I'm not invited—and you've made it quite clear that the invitation to be your guest no longer stands. Therefore, I am a servant. Believe that.''

Terri grabbed her bucket and headed for the door, hurrying into the dimness of the evening. *Think about that for a while, King Conaire!*

On the morning of the fourth day, Terri roused herself up out of the rushes and made her way upstairs to the sunny corner room. Its privacy and washbasin—and chamber pot—were the only luxuries she allowed herself.

But this morning, when she opened the door, she found the room looking a bit different.

The lids of both wooden chests were raised and leaning back against the wall. Inside, as though nothing had been touched, were all the treasures she had seen on her first evening there—the brightly colored wool and linen gowns, the carved leather belts and soft boots, the beautiful gold jewelry.

Beside the bed stood her tall black leather boots, and on the wool blankets, neatly laid out and clean, were her own gray riding breeches and white shirt. Her diamond wristwatch was right where she had left it on the table.

And in the corner was a large flat basin on the floor. It was big enough to sit in and filled with a several lovely inches of clean, clear, and oh, so inviting water.

Terri wrung her hands as she looked at it all. It was very difficult to keep from hurrying to the chests and lifting out their treasures. Though she was willing to work among servants, and wear rags, and sleep in a pile of rushes until she was invited once again to be a guest, she felt something almost like hunger at the sight of beautiful clean clothes: soft folded-leather boots, bright gleaming gold, and her own clothes, her own well-made riding boots. Oh, what she wouldn't give to bathe and dress!

But no. Obviously Conaire was trying to break down her

will. She had to let him see that she could not be bought! She would not ask him for anything.

Terri shut her eyes and turned away from the sight of such treasures, such luxuries, such enticements. No. Not yet. She would return to Conaire and his house on her terms, or not at all.

She fixed her eyes firmly on the floor and started to walk out—but the door opened before she could reach for it.

Conaire stood before her, smiling, extending his arm and waving it around the room. "Teresa Maeve, you have had enough of being a servant. You are once again my guest."

Terri stared at him, hardly able to believe her ears. Then she began to laugh. "You call that an invitation? You're still giving me orders like a servant."

He took a step toward her. "As you can see, I've had your own clothes and all the new things brought back to you—and even had a bath prepared. You can wash yourself and dress as a noblewoman should. I shall join you at dinner this evening." Giving her a brief nod, he started to back out of the room.

"Wait," she hissed.

He stopped, looking a bit surprised. "I'd be interested to know what made you change your mind," she said, her voice cold. "One minute I'm your guest and you're showering me with gifts. The next minute you take it all away and turn me into a slave. The next I'm your honored guest again. What next, Conaire? Will you want me to take up armor and fight? Sit in a corner wearing furs and jewels like a mannequin? Or go back to being a servant again?"

"You will never be a servant," he answered, walking toward her. "Yet these last three days, as you went about in filth and rags and did the worst of the tasks without complaint, you held your head high and kept your dignity about you. I could ask for no better proof of humility. You have passed the first test."

But Terri only glared at him. "The test of *my* humility,

you mean. I told you—if you tested me, I would test you in return. Where is *your* humility, King Conaire?''

He bowed his head, and smiled gently. ''I ask you to be my honored guest. I have greater need for your counsel and company than the slop jars have for you to empty them.''

She raised her eyebrows and stared him down, more than conscious of her rags, her dirt, her greasy hair, even as he stood before her in his fine linen, soft leather, and heavy gold. ''And what if I choose to be a servant? What if I reject your offer so that you can no longer hold it over my head?''

His face grew serious, and his brown eyes were solemn. He was not laughing or joking now. After a long time, he reached out to lift her sore and blistered hand, and spoke a single word.

''Please,'' he said quietly. ''Please.''

Chapter Ten

Terri squared her shoulders, and took a deep breath. It was so good to stand here with him again—so good to feel the touch of his strong hand upon her ravaged skin, soothing it, so warm and smooth.

Please, he had said.

At last she gave him her answer. "I accept your invitation. I will be happy to be your guest. However . . ."

She withdrew her hand and held it up as he started to speak. "I will keep at least one of the servant's tasks. I will feed the fire each morning. And I'll find something else to do here, too. I may be a guest, but I'll be a paying one. I will still earn my way."

Conaire grinned. The gleam returned to his eyes. "So you shall, if it makes you happy, Teresa Maeve. Now I will leave you alone in your room, but if I may, I will join you when the sun is high for a ride out. There is something I would like to show you—something I think you would like to see."

She nodded regally. "Thank you. I would like that."

He bowed, left the room, and closed the door. Instantly Terri turned and hurried over to the bath, fumbling with the iron brooch at her shoulder and finally tearing it from the old worn fabric. She kicked off the boots and pulled the heavy iron collar from her neck. In the next instant she had ripped

113

away the rags and was sitting in the clear water of the basin, scrubbing and scrubbing with the little lump of soap.

Dressed once more in her own boots and breeches and shirt, a small bundle tucked under one arm, Terri left the Great Hall and walked out across the lawn with long sure strides. It felt so good to be clean and fresh, to wear fine well-made clothes . . . so nice to be outside in the soft summer air, beneath the noonday sun, on her way to care for Firelair. . . .

She slowed, looking around her. Everywhere people stood and stared. Over the last three days they had all grown accustomed to seeing her in rags and working like a servant. They'd all but forgotten her strange and mysterious origins—until now.

As she walked on again, her thoughts took a serious turn. During her time as a servant, she had been worried about how and where she would fit in. She had been truly relieved, and grateful, when the servants had accepted her and allowed her to find a place beside them. But she had to admit that she did not want to be a servant.

No, not a servant, nor a queen. Was there nothing in between? Would she be forced to choose between the very lowest and the very highest? Would she ever be accorded the treatment she really desired?

She was not from this place, had not been born here, did not grow up here. Would she always be an outsider?

Firelair raised her head and trotted the few steps it took her to cross the small paddock, obviously pleased to see Terri. "Not half as glad as I am to see you!" Terri said, gently hugging the silver mare's neck.

She inspected Firelair's accommodations. She'd caught glimpses of the mare over the last three days, seen her enough to know that she was all right, but had been too busy to do anything more. Now Terri took a closer look.

The mare stood in a small paddock, maybe forty feet

square, with a small shed at one end. The shed was just high enough for her to raise her head a few inches before her ears brushed the tightly bound straw of the roof.

Still, it was better than the low close barn, designed for cattle and small Celtic ponies. The ground was smooth and clean beneath the mare's feet, there was fresh water in the big wooden bucket, and she was obviously well fed and groomed. They were giving Firelair the best they had, just as they had done for Terri.

But fine as the accommodations were, it was clear that Firelair was as anxious as Terri to get outside the fences and walls. Terri shook out the bundle she carried, unrolling the coarse, ragged linen clothes she had worn for the last three days. She was very pleased to find that the old pieces of fabric were ideal for rubbing and polishing the mare's fine coat, and even more pleased to know that no one would ever wear those rags again.

Firelair loved the attention, leaning into the pressure and twitching her upper lip. Terri finished the grooming job with a heavy wooden comb she found beside the water bucket, using the comb to carefully, patiently untangle the long silvery mane and tail.

At last the mare was saddled and ready, and Terri led her out onto the green lawn. Waiting there on their small sturdy horses were Conaire, Ros, and Sivney, and an elderly white-haired man whom Terri did not recognize.

"Will you ride with us, Teresa Maeve?" Conaire asked. "There is something we want to show you—something we think you will like."

"I'd love to," Terri said, her curiosity rising now that they were ready to leave. She turned to the white-haired man on his small black horse. "Good day to you, sir. My name is Teresa. Terri."

"This is our horsemaster," Conaire said. "His name is Sean."

Terri looked at the man again. He was aged, white-haired, with thick bushy silver-white brows. The horsemaster. "Sean," she said, grinning. "Of course!"

Conaire grinned back at her, and her heart lifted even higher at the sight of him there on his powerful red stallion. Then he turned away and sent the stallion galloping for the open gates, the rest of them quickly following.

Terri struggled to keep Firelair from racing past the smaller horses, since she did not know where they were going and had to stay in the rear. Conaire turned almost immediately into the heavy forest, and Terri had her work cut out for her in keeping the great mare from running over the heels of the horses ahead.

For a time they cantered single file through the cool dark woods. Though the fast ride was glorious, especially after the long days of heavy work and confinement, Terri found herself glancing left and right into the mysterious forest. How she would love to see it up close, explore it hour by hour, learn its every path and tree and leaf and flower!

Eventually Conaire eased his red horse to a trot and then a fast-moving walk. Though they were still deep in the forest, Terri realized now that the land was rising. They were traveling up into the hills.

She wanted to talk to Conaire and ask him where they were going—what this place was—where those faint trails led and what that small wooden house was that she thought she saw far away beneath the trees. But he only looked straight ahead and kept his stallion moving forward at a steady, determined pace.

An hour passed, by Terri's estimate, and then suddenly they were out of the woods and blinking in the bright sunshine.

They looked out over gently rolling hills, into a wide valley lush and green with grass and surrounded by heavy forest. A silvery river ran along one edge of the forest, and a few men and boys stood or sat near the trees beside their

small encampments. At the far end of the valley, wedged
in between the forest and some towering cliffs, was a small
cluster of buildings encircled by an earthen wall. It looked
like a miniature version of Dun Cath.

Below them, down in the beautiful sunlit valley, was a
herd of horses.

There were perhaps twenty of them, twenty small Celtic
horses like the ones Conaire and his men rode. But these
were all mares, broodmares, grays and bays and blacks and
browns and bright chestnuts, and every one of them had a
sturdy, glossy foal nearby. The long-legged foals followed
their mothers about, or raced and chased each other over
the lush green grass, or napped in the warmth of the sun.

Terri caught Conaire's eye. He was watching her carefully, waiting to see what her reaction would be.

She smiled at him and then walked Firelair forward, toward the beautiful green fields covered with mares and
foals, knowing that at last she had found her place. She had
come home. No matter what else might happen, she would
always have a place in Conaire's kingdom.

Later that afternoon the buckets and the basin sat waiting
once again in the comfortable corner room of the Great
Hall, and Terri was very glad to see them. She was hot and
dusty from the long ride, and greatly relieved to know that
now she could bathe whenever she wished. After her three
long days as a servant, she would never again take soap
and water and clean clothes for granted. She knew a little
of just how much work was involved in providing them.

Dorren came in, placing a stack of folded linen cloths
on the bed. "Thank you for setting up the bath," Terri said
to her. "I know how much work this is for you—"

The old woman held up her hand. "I do not object to
carrying water." She moved to the far wall, busying herself
with the buckets and basin. "I may be old, but I am strong,
and I have a good life here in Dun Cath with King Conaire.

My husband and my children and I are safe here. We even
have a small house and a few possessions of our own. None
of us are afraid of a bit of work, not for what we receive
in return for it.''

Terri smiled. Dorren's clothes were old and worn, and
her only jewelry was made of cold and somewhat rusted
iron; but she was safe and comfortable and well fed, as was
her family. "I should have known that Conaire would take
good care of everyone," Terri said.

"If there is anything you need from me, you have only
to ask." Dorren gave her a brief nod and started toward
the door.

One thing did spring to Terri's mind. "Well—now that
you mention it . . ." She ran her fingers over her smooth
gray breeches. "These aren't going to last forever. I'm going to need some new riding clothes. Could I get some cloth
and try to make some? Heaven knows I'm not much for
sewing, but I guess I can't just run down to the mall anymore.''

Dorren frowned at her. "Trews, is that what you want?"
She shook her head, her eyes narrowing. "Never will I
become used to seeing a woman running about in trews."

Terri lifted an eyebrow, but held on to her patience.
"Well, you're going to get used to seeing this one in—
trews. I can't very well ride Firelair in a skirt, even the full
ones you wear here! Now, how can I get some fabric? Can
I buy some, or trade for some?''

Now the woman only looked confused. "Buy?" She
turned away and began fussing with the folded linen on the
bed, as though it helped her to think. "There is wool cloth,
plaid, like what we use for most of the men's trews. Is that
what you want?''

"Plaid wool! No, thank you." She shuddered at the idea
of herself in plaid wool breeches. "I believe Conaire wore
some very fine linen trews just the other day. That would

be much better for the summer, and just a plain color. Is there any linen I could use?''

"I suppose." Dorren straightened up and turned to face her. "You will not have to sew them yourself. The king will send a servant to take care of that task."

"Oh. Well, that would be nice, but I don't want to take anyone else away from their work. . . ." She thought for a moment. "Do you sew, Dorren? Could you sew for me and let me do some of your other work?"

The woman almost smiled. "Sewing is the task I would choose if I had a choice." She looked down and ran her fingers across the wool covers on the bed. "I would sit beside the hearth, or on a bench on the lawn, and watch the children play as I worked with my fine needle and good thread and lovely cloth dyed so many bright colors. . . ."

Then she stopped abruptly and looked up again. "There is too much work to be done. Wood and water to be brought. I have not the time to sit and sew pretties when the rushes must be changed. The king will send someone to sew for you, one of the servants of higher rank than I." And with that she started for the door.

"Wait!"

Dorren slowly turned.

"I will ask—I will *tell*—the king—that I want you to sew for me and I will take no one else! Would you sew the new trews for me, Dorren?"

Terri was rewarded with a soft smile in the lined old face. "I will be pleased to sew them for you," Dorren said, and then left the room and closed the door behind her.

Terri sighed as she began pulling off her riding clothes, thinking that making Dorren's life a little easier at her age was the least she could do. She stepped into the basin and began to wash with the clean fresh water, her thoughts wandering.

The cool water felt good to her now, but in the winter it would need to be heated. There was a small hearth built into the corner of the room, like a small fireplace—well, when the weather got colder she could heat her own water there. She wouldn't want anyone trying to carry buckets of hot water up those steep stairs.

She smiled to herself. Already she was planning a future here. But there was going to be much more to this future than deciding how set up her bath.

Would she always remain alone in this room, pleasant though it was? Could she even consider Conaire's offer to make her his wife—make her his queen?

She stepped out of the bath and reached for the folded linen on the bed. Ah, Conaire. Never had she dreamed of finding a man like him—and she'd had some pretty substantial and imaginative dreams. What she really wanted was to find a way to keep him a part of her life without having to give up her newfound freedom in order to be his queen. But just how she was going to do that remained a mystery for now.

She dried off with the linen pieces Dorren had left, and wrapped one around her while she decided what she would wear to dinner with the king. There were riches in these chests such as she had never imagined, and they tempted her—such beautiful colors, such exquisite handworked embroidery. But after a moment of thought, she laid the brightly colored wools and linens back in the chest.

She was not going to dress like royalty. That would only feed Conaire's fantasy that she was his queen, conveniently sent here just for him. No, she was quite certain that she could do better than that.

Terri took out the simplest of the gowns, a solid cream-colored drape of light wool. There was a longer gown of linen, bleached almost white, to go beneath it. The belt was of dark brown leather, beautifully carved with a gold ring at one end.

She closed the lid on the fabulous hoard of jewelry. Terri was determined that the belt would be the only fancy piece she would wear. She would dress neatly, and comfortably, but would do her best to simply blend in. She would most certainly not dress like anything resembling a queen.

At last she was dressed, and sat down to comb out her wet hair with the heavy wooden comb. Her hair was coarse and curling, but the wide comb slid through without too much trouble, so long as she did not hurry. As she set the comb back on the table, she noticed her diamond watch resting beneath the edge of the bronze basin.

She picked up the watch, thinking how strange and out of place it looked among all these handmade clothes and furnishings—and almost smiled to see that it had stopped. Terri placed the watch down in the wooden chest, in with all the other fine jewelry, though she knew that she would not wear it again. Time, as all other things, had a very different meaning for her now.

Scrunching the damp hair into waves with her fingers, Terri walked toward the door and took a deep breath. Never had she felt so good! The hard work, the sweet fresh air, the beautiful green countryside, the good simple food, all combined to make her feel completely refreshed and renewed. Never had she felt so alive, alive as though the very fires of Midsummer were burning in her veins.

With a surge of anticipation, she thought of Conaire. She would be spending the evening with him again—they would be alone in his house, just the two of them.

She pulled open the door. A man stood there.

Terri blinked, and looked up at him. Light brown hair, blue eyes, smooth young face, dressed in a dark blue tunic—no, this was not Conaire, this was—

''Lonan,'' she said.

She remembered him well from the day she'd first ridden into Dun Cath. That seemed like ages ago, though it had only been four days. He had often been in the vicinity during her stint as a servant. She recalled looking up several

121

times during those days to see him standing there, watching her.

"Yes," he said, with a charming smile. "I am so pleased that you remember me."

She stepped into the *grianan* and pulled the door closed behind her. "I've not yet met many of the people here, but I hope to remedy that soon."

"Perhaps you can start with me." He smiled again. "If I may, I would like to walk with you, speak with you. There is something very much on my mind."

Now, what in the world could he want to talk to her about? Most of the people here tended to avoid her, giving her little more than intensely curious stares. Now she was the one who was curious.

She looked at him again. He was somewhat younger and more boyish than Conaire, and though she would ordinarily have considered him a handsome man, she found that he had none of the powerful, almost magical effect on her that Conaire had.

Yet she still wanted to know why he wanted so much to talk to her. She started to speak, then happened to glance down over the side of the balcony into the hall—and just at that moment the king walked in, his long red-and-gray mantle sweeping the rushes behind him.

Well, now! Did Conaire think she would not talk to any other men here in his kingdom? Did he expect to see her hurry away from Lonan just because Conaire was approaching? No. How many times had she told him that she was not his queen and not his property?

This might give her a small chance to start getting that point across a little more clearly!

Terri walked past Lonan and went to the railing. Leaning back and resting an elbow on it, she stood right where Conaire could not avoid seeing her. She tossed her head, flipping back her damp and curling hair, and tilted her head to smile up at Lonan.

"I would be glad to speak with you," she said. "Please, tell me what's on your mind."

He took a step toward her, his face turning serious. "Teresa, I am very distressed by the way King Conaire has treated you these last three days. No woman of your station should be treated so. You are no servant. You are a guest of Dun Cath, and should have been treated like one."

For a moment she almost forgot about Conaire in the hall below. At their first meeting, Lonan had clearly demonstrated his dislike and strong suspicion of her. What had happened to change his feelings?

But maybe it didn't matter. Her three days of drudgery had certainly changed the way Dorren felt about her. She'd even gained further respect from Conaire. The same thing must have happened to Lonan.

"It's very kind of you to say that," she told him, and meant it. She was proud of the way she had stood up to Conaire, met his challenge, and proven her point that she could take care of herself. Yet it was good to know that not every man here thought she had deserved such a test.

"I would like to make it up to you," Lonan continued, moving closer to her. "I will care for you as befits a lady—serve you, provide for you, see to your every need. . . ."

His face was only a few inches from hers. His skin was flushed and fair and his blue eyes glittered. She gazed into those bright blue eyes, thinking of how much he reminded her of her high school prom date—cute, and sweet, and fun to be with. Nothing serious, safe and harmless.

She almost felt tempted to kiss him, and why not? She knew that Conaire must be watching from down below in the hall. What better way to hammer home to him the fact that she was an independent woman who would do as she pleased, that she belonged to no man, not even—*especially* not even—the king!

Just then Lonan stiffened and pulled back. Terri looked at him in surprise, then realized he was looking over her shoulder at something behind her. His gaze had hardened into something between anger and fear.

She turned around, and there stood Conaire. His face was very still, showing no emotion; he merely stood and stared at Lonan.

The air between them tightened into tense silence.

It was like being caught between two warring bucks. Yet as the moments passed, and Conaire stepped up to stand beside Terri, she quickly became aware that this was quite an uneven contest. Conaire was the massive, powerful stag facing down the young spike buck, Lonan.

And face him down he did. Without a word, face red, glaring, Lonan ducked away and brushed past them, hurrying down the stairs and then stalking out the door of the Great Hall without once looking back.

Conaire's cold gaze followed him the whole way. At last, when the blue-clad figure had disappeared out the door, he turned to Terri and instantly his face changed. He relaxed, and smiled, and seemed as calm as if Lonan had never been there.

"Good evening, Teresa Maeve," he said. "May I escort you to dinner?"

Chapter Eleven

Slowly, cautiously, picking up the hems of her long cream-colored skirts, Terri stepped into the soft twilight of the king's house. It was a great circular house perhaps thirty feet across, with a pair of beautifully carved wooden poles framing its doorway, and it stood directly behind the Hall.

There was a stone hearth in the center, surrounded by heavy wooden benches. As in the Great Hall, the thatched roof had a hole cut in the center of it where the sweet-smelling smoke from the hearth rose into the summer sky. Around the inside perimeter of the house were tall screens of dark leather, laced into wooden frames and used to block off the house into rooms. The result was a neat, cozy, simple interior, with a thick bed of clean rushes on the floor.

"Welcome to my home," Conaire said. He was watching her closely, waiting for her reaction.

"It's a fine house, King Conaire," Terri said, stepping carefully through the rushes. She meant it: The home was solid, and protective, and gave her the same feeling of safety and comfort that Conaire himself did.

He offered her his hand, and she reached out to take it. He led her to the bench nearest the front of the stone hearth, and she sat down on the smooth wooden surface as he stepped to the edge. Waiting for them was a single wide gold plate and two round golden cups.

The food was the finest she had seen since coming

there—some kind of neatly sliced roasted meat, covered with a clear broth; a little mound of white salt beside the slices; and a flat loaf of bread, spread with dark yellow butter and sweet golden honey, with chopped dried apples sprinkled over the top. Conaire handed her one of the goblets and she found, to her surprise, milk! It tasted warm, but fresh, with a rich sweet flavor.

Conaire sat down beside her and drew a gleaming knife from his belt. With careful strokes he cut the slices of meat into long slender strips. He lifted one, touched it to the white mound of salt, and offered it to Terri.

She did not reach for it. Instead she leaned forward, tilted her head, and took the strip of meat from his hand with her teeth.

It was delicious, with a strong, rich flavor brought out by the salt. "What kind of meat is this?"

"Venison," he said, dipping another slice in the salt. "From the young buck we found on our journey home the night I found you."

He fed her another bite, then took one himself. "You are well dressed, Teresa Maeve, but I do not see any of the fine gold I sent to you. Do you not like it?"

She brushed away a bit of salt from her lip and took another drink of the milk. "It's all beautiful. Fabulous. I've never seen anything like it. If I'd had a treasure chest like that back in—back in America, I could have retired."

"So, if you like the gold pieces, why do you not wear any of them? They would look so beautiful against your skin . . . how the gold would shine against your dark hair. . . ." He reached out and gently stroked her hair, catching one end and touching it to his cheek.

With a little toss of her head, she pulled the lock of hair from his fingers. "I thought you said that a queen did not need 'decorating.'"

With a wide grin, he rose to his feet and stood close to her. "So, you acknowledge that you could be a queen, Teresa Maeve. I am so pleased to hear it. Shall we plan the wedding for tomorrow? Or would you rather wait a day or so?''

Terri turned away from him and sat sideways on the bench. ''I never said any such thing! I only meant that you were right when you said I did not need any gold or silver or diamonds or anything else to show the world what I am. Never have, never will!''

She reached back into the golden plate and broke off a piece of the buttered bread, thick with honey and dried apples. ''Besides, I thought you said you weren't sure you wanted me for your queen. Don't you have more tests lined up?'' She took a bite—it was like heaven, so sweet and rich.

''Why, so I do! You are so clever, Teresa Maeve. It's too bad cleverness is not one of my tests.'' He sighed. ''I suppose we shall have to put off the marriage for the time being.''

''Good.'' Quite pleased with herself, she swung both feet over the bench and reached for another chunk of bread and honey and apples.

He sat down close beside her, on the other side of the bench. ''Now I have another question for you,'' he murmured, so close that she could feel his breath on her neck. Her hand stopped halfway from the golden plate, still holding the bread. A thin line of honey began to fall from it.

''Lonan came to your door tonight. Do you wish to see him? To spend time with him as you have spent it with me?''

Her jaw tightened. ''I will see whomever I like. Not even a king will tell me what man I am allowed to see.''

''Of course not.'' She expected him to pull away from her, but he remained close—shifting ever so slightly so that now he was pressing the side of his body against hers. ''I will leave you to him. Shall I walk with you back to your room, or would you prefer to return alone?''

"No." She said it so quickly that she was almost surprised to hear the word. "No. I don't want to go back."

He leaned his head down close to hers. "Even as king, I would not ask you to go anywhere you did not want to go." His lips touched her cheek as he spoke. "I will be pleased to have you stay, if that is your wish."

Terri dropped the piece of bread. She turned to Conaire, breathing in his warm scent, brushing her cheek against the soft smoothness of his beard. "It is my wish."

Again, the lightest touch of his mouth on her face. "I am so pleased that you will stay here with me this evening," he said softly. Then he stopped, his lips almost touching hers. "But how can I stop you from seeing other men? There are so many handsome young warriors here at Dun Cath. I want to keep you for myself. How can I do that?"

"You can't," she whispered, her eyes closing.

He nodded, and shrugged his shoulders in resignation. "You are right. I cannot stop you. Then, I shall have to use other means to convince you—to turn your thoughts to me alone, to forget all other men."

Conaire lifted her up in his arms. Terri held on to him as he swept her away from the glowing hearth and carried her across the room, past the tall leather screens and into the darkness beyond.

It had been many days since they had first come together, and Terri pulled Conaire to her with all the fierceness she possessed. Here in the soft darkness of his room, safely closed away from any chance of prying eyes, she felt even freer than she had out on the sunlit hillside. The two of them rolled together atop the softest of furs on Conaire's large wood-frame bed, and Terri gave herself over to the pleasures of love as she never had before.

After a time, they lay together in the quiet beneath the single small, high window. Terri looked up at the distant shining stars and smiled to herself. She moved closer to

Conaire, stretching her body the full length of his, reveling in his smooth hot skin and sweet musky scent. With a sigh she rested her head on his massive shoulder.

The tension was easing now . . . her eyes began to close . . . she could sleep, now, sated at last, safe and warm and oh, so comfortable here in his arms.

But her eyes opened wide as Conaire suddenly began to move. He raised himself over her, his head moving in front of the window so that instead of the stars she saw only the gleam of his eyes.

"Surely you cannot be falling asleep, Teresa Maeve." He bent down to her, pulling her close with one strong arm, and began to kiss her neck with warm, insistent lips. "You will have no need of other men," he whispered, with quickening breath. "I will see to that . . . oh, I will see to that. . . ."

Terri felt as though she were melting. She caught her breath as he moved atop her and his weight pressed her down into the furs. She pulled him close, gripping his thickmuscled arms as he moved to thrust within her again, and again, making her his own, claiming her for himself even as she claimed him.

For the next several days, until one began to blur into the next and she could no longer recall how many days she had lived at Dun Cath, Terri followed the same routine—an exhilarating, dizzying routine that all but swept away any memory of her life before Conaire and the land of Eire.

Each morning she awoke the same way—in the darkness of her room, with Conaire sliding into her bed and embracing her with the strength only he possessed. He always left without a word just as grayness came to the sky. Terri would stretch luxuriously and lie blinking in the dawn, feeling as though she had just awakened from the sweetest of dreams.

After she had washed and dressed, she would make her

way downstairs and go outside to one of the storage sheds. There she would gather a pile of wood, as much as she could carry, and take it to the hearth in the center of the Great Hall. As the servants began entering the Hall or stirring in the rushes to begin their day's work, Terri kindled the dimming fire from the embers buried in the ashes.

When the fire blazed once more, she took a quick breakfast among the servants before leaving the Great Hall once again. Firelair always stood waiting, and Terri groomed her as the mare ate her morning oats. Shortly after, with the silver mare clean and saddled, Terri swung up and rode out across the green lawn. Always she felt a small surge of excitement as she watched the heavy gates of Dun Cath open wide to let her through, and waved to the watchman as she rode out into the fresh new morning.

Sometimes she would lead a quiet pack pony carrying food and supplies for the men and boys who tended the broodmares. On those days the trip would be slow and relaxing, in keeping with the old pony's pace; she and Firelair would drink in the sights and sounds and scents of the countryside, and time would slow to nearly a standstill as the three of them made their way across the hills.

But on the days when it was just Terri and Firelair and the wild free country, the two of them made the most of it. They were free to canter and gallop as they wished, to jump the ditches and streams and fallen trees to their heart's content. At first Terri stayed close to the well-worn trail she had followed with Conaire and his men, but soon she began exploring the smaller paths and shortcuts that led into the cool deep woods. Before long she felt quite at home in the forests between Dun Cath and the herd of mares and foals.

Once at the herds, she would greet Calva, the chief herder, and the four young men who helped him. They would tell her all that had happened since her last visit— where the best grazing was, where they planned to move the herd next, and how the foal with the injured knee was doing. She would remember it all so that she could describe it later for King Conaire.

She always returned to the dun in time for lunch—and in time to spend another delightful half hour alone with Conaire. ''Will you tell me now that you need no other man, Teresa Maeve?'' he would whisper. *There is no one but you, no one I need but you*, she wanted to tell him—but she could not bring herself to say the words.

She could not let him have that hold over her. She wanted him, but did not want him to know that she was also beginning to need him—need his strength, his passion, his all-encompassing protectiveness that felt so very much like love. And so she would only hold him close, and revel in his strength and passion, and hope this lovely dream might never end.

In the afternoons she went out to the paddocks to see which of the colts old Sean wanted her to work with that day. Terri loved working with the young horses, teaching them to lead, stand quietly for grooming, and wear a bit and bridle. Most importantly, she taught them that humans were their partners and protectors, and could always be obeyed because they could always be trusted.

Sean would watch her from the other side of the fence, content to relax there in the warmth of the afternoon sun. Terri knew that she was gradually taking over much of his work, and was careful not to make him feel that he was being pushed aside. She always heeded his advice, and followed his lead, and it was not long before the two of them had become good friends.

Every evening, no matter how late the hour or how long his day had been, Conaire always came to her bed to take possession of her once again. He never failed to remind her that she'd found the man she had never hoped to find—the man of unquenchable passion, boundless masculine strength, and never-ending devotion who was hers and hers alone.

One sunset, just as Terri was turning loose the year-old chestnut filly she had been leading, Conaire came out to the paddock. He leaned across the wooden fence and smiled at Terri as she walked over to him.

"Good evening to you, King Conaire," she said, gathering up the length of rope. Even after all these weeks of intimacy, she still felt as though she were seeing him for the first time whenever he approached. Now he stood casually before her, one elbow on the topmost rail of the fence, and she drank in the sight of him.

As always, he looked every inch a king. He wore a dark green tunic of beautiful woven linen, embroidered in stunning interlocking patterns with gold thread so heavy it was almost like shining wire. A heavy gold neck-piece rested at his throat, and more gold gleamed at his massive wrists and strong fingers. But even had he worn nothing but servant's garb, there would be no mistaking him for anything but a king. One glance at that noble face—at those sharp and shining brown eyes, the firm jaw beneath the red-brown beard, the expression of will and strength—would tell the whole story.

He gazed at her, and grinned, making the fine lines crinkle beneath his eyes. "Good evening to you, Teresa Maeve. And may I say you are looking exceptionally lovely this evening."

Terri stopped. Was he making a joke? She was suddenly self-conscious about her worn gray breeches and plain linen tunic, both of which were covered with dirt and sweat from her long day of hard riding and horse training. Next to Conaire, in his fine clothes and heavy gleaming gold, she looked almost like a servant again.

But she looked up at him and refused to be embarrassed. "I wore nothing but mud and rags in front of you for three solid days. I'm not about to be ashamed of wearing plain clothes and putting in an honest day's work.'' She finished coiling the lead rope, glaring at him from beneath her lowered brows.

''So you did.'' He grinned wickedly, his white teeth gleaming. ''But do not forget, beauty is one of the things a queen must have. Especially my queen.''

Instantly her temper flared. She knew he was baiting her, but some things simply could not go unchallenged. ''Conaire—listen to me. Do you know what I have been talking to Sean about today?''

''I could not begin to guess. Please, tell me.''

''You know how much everyone admires Firelair. Wouldn't you like to have more horses like her for Dun Cath?''

His eyes shone. ''I would. But there are no others like her. If she was taken to any of the stallions here, her foal would still be smaller, more like our own horses.''

''Yes. But over the years, with careful selection, you would begin to see horses of her type. And most of all, you could get another true mare—another mare who is the seventh filly foal in an unbroken line of filly foals. Sean says there have been none here, at least none that anyone knows of for sure. I could keep track! I could set up a program to breed the finest horses ever seen in all of Eire!''

''That would be wonderful indeed, Teresa Maeve.'' His face was solemn now. ''That would be enough to keep anyone busy for a long time. Perhaps even a lifetime.''

''Oh, but that's only a start! You can't know the best horses just by looking at them. You've got to train them, ride them, test them!''

''Test them.'' Conaire gazed at her, but she only glared back. ''And I am certain you intend to do all of this yourself.''

''Yes! You know there's no one better qualified to do this! I could teach you what I know about horse care—how to breed them, how to train them. How to ride with stirrups!

133

No one would love to do this more than I would."

"I see." He was quite serious now. "You would rather be queen of horses than queen of Dun Cath?"

She smiled in relief. Had she broken through to him at last? "Yes! Yes, you could look at it that way," she said to him. "Unless you tell me that I can do all this while still being queen of Dun Cath?"

He hesitated. "The king—and the people of the dun— have greater need for a queen than do the horses." Conaire reached out to her, across the fence, and took her hand. "Could you not consider a compromise? Surely the queen could allow others to run the breeding. Surely the horse boys could count the number of filly foals born in a row." He tried to smile. "And even a queen may ride out alone on her favorite mare from time to time."

Terri shook her head. "It would not be the same. You know that no one can do this better than I. Are you going to forbid me to work with the horses, Conaire? Are you going to make me a servant again, thinking that I'd rather marry you and be your queen than empty the slop buckets again?"

His voice was quiet. "You are a free woman. You were willing to work as the lowest of servants, and so you have earned the right to take on the tasks you want. You are free to live as you wish, within our laws." Conaire paused, and took a deep breath. "I will not have an unwilling queen."

"Free." She looked up at him. "Nothing is more important to me than my freedom. You must understand that. I spent all those years locked away, doing what everyone else wanted me to do and never what was important to me. Now I have all that I ever could have wanted—a job to do and a beautiful land to live on."

She gazed at him, and her voice softened. "Why could it not go on the way it is now? We are so happy together. I have my work, and you have yours, and the rest of the time is ours." Terri hesitated, then thought of all those mornings and afternoons and evenings when Conaire had sought her out—he was always there, waiting for her, ready for her. "I will admit to you that I need no other man."

She saw the faint gleam of satisfaction in his eyes. "I am very glad to hear it." But his face did not change. "I, too, am happy with you, Teresa Maeve. But it cannot go on this way forever. I am bound to take a queen, and take one soon. Enough time has passed already. If you are not that queen, you will have to find another man. Or you will have to live alone and I will come to you only in the night."

A faint chill passed over Terri. "Come to me only in the night?" She withdrew her hand and shook her head. "I will never live like that."

She backed away a step. "I don't know what to tell you. You know how I feel. I don't know what else I can do to change your mind, but I can tell you one thing that is certain: I will not give you my freedom, King Conaire. I will not give you my freedom."

Chapter Twelve

An hour past dawn the next day, Terri led Firelair across the lawn to the small white building that held the blacksmith's forge. Sean walked beside her, shaking his head as he looked at the strange object in his hand: one of Firelair's steel shoes. The loose broken nails in it rattled as he turned it this way and that.

"I found it in her paddock this morning," Terri said. "They've got to come off. She can't wait any longer. I know you can't put them back on—I wouldn't know how, either—but I can't let her go around with only three shoes, or wait till she loses them. They'll be falling off soon anyway. That left front one is loose already."

"So it is." Sean looked up as the smith stepped out of the forge-house. "Now, how do you expect this to be done?"

"Well . . ." Terri thought back to the work she had seen done on the riding-school horses back in her own time. "The main thing is to cut the clinches—the nails, here, where they're bent over on the outside of her hoof—and then pry the shoe off and the nails with it, out through the hoof."

"Sounds brutal to me," Sean grumbled. "Driving nails through a horse's foot!"

The smith reached out and took the shoe from Sean. "It's well made, I'll say that," he remarked, turning it over and studying it closely. "Never seen the like of it. May I keep it?"

"Of course," Terri said. "I'm very grateful for your help. I sure wouldn't want to try this on my own."

Sean glanced at her, scowling, but said nothing.

"All right then," said the smith. He was a slender man of medium height, with years of hard work etched into his face. He disappeared into the forge-house with the shoe, and came back out with an enormous hammer and a small square of steel. "I think I see the way of it. Bring her here, to the tallest stone."

He walked to one of the large stones, nearly as big as boulders, which sat outside the forge-house door and served as benches. Terri led the mare close. The smith reached down, pulled the mare's front leg forward, and placed her foot on top of the stone. Bracing himself, he set a thin square of steel snugly against the outside of the mare's hoof, beneath the row of clinched nails, and struck each nail with a hammer.

One by one the ends of the nails went flying. Firelair looked somewhat baffled at having her foot placed on top of a boulder, but stood still as the smith struck the nails.

Terri held her breath. She wanted to close her eyes, but could not. That hammer was huge, bigger and heavier than anything a modern horseshoer would use for such a task. If his hand slipped, if the mare should jerk her foot as he struck—

The smith changed sides and placed the square of steel on the other side of the hoof. The hammer struck again, once, twice, a third time. Then he took down the hoof and bent it up until he could see the bottom of it. He forced the thin square of steel between the hoof and the shoe and began working it up and down, prying off the shoe and drawing its nails from the mare's living hoof.

"Careful—don't let the nails catch—" Terri nearly reached for his arm, but managed to restrain herself. Firelair seemed unconcerned, and at last the smith stood up with the nail-spiked shoe in his hand.

Holding her breath, Terri forced herself to look at the hoof. She was terrified that it would be broken and torn from the force of the smith's tools, unfamiliar as he was with such a task. But he was a man of great patience and had taken great care with his work. Firelair's hoof was whole and sound, with only three neat holes on each side of it where the nails had been.

She breathed a sigh of relief. And as she watched, the mare's other front foot was done, and then the one hind foot that still had a shoe on it. The smith gathered up the three shoes he had just removed and took them back into the forge-house.

"I still don't see the reason for it," Sean said. "Our horses are not nearly as large as this one and they need no such things on their feet. They already have feet as tough as stone."

Terri smiled, and patted the mare's neck. "It's just the custom, where we come from, to shoe the working horses. She has to work on paved—ah, very hard roads sometimes, and the shoes also help her when she's jumping."

"Jumping?"

"Yes, she was a hunter. Firelair could jump a fence as high as your head, or even higher." Well, Terri felt sure that she could, though of course she'd never seen her do any such thing. "The shoes protect her front feet on landing from such high jumps, and can be specially made to help keep her from slipping."

"She could jump as high as my head?"

Terri glanced up at the mare. "Of course." Well, couldn't any Irish hunter as fine as Firelair jump six feet? "I'll show you sometime," she said, and patted the mare's neck, not believing what she had just said.

The smith came back out of the house holding all four shoes, now free of the sharp broken nails. "Strangest things

I've ever seen," he commented, looking closely at the machine-made steel shoes. "I'd give something to know how these were made. Do you want them back?"

"No . . . you keep them." Terri could see how interested he was, and neither she nor Firelair would have any further use for horseshoes. "You can hang them over your door for luck."

"Hang them?" He glanced up at her. "No, I'll study them, and then maybe give them to my sons. I know they've never seen anything like this."

Sean crouched down and looked closely at the mare's hooves. "Not much damage done, but I'd say you should not ride her until her hooves have grown accustomed to going about naturally. I'd give her at least a fortnight."

"A—what?"

"A fortnight."

"How long is that?"

Sean and the smith glanced at each other, and then Sean looked back at Terri. "Perhaps you had a different word for it in Merrica. It means fourteen nights. Fortnight."

She grinned. "A fortnight. Yes, I think you're right— give her a couple of weeks to let her feet grow out and toughen up."

Terri turned and led the mare back toward the paddock, very relieved that this ordeal was over. She almost felt like laughing. Fourteen nights! Of course.

The next morning, Terri set out for the broodmare herd, but not on her trusty Firelair. As she rode through the gate she steadied herself on the bare back of a small bay stallion. Scallan was a young and fiery chariot horse, barely three years old. He had had little experience with carrying a rider, or with going out alone, but there were not many spare horses in Dun Cath and he was the only mount available this morning.

Terri knew it would take some time for the two of them

to get accustomed to each other. She just hoped that she could get him there and back again without a major battle, for she was not about to go back on her promise to ride out to the broodmare herd each day.

She needed two strong hands on the reins to guide him, and could have used another to grab hold of his mane as he constantly snorted and shied and started and stopped. But the combination of her insistent hands on the reins and hammering heels on his sides kept Scallan moving in the right general direction, and after a long and tiring trip she finally reached the herd.

But the real struggle began the moment they rode out of the forest and entered the lush green field. The young stallion completely forgot about his rider at the sight of twenty lovely, tail-swishing mares, and immediately began whinnying loudly at them and showing off with all the prancing power he could summon. Terri had her work cut out for her as she pulled and pushed him on his way until she could complete her circuit around the herd. Everything was in order, the mares and foals at peace beneath the blue skies with puffy white clouds, and after talking briefly to the herders, Terri headed back home.

When she was almost in sight of the dun, she pulled Scallan off the trail toward the river. As she approached the rushing water, the stallion raised his head and neighed, long and loud, and started to trot off along the bank. Once again she wrenched his head around and pushed him where she wanted him to go. Though she loved a challenge—and this half-wild creature was certainly going to teach her a lot about training a young horse—she would be very, very glad when she could once again ride out on Firelair.

The stallion stopped short at the edge of the river and slammed his head down to the water to drink, almost sending Terri sprawling over his neck. She braced herself with her hands, pushed herself back up, and reached for the leather flask of water slung over her back. She found it

140

much easier to drink from the flask instead of having to get down on her knees at the edge of the rivers and streams.

She'd barely finished her first swallow when the stallion threw his head up and neighed again, the force of his cry shaking his whole body. Quickly she took up the reins, but Scallan stood rooted to the spot with his head up and his small black-tipped ears pricked in the direction of the dun.

Now she heard it, too. There was a horse stepping through the thick brush on the other side of the narrow river—breaking through to the water's edge—a short seal-brown horse with a rider who was familiar.

"Lonan!" Awkwardly, still trying to steady the young stallion, Terri managed to close the leather flask and sling it back over her shoulder.

She was greatly annoyed with herself for not knowing the man was there. She was normally quite aware of what was going on around her—the result of living and working for many years in a big city—but this time she had been so preoccupied with the horse that Lonan had just walked right up on her.

"It's, ah, nice to see you," she said, struggling to keep Scallan from plunging into the water and joining the other horse.

Lonan made no reply. He sat watching her from the other side of the narrow river, his blue tunic standing out against the soft green of the trees.

The stallion neighed again and Terri forced him this way and that. She was now thoroughly soaked from his splashing in the knee-deep water. Finally she got him on the grass, slid down from his back, and jerked the reins sharply, getting his attention and giving her a chance to catch her breath.

"Good morning," she called, stretching her legs and trying to brush the wet horsehair from her breeches. She was going to be stiff and sore tomorrow from this wild bareback ride, she could tell that already.

141

The seal-brown horse began splashing across the shallow river, and Terri took a firm hold of Scallan. But having Terri at his head instead of on his back seemed to steady him, and he stood alert but unmoving as Lonan stopped a short distance away.

She looked up at him, expecting him to speak to her, but still he said nothing. His silence began to unnerve her. First he had sneaked up on her, and now he sat staring, silent as a stone.

"I'm just on my way back to the dun," she said, trying to make conversation. "What brings you out here today?"

He slid down from the brown horse's back and dropped the reins. "You," he said, walking toward her. "I've come out here for you."

Terri took a step backward. "Me?"

"You, Teresa. Only you." He was so close now that he could reach out and touch her if he wished. She backed up until she stood pressed against Scallan's damp and quivering shoulder.

"I have come for you, to take you from the man who has treated you so badly."

For a moment, she blinked. "What man? What are you talking about?"

"Conaire." His face became dark and cold. "Conaire, who has demeaned you, who has stolen you away from me—Conaire, who has stolen my—my—"

She stared at him, trying to register what he had said. "Conaire? Treated me badly?"

Terri thought of the last time she had seen Conaire . . . it had been this morning, in her room, on the wonderful soft bed beneath the smooth linen covers. . . . She shook her head. "King Conaire has given me everything I ever could have wished for. Why do you say he has treated me badly?"

"You are a woman of the Otherworld, but he treats you like a servant—like one of the horse boys. He has no love

142

for you. He is merely in need of a queen and has been unable to obtain one. Now he thinks to buy you with gold and gifts and promises, even while working you like the meanest of the servants—like a slave.''

After a moment of shocked silence, Terri burst out laughing. The stallion jumped a little, but Lonan only looked at her, his eyes widening and his face growing pale.

''I am the one you should look to, Teresa!'' he insisted, his voice rising. ''I am the one who cares for you! Come with me. I will care for you. I will show you—''

She turned her back on him, still chuckling, and started to gather up Scallan's reins. ''Thank you, but no. I know how to deal with Conaire, and I am quite happy with the way things are. If I change my mind, I promise you'll be the first to know.''

She froze as he grabbed her arm.

''Why do you turn away from me? You belong with me, not with Conaire—never with Conaire, nothing for Conaire—''

''Let go of me! What are you doing?'' Terri tried to wrench away, but he dragged her around to face him and caught her other arm, too.

''Come with me,'' he growled. ''Come with—''

With a shriek of rage and a superhuman effort, Terri got her right arm free and punched the side of Lonan's face as hard as she could. The stallion leaped back, but she held on to the reins, her sudden violence startling the man into letting go. Quickly she grabbed Scallan's black mane and vaulted onto his back.

She caught a glimpse of Lonan's face as she swung the stallion around. That face was dark, cold, furious. But he was not half as furious as she was.

''If you ever lay a finger on me again, I swear I'll kill you myself! I've never harmed a soul in my life, but for you I will make an exception! I'm not afraid of you! Don't you *ever* try to tell me what to do *ever again*!''

She released the stallion and he sprang into a mad gallop, racing her back to Conaire and Dun Cath.

On the wide green lawn of the dun, Terri pulled Scallan to a halt and leaped down to the grass. A young stable boy dashed up to catch the reins. Shaking with anger—she'd had the entire half-mile ride back from the stream to nurse her rage—Terri headed straight for the Great Hall.

Her damp hair flew wild around her face and her clothes were covered with sweat and horsehair, but she did not care. Right now nothing was more important than finding Conaire. If she had to drag him away from his men with her bare hands, she would make him stop whatever he was doing and speak to her.

In an instant she was stomping up the two wooden steps to the Hall and standing in the doorway. "King Conaire! I want to talk to you *right now*!"

Terri stood glaring with her hands on her hips, the recipient of a dozen astonished glances. Conaire and several of his men, Ros, Sivney, and Brann among them, sat on benches near the hearth. They were obviously in the middle of some sort of discussion. No one moved, although Terri did see a few glances flick towards Conaire.

"Right now!"

At last Conaire got up and took a step towards her. "We are in the midst of something rather important, Teresa Maeve," he said carefully, looking at her with a slight frown. "I will speak to you as soon as we are done. Perhaps we can eat together, in my house, after you have—"

"No! I'm not looking for a lunch date! I demand to speak to King Conaire *right this minute*! *Alone*!"

His face did not change, but she could see his chest rise and fall in a deep sigh. "So you shall." Conaire turned to his men. "I will send for you when we are finished talking." After a brief pause, and a few glances at each other, the men all got up and walked out the door. Not one of them looked at Terri, who had to step aside to let them pass.

Finally they were alone in the empty hall. Even the servants had vanished. Conaire stood his ground, arms folded across his chest. "So. Tell me what it is that is so important. I am sure you would not interrupt the king's business with his men without a very good reason."

"Of course I wouldn't!" She pulled off the water flask and threw it down into the rushes. "I've got a very good reason! I want someone killed."

He never moved, but his eyebrows raised. "Killed? Why? And who?"

"Lonan, that's who! And why? Because he just sneaked up on me and grabbed me! Said I belonged to him! If I hadn't hauled off and slugged him, I don't know what he might have done!"

"Did anyone else see this?"

"No! No one! He sneaked up on me because I was alone! He was waiting for me!"

Conaire walked over to her, touched her for the first time. "You are not hurt?"

"No, but I sure wish *he* was," she growled. "I want him dead! If he isn't stopped, he'll do it again, to me or to some other woman! There are too many men who've gotten away with that kind of thing, but this one won't—not if I have anything to say about it!"

Conaire led her to one of the benches. He sat down, but she remained on her feet. "Please, sit down," he said. When she only glared at him, he repeated his request. "Please."

She dropped to the bench, still glaring. "So? Are you going to do it, or do I have to?"

"Teresa Maeve—listen to me for a moment. I cannot go out and kill Lonan."

"Why not? I thought you were the king! You can do whatever you want to do!"

"I am the king," he said, sitting down beside her. "But I am not the law. It may be different where you are from, but here no one is above the law—not even the king."

"But don't you have laws against men attacking women? Don't you have laws allowing women to defend themselves?"

"We do. And a trial can be held, but I warn you, if there were no witnesses, it will only be your word against his. Do you want me to order a trial? The decision must be yours."

"I want you to make sure Lonan never tries to harm any woman ever again! And I want you to do it now!"

He placed a gentle hand on her arm. "If you do not want a trial, there is nothing I can do. I simply cannot walk out and kill one of my own men."

"Even though you're king?"

"Especially because I am king. In many ways a king is more restricted than other men in what he does. A king must think about the consequences of his actions . . . if he wishes to remain a king."

"But I want—"

"A queen, too, must think about what she does. She must think of how her actions will affect her people . . . and her king."

"I am not anyone's queen, as I have said so many times before," Terri snapped. She stood up again and scowled down at Conaire, arms crossed. "But you're right—I don't want a trial. I haven't got any proof; it's just my word against his. But I'm not going to let him get away with this!"

He rose to his feet. "There are things worse than death."

"Oh? Like what?"

"Like humiliation."

"Humiliation?" Her temper flared again. "What you did—or tried to do—to me, when I was a servant? That did me no harm. I don't consider a little work to be worse than death!''

''That was not humiliation, dear Teresa Maeve.'' Conaire actually laughed. ''That was merely a small lesson in humility, a very different thing. I'm talking about real humiliation—disgrace, loss of honor, making a once-respected man a figure of ridicule.'' He got to his feet and stood close to her, his eyes gleaming. ''Satire.''

She looked at him, cocking her head slightly. ''And how is such a thing done?''

He shrugged. ''In any number of ways. A satire can be a song, or a poem, or a story, all illustrating the misdeeds of the one in question and detailing why he is no longer worthy of anyone's respect. But I have often found that it is not even necessary to do that much. Many times the subject of a satire ends up being a willing victim. If he is truly deserving of a satire, he will walk right into it and none could stop him if they tried. You have only to be ready for him.''

''I see,'' Terri whispered, her face brightening. ''I know exactly what you mean. And I'll be ready for Lonan.''

Chapter Thirteen

The next afternoon, Terri finished grooming Firelair and turned her loose in the paddock to eat her oats. The dun was quiet today, almost sleepy in the warm summer sun and still, humid air. Conaire had gone hunting with most of his men. The rest of the people stayed inside to rest or to do their simplest indoor tasks.

Terri glanced up at the sky, where the sun made its lazy way toward the west. She was hot and tired and dusty and sweaty after a long day of riding out to the broodmare herds and then taking a turn at working in one of the gardens.

At this moment, there was nothing in the world she wanted more than a bath. The bronze saucer with its few inches of clean water would be waiting for her in her room, but as she lifted her damp, heavy hair off her neck she knew that it simply wouldn't do—not today!

She thought of the clear, cool river that tumbled gently over smooth rocks just a short way from the dun. It was sheltered beneath the trees, dappled with the sunlight which filtered through the forest: clear rushing water deep enough to swim in.

Quickly she ran up to her room and gathered what she would need—several pieces of clean linen to serve as towels, her heavy wooden comb, a lump of soap. Terri stripped off her boots and work clothes and pulled on a clean linen undergown; then, grabbing her things, she left her room and headed on foot for the gates of Dun Cath.

"Ahhh . . ."

Terri stood in the dappled shade of the riverbank, gazing in delicious anticipation at the crystal clear water. At the base of a tiny waterfall a pool had formed, lined with smooth clean rocks just a couple of feet beneath the surface. The rushing water sparkled in the stray sunlight that shone down through the trees.

She had walked several yards downstream from where the drinking water was drawn, yet not so far that a shout might not bring someone running. She set down her things, pulled the linen gown off over her head, and stepped down into the water. Settling herself against a large smooth rock, Terri closed her eyes in bliss as the water rose up to her chin and the cool currents caressed her beneath the bright surface.

She'd been grateful for the bathing arrangement set up in her room each day; she well understood that such things were a luxury here. But there was still nothing like immersing herself in clean, clear rushing water, from her long dark hair to her tired aching feet, and after a moment she slid beneath the surface and let the cold water close over the top of her head.

After a time she broke through the surface and caught her breath, then moved to the edge of the pool and reached for the soap. She spent the next several minutes scrubbing and scrubbing in the pool, and then rinsing beneath the little waterfall. At last she sat back against the rocks to let the cool current give her one last gentle massage. It was so relaxing. She could see only the soft green forest and the bright surface of the water, hear only the rushing of the waterfall behind her.

Then, through half-closed eyes, Terri caught a sudden

149

movement on the bank. Quickly she sat up, and there he was.

Conaire rode through the trees, tall and proud on his red stallion, grinning with delight at the sight of her. She smiled back at him—now, here could be the perfect ending to the perfect day.

Suddenly she shrank back in horror.

Conaire was not alone. Following him in single file down the riverside path came twelve, fifteen, twenty of his men. They stopped their horses and lined up on the bank. All of them sat staring down at her, and not one of them had a bigger grin on his face than Conaire.

Terri could not believe her eyes. "What do you think you're doing?" She sank to her chin in the water, trying to hide within the foaming waterfall. "Conaire! What are you *doing*?"

He slid down from his horse and tossed the reins to one of the other men. "Good afternoon, Teresa Maeve," he said, still grinning. "Lovely day for a swim."

She gave him her fiercest glare. "I'll appreciate it if you will take your men and leave me in peace. Surely you can see that I'm not dressed."

He raised himself up a bit, peering closely down at her. "Why, so you're not. I can see that from here," he said. "But you are still hidden well enough from the men on the bank—so long as you stay in the water."

"You can't be serious!"

"Oh, quite serious. Never more serious." And as he spoke, his face became somber, and he stood up with his arms folded across his chest.

Her rage began to swell. She clenched her teeth. "King Conaire—I am *asking* you to take your men and leave me in privacy!"

Conaire glanced around him, at the trees and the grass and the lovely rushing stream. "Why should we leave?

This is the perfect spot for us to stop and rest and have a bit of food," he said.

"You're practically in sight of the dun! It's right there on the other side of those trees!"

He shrugged. "We had no chance to stop today, the hunting was so good. The men are hungry and so am I." Conaire paused, glancing up at the lovely forest. "I think we will stop right here."

"What do you expect me to do? Stand up naked in front of twenty of your men and stroll ashore to get my clothes?"

He laughed. "Teresa Maeve, I would never expect one such as you to do any such thing." Then, to Terri's horror, he picked up her gown and her linens and began to walk downstream, away from the men. When he was many yards away, almost out of sight, he tossed the clothes behind some bushes.

"I'll just leave your things down here, behind these tall bushes. You can stay in the water and make your way down to them without too much trouble, I think."

"I can't possibly swim the whole way!" she shouted, her voice shaking with outrage. "The stream is only a few inches deep between here and there!"

"Well, then," he called, starting back toward her, "I suppose you will simply have to stay beneath the water until we are gone."

Her fury boiled over. "Why are you doing this to me? How *dare* you do this to me?"

Conaire stopped, and shrugged. "Why? Because again I am testing my queen—and that is also why I dare. There is nothing I would not dare to ensure the future of my people. Humility is a very important thing to find in a queen, and I see another chance for you to prove yours." And with that he turned his back on her and walked away, back to his men.

"*King Conaire!*" White with anger, Terri began to raise herself up, stopping when the water bared her shoulders.

151

"I have told you that I will never be your queen. And since you have chosen not to believe what I say, maybe you'll believe what I *do*!"

With that, she rose up out of the water and stood as tall, and as proud, as she had ever stood in her life. The cold clear water streamed off her hair and ran in little rivers down her bare skin. Locking her gaze with the king's, she walked straight to the rocky shore and stepped boldly onto the bank.

Any hint of embarrassment she might have felt was replaced with sheer satisfaction at the look on Conaire's face.

After a moment of shocked silence, his men began to roar with laughter. Terri continued striding up to Conaire, wearing nothing but glistening beads of water and the cool forest breeze. One corner of his mouth began to curl up even as he stared at her.

After standing and gazing coolly at him for a moment, she turned aside and walked slowly, almost lazily, down to the bushes to find her gown and linen towels. Upon retrieving them, she began walking back, never taking her eyes off of Conaire.

Suddenly she heard the sound of a horse galloping up the path where the others had come. With a flash of new anger she saw that it was Lonan, apparently a little late for lunch.

Immediately she turned her back to him, pulled on the gown, and wrapped one of the long pieces of linen around her shoulders like a shawl. Covered now from neck to ankles, she threw Lonan her coldest glare and then turned and walked back toward the king.

If the men were laughing before, they were practically falling off their horses now, but now they were laughing at Lonan. Terri went straight to Conaire and gave him her haughtiest look.

He shook his head slightly. "Well, Teresa Maeve, you

seem to have taken to heart the things I mentioned to you last night.''

''About what?''

''About satire. And humiliation.''

''Ah. Yes. And I must say that you were right. Sometimes humiliating a person really can be more satisfying than killing them.''

''Well. I am very glad you had no wish to kill *me*.''

She raised her chin. ''Don't bet on it.''

''But I must ask you a question,'' he continued. ''Was this a proper action for any modest woman, much less a noble lady—or a queen?''

''Oh! I forgot. This was to be another test of my humility. Are you saying I have not passed it this time?''

''Well, I should hardly think that parading naked in front of twenty men is an act of humility, or modesty.''

''Then let me tell you what *I* think. You already tested my humility once, remember? I am not going to prove it to you again. I have nothing to prove to you.'' She stabbed her finger at him. ''Never test me again.''

She started off down the path to the dun, head high, but heard Conaire's voice behind her. ''You may not wish any more tests, Teresa Maeve, but I must tell you—you have already passed another.''

''Oh? And what would that be?''

''Beauty.''

Her lip curled in a half smile. Terri continued on her way to the dun, her head held high in triumph.

The day faded into early darkness as storm clouds blotted out the sun. A heavy rain began to fall, and the people of the dun took shelter within their houses and inside the Great Hall.

Hearth light and torchlight glowed from the doors and windows of those warm dry homes. The smell of wood smoke and roasted meat and freshly baked bread drifted across the grounds, even through the cold steady rain. Servants and warriors, women and children, druids and a king and a would-be queen—all the inhabitants of Dun Cath were safe and comfortable on this stormy summer evening.

All except one.

Huddled beneath his heavy woolen cloak, Lonan crouched in the shadow of the dun's high wooden wall as the rain poured down. He watched the others as they ate and drank. He listened to their laughter and knew they were laughing at him.

And no one laughed louder than the red-bearded king.

Lonan pulled the top edge of the rectangular cloak farther over his head, ignoring the rain that dripped from the woolen edges. His anger simmered, and flared, and burned, until it seemed that the rain that struck him must surely turn to steam.

She had laughed at him. Laughed at his offer to take her for his own, to marry her, to provide for her. And then set everyone up for the biggest laugh of all out at the riverbank. She had dared to walk naked in front of the men, and then only covered up when she saw *him*.

How could she refuse him and run to Conaire instead? Didn't she realize that Conaire had no right to her? Had no right to take a woman of the Otherworld as his queen? Had no right to take a queen at all?

He, Lonan, was the one who should have been king. And since the kingship had been unfairly denied him, the least he deserved was the king's woman. Conaire treated her like a slave—worse than a slave. And yet she invited him into her bed every morning and every night. What was wrong with her that she preferred such treatment to the life of ease Lonan could provide?

He almost smiled. If she became his wife, she would never have to work, never have to lift or carry or handle horses or ride out alone the way Conaire expected her to do. No, the hardest work she would have to do would be to lie on her back and let him provide her with children.

But best of all, Conaire would have to stand by and watch as the woman he had wanted was taken as a wife by another man.

There had to be a way to make her understand. He wasn't about to give up yet.

Lonan let the cloak fall back to his shoulders and pushed himself off the wall. He stalked through the cold rain, not caring that it pelted his bare head. He saw only the sodden ground and the heavy drops still splattering onto it.

In a moment he found himself at the door of the Great Hall. Yes, over there together in a corner, just finishing their fine meal with the other happy members of the dun, were Brann and another man—Fearghan, he saw, Fearghan the gatekeeper.

Lonan slipped inside the Hall. No one took any notice of him. He went straight to Brann and Fearghan and stood over them, his hair still dripping with rain.

"Come with me," he said.

At first the two of them only stared blankly at him. But when he remained standing there, making it clear that he had no intention of leaving until they came with him, the men set aside their plates and got slowly to their feet.

The silent group left the Hall and set out through the rain. Eventually they came to Lonan's small, cold house—the house he shared with Brann, since neither of them had a wife. All three men stepped inside and shrugged off their heavy wet cloaks.

Lonan went to the hearth at the end of the room and stirred the fire, providing a bit of heat and light. Brann pulled out a rickety bench, and Fearghan stood behind him.

"So," Brann said, as he settled himself on the bench, "why have you brought us here?"

Lonan leaned against a corner of the shadowy little house. "Well, neither one of you had the opportunity to laugh until you fell off your horses today, since you didn't go out with the hunt. I thought you might like to do your laughing now.''

Brann gave him a blank look. He twisted around to glance over his shoulder at Fearghan, and then turned back to Lonan. "No," he said. "No, we did not come here to laugh."

"Although we do know what she did this afternoon, out there in front of all the men," growled Fearghan. "They're talking about nothing else."

Lonan stared hard at them from the shadows. "Something must be done about her," he said.

"It must," Brann said, nodding his head.

"I agree," added Fearghan, stroking his rough yellow beard.

"And have I not said that from the beginning?" Lonan asked, his voice rising with anger. "Have I not said it from the moment she and that unnatural animal first set foot in Dun Cath?" His rage began to boil again, but now it was tempered by curiosity—and a glimmer of hope. "Why do you agree with me now?"

"Because you are right," said Fearghan in his rough voice. "The woman is barely civilized. She walked naked in front of Conaire's men. She rides out alone every day. And she spends no time among the other women, no time at all. She prefers the company of horses and horse boys."

"And the king," Lonan added softly.

"Yes. The king," Brann said. "He has begun to spend more of his time following her about than he does taking care of his people."

"And are the people beginning to talk about this?" Lonan asked, his voice carefully neutral.

"They are," Fearghan said. "First one, then two, then many. They have begun to talk."

"Conaire says he wants her as his queen, but she keeps putting him off," Brann said. "And every time she refuses, she keeps him running back to her." He shook his head.

"So long as she does this, Dun Cath will never have a queen."

"Yet there must be a queen," Lonan said, watching them closely. "If Conaire has no sons, there will only be fighting over his successor. He has no other eligible male relatives. It could destroy the dun, yet he will not take another. He would see the dun divided and destroyed before giving up this wanton, unnatural woman and finding a suitable queen."

He spread his hands wide. "You know that I myself have offered to marry her. I offered to make her my wife, to build her a house of her own, to give her everything any woman could ever want—but she refused!"

Fearghan frowned, his expression fierce. "She refused you, too?"

"Yes! Even after the way Conaire treated her, forcing her to work as the lowest of the servants. What kind of woman would choose filth and rags and the work of five men over the life of a warrior's wife?"

Brann sighed. "It makes no sense."

"Of course it makes no sense!" Lonan was shouting now, but his spirits were rising as well. "She should not be queen. She should not be Conaire's! She should be mine!"

Fearghan turned his heavy stare to Lonan. "You would still want her, even after the way she behaved today out at the river? After the way she treated you?"

Lonan laughed. "Of course! I would be doing the entire dun a favor! Do either of you want to see her be your queen?" His voice lowered ominously. "She could yet change her mind and accept Conaire's offer. He does have a great deal of gold and fields full of horses and cattle to use as bait." Then Lonan stood tall, and stared straight into both sets of eyes. "Do you want a king who would have her for his queen?"

After a long moment, Brann and Fearghan glanced at

each other, and then back at Lonan. "Some of the people do admire her," Brann said. "They have never seen any woman with such strength, such spirit—"

"Then we will have to show them what she is really about," Lonan interjected smoothly.

The two of them looked at him again. "I promise you, I will stop at nothing to show the dun what sort of woman she really is." His lips moved into a thin smile—a smile he actually meant. "And after I do that, I will keep her for myself."

"She has already refused you," Brann said. "The king has said she is a guest, a free woman. You cannot force her to stay with you."

"Why, I assure you, force will not be necessary, dear foster-brother," Lonan answered. "Only persuasion."

"Persuasion?"

"Persuasion. The right sort of persuasion." Lonan smiled at them again, picked up his damp cloak, and walked back outside into the rain.

Chapter Fourteen

Though it seemed to take forever, the fortnight did pass, and to Terri's great happiness—and relief—she found herself swinging up once more on the lofty back of Firelair. The morning was as soft and silvery gray as the mare's fine coat, but charged with an undercurrent of energy and excitement. Terri quickly took up the black leather reins as Firelair pranced and danced.

It was easy to understand the mare's eagerness. After being cooped up in her small paddock for two weeks, she was suddenly out on the lawn of the dun with a rider on her back, and surrounded by the twenty men and horses of the king's hunt. She snorted at the pair of huge, gray, rough-coated hounds that pulled and frisked at the ends of their leashes, closely held by Ros as he sat on his horse.

Terri spotted a tall red-bearded man, dressed in a plaid tunic of finely woven black and green wool, standing near the gates. Heavy gold gleamed at his throat and wrists and bare arms. When Terri saw him vault onto his horse's back, she guided Firelair through the crowd and then rode out of the gate at the side of the king.

Conaire smiled up at her, his teeth white beneath the soft beard, the fine skin of his face and arms burnt almost red-gold by the sun. She returned his good humor, feeling as though life couldn't get any better. Here she was, riding at the side of this handsome, powerful man, a man who fulfilled her every want and desire in ways she had never even imagined. No, she would never allow anyone to take this happiness, this freedom, away from her—not even Conaire himself would ever take it away!

"So, today we will see what this lovely creature can do," Conaire said.

Terri glanced down at him. "I beg your pardon?"

"Firelair. We've heard a lot of what she is said to be able to do, but I expect that today we will have the chance to see it."

Terri shortened the reins a bit, doing her best to keep the high-stepping Firelair from leaving the short-striding ponies far behind. "Of course you will," she said with a serene smile. She glanced over her shoulder. The eyes of every man were upon her; every one of them would be watching to see if the mare could do even half of what Terri had claimed.

"Is it true that she's never been bested in a race?"

Terri looked at Ros, who rode just behind the king and held the leads of the enormous dogs. "Now, does it look like any horse here could match her stride for stride?" she asked.

Ros only grinned, and shook his head. Terri realized that she now understood the old Irish habit of answering a question with another question.

"Could she really jump as high as a man's head?"

That would be Sivney. "Haven't I said that she could?" Terri answered, as casually as possible. "That's easy, for her."

"I'd like to see that!" cried another man. The rest of them laughed and called out, "So would I! So would I!"

She smiled at them all. "If you see an obstacle of that size, you'll let me know, won't you?"

"That we will! We will!"

Terri faced forward again, chuckling to herself. It did not seem likely that she would have to prove Firelair's abilities

160

any time soon. This was ancient Eire; except for the enormous earthen walls and thorn-filled moats of Dun Cath, there wasn't a wall or a fence to be found anywhere in the land. And there wouldn't be a horse show with a jumping course held in these parts for oh, another fifteen centuries or so.

There was a sudden gasping and whining from the dogs behind her. "Well, I think we're about to see some of what she can do right now," Conaire said as his stallion raised his head. "Get ready."

Terri quickly shortened the mare's reins and glanced back. The pair of hunting dogs strained and pulled frantically at their leads, nearly dragging Ros from his horse. But he hauled them back, reached down, and slipped the leather leads over their heads. They were off like a shot, and vanished instantly into the forest.

The riders turned and galloped after them, sliding into single file behind the king as they swept into the sun-dappled dimness of the forest. Terri nearly pulled Firelair to a stop to keep her from running over Conaire's small red stallion. After a moment the mare settled in and stayed in her place in line, though Terri knew she could easily have left the entire hunt far behind.

As they followed the narrow trail, the red stallion stretched himself out and flattened his ears as he raced with all the speed he could summon. Conaire crouched low over his neck, letting the horse pick his own path. Terri let Firelair out a notch. Far in the distance, she could hear the breaking of brush and see the movement of the bushes and trees as the huge hounds ran down their prey.

She realized that she heard no barking from them; they were gaze hounds, chasing their quarry by sight alone, racing too fast to waste any energy in making noise. But suddenly the forest was filled with a roaring bellow and a ferocious growling and snarling.

In a moment Terri saw it. The horses of the hunt went

flying past a thrashing tangle of dogs and bushes and an enormous antlered stag. Quickly the men began pulling up and leaping to the ground, leaving their wild-eyed, snorting horses to shy away from the scene and mill around beneath the trees.

By the time Terri managed to get Firelair stopped and turned around, the bellowing stag was surrounded by shouting men dragging off the dogs. She saw Conaire seize the stag's head by its antlers. A dagger flashed in his hand, and with a final cry the creature fell silent.

Terri's heart pounded. Firelair, tense from the excitement of the chase and snorting at the smell of blood, jogged in and out of the trees as Terri craned her neck to see what was happening. Finally she got the mare to stand still, and was able to get a look at the result of the hunt as the crowd of men began to disperse and the panting hounds were led away.

The stag lay still in the torn-up bushes. A small red river ran from beneath its throat. She was amazed at size of the animal—somewhere near five feet tall at the shoulders, she felt sure, with new three-pronged antlers still covered in velvet.

"This is a young one," Conaire said, walking up beside her. He still held his dagger in his hand. "Not yet reached his full growth. Only three tines on his antlers, and not nearly as tall as some I've seen."

"Well, I can tell you it's the biggest deer I've ever seen," Terri murmured. Then she rose a little in her stirrups and looked closer, studying the animal's short thick neck, massive shoulders, and wide heavy antlers. "Wait a minute—that's not a deer at all! Back where I'm from, if I remember right, we'd call that an elk."

Conaire placed the gold-hilted dagger back in its sheath at his belt. "That is a new name to me," he told her. "We have always called these creatures the red deer—see there

162

how his summer coat looks red-brown. In the winter it will turn to gray.''

"Two names, same animal," Terri said, smiling. "I guess it's good to know that even across the worlds, some things remain the same.''

"Many things remain the same," he said, turning to her and resting his hand on her knee. "A great many things. Names may change, but the things themselves never do.''

She looked down into his gleaming brown eyes, feeling the heat of his hand even through her tough linen breeches. "No," she said softly. "No, they don't.''

Then she quickly looked away and walked Firelair forward a few steps, forcing Conaire to let his hand slide off of her knee. Glancing back at the dead stag, she saw the men approach with enormous knives and knew what was coming now. She guided Firelair a little distance away, into the peaceful forest, and heard the footsteps of a man and a horse following close behind.

"Huge dogs, giant deer," she said, turning the mare to face him. She looked boldly into his eyes. "When are you going to start breeding some big fine horses, Conaire?''

"I will do that when you start breeding some big fine children, Teresa Maeve," he said, with a pleasant smile.

Terri stared at him in shock. If any man back home had ever dared talk to her like that—

But all she could do was swallow her anger. She knew he simply wanted to see her lose her temper, and she refused to give him the satisfaction. "I keep telling you that I can raise horses for you that will be as fine as Firelair. Aren't you interested?''

"Oh, I am interested. I am always interested in anything to do with you and breeding, Teresa Maeve." He grinned wickedly, and Terri felt the heat of her anger rise. But she said nothing, simply waited for him to go on.

He cocked his head. "But tell me—why do I need you to begin breeding big fine horses? All I need is Firelair.

163

We simply let her join the broodmare herd, and wait for the big gray foals each spring.''

She gave him her coldest look. "Two reasons. One, Firelair is not yours and she goes nowhere without my say-so. And two, I will never allow her to go into the broodmare herd unless I have your permission to begin supervising the breeding.''

"And why do I need you for that? Are not my own horsemasters skilled enough?''

"Of course they are. That's not the point. I am telling you that Firelair and I go together. You cannot have one without the other.''

"A queen may certainly keep her own horses.''

"But a queen may not ride out every day to select and train them!'' She glared fiercely at him, waiting for his response, but he said nothing.

At last she stepped down from the mare and faced him directly. "Conaire, I have been here many weeks now— I'm not even sure just how many. But the time has come when I must decide my future. I want that future to be here, with you, with the people of Dun Cath and the horses that I could raise and train for you.''

He reached for her, but she drew back; this was not a time for lovemaking. She wanted him to talk to her; she wanted to hear what he had to say.

Conaire stepped close, and she retreated until she stood against the massive trunk of a tree. He took her face gently in his powerful hands. "We are at a crossroads, you and I,'' he said, and she was amazed to hear the gentleness in his voice. "I must have a queen. I must have children, sons, from which to choose the next king.''

She frowned. "I thought that kingship here wasn't hereditary, and automatic, the way it is—like it is back where I'm from.''

"It is not,'' he said patiently. "You are right. But the next king will still be chosen from among the men who are my blood kin. The more sons I have, the greater the chance that it will be one of them.''

He withdrew his hands. "I have said that I believe you are the one to be my queen. But I cannot force you. If you do not want to marry me, you may continue to live and work as you do now at Dun Cath, for as long as you wish to do so. Firelair may go into the broodmare herd and you may begin raising my big fine horses. But I will take another for a queen, and come to you only in the night . . . or perhaps in the deep of the forest, when there is no one else to see.''

An awful coldness, an almost paralyzing sense of pain, began to spread through her. "No, Conaire," she whispered. "If you cannot marry me without taking away my freedom, then you will not marry me.''

She swung back up on Firelair. "And neither will I stand by and watch you take another in the bargain. If you turn away from me, and choose some docile housebound creature in my place, then hear this, King Conaire: You will never find me waiting in the dark. I will take Firelair and I will go and find another place where I can live—even if it means I live beside the horse boys and the broodmares.''

She turned the mare around, forcing him to step back. "I will give you anything but my freedom. Anything but that.''

Conaire reached up and clamped his hand over the reins, halting Firelair. "You are forgetting something, dear Teresa Maeve. There is still one of my tests that you have not yet passed." When she stared down at him in disbelief, he actually grinned at her. "Courage.''

Her rage exploded. She slammed her heels into Firelair's sides, breaking Conaire's hold as the mare charged into a wild half rear and then a thundering gallop down the path.

Terri felt that she could not get away fast enough. But even as she raced into the forest on the streak of silver that was Firelair, she heard behind her, all too clearly, the deep hearty laughter of Conaire, the king.

She'd never been so angry in her life. "He didn't hear a word I said! Not one, single, solitary word!" Her shouting only drove Firelair on faster, but Terri did not care.

All day she'd had to hold the mare back, trying to keep her from leaving the short-legged Celtic ponies in the dust. Now the two of them were free to race as fast as they cared to go through the forest, even though the faint and sometimes winding trail—a trail Terri had never ridden down before—still kept the mare from reaching anything like her top speed. But Terri had explored these forests so often that she felt safe and at home within their sheltering trees, and she allowed the mare to follow the path as she wished. Right now, all Terri wanted to do was put as much space as possible between herself and Conaire.

At last they reached the edge of the forest and galloped out into a long, narrow meadow. It seemed somehow familiar, though Terri was sure she'd never seen it before. But right now it did not matter. Firelair stretched her neck and ran as she had tried to run all day. The very ground shook from the pounding of her hooves.

Terri reveled in the flying speed, watching the tall trees on either side of the long meadow flash by them. At last she sat back in the saddle and began to pull the mare up. It looked as though the meadow was narrowing down to a point—and again, it looked familiar. There was some kind of structure there—a circle, tall earthen walls.

Of course! It was the horse boy's *rath*, sitting beneath the cliffs at the far end of the broodmares' grazing land. She had always ridden up to it from the other direction, and now she was seeing it from a different side.

The mare eased down to a walk. A sense of peace came over Terri, as it always did when she visited the beautiful lush fields that were home to the mares and foals. These lands were hers. They were her home. She was meant to be here; she was as much a part of this place as anyone who had been born on it.

How could Conaire ask her to give all this up? How could he ask her to shut herself up forever inside the walls of Dun Cath, locked up like an imprisoned broodmare in a gold-fixtured barn?

A profound feeling of sadness began to close over her. Just when she thought she had found the perfect place, the perfect man, the perfect life, she was being forced to decide which was most important. And she found it impossible.

If Conaire loved her, how could he ask her to choose? That was the question that brought her the most anger, the most confusion, the most pain.

Could she really take Firelair and go, as she had told Conaire she would? Could she make herself turn and walk away from him forever?

Terri closed her eyes, rocking gently to Firelair's long-striding walk. Why didn't she put a stop to this right now? Why didn't she turn Firelair around and gallop away, leaving Conaire and all thoughts of him far behind?

The mare slowed and stopped. Terri looked up. She had reached the walls of the horse boy's *rath*.

She stood in her stirrups and peered inside. The earthen walls were only about six feet high, and she could easily see over them from Firelair's back. There appeared to be no one inside; she saw no activity near the little round house or either of the two low-roofed sheds. The tall wooden gate, solid like the ones at Dun Cath, was tightly closed.

Of course, at this time of day all the herders would be out among the broodmares. The *rath* was quite deserted.

She thought briefly of turning around and going back to Conaire and the hunt, but right at this moment she could not bear the thought of seeing him again. She wanted only to ride out and see her beloved mares, and then ride home in peace. Once she got past the *rath,* she would know right where she was, she would be on her own land once again.

The *rath* had been carefully built to close off the long meadow from the mares. The small circular fort sat wedged between the high sheer cliffs on one side and the rocky bed of the river on the other. The river rushed by just a few inches from the wall of the *rath,* and thick dark woods came right to the edge of its opposite bank.

Carefully, mindful of Firelair's newly unshod state, Terri began edging the mare around the wall of the *rath* along the rocky, gravelly bank of the river. The water here was wider and deeper than the small stream at Dun Cath; it raced and tumbled over the rocks and boulders. Some places were only a few inches deep, while in others the fast water had created holes and drop-offs. She breathed a sigh of relief as Firelair got past the wall and stepped up onto the soft thick grass once more.

They stopped, and Terri looked out calmly at the beautiful fields. Here the cliffs veered away from the *rath* and the river, opening into vast acres of long, green, life-giving grass. Though the mares were out of sight just now, their meadow empty, it did not matter; she was here on this part of their sweet and peaceful land, and she was home.

Terri swung her leg over Firelair's back and slid down to the ground, welcoming the feel of the soft thick grass beneath her hard leather riding boots. Lifting one of the mare's front feet, she examined it closely—yes, it seemed to be just fine; the new growth of hoof was strong and flexible and not wearing down too quickly—

Suddenly the mare threw her head up and snorted. She swung around, jerking her foot from Terri's hand. Terri quickly turned to see where she was looking.

The gate of the *rath* had been pushed open from the inside. Galloping through it was a small brown horse with a blond-haired rider.

Lonan.

Her first reaction was shock. What was he doing out here alone? He had not been with the hunt this morning. He'd hardly been around at all for the last several days. The *rath* was deserted—how had he gotten inside? And why had he been hiding in there?

But as the brown horse galloped straight toward her, and as Firelair grew increasingly agitated, Terri's sense of shock was replaced by a single, pure emotion.

Rage.

Rage at this intruder, this bully, this criminal who had invaded her life and her land. She held tightly to the reins as the mare continued to snort and pull backwards, standing her ground as Lonan rode up to her. Once and for all, this would be ended now. Right now.

Lonan slid down from the small brown horse and let go of its reins, not caring that it trotted off. Terri pulled her small knife from her belt.

He stopped, but merely grinned at her. "You think that will help you now?" He took a step closer. "Breeches-wearing bitch. It's going to take a lot more than that."

She began to shake with anger. All she could see was the satisfying picture of her knife hurled deep into his chest, quivering there.

"I knew that if I waited out here long enough, I'd catch you one fine day." Another step. "Oh, you can scream all you wish. There's no one to hear you. They're all gone, on the far side of the grazing lands all this week." He grinned again, cold and leering. "Now you'll give me what you've been promising."

Lonan took another step, even as she gripped the knife tighter. "Everyone saw how you walked naked in front of a band of twenty men," he said, in a voice suddenly fierce with his own anger, his own hatred. "You would do anything for attention. Do not complain now that you're getting it."

He lunged for her, and with a cry of outrage she slashed

169

down at him with her knife. But he grabbed her wrist, stopping the knife and forcing her to drop it. He turned her away, locked his arms around her, and began trying to drag her toward the *rath*.

"You might well like me better than Conaire, once you've had a taste." His voice was rough in her ear. He held her so tightly she could hardly breathe. "You practically rolled over on your back for me the first time I spoke to you—it was up on the *grianan*, you remember it, don't you?"

With a scream Terri lashed out at him, kicking, fighting, struggling to break free of him any way she could. But he only laughed. "It will be your word against mine, just as before," he said. "Just as before."

Chapter Fifteen

Terri knew she was in trouble. Even in her rage she was no match for a warrior, a man trained practically from birth to fight hand to hand with other men. She would have to find another way, and quickly.

Even as she fought, she tried to look around her. Though she had dropped Firelair's reins, the mare was still standing right alongside—and so was Lonan's small brown horse. As Terri watched, the horse walked up behind the tall gray mare, sniffing at her flank and nickering to her.

The mare's ears went flat against her head. She bared her teeth and squealed. Instantly Terri ceased her struggling and sagged sideways, as if she were fainting—fainting right under the brown horse's nose.

Lonan stepped forward in an attempt to lift her up. He stood right between Firelair and the horse. And right at that moment the gray mare lashed out hard with a powerful hind leg, determined to put the intruding little horse in his place!

But the horse was never touched. As Terri had intended, Lonan was squarely in the way—and he took the full force of Firelair's angry kick.

"*Aahhh!*" Instantly Lonan dropped Terri and fell to the ground. She scrambled to her feet and wasted no time in catching Firelair, getting a foot in the stirrup and swinging up into the saddle.

She looked down at Lonan as she swung the mare

around, away from the *rath*. He lay writhing on the ground, clutching his thigh, and glared up at her with nothing but hatred in his eyes.

"My word against yours?" she hissed. "Well, I think you just heard what I have to say. And if you come back again, you'll find out there's plenty more where that came from!"

She galloped away from Lonan and the *rath,* heading toward the broodmares' fields and the familiar trails that led back to Dun Cath. Glancing over her shoulder, she saw that Lonan had gotten to his feet, caught his brown horse, and climbed up onto its back. He forced it into a gallop straight toward Terri.

She was not worried. Firelair would have five miles on that little horse before he could even hit his stride. But as she looked ahead toward the trail, another movement caught her eye.

Riders. Two, three—five—five riders, materializing out of the forest. Each one blocking any path she might have taken.

She began to slow the mare down. Who were they? Fearghan, that was one; he was the gatekeeper with the rough yellow hair and beard. She didn't know the names of the others, though she knew she'd seen them all at Dun Cath.

Lonan's men, every one of them.

For a moment she considered trying to race past them. But they were already far ahead and sweeping in now to surround her—she saw the flash of swords and for a moment had a vision of Firelair cut down, her silver coat running with red.

In that instant, Terri made her decision. She turned the mare around, avoiding Lonan in a wide sweep, and galloped back at full speed toward the *rath*. Fixing her eyes on the solid earthen wall, she pulled the reins up short and leaned forward over Firelair's flying mane.

The wall loomed before her, all six feet of it. Never

before had she faced such a height. Back home in her weekly riding lessons, the tallest obstacle she'd jumped had only been about three feet. But now, coming closer at every stride, was a massive solid wall at least twice that height.

Firelair saw it. She knew what they were about to do. She pricked her ears, dug in hard with her powerful hind legs, and galloped toward the wall as though it were a magnet pulling her in.

One last stride. Terri locked her fingers in the silver mane and held on tight as the mare took off. Over that tremendous wall she flew, higher and higher, hanging at the very top, and then diving gracefully back to earth.

Terri sat back against the hard jolt of landing. Now they were inside the *rath,* among the haphazard sheds and the small round house. But Terri sent the mare past the obstacles, two strides, three, four, five, and then they were flying again over the other wall of the *rath.*

True mare . . . true mare . . .

But just as she landed, Terri saw a big group of horses approaching. For a moment her heart nearly stopped. More of Lonan's men?

No! It was the hunt. It was Conaire and the hunt, following the same path she had taken, now jogging straight toward the horseboy's *rath.*

Lonan and his criminal men were left far behind. As she cantered down the long sunlit meadow, all Terri could see now was the face of Conaire, riding out to meet her on his fine red stallion. Conaire, who had nothing in his eyes for her but awe, and respect, and love.

"Teresa Maeve," he said to her, his brown eyes gleaming as she rode up to him, "we will doubt you no more concerning this mare's abilities. Never have I seen any horse fly like that."

"Well, I didn't do it to impress you," Terri said, looking

over her shoulder as Firelair came to a halt. "I rode straight into an ambush."

"Into a what?"

"They were waiting for me! It was a trap!"

His face became deadly serious. "Who was waiting?"

"Lonan." She took a deep breath, controlling herself as her rage threatened to boil over at the mere mention of his name. "Lonan and five of his men."

"Five?" The astonishment was evident in Conaire's voice. He turned his stallion and looked out beyond the *rath*. "Where are they now?"

She glanced over her shoulder. As she had expected, the fields beyond the *rath* held nothing but grass. "Gone. I'm sure they vanished the instant I went over that wall. As Lonan said, it's nothing but my word against his—just like the last time."

"Tell me what happened." His eyes became hard, his voice tight with rigidly controlled anger.

She pushed the damp strands of her hair back from her face. "It was just like the first time. He was waiting for me. He tried to drag me away—into the *rath,* I guess. But this time Firelair helped me out. She kicked him."

"Kicked him?"

Terri smiled, with no small satisfaction. "Nailed him right in the thigh. I hope she broke his leg."

Conaire smiled for just a moment. *"And her rider will never come to harm,"* he said. "That is what you told me the day you came to Dun Cath."

"Yes," Terri said, gently touching the silvery neck. "Yes, I remember."

"But I cannot entrust your safety only to Firelair, no matter how wonderful she may be. Are you ready, now, to order that Lonan be brought to trial before the druids?"

Terri turned the mare away from the *rath* and began walking her back toward the men of the hunt. "What good would it do?" she asked, her voice calm. "There were no witnesses. Everyone knows that I ride out alone almost every day. I have no proof of what he tried to do. He could make up any story he wanted about how he hurt his leg.''

''Yet this cannot be allowed to continue. Under the law, he can be punished.''

''But can he be stopped?'' Terri looked at Conaire, and was surprised when he did not meet her gaze but looked back toward the *rath* instead.

''The law can punish him, but you are right—it cannot stop him.'' For a moment he seemed to be looking at something very far away, and his face was a mask.

''He's never tried to harm any of the other women, has he?''

Conaire turned back to her. ''He has always kept to himself. He seems to prefer staying in the background. He has never broken the law before, not that I know of.''

''I think he'd be quite happy to have a trial. He practically dared me to call for one. He knows I can't prove anything, and I think he'd love to see me humiliated.''

She gazed out at the fields beyond the *rath*. ''But he also said that before Firelair kicked him and left him sitting there to watch as she jumped that wall like it was nothing. I think we taught him a lesson today.''

''But surely you will agree to stop riding out alone.''

Terri looked at him, horrified. ''I cannot let him turn me into a prisoner. I cannot hide inside the dun just because he might be lurking somewhere! If that happens, he really will have won. No. This has only made me want to ride out on my own more than ever.''

''I will not stand by and watch you place yourself in danger. I will not see you come to harm—but I can do nothing without a trial.''

She lifted her chin. ''And I will not let him win. If he's crazy enough to bother me again, I'll see to it that Firelair breaks both his legs.''

One corner of Conaire's mouth moved in a small smile,

and he sighed. "Well, now. With such a threat, how could anyone think of bothering you?"

She smiled at him, her confidence restored. She had faced the worst that Lonan could offer and she had won. *He* had been the one left lying beaten and helpless on the ground. And as she and Conaire rode back into the forest together, the riders of the hunt fell into line behind them. Terri took great satisfaction in listening to the men as they rode along behind her.

"Did you see that? Did you see?"

"As high as my head!"

"Never thought to see a horse leap so high!"

"And how did she stay on?"

"Must have been tied on!"

All of them laughed, but Terri could hear the awe and respect in their voices. She knew that she now rode with Conaire as a fully accepted member of Dun Cath—as someone who was very nearly the equal of the man she rode beside.

In the darkness and quiet of the still summer night, King Conaire walked alone across the deserted lawn of the dun. He went straight to one of the small white houses and, with a single massive kick, broke down its wooden door.

He saw Lonan scramble to his feet near the small smoldering hearth. Without a sound Conaire lunged past the other men in the house and slammed him up against the far wall, his hands locked on Lonan's throat.

The man could only gasp at the pressure on his neck. Conaire took great satisfaction at the shock and fear in Lonan's eyes, at the trembling and weakness in his arms.

"I am told that someone has been following one of the women of Dun Cath," Conaire said, his voice low. "I am told the man has even tried to harm her. Do you know anything about this?"

Before Lonan could answer, Conaire again slammed him

hard against the wall. His iron fingers clamped harder around the pale neck. "Of course you don't. You are well aware that I would never tolerate any man treating a woman in such a manner."

Viciously he threw Lonan to the damp dirt floor, quite pleased at the solid thud he made. Two other men rolled quickly out of the way to avoid having him land on top of them. "And if any man of Dun Cath were to harm any woman, I would of course have no choice but to kill him. You do understand that?"

Lonan coughed, and gasped, and got slowly to his hands and knees. Glaring, he gave a slight nod.

Conaire returned the nod. "Good." He reached down and caught Lonan's wrist, pulling him to his feet—and just as the man peered up at him, with nothing but fear and hatred in his eyes, Conaire struck him a crushing blow on the jaw with his tightly clenched fist.

Lonan's eyes rolled up in his head and he dropped to the floor. "I'm glad we understand each other." Conaire turned and glared at the other men in the small close room. "How many of you? Eight?" He locked his gaze with each and every one of them. "Is there anyone else here who has anything to say to me?"

No one moved. No one spoke.

He gave them a pleasant smile. "Then, do go on and enjoy the rest of your evening." With that, Conaire stepped over Lonan, kicked the remains of the broken door out of his way, and walked out into the night.

The next morning, in the grayness of the dawn, Terri awakened to the sweet morning breeze and rose to face the day with a new determination.

Never again would she ride out with even the slightest trace of fear or apprehension. She had faced the worst that Lonan had to offer, and she had fought him off and won. The whole episode had only made her stronger. She and

177

Firelair would not give up the smallest part of their freedom—not now, not ever.

Looking forward to another day of work—and another evening spent with Conaire—she quickly pulled off her long linen gown and began getting dressed. Her own cotton underwear and sports bra, which she had been wearing on the day she arrived here, had long since worn out. She had taken the threadbare bits of fabric to the refuse pit herself, since she could only imagine what the other women would have thought of such strange garments.

Her boots and breeches and tailored white shirt had been accepted by the people as odd, and interesting, but not terribly different from the kinds of things they were capable of making for themselves if they wished. Terri was just glad that her breeches had been the button-up sort; she had no wish to try to explain a zipper to anyone here.

Now she slipped on one of the several pairs of short drawstring pants that Dorren had sewn for her. Made of lightweight linen, they were perfectly serviceable as underwear. And since she'd quickly learned that she simply was not comfortable going around without some means of support, she had fashioned for herself the simplest and most comfortable of brassieres. Taking a long strip of linen, Terri pulled it around the back of her neck, crisscrossed it over her breasts, and tied it securely behind her back. One size really did fit all!

Dorren had made her three pairs of "trews," or breeches, all in a soft light-gray color much like her original pair. But these were made of a durable wool-and-linen fabric, loosely fitted with a drawstring at the waist. And there were linen tunics, too, six in all, in bright colors that she loved. Dorren had made them in dark red, in bright blue, in green as dark as the forest, in yellow as bright as the sun. Two were in riotous plaid—one green and brown and white, one red and blue and yellow. They were all cut the same, hip-length and long-sleeved, needing only a belt to cinch them in tight around her waist.

Not that fit was a problem anymore, she thought, tying a brown leather belt snugly around the bright yellow tunic. Back in her old life it had seemed that she was always a few pounds over her best weight; but now, with all the hard work and hours of riding she did each day, her body had become tight and slender and firm. She could eat as she pleased, and found the food delicious—roasted meats, hot flat bread, golden honey, dark yellow butter, fresh milk, sweet dried apples, and strange white root vegetables that looked like carrots but were not.

At last she pulled on her black leather boots, stood up, and straightened her bright yellow tunic over the gray trews. It was not the sort of outfit that she had ever expected to be wearing, but she was actually quite pleased with her simple wardrobe. The tunics and trews, combined with the lovely gowns and softly glowing gold safely tucked away in the carved wooden chests, were all the clothes she could ever need for her life here in Dun Cath, here in ancient Eire.

Simple fare and simple clothes . . . but it was enough, it was all she needed, it was the bounty of the whole world.

Her only real concession to decadence was the beautiful gold jewelry that Conaire had given to her. She was especially fond of the wide solid bracelets and of the strange earrings that looped over one's ear and then dangled below. She would often wear a piece or two of the gold in the evenings, when she had bathed and then dressed in one of the clean linen gowns. But of all the priceless jewelry, none of it meant more to her than her golden ring.

The ring had become a very special piece. It was the one thing from her old life that meant something to her and she had never removed since she'd come here. In a very real way it was the link between the two worlds, found in the

179

old world and then transformed, somehow, by Conaire in this one.

She had long wondered what Conaire had done to it on that first night when he had tossed it through the flames. Something special, almost magical, had happened to the ring after that. Was it just her imagination, or had he worked a bit of magic? She'd never seen him do anything like it since. But that had been a very special night, a night like no other, and there did not seem to be any use in examining it too closely. It was enough that she was here, and that the ring remained on her finger. It was enough that Conaire was now the best part of her life.

Terri left the room, closing the door quietly behind her, and walked down the steps into the gray pre-dawn dimness of the hall. No one else was stirring yet. A few servants still snored gently in the shadowy corners, curled up in the deep rushes, while most of the other folk were still safely tucked away inside their small homes.

She set out through the quiet dun. Traces of mist rolled across the empty lawn, lingering in spots near the houses. The cloudy eastern sky was just beginning to turn silver. From the nearby forest she heard the first sweet notes of the birds.

Walking over the soft wet grass, Terri found herself wondering what day of the week it was. In her old life, everything had revolved around the rhythm of work five days and take the weekend off. But here there was no such thing as a weekend. The routines continued each and every day, though she had no doubt they would vary as the seasons changed.

And she couldn't wait to see how.

Now she had reached the old shed where the wood was stockpiled, and, as she did every morning, Terri gathered an armload of wood and carried it back to the Great Hall. Once there, she stirred the sleeping fire in the central circular pit to uncover the glowing red coals, and fed them generously with the wood she had brought. When the fire had been stoked and was once again crackling with a low steady flame, she set off again, this time to feed and groom Firelair and ready her for the morning's journey out to the broodmare herd.

The pale golden sun sat just above the horizon when Terri led the mare out to the lawn. She gathered up the reins and prepared to mount. But just as her foot touched the stirrup, she heard a shouting and commotion from the Great Hall.

It sounded like an argument. There were several excited men's and women's voices—and one familiar deep male voice calling her name.

"Teresa Maeve!"

Conaire walked out of the Hall, followed by a little group of servants, and headed straight for her. Terri set her foot back down on the ground.

She welcomed the sight of him. Though he never failed to come to her at least once each day or night—and sometimes more than once—she was always stirred by the sight of this powerful, broad-shouldered man, his red-brown hair and soft beard glinting now in the new light of the sun.

Ordinarily he would have been just as pleased to see her. But from the look of concern in his sharp brown eyes, serious now beneath the thick brows, Terri knew that something was very much amiss.

He placed his hand on her arm, gently detaining her. "Have you changed your mind about lighting the fire in the Hall each morning?"

Terri frowned. "What are you talking about? No, I haven't changed my mind. I lit the fire this morning, as I always do. It was burning and well fed when I left, as it always is."

Conaire shook his head as the servants crowded close. "I am sorry to tell you, but it's not lit now."

Her brow deeply furrowed, Terri tossed Firelair's reins

to one of the startled servants and stalked back inside the Hall with Conaire close on her heels. To her astonishment, she saw that he was right—the fire was out. But when she looked closer she made a startling discovery.

"Look at this! The ashes are still hot—and they're damp! Someone has put the fire out!"

Conaire shook his head slightly. "Perhaps the wind—"

"The wind doesn't dump water on a fire. I *didn't* forget to light it this morning, and I sure didn't put it out myself."

"Then what could have happened?" He turned to the assembled servants. "Did any of you see anything?"

Terri's gaze flicked across their faces, but they all looked straight at their king. "We saw nothing, Ri Conaire," said one of the women. "The fire was dead when we came in this morning."

Confused, her annoyance building, Terri turned and walked out of the Hall. She went back to the shed and gathered the largest stack of wood she could carry. Then, in front of Conaire and all the servants, she rekindled the fire and fed it until it blazed like an inferno.

"I am sorry the fire went out," she said, as formally as she could, to the king and his servants. "I am quite certain it will never happen again."

Conaire did not quite grin—the servants were watching, after all—but she saw his eyes gleam. "Thank you, Teresa Maeve," he said. "I am equally certain there is no one better qualified to handle fire than you."

Terri raised an eyebrow at him, then turned and walked quickly back to the lawn. She was already late riding out this morning. Now, where was that servant with Firelair?

Oh, there, near the gate. But holding the reins—

She stopped cold. And then the irritation she had felt over the matter of the fire boiled into anger.

Lonan stood at Firelair's head, patting the mare's nose, straightening her mane, crooning nonsense to her, even as the horse fidgeted and her expression grew increasingly sour. He looked up just as Terri approached.

"Why, good morning to you, Teresa," he said, with a pleasant smile. "Lovely day for a ride, isn't it?"

She gave him her coldest glare and grabbed the black leather reins out of his hands. It was with some pleasure, though, as she mounted the mare, that she noted the bruises on his face. Just as she had told Conaire, she was the one who had come out the victor when Lonan had stalked her yesterday. It seemed that he would bear the memory of that day for some time to come.

Chapter Sixteen

Later that afternoon, Terri rode back into the dun and found that all was calm and orderly. Yet her suspicions remained aroused. Someone had deliberately put her fire out, but who? And why?

As quickly as she could, she unsaddled and groomed Firelair, turned her loose in the small paddock, and hurried inside the Great Hall. There she found only servants going quietly about their usual tasks. Two of the men were running an iron spit through several large cuts of meat—venison, probably, she thought. The fire burned steadily, as always, the smoke escaping through the opening far above in the heavy straw roof.

Yet she noticed the servants glancing up at her, their faces very still. No one greeted her, as at least one or two of them usually did. It was clear that she was not the only one who felt suspicious.

Terri sighed, and walked over to the group. She would have to try to put things right and soothe the ruffled feathers if she could. "I'm back a little early today," she told them, with the friendliest smile she could muster, "so I'll come back down and help you make supper. I'll turn the meat on the spit. I promise I won't leave the spot until it's done."

They all looked quickly at each other, and finally back at Terri. "Thank you," said one of the women. Terri had seen her many times, but did not know her name. "The

184

king dines with his men tonight,'' the woman went on, ''and there is much to be done.'' And they all turned back to their work.

''You're welcome,'' Terri said, and went upstairs to wash and change her clothes.

She came downstairs, clean and refreshed, in a new light-weight wool gown woven in a soft plaid of gray and green and black. Over her arm she had tossed her original pair of gray riding breeches and her white tailored shirt. Both were showing torn seams and loose buttons, but even though the garments were close to threadbare in spots, she wanted to keep them for as long as she could. She also carried a small basket, which held wooden spools of fine linen thread and three of the best bone needles.

Terri sat down on the edge of the low stone wall that formed the great circular firepit. As soon as they saw her, two men came over with the heavy iron spit, weighed down with meat, and lifted it into place across the flames.

Terri smiled at them and accepted a large wooden bowl from one of the women. The bowl was filled with thick dark honey and had a long wooden paddle stuck into it. She lifted out the paddle and began coating the meat with the honey. The idea of basting meat with honey had never occurred to her before, but one taste of the finished product had convinced her. The honey formed a thick glaze that sealed in the flavor and the juices. Her mouth began to water, and she could not resist touching her finger to the edge of the bowl for just a taste of the honey. Delicious!

It was only necessary to baste and turn the meat every ten minutes or so—though she would have to guess at the time, since her watch had long since stopped working—and so she would be left with plenty of time to get her sewing done.

With a sigh, she settled herself comfortably on the stone wall, set down the gray breeches and white shirt, and began rummaging in the basket for her needle and the right color of thread. The thread she had no trouble finding, but even after taking everything out of the small basket, there was no sign of the needles.

They had been carefully inserted into a small square of red wool for safekeeping, but the scrap was empty now—there was nothing in it but holes.

Now, how had she managed to lose all of her needles? She had always been very careful with anything she'd ever been given, for she was well aware that every last thing—every gown and needle and plate and knife—had to be carefully, individually, painstakingly made by hand. No one could just hop into a car and drive down to the local mall to pick up whatever might be needed.

Well, maybe she had just left them up in her room. She got up, leaving the clothes and basket and honey bowl sitting on the stone wall, and trudged back upstairs to her room.

There, to her amazement, she found her three needles. They were carefully laid out on the windowsill as if they'd always been there.

Completely baffled now, she gathered up the needles and went back downstairs. As she crossed the room, heading back towards the firepit, she stopped short as a man walked right across her path.

"Oh! Good evening to you, Teresa."

She looked up, and frowned in confusion. "Good evening, Brann," she said, edging around him.

He was usually oblivious of her, but now he was all smiles, standing there in his fine blue tunic with his full attention directed at Terri. "A very beautiful evening, would you not agree?"

She looked back over her shoulder at him. "Yes," she answered. "Yes, it's very beautiful." More puzzled than ever, she went back to the firepit and quickly set to work.

At last, all seemed to be in order. Brann disappeared, and Terri spent the remainder of the late afternoon beside the fire. Every so often she would turn and baste the meat with the honey and then go back to sewing up her breeches and shirt, one patient stitch at a time. She was careful not to let the honey touch her fingers, not wanting to have to wash the sticky stuff out of her clothes.

The sewing was done just as the meat was ready. The two men lifted the heavy spit from the fire and carried it away for carving. Terri helped the other servants drag out the large flat wooden squares from the corner and set them down on the rushes. The squares served as a table, and thick furs were tossed down for everyone to sit on.

As the men began filing in, Terri poured water into gold cups and set them down on the squares. With everything ready, she smoothed her dark hair with her hands, shook it back, and waited for Conaire to arrive.

She had not seen him all day. This morning, while she was riding out to the broodmare herd, he had remained in the dun, attending to the various mysterious things a king must attend to. This afternoon, before she returned, he had already left with his men for sword and spear-throwing practice. This evening, as was his custom after such practice, he would dine in the hall with his warriors and their wives and ladies.

Now he walked inside the torchlit hall, dressed in his fine dark green tunic and gleaming as always with heavy gold. But even his gold could not match the gleam in his brown eyes when he looked at Terri.

She smiled at him, and together they sat down on the soft furs. The other men took their places, most of them sitting with their wives or favored ladies. The hall was filled with pleasant conversation and the delicious smell of good food, and as the servants began to move among them with platters of meat and plates of bread and butter and vegetables, Terri almost had the old feeling of being out on a date in some fine restaurant. But unlike the dates of long ago, she knew quite well how this one would end! And with a happy rush of anticipation, she reached for a long strip of the honey-roasted meat and took a generous bite.

Her eyes flew open wide. What was this? The meat tasted vile, spoiled. Quickly she dropped her head to spit the offending bite into the rushes, and grabbed for her goblet of water.

As she took a drink, she realized that nearly everyone else at the table was doing the same thing. She looked up at Conaire, who had not yet touched his meat—he had been waiting for her to begin first.

"Something's wrong with the meat," she told him as the murmuring and grumbling began to grow from the other people around the low table.

Conaire frowned and looked closely at the meat on his own and Terri's plates. He raised a piece of it nearly to his thick red-brown mustache, then threw it back down on the plate. Getting to his feet, he sought out the servant woman Terri had spoken to when she came in that afternoon.

"What has happened to this meat? Why are you serving spoiled food?"

The woman's eyes widened in confusion. "The meat was not spoiled, Ri Conaire. I brought it up from the *souterrain* myself, and it was cool and fresh, as it should be."

"And who prepared it?"

After a moment's hesitation, the servant woman looked at Terri—and so did Conaire.

Terri got to her feet. "That's right. I did watch the meat. But it was perfectly fine while I turned it! I must have spent two hours basting it—maybe three!"

"What did you baste it with?"

"With this." She went to the firepit and caught up the sticky bowl of honey, nearly empty now. Conaire took the bowl and peered closely at it, then touched his finger in it and took a cautious taste. Making a face, he threw the bowl into the rushes. "Orna! How could this happen? Why did you give her this to prepare the meat?"

Orna looked a little pale, but remained insistent. "It is honey, new and fresh. I filled the bowl with it myself."

Conaire stared hard at her, and at all the servants. "Honey mixed with something spoiled, something rancid!"

Terri walked over to stand beside Orna, but the woman only glanced suspiciously at her. "She's right!" Terri said. "It was honey! I know, I tasted it myself!"

Behind them, back at the table, people were getting up and crowding up behind the king. Terri could hear their muttering and complaining.

"How could she spoil the meat like that?"

"It's not fit to eat!"

"What does she expect us to eat now?"

"Nothing like this has ever happened here before."

"Not until *she* came."

"Maybe she ought to go back to carrying buckets."

"Enough!" Conaire's single shout was all it took to silence the crowd. "No one knows how this happened. Perhaps the meat was bad to begin with, and ruined the honey. Now, I want to hear nothing more about it! Throw the meat into the refuse pit! You can do with bread and butter for your supper just this once. *Go!"*

After a sullen silence, the warriors and their women made their way back to the boards and sat down. Conaire joined them, remaining on his feet until Terri could join him on the furs.

She sat down beside him and reached for the bread, but inwardly she was seething. That meat had been good and that honey had been sweet. What could have happened to it?

She peered up from beneath her brows, and her angry glare landed straight across the boards—straight on Lonan and Brann.

The two of them gave her the kindest of expressions, the politest of smiles. Lonan held out a small golden bowl to her and asked, "May I offer you some honey, Teresa?"

* * *

Two days went by, and though Terri was apprehensive, there were no further disasters. The fire continued to burn, and the food was good as always. Maybe she'd just been experiencing a run of bad luck.

But on the morning of the third day, the fire went out again.

Terri had given Firelair and herself the day off from riding. Nothing more would be needed at the broodmare herd until tomorrow. Firelair grazed eagerly in the fields outside the dun under the watchful eyes of young Evin, while Terri was in the shed with a young black mare, working patiently on teaching the flighty creature to stand tied to a post for grooming and handling.

But her concentration was interrupted by shouting and a commotion outside. It seemed to be coming from the direction of the Great Hall.

She turned the black mare loose and looked outside the shed. A group of servants had spilled out onto the lawn and were embroiled in an argument.

Terri walked over to them. "What's going on?" she demanded—but in her heart she already knew.

They all fell silent and turned to look at her. "The fire—" one of the men began.

Terri closed her eyes. "Don't tell me. It's out again."

The man nodded. "All right," Terri said, sighing in frustration. She wasn't sure that anything else that happened around there could surprise her. "Then I'll light it again." She started off toward the woodshed, but one of the women—her name was Orna, Terri recalled—stopped her by placing a hand on her arm.

"The fire has already been rekindled."

"Already?" Terri frowned at her. "Who did that?"

"I did," the woman said, withdrawing her hand.

"You? But I told King Conaire that I would light the fire in the mornings!"

The man beside Orna shook his head. "Only some mornings, it would seem."

Terri turned on him. "I lit that fire this morning, just as I've lit it every morning! You'd better start watching to see who's putting it out!"

She waited for the man's response. But the people of the group only looked at one another and began murmuring their replies.

"No one is putting it out."

"It's never lit in the first place."

"We are the ones who are blamed when the food is late because the fire is not ready."

Terri could not believe her ears. "Now, listen here, all of you! I—"

She was stopped by a powerful hand on her shoulder. "What is going on here? I had to leave my men at sword practice because of all the shouting. Tell me!"

Terri turned and looked at Conaire. He cut a powerful, almost frightening figure in his leather fighting gear, his red-brown hair damp and wild, a heavy wooden sword gripped tightly in one hand. The servants saw their king and crowded close, eager to tell him their story.

"The fire is out again!"

"The food will be late, but it is not our fault!"

"Someone else must be put in charge of lighting the fire!"

"All right!" Conaire raised his hands to quiet them. Terri could hear the increasing annoyance in his voice. "I will tell you what you will do. From now on, Teresa Maeve will light the fire as she always has, but she will not leave the hall until you have come and someone is there to watch the fire. Do you agree to this?"

They all glanced at one another. "We agree, *Ri* Conaire."

He turned and looked at Terri. "And you, Teresa Maeve? Will you agree to this?"

191

Her lips tightened. "If that's what it takes to satisfy everyone, then yes, I agree," she answered. "I will do whatever it takes to make everyone happy. If they don't believe I've been lighting the fire, then they'll just have to see it for themselves."

"Thank you." Conaire drew himself up and looked back towards the lawn—only to have his brows pull together in a frown. The group of men he had been training with were now walking towards him.

"What is this?" Conaire said to them. "The practice is not over yet!" He looked at a grim-faced man with long dark hair. "Niall, you and I are still to go hand-to-hand!"

But the dark-haired warrior shook his head. "The druids are waiting for you," he said. "It is their day to speak with the king." Niall glanced first at the gathering of servants, and then stared hard at Terri. "There is not enough time—now—to finish the practice."

Conaire clenched his fists, and his face was grim, but he made no other outward show of the increasing irritation that Terri knew he felt. "Then we will have to make up for it tomorrow."

He gave everyone around him a hard look. "All of you! Back to your tasks. The day has hardly started yet. We've wasted enough time already."

Slowly, reluctantly, the servants went back into the Hall. Conaire's men moved off to put away their weapons. But Terri felt their eyes upon her as they left, and knew that all of them blamed her for what had happened.

As the sun wheeled high overhead, making yet another long summer journey across the sky, King Conaire and his druids and the other free men of Dun Cath left the close hot confines of the dun and walked outside under the cool canopy of the forest. The men sat down in the deep shade of the trees, along the banks of the rushing stream, and prepared to listen to their king.

"Ah, now, this is much better," Conaire said, leaning against the rough bark of a tall tree. "We can all think better out here in the fresh air, where it's cool and clear."

Brann walked over to stand behind the king and whisper in his ear. "The two are ready for you to hear them, Ri Conaire," he said.

Conaire nodded, and pushed himself away from the tree. "Good. Bring them forward."

Brann made a small gesture to two men who were sitting and waiting out in the midst of the assembly. First one and then the other got up from the crowd and approached their king.

The first was Egan, a handsome brown-haired youth in a dark green tunic. Intricate embroidery in red and blue and white wound its way around the cuffs and neckline of the fine garment. Handsome pieces of gold gleamed at his throat and wrists. There was no mistaking that he was from a family of some prosperity. He stood before Conaire with his head up, his brown eyes intense and unwavering.

From the other side came Bellagh, a thick broad-shouldered man with dark brown hair. He wore an una-dorned brown wool tunic, and his only gold was a pair of wide plain bands on his forearms. He, too, stood before his king, but he was sullen and staring, occasionally shifting his gaze to his rival.

"I would hear both your stories," Conaire said. "Egan, you may begin."

The intense young man stepped forward. "My king, one of your warriors is not fit to serve you. I ask you to decide whether he still belongs in your service."

Bellagh looked at him with murderous intent. And as he did, there was a shifting among the men. Conaire felt a growing apprehension as he saw a few of his warriors sur-reptitiously move to sit nearer to Bellagh, while a few more placed themselves on Egan's side.

"Why do you say he is not fit?"

"He is a liar, my king."

"A liar."

"And a thief!"

"Can you prove any of this?"

"Of course he can't prove it!" shouted Bellagh. "*He* is the liar! *He* is the thief!"

There were now two small, but distinct, clusters of men sitting on the forest floor—one near Bellagh and one near Egan. Conaire glanced at those who still sat between the two groups. Their eyes shifted from one side to the other, clearly uneasy at the growing division. At last they looked at their king—and he knew that they were waiting for him to choose, to make a decision, to put this rift back together any way he could.

He turned his attention back to the two men who stood before him. Without looking away, he spoke over his shoulder at Brann, his chief druid. "What shall be done?" he asked.

"There must be proof of these accusations, *Ri* Conaire."

He continued to gaze steadily at the men. "Bellagh. Egan. What proof do you have?"

Both began talking at once, shouting and accusing and pointing and interrupting. Conaire frowned, trying to control his own temper. Nothing would be solved by losing patience with these two young idiots.

"Listen to me, both of you! Listen—"

But even as he tried to quiet them, he realized that all of his men were getting to their feet. They were looking intently down the path which led from the dun into the forest. Many had placed their hands on the hilts of their swords. Everyone fell silent.

Someone was coming through the forest.

Chapter Seventeen

Conaire walked directly out to the path, drawing his sword as he moved. But out of the forest there emerged nothing more than a pair of riders on slow, quiet horses. One of the riders was a bent and gray-haired man, the other a fresh-faced boy not more than twelve.

"Calva!" Conaire put away his sword. "Why are you here? Is something wrong?"

The old man, chief herder and guardian of the mares, slid down from his horse and handed the reins to the boy. "Yes, something is wrong, *Ri* Conaire," he said slowly. Then he looked around at the assembly. "But perhaps it should wait."

"It will not wait," Conaire said. "Tell us what has happened. You would not have ridden all this way yourself if it was not important."

Calva took a step forward. "We are in need of food, my king," he said quietly. "We are down to our last two days of grain and cheese. The dried fruit is gone."

"Last two days?" Conaire frowned at him. "I don't understand. Has not Teresa Maeve been bringing you supplies? I have seen her leave with a fully loaded pack pony every fourth day, without fail. What has happened to the food she has brought to you?"

Calva and the boy looked at each other. "She has brought us food," Calva said, "but of the last two loads,

195

none has been fit to eat. The grain is contaminated with filth, and the cheese ruined. It reeks of spoiled meat. Even the last sack of dried apples was riddled with maggots. We have had to burn it all."

Conaire stood very still, staring at the old man and the boy, unable to believe what he was hearing. "Burn it all," he repeated.

"All, *Ri* Conaire. We have been catching fish from the river and collecting some food from the forest, as always, but we must have some grain and cheese and dried fruit to provide enough for all."

"Of course." Conaire glanced back at his warriors, trying to think. How could Teresa Maeve take spoiled food to the horse boys? She was intensely devoted to the mares and foals. Why would she do anything to harm their caretakers?

"Bring her forward," said a voice from the crowd.

Conaire looked quickly in its direction. "What did you say?"

Lonan stepped forward, coming to the head of the crowd. "Bring her forward," he repeated. "Bring Teresa here and let her answer for what she has done."

Brann moved to stand beside him. "We should hear this now, while all are here. The herders will have to return home before dark. Bring her now."

All of the rest of the men stood and stared intently at Conaire, even Bellagh and Egan. It was clear that all of them were in agreement—something must be done about this now. Conaire felt a great pain somewhere deep inside his chest at the thought that he would have to bring Teresa Maeve before these men, that he had no choice but to require her to answer their charges.

But even worse was the way that his men were beginning to divide themselves. No one could fail to see that some gathered near Lonan, while others deliberately distanced themselves from him. And still others milled about in the center as if totally undecided.

Conaire turned to Brann. "Find her," he said. "Find her and bring her here. Bring her now."

Immediately Lonan turned and began running back toward the dun, gathering up Bellagh and Fearghan and taking them along. Conaire's mouth tightened. He would have preferred one of his own men to go along with Lonan, but he could not call them back now without a disruptive confrontation.

He closed his eyes. Already he was thinking in terms of his men and Lonan's men.

Nothing could be worse than a division of the dun. It would lead only to his own men making war on each other. Nothing could be worse than that. He would die before he would let that happen.

The sun began to make its long slow descent. Beneath the cool shade of the forest, the king and his warriors sat down to await the return of the men who had gone to find Teresa Maeve.

They waited. And waited. There was plenty of discussion of other matters concerning Dun Cath, and some pleasant time spent in telling outrageous stories, but nothing was done regarding the woman who had all but turned the entire dun upside down.

Gradually the conversation began to taper off. Silence, and its accompanying tension, replaced the talk and laughter that had earlier filled the sun-dappled forest. *Where was she?* It had never been difficult to find Teresa Maeve before, but Conaire knew he couldn't wait much longer.

The sun was beginning to approach the horizon when at last he stood up. "Calva," he said, "go now and get what supplies you need. It's going to be very late before—"

"King Conaire!"

That shout, filled with rage and frustration, instantly made him look up. And it was only with the utmost control that he kept himself from laughing out loud.

197

Red-faced with anger, she walked between Lonan and Bellagh, with Fearghan close behind. The three of them were doing their best to herd her along, but she was extremely reluctant, to say the least. When Lonan tried to place his hand on her arm to guide her, she wrenched away and slapped him across the jaw with all the strength and viciousness she possessed. Conaire noted with satisfaction that Lonan turned away and nearly fell as he covered his jaw with his hand.

That jaw must be pained, indeed.

But his attention was drawn to the furious Teresa Maeve. Dressed as always in her gray trews, black boots, and linen tunic—bright blue today, a fine choice, for it brought out the blue in her clear gray eyes—she had clearly been working, for she was streaked with dirt. Her dark hair was caught up high with a soft leather thong and hung in a long thick tail past her shoulders.

At first glance, she looked almost like a servant. But the sheer force of her spirit made it clear to all who saw her that she was anything but. Tall enough to look Lonan in the eye, she was strong and absolutely fearless, with courage enough for four men and the stallions they rode. It struck him again that this woman was, now and always, something very different from any woman Conaire had ever known before. And he got the same feeling every time he saw her, no matter how long it had been since the last time they'd parted.

She had seen him now. Shaking off her tormentors, she walked straight to Conaire and stopped right in front of him, a ferocious look in her eyes. "What is the meaning of this? I was at work with the young horses in the barns, when *these* three"—she looked at them with the coldest contempt Conaire had ever seen on the face of man or woman—"came in and insisted I go with them! Refused to tell me why! Practically dragged me off when I didn't want to go!"

"We could not find her," Lonan said in a near-whisper, gingerly placing his hand to his jaw. "No one had seen her."

"That's a lie and you know it," raged Teresa Maeve. "I was in the barn the whole time! I'm always there at this time of the day! Everyone knew I was there. All you had to do was ask!"

Bellagh and Fearghan looked up at Conaire and shook their heads. "Nowhere to be found, Ri Conaire," said Fearghan.

Terri nearly struck him, too, but Conaire gently caught her arm and drew her forward to stand beside him. After one last murderous glare at her three escorts, she began to look around and take in the rest of the scene—and then she realized who else was there.

In an instant her expression changed from rage to confusion. "Calva! Donnan! What are you doing here?" Then a look a fear came into her eyes. "Is something wrong? Has something happened to the mares? What's happened?"

"Nothing has happened to the mares," Conaire said quickly. "You are here because we must ask you a question."

"Ask me a question? What are you talking about? What is this all about?" She could not keep the disgust out of her voice.

Conaire answered her as gently as he could. "Calva says that all the food you have brought them on your last two trips has been spoiled. They are here because they are nearly out of supplies."

She looked at Calva and Donnan for a long moment, blinking. Then, with her dark brows pulled together in a frown, she turned back to Conaire and shook her head emphatically. "But that's not true! Calva! Why would you say such a thing?"

The old man looked away. He could not meet her cold

gray gaze, which was as hard as iron. Conaire touched her gently on the shoulder.

"I am sure that you did not mean to take ruined food to the horse boys. But no matter how it happened, they must have more supplies now. Will you take them?"

Still flustered, she looked at the old man and the boy again, as if hoping they would tell her it wasn't true. "Well, of course! I'll get Firelair and a pack horse and go right now!"

Teresa Maeve started off for the dun, but Conaire restrained her. "Someone will have to go along with you while it is loaded, to make certain that the food is good when it leaves here."

She looked up at him. He saw first surprise and then anger in her clear gray eyes, and her face began to flush red. "Go with me? You mean—you don't trust me?"

Conaire closed his eyes. "It is simply to satisfy everyone, Teresa Maeve—and to protect you. It will prove that you are taking good provisions."

"It will prove that I cannot be trusted! That the king himself does not trust me!"

His heart tightened at her accusation, but he held his ground and made no reply. He was the king, after all. The good of his people must come before what he himself wanted.

She continued to stare him down, but when he offered her only silence, she finally turned away. And though she looked angry enough to kill the whole lot of them, she somehow managed to restrain herself and stalked off toward the dun.

"All right, then!" she shouted, without looking back. "Who's going with me?"

Lonan started to follow her, but in an instant Conaire had locked an iron hand on his arm. "Thank you, Lonan," he said smoothly, "but you have done enough today. Ros! Sivney!"

His two most trusted men got quickly to their feet and came over to him. "Go with Teresa Maeve. Help her gather the supplies. See to it that all of it is good, and ride with her and Calva and Donnan to the horseboy's *rath*."

They left with Teresa Maeve, and she went along with them—but not before throwing Conaire a glance so cold that it seemed as if the winds of winter had suddenly blown through the warm summer day.

Darkness shrouded the dun. Terri welcomed it as she would a comforting blanket. She stood in the shadows beside the paddock fence, listening to the familiar sound of Firelair grinding her hay—her share of the precious store of hay that Conaire had ordered she might have. The only light came from the torches scattered throughout Dun Cath, and from the stars whenever the drifting clouds allowed the glittering points of light to shine through.

Out of the darkness walked a shadow. She tensed, and then let out a sigh when she realized who it was.

"Why do you stand out here alone in the darkness, Teresa Maeve?"

Terri turned her back to him, lifting the hem of her soft woolen gown so that she could place one foot on the bottom rail of the fence. "I'm not alone, Conaire. I'm here with Firelair."

She could feel the warmth of his presence, and knew he was smiling at her even though she could not see his face. "Of course. You could have no better friend than the true mare."

"I'm beginning to believe that."

"I, on the other hand, am in great need of a friend right now," he said She felt him take a step toward her. "Very great need."

"And what is it you want me to do for you, King Conaire? The food has been delivered to the horse boys and certified as being fit to eat. Is there water to carry? Dinner

201

to cook? What more can I do that I have not already done?''

He paused. ''Please. Do not misunderstand me. I know better than anyone how hard you work for all of Dun Cath. But . . . some of the people do not understand. Some are confused . . . and some are angry.''

She whirled to face him. ''Angry? Angry about what? What more do they want me to do?''

''So much of what you do is for yourself alone, Teresa Maeve. All of us must work together to help the dun survive. And there is nothing I want more than to have you be a part of Dun Cath—truly a part.''

Terri looked up at him in shock. The faint starlight glittered off the gold at his neck and wrists. ''What are you talking about? Not a part of the dun? I light the fire and I ride out to the mares and I train the young horses and I pitch in and do whatever else might need doing, from carrying firewood to setting the table!'' She began trembling with anger and pain. ''How can you say that I am not a part of Dun Cath?''

His voice was so soft that she could scarcely hear him. ''The fire goes out, Teresa Maeve. The horse boys get no supplies. The meat you prepare is spoiled.''

She could hardly believe her ears. ''You know none of that is my fault!'' she cried. ''I told you, someone is sabotaging everything I do! It's almost certainly Lonan and his miserable pack of lowlifes. Why don't you find out why they're trying to drive me out and turn everyone against me!''

Conaire shook his head. ''You must understand—it doesn't matter why those things happened. It only matters that they did happen, and that the blame has been laid at your feet. There is nothing I can do to change that.''

He took a step toward her. ''The people—some of the people—still see you as an outsider. You remain the stranger, the different one, the woman from the Otherworld

. . . the one who rides alone and does everything in her own way, only in her own way. But there is one thing that you can do to be accepted. One very important thing.''

"And what is that one important thing, King Conaire?" She set her teeth. "Oh, don't tell me—*I'll* tell *you*. If I marry you, and become your queen, you'll be able to lock me up here inside the dun and keep me under control. Then I won't trouble you or anyone else ever again. Am I right? Is that what you want me to do?''

"Teresa Maeve . . .'' His voice was weary, and for the first time she began to sense something new in this powerful, unshakable man—a feeling of despair. "I have no wish to lock you away. Far from it. I am a king, and I need a queen—a strong and beautiful queen—a queen like you. Why do you refuse to help me?''

"I would help you, King Conaire. I would help you in any way I could. I thought that I was helping you, you and all the people here. But you ask for too much. You want me to give up my own life in exchange for accepting yours.

"That's not a partnership. That's not an even exchange. That's not an agreement to help one another. You want nothing more than my freedom, my future, my very life!''

"Are you saying, then, that you do not want to share your life with me?''

She paused, trying to control the shaking in her voice. "Is that what you're asking, Conaire? You've never asked me that before. All I've ever heard is that you want me to be your queen, as if you thought I might be available for hire.''

"I do want you to share your life with me.'' He closed the distance between them and took her hands in his. "There is nothing I want more than for you to be my wife.''

For a long moment, she stood within a heartbeat of him. She felt a tremendous longing to lean her head against his broad chest and rest there, where she could be safe and warm and protected and loved . . . but she only tightened her fingers on his hand.

"For as long as I can remember, I have always said that I would never marry," she said. "The last thing I wanted was to trade my freedom so I could be tied down to a man—any man. But now . . . now . . ." She breathed deep, and looked up into the shadowed face of the one man who had the power to bring about such a change of heart.

Her voice trembled, though she tried mightily to steady it. "I was actually starting to change my mind."

His hand tightened around her fingers. "Can you not understand that I don't want to own you? Do you not see that we need each other, that we would complement each other as the day does the night?"

He went on, urgently, as though she would understand if he could just get the words out quickly enough. "Nothing worth having is ever won without sacrifice, Teresa Maeve. You and I would love and protect each other as no man or woman ever have before, or ever will again.

"The people of the dun would need you here. I would need you here. But I would be here for you also.

"I want you to be the mother of my children. I do not mean that you must have a baby every year, as some of the women do. I want only a child or two that I would know for my own, who could follow us in time and continue to guide the dun in the years to come."

She closed her eyes. He made it sound so wonderful . . . sharing their lives, loving and protecting each other for all the rest of their days. And children—yes, she could almost see herself willing to have a child with Conaire. A son, wise and powerful, or a daughter, fearless and strong . . . the idea touched something, somewhere, deep inside her. She could imagine how happy he would be to see a child of his . . . of theirs.

Terri looked up at him. "I would be happy to make you the only man in my life, for all the rest of my life."

"Then marry me. Become my wife. Be no longer an outsider, but truly a part of my life and the life of us all."

"Your wife . . ." She drew a deep breath. "Being your wife, Conaire, I could accept." She almost smiled. She knew she was enough of a match for him to keep her freedom as his wife.

"But not my queen."

She raised her chin. "As your queen, I would belong to you in ways that a wife never would. And not just to you. I would owe my presence and my loyalty and my very life to the people of Dun Cath, just as you do. But you would still be first over me in the eyes of the people. Even if a man doesn't own his wife here, the king certainly owns the queen. And there's not one person here in the dun who would ever believe any different. Am I right?"

He sighed softly, and turned his face away from her. "Teresa Maeve—what is it that you truly want?"

What indeed? "I want to keep my life as it is now. I want to have the freedom to ride out when I wish, the freedom to make a lifelong career of something I could only dream of back in my old world—raising and training magnificent horses, horses like no one in this place has ever seen.

"And I want you in my life. I want to know that when I get up in the morning or ride back home in the evening, you will be there for me—only for me. That is what I want, King Conaire."

"Yet you are willing to give nothing in return."

Her temper began to flare, but she held on to it. "You mean I am not willing to give up everything."

"You well know that I am a king! You cannot be my wife without also being my queen!"

So, even the great laughing king has a temper! "Yes, I know what you are, just as I know what I will be if I marry you."

As she looked up at him, a slow feeling of surprise came

over her. "You know—there are some parts of being a queen that I would not object to. I would accept the title, if it made the people happy. I would stand at your side during the ceremonies. I would have children with you, not only because I love you but so that the family of the king could go on. I would accept all this for you—so long as I did not have to give up my freedom in return."

"Is it just that you want to ride out and see the horses every day?" he asked. She could hear the exasperation, the very real confusion in his voice. "Is that what this is really about?"

"This," she said as firmly as she could, "is about the freedom to ride out and see the horses every day—or not ride out and see them—as I choose."

She looked away, into the darkness and the black shadowed hills. "You've got to understand something. Back in my world, women were oftentimes forced to choose between marriage and career—between having a family and having their dreams. They had to trade their independence for the 'prestige' of being attached to a man. I thought that here, in this place, in this time, I would not have to make that decision."

Terri faced him once again. "This is about my having the freedom to choose what I want to do with my life. If I were queen, that freedom would be gone, for my life would belong to the king and his people. And I told you before, King Conaire—I will not give you my freedom."

He turned away from her. "What do you want me to do? Do you think I will walk away from the dun just so we can be married? Choose you over my people and my kingship?"

She stood where she was. "But if I stay, how can you ask me to give up my future? My horses? My plans? I would have to give up my life to go and stay all day, every day with the women and the children and *occasionally* the king, as much a servant to him and to the people of the dun as I was when I wore rags and carried slop buckets.''

She heard him sigh in the darkness. ''Then there is something I must ask you, Teresa Maeve. Are you be willing to stay and serve the new queen? If you will not agree to be my wife, then I will leave tomorrow to resume the search for one. It has been too long already. The dun can wait no longer.''

Terri looked at him in shock. The words echoed in her ears. *''I will leave tomorrow . . . tomorrow . . . tomorrow . . .''*

She realized suddenly that somehow she had thought she would be able to change his mind—that he would see how important this was to her, that if he loved her the way he said he did, he would never ask her to give up her life for the title of queen.

But he had given her an ultimatum instead. *Give up everything for me, or I will leave you and choose another.*

Pain began to grow within her chest. She pressed her hand to it. How strange . . . she actually felt that pain within her heart, just the way the old songs and stories had always said that people did. She'd thought that *broken heart* was nothing but an expression . . . until now.

Always before, her ferocious strength and unbreakable defenses had served well to keep any man from wounding her heart. But now that strength was nowhere to be found. One man had, at long last, found his way past those barriers.

''So, it has come to this,'' she whispered. ''I have to choose, or else.'' She glanced up into the stars, at the glittering display in the blackness of the night. ''I understand now. I can stay, and have my freedom and my horses, and even enjoy your company from time to time, King Conaire—but I will have to stand and watch you marry another, and know that I will stay always in the background, always at the edges of your life.''

She looked at him, and slowly shook her head. ''I cannot

do that. I cannot watch you marry and live with another woman.''

He took her hand, and his voice rose with hope. ''Then, you will accept me? You will marry me and become queen of Dun Cath?''

Terri withdrew her hand, sliding it out of his strong warm grip. ''I do not accept. If you really mean to find someone else, then I will leave. I will take Firelair and I will go before I will ever see you do such a thing.''

She turned away from him and ran out into the night. Though she had no reservations about letting him see her working like a servant, or covered with dirt, or naked in front of twenty men, or with her temper at its worst, she would never, ever let him see her cry.

Chapter Eighteen

The night was still, and silent, and emptier than Conaire could ever remember it having been. He sat on a pile of furs on the ground outside the door of his house, shrouded in darkness, with only Ros and Sivney standing with him for company. At that moment he wanted nothing but the shelter of the night and the comfort of his two closest friends.

"How shall I solve this?" he whispered.

He could feel the two of them shift slightly in the darkness. "Solve what?" Ros asked quietly. "The hatred between Egan and Bellagh? The unrest that many lay at the feet of Teresa Maeve? The lack of a queen, and a son, for the king? The dividing of the dun into those who are loyal to you and those who blindly follow Lonan? Which of those do you want to know how to solve?"

"Some would say that those problems are all the same problem," said Sivney.

"To be solved in the same way," finished Ros.

Conaire glowered at both of them. "Solved in what way?" he asked. He could not keep the bitterness from his voice. "By exiling her?"

Sivney shrugged. "Perhaps by marrying her."

"Either way, she would no longer be an outsider," Ros said. He leaned back against the door frame of the house. "She would either be an accepted member of Dun Cath, the wife of the king and the queen of the people, or she would be gone.''

Conaire closed his eyes.

Sivney took a step toward him. ''Do not misunderstand—many of us admire her as much as others fear and resent her. The problem is that there appears to be no middle ground.''

''She cannot go on the way she is now,'' said Ros. ''She cannot be forever the strange visitor who may or may not be from the Otherworld.'' He paused, and then smiled. ''But I also know how hard she works to earn her keep. I have no objection to her, and neither do many of the others. A woman of strength and spirit is always to be admired, even if that spirit is displayed in some—rather unusual ways.''

Conaire nodded slowly. ''You are right,'' he said. ''It is that very spirit that causes some to love her and others to hate and fear her.'' He sighed, and bowed his head, as though he felt the weight of the whole night sky pressing down on him. ''I have told her that her life cannot go on the way it has up to now. If she will not accept me, I will go tomorrow and continue the search for another queen.''

The two of them looked down at him. ''You have given up on her?'' asked Ros.

''I have not. I know in my heart that though I were to look at every woman in every dun in all of Eire, I would not find any to make me forget Teresa Maeve. I only hope to make her choose—and I am gambling that she will choose me.''

''But what if she does not? If she refuses to marry you, and insists that she will go on with her life as it is—what then?''

Conaire almost smiled. ''She may attempt to do just that, though she has threatened to leave Dun Cath if I bring in another woman to marry. But I believe that time is on our side—on my side.

"The summer will not go on forever. In the worst of the winter she will have to stay inside the dun, as everyone does, and in the spring that mare of hers will join the brood-mare herd far out in the high pastures. She'll have to take one of the dun's horses if she still wants to ride out."

He paused. "She works very hard to fit in and be a member of the dun. She wants to belong and is learning more and more of our ways all the time. She's even dressing like the other women, right down to the way she ties her belt and laces her boots."

"And she has even *remained* dressed for many days now," said Sivney.

Conaire laughed. "So she has. I do not think there will be a repeat of that performance. She was merely testing me, just as I have tested her."

He searched out the faces of his men in the darkness. "I have always known that I could not have it both ways. I said I would find a strong queen for the dun—and I well knew that the one I wanted would be no meek and subservient creature. You cannot expect a woman who meets my requirements to be docile and housebound, can you?"

Ros smiled back at him. "I suppose not. But here is the trouble: We can accept her wild spirit because we know it is the source of her strength. Yet the question remains—can the others understand it?"

Conaire shook his head. "I never fail to believe that they will. Perhaps it is because I cannot help but think they will see her with my eyes . . . see her great strength and her beauty and her bold and fearless heart. I cannot believe they would want any other for their queen, even as I can want no other."

"Perhaps you are right," Sivney told him. "Surely, by the spring, all of this will be resolved, and we will be holding a wedding feast for you and Teresa Maeve."

"There is nothing I would like better. And I feel certain that she only needs time. Think of it: She has lived among

us for less than one season. She is still new to us, new to
Dun Cath, new to everyone here. Giving her a few months,
a few seasons, seems such a small thing for her to ask of
me or any of us . . . and a very small thing for us to offer
to a guest.''

He looked up into the sky. The clouds had drifted away
and the stars were now a bright glittering river against the
endless night sky. ''I swear it: I will see that she is given
all the time she needs, though I am certain that all will be
decided by the spring.''

Conaire looked up at the shadowy figures of his men.
They made no reply, but he could see them nodding in the
darkness.

And then they heard it.

From somewhere outside the walls, deep in the blackness
of the night, came a distant wailing scream. It was a scream
filled with loss and anger and pain, as though all the anguish of the world had been loosed in that one, long, terrible cry.

The scream faded, leaving only a shattered silence in its
wake. Conaire and his men sat absolutely still in the darkness. He sought out their eyes, and even by the starlight he
could see that they were as shocked and unnerved as he
was.

Abruptly Conaire got to his feet. Slipping a little on the
damp grass, he raced past the Great Hall and headed toward
the lawn of the dun with Ros and Sivney close on his heels.

A crowd of people had already gathered on the shadowed
lawn. They stood facing the river and the woods, shifting
nervously and whispering to one another. The whole group
turned quickly at the sound of running footsteps.

''All of you heard it?'' Conaire asked. Everyone nodded,
though no one—even the warriors—spoke so much as a
single word. In the glare of the torches Conaire could see
their wide staring eyes and pale faces.

"We have to go and see what it was," he said firmly. "Someone may be out there. I want five men. Who—"

He was stopped by a hand on his shoulder. Brann stood behind him in the darkness, his face serious but showing none of the fear that kept the others still and silent.

"No one is out there," Brann said. "It was the *ban sidhe*."

Conaire looked closely at him. *"Ban sidhe?"* he asked.

"The woman-spirit. She cries out before a death, lamenting it now, for she knows it is certain to come."

"Whose death? What are you talking about?"

"None can say," he murmured. "But you will find nothing there." With that, he turned away and walked back into the darkness.

Conaire watched him go, and then glanced once more toward the night-shrouded woods. Quickly he looked back at his people. "No one is going to die!" he cried, demanding their attention. "Listen to me! Check your families. Make sure everyone is safe. If we must go out, we will, but most likely the sound was made by some animal. It's over now. Go back to your beds, go back and sleep while you can."

Amid low murmuring and uneasy glances, the people began moving off to their homes. At last Conaire stood alone on the starlit lawn.

Despite what he had said to the people, he knew that the wailing scream had been made by no animal. It had sounded human, but a human in the grip of the worst kind of pain and terror.

And Brann had been no help at all with his vague warnings of spirits and death. "No one is going to die," Conaire whispered, but he was not quite sure just who he was whispering to.

He knew that the people would check on their own family members and quickly inform him if anyone was actually missing. But there was one person who remained foremost in his own mind, one who had never left his thoughts from the moment he had heard that bone-chilling wail.

Conaire walked to the dimly lit Great Hall. Inside, the servants remained huddled together in small whispering groups. Paying them no attention, he lifted one of the small torches from the wall and started up the steps to the *grianan*.

The last door was tightly closed, but not locked. It opened smoothly at his touch.

Shadows jumped in the room from the flaring light of the torch. He could just make out her curving form beneath the light wool cover, her long dark hair spilling over it.

He was drawn to her now more strongly than ever. They had parted on such bitter terms, with so much uncertainty between them . . . and then that terrible wailing scream had invaded the dun and terrified them all. Even he had been unnerved by it, and he was not ashamed to admit it to himself. He was a warrior and a king and he well knew that recognizing fear was not a weakness.

Conaire took a step inside the room. How he longed to reach out and touch that soft, sweet mass of dark hair. How good it would be to pull her close, breathing in life and strength and comfort from the woman who had claimed his heart.

But she was so still, sleeping so peacefully, that for now he decided to let her remain undisturbed. She had been so angry when they parted earlier that evening; no doubt some of her anger still remained. Best to let it fade away in sleep. And he saw no reason to make her hear of that terrifying sound tonight, not if she had already managed to sleep through it.

He reached for the door. "Sleep, dear Teresa Maeve," he said softly. She did not respond, and after a moment he closed the door behind him and set out for his house.

*   *   *

The next morning, Conaire took Ros and Sivney and walked out into the dark blue-gray of the dawn. As they fetched their horses, Conaire noticed that Firelair was not in her paddock. He knew that Terri always left very early, but he had still thought he would see her this morning. He had wanted her to see him ride out, wanted her to spend the day thinking about him searching for another woman to be his wife, his queen.

But she had already left the dun.

Well, he would, on his journey today, just happen to ride out past the broodmares' fields. No doubt he would find her there.

They rode out past the river, following it for a time. They rode past the place where that terrible scream had come from. Now, though, they heard only the pleasant trickling sound of the water and the floating calls of the birds. Everything was as it had always been.

The day turned as lovely as any Conaire had ever remembered—the sky a clear blue, the sun warm and golden, the wind sweet with the scent of grass and leaves. But as the morning passed into afternoon, he took no pleasure in its beauty.

He and his men rode home from the broodmares' pastures in tense silence. Conaire heard only the jogging hoofbeats of the horses and felt only his own growing apprehension.

Terri had not been out to the pastures. None of the horse boys had seen her. It was the first time she had failed to appear, and she had even promised to come back first thing this morning to make sure the food she'd brought yesterday afternoon was still satisfactory.

She had never arrived.

He urged his horse on faster. Faster. The men were left behind. And when at last he galloped through the gates of the dun, he leaped down and left the sweating red stallion alone in the middle of the lawn.

Conaire ran first to the Great Hall. Upon seeing him, the servants frowned and stopped their work, and began to walk over to him in little groups of twos and threes.

"It has happened again, Ri Conaire."

"There was no fire this morning."

"It was never lit!"

"This was not our fault! Do not blame us—"

"Where is she?" Conaire's shout cut off their petty protests. *"Where?"*

There was only silence for a long moment. Then one of the old men said, "She has ridden out, as she always does."

"You are certain of this? You saw her?"

The old man glanced at the others. "I saw nothing. She leaves so early—"

A woman took a step forward. "She must have gone out, Ri Conaire. The mare is gone. No one would take that mare out but she herself."

Conaire's glance flicked over them. "Did she take provisions? Is there anything gone from the storehouses? Go and see!"

One of the other men hurried away. Conaire turned away from the tense little gathering and hurried up the steps to the *grianan*.

Her door was closed. He rapped on it. "Teresa Maeve? Are you there? Do you hear me?" He waited a long moment, but there was no response.

He pushed the door open. And thought his heart would stop when he saw that she still lay in her bed.

"Teresa Maeve!" He rushed to her side, and reached out to touch her long dark hair. "Why are you still here? Why—"

He snatched his hand away. It was not her hair at all. It was a black horse's tail, tied off at one end and stuffed under the wool cover.

216

He ripped back the cover. There was nothing under it but a couple of plain black cloaks, servant's cloaks, tightly rolled into long slender bundles.

Rage and fear flooded him all at once. How could this happen! Where could she be? Who could have done this?

Conaire threw the cover down and raced out of the room, down the steps, out of the Hall. "Sivney! Ros!" he shouted as he ran for the barn. "Get your horses! Now! We're going back out!"

"King Conaire."

He looked up, ready to give this latest interruption the full force of his temper. "What is it? What—"

Lonan stood calmly in the doorway of the barn, as if he'd been waiting there just to speak to the king. "You will not find her," he said.

Conaire grabbed him by the shoulders and shoved him back against the rough wooden wall. "What do you mean, I will not find her? Where is she? *Tell me!*"

Lonan gasped, but kept calm. "She has run away," he said, straining against Conaire's iron grip. "She and Dary. They're gone."

"Dary? What are you talking about?" Dary was one of the youngest of his warriors, a handsome dark-haired man with a boyish face. He'd seen Terri speak to him once or twice, but no more than she spoke to any of his men.

Conaire punched his fist toward Lonan's face, stopping only at the last instant. "That's a lie! Now tell me where she is or I will kill you where you stand!"

Slowly, Lonan opened his eyes, and shook his head. "They left last night. Late. Not long before that awful scream was heard." He smiled, lips pressed tightly together. "The *ban sidhe* was right, it would seem. How long do you think your Teresa can survive out there alone, with only Dary for company? I do not think you will see her again, King Conaire."

With a cry of rage, Conaire threw him to the ground.

"You're lying! I don't believe you! Why would you say such a thing to me?"

Lonan stirred, and with some difficulty got up to his knees. Cold rage showed in his eyes, but now it was mixed with pure satisfaction. "Ask Fearghan," he said. "He was on the gate last night. She demanded that it be opened, said she'd tear down the walls to get out if she had to. So he opened it and watched her gallop away on that monstrous gray beast of hers, with Dary on his own horse close after." He slumped back against the wall. "And I say that we are well rid of her."

Conaire's fist clenched again, but then abruptly he turned away and left Lonan sitting in the dirt. "Ros! Sivney!" he bellowed. The two men came running toward him from where they had been watching on the lawn. "Get the horses! Get some food and two more men! We're going out again now! Hurry!"

He watched them scurry off to follow his orders. Lonan got slowly to his feet, trying to brush the dirt from his fine blue tunic and black trews. "You cannot leave your people today, *Ri* Conaire," he said, with sneering sarcasm. "You have promised to finish hearing the case of Egan and Bellagh."

Conaire's fists tightened. "It will have to wait."

"A case already interrupted once by Teresa Maeve, in case you have forgotten."

Conaire turned on him. He was grimly pleased to see the man flinch and step back. "Say one word more, and it will be many days before you can speak again."

Lonan started to open his mouth, then thought better of it. He limped away, heading toward his house, and did not look back.

Conaire turned away from him and watched as his men rushed about, following his orders. It was impossible. He did not for one moment believe that she would run away with a strange man in the middle of the night, no matter how angry she had become.

But where was Firelair?

For just a moment he closed his eyes, trying to think, trying to breathe, trying with all his strength to keep his inner panic from showing through.

Never had anything reached out and seized him the way this had. He had no fear of warring tribes or dangerous animals; those threats he could face with easy courage, for he was a man well trained in courage, in wielding sword and shield, spear and sling, stallion and loyal men in defense of his people and his land.

But if she was gone—if she had truly run off as she had threatened to do, with Dary or anyone else, or if a worse fate had befallen her—none of those things could help him now. He would have no choice but to let her go; he would have to accept that she would never be his queen, never be his wife, would be forever gone from his life.

Not for one moment had he ever known what true fear felt like—never, until now.

Ros hurried up to him, leading his horse and Conaire's red stallion side by side. "Do you really think she has gone?" Ros asked.

Conaire closed his eyes. "I cannot believe it," he whispered. "But I may not have any choice."

He touched one hand to his chest. He seemed to be filled with emptiness, as though all his strength and heart had left him and galloped away on the back of a great silver mare.

For the rest of the afternoon, Conaire raced the sun, determined to find Teresa Maeve before the day outdistanced him. With the four men behind him pushing to keep up, he galloped his red stallion through every corner of his kingdom in the most desperate search of his life.

He saw so many of the places where they had spent time together—the broodmares' pastures which she so loved; the

219

place deep in the forest where they had killed the stag; the spot at the river where she had walked beneath the sun-dappled trees wearing nothing but her beauty; the hilltop near the dun where she had first come to him as a woman in love.

She had become such a part of his life that he could hardly remember what it was like before she had come. And now she had vanished into the night without a trace.

Deep in the forest, shadows lengthening, they stopped at a small stream to let the horses drink and catch their breath. "We can check the high pastures again," Conaire said, sliding down from his horse and dipping up a handful of water for himself, "and all the trails which lead to them—there are at least two more we have not searched—"

"The day has ended, *Ri* Conaire," Ros said quietly.

Conaire stopped and looked up at him. The other three men sat unmoving on their horses, staring down at their king. The water began to trickle out from between Conaire's fingers as he stared back at Ros. After a long moment, Ros looked away, saying nothing.

Conaire swung back up on his stallion. "If the day has ended," he said, "then we will start anew with the night." He turned the stallion and sent him into the dimness of the woods at a fast trot, leaving the men to scramble after him before he disappeared.

He had seen a faint trail leading away from the stream and into the forest. It might have been only a deer path, but it was one track that he had not searched. And he would search every last deer path and cattle trail and wolf trace in his kingdom until he found her.

Chapter Nineteen

There—

Conaire stopped his stallion and leaned forward, peering down at the damp mossy trail. In the near-darkness it was difficult to see, but there was no mistaking that hoofprint— larger than any that could have been made by one of his own horses.

It could only have been made by a horse the size of Firelair.

Carefully he urged the stallion on, stepping him as rapidly as possible down the darkening path and searching for more hoofprints. He found one more, and near it, a smaller, normal-sized print. Then, further on, the path widened a bit, and in the bare earth he could clearly see Firelair's large hoofprints surrounded by many smaller ones. All of them pointed the same way he was headed.

He drove the stallion forward. With a leap the animal raced down the trail. Conaire could hear the pounding of the others some distance back.

For a few long moments the stallion cantered down the dim and narrow trail, weaving cautiously in and out of the trees. Then suddenly he threw his head up and slid to a stop, and let out a loud, ringing neigh that echoed through the towering trees of the forest.

Conaire loosed the reins and let him go. The stallion swung to the right and trotted off, ears up, head high, and neighed again, clearly very interested in that particular direction. Conaire grabbed a handful of thick red mane and hung on tight as the stallion ducked and dodged his way around the trees and heavy underbrush, his fatigue now entirely forgotten.

They approached a clearing. Conaire could just make out the dark outlines of a small wooden house at the center of it, with two horses tied beneath the trees on one side. On the other side of the house, chafing at the tie rope and nickering with great anxiety to him and his stallion, stood Firelair, her head high and her large eyes glittering with fright.

The stallion made a great charge toward the clearing. Conaire dragged him to a halt. His heart pounded as he forced the animal back into the woods and hid him within the darkness of the trees. His men came riding up beside him, but he could not take his eyes from the wooden house in the clearing, barely visible now in the gloom.

She was there. He had no doubt of it. Right there, not a hundred paces away, hidden inside that small dark house, waiting for him to find her and help her get free. But he must be careful. He could not simply go charging in there. She was guarded, they would be waiting for him—

He slid down from the stallion and handed the reins up to Oran. "Sivney—Ros—come with me. Give your horses up to Falvy. Stay quiet." Conaire drew his sword from its wooden scabbard, and heard the other two men do the same as they started after him.

The night sky was heavy with clouds. The darkness in the clearing was nearly total. But from around the frames of the tightly closed door and single tiny window came a faint glow, as if a fire burned in the hearth. Conaire and his men crouched down and began to walk slowly and silently through the knee-high brush of the clearing.

He knew that she was not there by choice. If she really had run away as she had threatened to do and was simply hiding in this house, she would never have left Firelair sweat-stained and frightened and tied to a tree with no feed or water in sight. The rough rope about the mare's fine head was someone else's work, not Teresa Maeve's.

The mare stood tall and quivering, watching them. Her silvery coat glowed in the deep twilight like a drifting patch of mist. She nickered softly and anxiously at them as they approached the house.

The door slammed open wide. And from within the dimly lit house rushed two tall black shadows with swords gripped tightly in their hands.

"Stop!" For a desperate instant Conaire held his sword, trying to see just who it was who had come bursting through the door of the house. But they rushed at him and raised their swords, and he had no choice but to raise his in return.

He slashed at the first one. Ros and Sivney together struck at the second. The first man fell at Conaire's feet, his sword knocked out of his hand, and began scrambling to crawl back inside the house. When the man was half way across the doorway, Conaire bent down and grabbed him by his long dark hair, jerking his head around so that he could see him.

A young face, with fierce and frightened eyes. "Dary!" Conaire could not hide his astonishment. He had been so sure that Lonan had lied to him. "What are you doing in this place? What is going on here?" He jerked the man's head again. *"Where is Teresa Maeve?"*

The youth gasped, and made no answer. But his eyes flicked toward the inside of the barren little house. Conaire threw him down and dashed inside. He was cold with fear at what he might find, but even more afraid that he might find nothing at all.

She lay struggling on a pile of straw before the fire, bound at the wrists and ankles, a rag tied around her mouth.

She was still in the red and white wool gown that she had worn last night, though now it was torn as though a knife had slashed it from hem to knees. Conaire pulled away the gag and cut her bonds. In an instant she was sitting up and holding him tightly in her arms.

Just then Ros and Sivney crashed in through the door, grabbing Dary before he could get up. "No! Don't kill him!" cried Teresa Maeve. "He's a victim, too."

Conaire glanced at the men. "Hold him. We'll take him back and let him be tried." Ros gave him a quick nod, and then he and Sivney dragged Dary back outside.

He turned back to the woman in his arms, holding her close for a long moment. He could feel her trembling as she pulled him to her, but she did not weep, or say a word.

"I feared I would not see you again," he said gently. "When I discovered you were gone, I thought that my heart had gone away with you . . . and left me only an empty shell."

She shook her head emphatically, her dark matted hair flying left and right. "I didn't go anywhere. It was Lonan. Lonan and his cronies, those pathetic men who would do anything he told them to. They need someone to do their thinking for them and he's more than happy to oblige."

He caught her by the shoulders, feeling the rage building in him—rage replacing fear now that he knew she was safe. "Lonan was the one who did this? He kidnapped you, forced you to come here?"

She nodded slowly. "He grabbed me near the paddocks last night. It was him and at least two other men. I don't know how many, I couldn't see them. They pulled a piece of wool cloth over my head. They put me up on Firelair and tied my hands to her mane and led me from one of their own horses. Just as we got to the stream, I managed to work the gag off my mouth and I screamed—screamed as loud as I could, before they stopped and tied it back on. But no one heard me."

Conaire could only stare at her. He had heard. And so had his men and the servants and practically everyone else in the dun. They had all heard that terrible wailing scream and they had believed Brann's story about the *ban sidhe,* the woman-spirit who cries before a death—a death—

He placed his hands gently on either side of her face, looking into her eyes. "Oh, Teresa Maeve . . . I should have gone right then . . . I should have . . . ."

But she sat up straight, pushing back from him. "Fire-lair—where is she? Is she all right? I could hear her outside all day long, nickering and pawing. I know they haven't done anything to take care of her. I swear, I'll kill them myself if she's hurt by this!"

"She's all right. She's outside with my men. We'll take care of her. We'll get both of you home. But why did they do this? Why?"

She looked at him again. Something like pain coursed through him at the thought that he might never have seen that face again . . . never touched that smooth cheek, or kissed those warm full lips, or looked into those eyes . . . those clear gray eyes without a trace of fear in them.

"He wants your kingdom, Conaire. For some reason he thinks it should have gone to him instead of you. He wanted to get back at you by getting rid of me. He wants your kingdom, but since he can't have that, he thought he'd take your woman instead. I heard them talking about selling me off—me and Firelair both. They were going to sell me as a slave. That way they could still come and visit me from time to time." A shiver ran through her, and she turned away. "I didn't know you had slavery in this place."

"Criminals are sometimes made slaves, instead of being put to death." His fingers tightened. "Are you all right? Your gown . . . what have they done to you?"

She glanced at him and sat back, rubbing her wrists. "Nothing yet. They ripped my skirts so I could ride. But

Lonan and the rest of them were going to come back to-night. If you had not come—"

"But I did come. And now we are going home." He caught up a long stick of firewood and held it in the coals long enough for it to start its own flame. Holding the make-shift torch over their heads, he helped Teresa Maeve to her feet and pulled her close to him as they walked toward the door.

Together they stepped out into the darkness. Within the small light of Conaire's smoldering stick of wood stood Ros and Sivney, standing over Dary with swords drawn. Facedown on the ground beside them lay the second man, unmoving and ignored.

"Who is this?" Conaire asked, though he knew that the answer—whatever it was—would be like a knife in his back.

Ros reached down and turned the man over. The eyes stared up, unseeing; the hands fell back, empty.

"Kealan." Conaire stared down at the dead man, low-ering the torch. "First Dary, now Kealan. How many more? And why?" He looked up at Ros. "Why? These were men I knew, men I trusted! Why would they do this?"

He let go of Teresa Maeve and turned to Dary, thrusting the torch high over the cowering young man's head. "Why, Dary? Why would you do this? You were one of my sworn men! I knew your father, I knew your uncles!" He reached down and grabbed him by the front of his tunic. "Give me one reason why I should not kill you right now!"

Dary remained still, and looked him straight in the eye. "You should kill me, my king. I sold myself to another, sold myself like a slave. Another man bought my loyalty when it belongs by rights to you."

"Bought you?" Conaire said fiercely. "Who bought you? And what did he pay you with? Gold? Cattle? What?"

"The life of my child," Dary answered.

"What?" Conaire eased the youth back down to the ground, and let go of his tunic. "Your child?"

Dary looked away. Ros took a step forward. "It was Lonan," Ros said. "Lonan threatened to kill Dary's young infant if he did not help to carry out this kidnapping. Kealan's, too." He paused, and looked down at the young warrior. "Dary woke up one morning to find a knife in the sleeping child's basket. He was convinced they would strike if he refused to help them. Kealan feared the same."

"But they were among the most trusted of my men!"

"Exactly why Lonan chose them. He knew you would never expect it of them."

From out of the darkness came a demanding whinny and the sound of the ground being pawed by a big round hoof. "Firelair!" cried Teresa Maeve, and with a touch on Conaire's arm she turned away from him and dashed into the blackness beyond the torch.

"See to her, Teresa Maeve," he whispered. "We will see to Dary."

In the darkness, with only the light from a couple of makeshift torches to guide them, the company made ready for the journey back to Dun Cath.

Terri quickly untied Firelair and led her near the front door of the house, into the circle of light. "Look at this— look at this!" she hissed, loosening the coarse makeshift rope on the mare's skinned and bleeding head. The black leather bridle and saddle lay in a heap near the door of the house, and now Terri breathed a sigh of relief as she pulled off the rough biting rope and replaced it with the smooth leather straps of the bridle.

She rubbed off the mare's back as best she could with her hands. Across from her, at the edge of the torchlight, Conaire's men led their horses up and placed the body of Kealan across one of them. Dary sat on the ground beside his own horse, keeping very still, looking down and saying nothing.

Terri's eyes burned. Inwardly she began to shake, thinking back on her ordeal of the last day and night. For just a moment she leaned her head against Firelair's smooth neck.

A strong hand rested gently on her shoulder. "Teresa Maeve," said a deep soft voice. "Are you sure you are all right?"

She gave a hesitant nod, her face still hidden against the mare, and then nodded again, more firmly this time. "Yes," she answered, turning to him. "Oh, yes, I am all right now. . . ." Terri reached for him and he started to pull her close, but she placed her hands firmly on his arms and held him back so she could see his face.

"I'm so sorry," she said.

His arms tensed, and a puzzled expression crossed his face. "Sorry? How can you be sorry? You have done nothing! Why do you say you are sorry?"

Terri glanced over her shoulder. "I am sorry for them. For Kealan, and for Dary. They were forced into this just as I was."

She let him go, and drew a deep breath. "They watched over me all day. They stayed with me, even though all Lonan wanted them to do was help with the kidnapping. Their work was done; they could have gone back to the dun and left me here alone. But they didn't. They stayed, and gave me water and food, and even made a bed of straw for me to lie on. They said they would stay with me until I was sold and then find a way to let you know where I was.

"They couldn't rescue me. Their own families would have been killed. I don't have any doubt of that. But I am just as sure that Lonan would have had them both killed once I was—disposed of. He's not the type to want any witnesses."

She looked up into his eyes. "They tried to give me what

help they could, and Kealan paid for it with his life. What is it going to cost Dary?''

Conaire stared back at her, and slowly shook his head. ''Any other woman would be shaking with fright after such an experience, filled with fear and loathing of her captors. Yet you try to understand them, even show compassion for them.'' He smiled. ''You are an exceptional woman, Teresa Maeve. Most exceptional.''

Terri looked away, though she did smile faintly in return. ''Oh, I'm shaking, all right. I expect I will be for a long time yet.'' She raised her chin. ''But there is a question that must be answered now. What will happen to Dary?''

Conaire shrugged. ''We'll take him back with us. He will be under my protection. Unless you want him to be tried, he will remain a free man.''

Her eyes widened, and she reached out and caught his arm. ''We can't take him back! Don't you understand? It's Lonan who's got to be dealt with! Lonan is the one behind all of this! He's like a snake in your kingdom. You've got to get rid of him once and for all!''

''He's like a—what?''

''A snake! An evil, slithering, poisonous snake!'' At his blank expression, Terri sighed. ''Of course. There are no snakes in Ireland . . . and I guess there never have been.''

Conaire smiled gently, but his eyes were serious. ''I am not sure what a 'snake' is . . . but I will take your word that it is a foul creature if you compare it to Lonan.'' He reached up and gently touched her hand where she held his arm, and then moved away from her towards the torchlight.

Dary still sat alone on the ground. ''Stand and face me, Dary,'' Conaire said. Slowly the young man got to his feet, though he would not meet his king's gaze.

''You may kill me where you stand, Ri Conaire,'' he said, ''and well you should. But I will not return to Dun Cath. Lonan's men are everywhere . . . many follow him in

229

secret. I do not even know all of them for certain . . . and I will not see my child killed.''

''Go,'' Conaire said.

Dary looked up at him.

''Take your horse and go. Hide in the forest if you must. We will say that I gave you a choice of exile or death, and you chose exile. And when I have rid Dun Cath of the poison that is Lonan, you will return and you and your family will be safe.''

Dary stared back at him, the relief—and disbelief—plain to see on his face. Then his gaze shifted to Terri.

''Go,'' she said. ''I know you had no choice. We'll see you again—and so will your child.''

The young face changed, and into Dary's eyes came an expression of such intensity, such devotion, that Terri felt deeply touched. She thought she had known what loyalty was, but she had never seen anything like this. This was loyalty born not of corporate politics and lip service, but of heart and soul, life and death.

''I will go,'' he said, to her and to Conaire, ''but I will return. I swear it.'' He reached out to clasp Conaire's wrist. Then, in an instant, he mounted his horse, swung it around, and lashed it into the night.

It was a long, slow journey back to the dun. Every member of the company kept silent. The only sounds were the hoofbeats and snorting of the horses.

The darkness and the deep forest and the dead man tied across his horse forced them to stay at a careful walk. Terri's weariness after the long and terrible day began to catch up with her. She swayed in the saddle as Firelair walked along, nodding off and almost sleeping as she rode.

She came suddenly awake as Firelair stopped. In the damp and misty darkness, the gates of Dun Cath were slowly swinging open.

Never had she been so glad to see the place. They rode

inside and stopped on the wide lawn, where a few scattered torches cast their flaring light onto the mist and wet grass. Terri moved past the others and steered Firelair toward her paddock, thinking that for once she would just unsaddle the mare and turn her loose and give her a good grooming in the morning. . . .

The lawn suddenly grew brighter. Blinking, Terri looked up to see a crowd of torchbearing men moving toward them, surrounding them. And to her astonishment Lonan walked straight to Conaire's horse and caught it by the bridle.

"So, we see what kind of man you are," Lonan sneered. His face was distorted, ugly, in the glaring torchlight. "You have brought back the cause of all our trouble."

Conaire swung down to the ground. Lonan let go of the horse and stepped back a pace. "I am the same man I have always been," Conaire snarled, "except for carrying more rage than I ever knew it was possible to carry."

Lonan cocked his head slightly, but stood his ground. "Rage? Why? Oh, of course; I understand. You are angry for the same reason *we* are angry—because our king no longer cares to rule his dun! Because he sees nothing and follows nothing but the backside of a woman, a woman who has caused nothing but disruption and trouble from the day she arrived at Dun Cath!"

"You kidnapped her!" Conaire shouted. The red stallion flinched, but stayed by his side. "You stole her in the night so you could sell her for a slave. You are a criminal and a poison and you will not escape me this time!"

Lonan only shrugged. "I kidnapped no one. She got on her mare and rode off into the forest with Dary, just as I told you she had. Ask Dary. If you found her, you must have found him. Or are you afraid he'll tell you the truth?"

"Dary is gone," Conaire answered through clenched teeth. "He was there with her, guarding her. I gave him the choice of death or exile. He chose exile—but Kealan chose death.''

He jerked his head toward the men behind him. Sivney led forward the horse that carried Kealan's body, and eased the dead man down to the ground. Lonan stared at it, frowning, and from all around him came the stirring and murmuring of the men with the torches. *"Kealan! Kealan is dead . . . dead . . ."*

Lonan looked back at Conaire, and smiled coldly at him again. And Terri realized, to her amazement, that the crowd of men had begun to shift. It almost seemed as if the majority of them were grouped behind Lonan.

In the darkness, she began to shiver.

Chapter Twenty

"Well, then. All very convenient. It's just her word against ours, isn't it?" Lonan's eyes narrowed, and his face became filled with hatred. "And we say she is a liar and a trouble-maker who is bent on the destruction of the dun. She cares only for the gold you give her and for that freakish animal she rides—and for the attention she can get from others! We all know, all too well, that there is nothing she would not do for attention."

"That's a lie!" Terri shouted, but no one heard her— her cry was drowned out by Conaire's roar of rage as he pulled his sword from its scabbard.

The crowd of men fell back. Terri caught her breath. But Lonan made no move, even as Conaire stood over him with sword in hand. "There is something you should see before I kill you," Lonan said.

Without taking his eyes off Conaire, he made some gesture to the men behind him. And as the company held its breath, four men came through the crowd. Each pair carried something long and heavy between them. They laid down their burdens at Conaire's feet and then stepped back— leaving the torchlight to flicker on the faces of two dead men.

One was Bellagh.

The other was Egan.

"They fought after you left!" Lonan shouted. "Bellagh

233

killed Egan outright, and then died of his own wounds before the sun went down." He smiled again, a cruel grimace of rage and cold satisfaction. "You could not be troubled to hear their case! You could spare them no time! You could not turn your eyes from that woman's backside, and now three good men lie dead at your feet!"

Conaire lowered his sword. His face was pale and very still, and it seemed to Terri that all the fight drained out of him as he stared down at the bodies.

One of the men still with Conaire pushed forward to stand beside his king. "He provoked them, *Ri* Conaire," the man said, pointing his sword straight at Lonan. "He told each one lies about the other and then made certain they crossed paths. There was no stopping them after that." The man lowered his sword, but never took his eyes off Lonan. "You are not to blame, *Ri* Conaire. Bellagh and Egan are to blame—and so is that one." He thrust the sword point at Lonan.

"I accept blame for nothing," Lonan cried. "This was something only the king could have prevented. When those two men began to fight, the king could have ordered his men to stop them and keep them from killing each other. He could have ordered that a trial be held then and there and put an end to the matter once and for all.

"But your king was not here. Your king was following that woman."

There was a great murmuring and discussion among the men. And to Terri's horror, they further split themselves up, until only a handful stood with Conaire and all the rest were scattered across the lawn behind Lonan.

Terri quickly turned Firelair towards Conaire. But Lonan spread his arms wide and turned to the men gathered around him.

"You know I am right!" he shouted to them. "Look what has happened to Dun Cath since Conaire brought her here. Interference and unrest among the servants. Among the horse boys. Among the warrior men! And who could blame them, when she parades herself naked in front of them and behaves worse than a bitch-dog in heat!

"She has disrupted every aspect of life in Dun Cath. Worse than disrupted—destroyed! She is a destroyer of the king, a destroyer of the dun. And if you want proof, you need only look down at the ground where he stands, where three honest men lie dead! The dun has already started to die. How much more proof do you need?"

The entire gathering stood in absolute silence. Terri knew there would be no going back from this point. Lonan had defied the king and was now laying claim to his kingship.

Conaire would have to do something. He would have to fight back, or else risk losing the dun—but so few of his men stood with him. How could so many of them stand with Lonan? Where was their loyalty?

She saw their eyes in the torchlight. Their gazes flicked from Lonan, to Conaire, to her, and the confusion and uncertainty on those faces was plain to see.

A terrible feeling of dread began to creep over her. Lonan had, at last, found the one weapon he could use in his long feud with Conaire. He could not defeat him with weapons, or laws, or traditions; but he could plant the seeds of mistrust and uncertainty and doubt, and so he had. Bigger kingdoms than this one had been brought down in just that way, had fallen to just such devious weapons.

Lonan meant to destroy Conaire and take his kingdom for himself. The men were divided, and Conaire all but alone. Terri knew that he would never walk away from Dun Cath, never give up, never surrender.

The only thing waiting for him now was a battle to the death.

Lonan let his arms drop to his sides. Then, with a violent gesture, he pointed straight at Conaire.

"You are no longer fit to be king," he sneered, as the

silent men of the dun moved ever closer behind him. "Your will has been broken. Your mind has been taken hostage. Your strength of spirit is weakened and diseased. It is as if you had lost an arm, or a foot, or had the bones of your legs crushed. You are no longer whole, you are no longer complete, you are no longer fit to be king!"

The murmuring began again as the men reacted to these words. Their wavering torches sent the shadows jumping throughout the dun. But they fell silent as Brann pushed his way through them and stood beside Lonan.

"My foster-brother is right," Brann said. "The law says that a king must be free of infirmity, free of disfigurement, in both body and mind." He stared at Conaire, his face devoid of expression. "And when the mind no longer has the will to resist that which turns it from the people, it is as if that mind were weak ... and broken ... and crippled."

Now all of the men behind Lonan turned to look at Conaire. With a shiver, Terri heard the sing of metal on metal as some of them drew their swords from their scabbards.

She looked quickly at Conaire. With him stood exactly eight men. They were tall and fearless beside their king, staring fiercely at Lonan with their own swords in hand, but they were only eight, and they faced an armed and angry mob of not less than fifty.

Lonan grinned at the sight. The wild light of victory already gleamed in his eyes. And to Terri's revulsion his gaze shifted to her, and he walked over to stand almost at Firelair's feet.

Conaire and his men turned as if to follow him, but made no move to approach. Conaire's eyes, fierce with anger and frustration, burned right into Lonan. The sword trembled in Conaire's hand, so tight was his grip on the hilt. He took one step toward Lonan, but stopped when the mob raised its weapons.

"So, it has come to this," Lonan said. His voice was

smooth with satisfaction. "Justice has come at last to Dun
Cath." He turned and ran his finger down Terri's ragged
red gown, from her knee to her ankle, and then looked back
at Conaire and smiled.

"You have a choice," he said. "You can have this
woman. Or you can have your kingdom. But you cannot
have both."

Terri's blood ran cold. She turned to Conaire and his
men. *We have to stop this!* she wanted to shout to them.
*We can't let this happen! We've got to do something! I'll
never go with him! And you can't let him take your kingdom!*

But Conaire made no move. His eyes shifted from Terri
to his men, and back to Terri again.

She heard the low voice of one of his men. "We will
not let him do this, Ri Conaire," the man said urgently.
"We are only eight, but we are your best! Say the word
and we will cut them all down like the dogs they truly are."

Yet Conaire only shook his head, though his sword remained tightly clenched and trembling in his hand. His eyes
never left Terri.

Lonan pushed himself away from the silver mare.
"What's wrong, Conaire? What are you waiting for? Aren't
you willing to fight for your Teresa?" He took several steps
toward the king and spread his arms wide. "Have you not,
at last, found the woman worth dying for?"

Conaire shouted his rage and started to raise his sword.
Terri cried out and Firelair jumped, startled.

For an instant she was certain that everything she knew
was over. Conaire was a trained warrior, a powerful king,
a hardened man in a violent time. He could never put away
that sword. He would die first. All of them would die.

But to Terri's astonishment, Conaire lowered his sword.

His teeth were clenched, and his murderous glare remained fixed on Lonan. But although he shook with anger,

and from the effort of keeping that anger under control, he shoved his sword back into its scabbard.

Lonan frowned at him. "What's the matter, Conaire?" he asked, his confusion plain. "Why do you put away your sword? I ask you again: Haven't you found the woman worth dying for?"

"I have not," he answered. He looked up, and his gaze locked with Terri's. "But I have found the woman worth living for."

Terri's heart pounded. It was the last thing she had expected to hear. *". . . worth living for . . ."*

The warrior had chosen life. In a choice between her and the kingdom, the king had chosen her.

A shocked silence descended over the dun. Everyone stared at Conaire. There was not a sound, or a movement, except for the snapping and flickering of the torches.

"You may have the kingdom," Conaire said, straightening. "It seems that I have lost it already." But as Lonan smirked, Conaire fixed him with a gaze cold as steel. "You may yet find that this kingdom is not worth having."

He walked off a step or two, ignoring Lonan's tense and heavily armed mob of men, and caught his stallion by its trailing reins. "Every field needs weeding from time to time," he said, "and I should thank you for doing mine for me."

Conaire gathered up the reins as Lonan began to frown. "I will take Teresa Maeve, and my loyal men, and we will go. And I will kill any men of yours who try to ride after us."

He vaulted onto the stallion's back, and turned the full force of his hatred on Lonan. "I am well rid of any man who would follow you!" he cried, his voice rough with anger. "I want only the men who choose, in freedom, to follow me. We will take only our own horses and possessions. And if you try to stop us, you will have to kill us all in cold blood, right here in front of everyone—and then let the bards sing of that through the ages to come.''

Terri felt as though her life had just passed before her eyes. Though she knew they were still in great danger, an enormous relief flooded through her. It wasn't over. Conaire would live. All of them would live. Instead of charging blindly into a horrible, deadly battle for the sake of ''honor,'' as she had expected, Conaire had chosen life— chosen the future—chosen her.

If ever she had doubted her love for him, her respect for him, she doubted it no longer.

But Lonan was not finished yet. He turned again, and this time he pointed straight at Terri. ''So, even Conaire has admitted that I am right. He has said that having this woman is more important to him than leading his people, more important than being a king.''

He looked back at his men, and almost laughed. ''After all the time he spent searching for a woman fit to be queen, this is the one he chose? This is the best he could do?'' He spat on the ground. ''*She* came here only for wealth and praise, riches and attention. And she used the bed of the king to get them. We are well rid of them both!''

Shocked, Terri broke the silence of the men and shouted right back at Lonan. ''That's not true. I care nothing for gold or money or things! I care only for Dun Cath—and its horses—and its king!''

But Lonan only laughed, cold and disdainful. ''Oh, she was a prize, indeed. When she had taken all she could from us, what did she do but run off with Dary, who promised her even more gold.''

Her shock boiled into rage. ''I should have killed you myself!'' she shouted at him as Firelair shifted and tossed her head. ''I should have!'' She glared at him, wishing she could run the mare straight over the top of him and blot out that evil grin once and for all.

But then she grew conscious of the many eyes watching her, waiting for her reaction. Well, she would let them all know where she stood. "I'll show you how much jewelry means to me! I'll give you my very last piece!" And with that Terri reached for her shining gold ring, twisted it off her cold finger, and hurled it straight at Lonan's head.

The ring flew through the air, glinting in the torchlight. For an instant Terri hoped it would strike Lonan right in the face—*serve him right!* she thought.

But with this act of defiance, she felt something go out of her. Her vision swam and she felt dizzy, exhausted. She let her head fall forward and locked her hands in Firelair's mane. This day had been so long, so terrible, it was no wonder she felt so drained. . . .

But then she breathed deep of the damp night air, and raised her head to look at Lonan. To her satisfaction she saw that he held one hand pressed against his face, as though something hard and stinging had struck him on the cheek.

"There!" she said to him, shaking her hair out of her face. "I don't have any more jewelry to throw at you, but I'll be glad to hit you with just about anything else I can get my hands on. What do you say to that?"

She glared down at Lonan, almost eager for him to reply so that she could let go at him again. But he made no response at all. He took his hand down from his face and simply stared at her, as though he hadn't understood a word she'd said.

"What's the matter?" she hissed. "Are you only brave enough to talk to me when you've got me bound and gagged?"

Still he made no response. Terri looked over at Conaire. He, too, stood and stared at her, but now his expression was one of loss, and pain, and despair.

"Why are you looking at me like that?" She glanced quickly from Conaire to Lonan and back to Conaire again. She was suddenly afraid that in the tense silence they might lunge at each other and start a battle that could not be stopped—but the two of them just stood watching her, as did Ros, and Sivney, and Brann, and all the rest of the men in the gathering.

Then, at last, Conaire spoke.

At first she thought she simply had not heard him. None of his words made sense. She frowned and shook her head slightly, prompting him to repeat what he had said—but when he did, she felt a coldness and aloneness creep through her, a coldness that was something like fear.

"Why are you speaking to me in Gaelic?" she demanded. Her voice began to shake. "I can't understand Gaelic, you know that! Why are you doing this?"

Lonan said something, and laughed. Ros and Sivney turned and spoke to one another. And Conaire walked his stallion over to her, placed his hand on her knee, looked up into her eyes, and spoke beseechingly to her, but she could not decipher one word he said, or that any of them said, and it was equally plain that they could not understand her.

"Why are you doing this to me? Speak to me in English! Speak to me so that I can understand you!"

But none of them did. Lonan's men began shouting and raising their weapons, and pressing closer.

Conaire turned and spoke quickly to his own men, and then shouted something to Lonan—shouted again and again. The mob of men quieted, and then grudgingly they parted to allow Conaire's eight men to pass through them. The little group disappeared into the black shadows, hurrying toward the houses at the back of the dun.

For a moment Terri felt a rush of fear. Where were they going? Had they, too, decided to desert their king? It was maddening not being able to understand what they were saying, not knowing what was going on. But Conaire looked straight into her eyes and held her gaze for a long moment, and even smiled just a little.

Wait, he seemed to be saying. *Trust me. Just wait.*

She took a deep breath. Now she understood, or thought she did. The men would come back. No doubt they had gone to grab what possessions they could. And she and Conaire were hostages against their return.

The moments passed. Terri found herself trembling. But Conaire waited calmly, his face like stone, and just when she thought she could not wait another second, she caught sight of something moving far across the dun.

She was the first to see them coming, sitting high as she was atop Firelair. Conaire's men were returning, as he had known they would. Each was leading a horse and carrying a tightly wrapped bundle. But Terri's heart sank when she saw what else they were bringing.

Three young women walked in their midst, their eyes wide and their faces white. Of course. The men would not leave without their families!

Or would they? Why were only three of them bringing their wives? She saw no children with them, and then realized that the women appeared quite young. They surely were newly married and had no children yet.

But the other five men—where were their families? Terri shivered. They must be leaving them behind, but how could they? How could they choose Conaire over their own wives and children, and leave them here with Lonan?

And then she realized that they had done no such thing. No man of Conaire's would abandon his family. Of all his loyal men, only the five who were not married, and the three who had wives but no children, had dared to stand with their king. The rest were scattered among the mob, but they could not identify themselves for the same reason Dary and Kealan had gone along with her kidnapping.

They wanted to see their children remain alive.

She looked again at the torchbearing mob of men. Some of the faces she recognized, and she knew without a doubt that those men were loyal to Conaire. She was just as sure that others belonged to Lonan. But the rest—she honestly could not say.

Did the men themselves even know for certain who was loyal to whom? If Conaire and his advisors had been caught unawares, the rest of them could only be filled with suspicion of one another. The fear and doubt and mistrust that Lonan had planted had done their work exceedingly well, thriving in the atmosphere of whispered secrets and furtive conspiracy.

The eight men got on their horses and pulled their belongings and their wives up behind them. For an instant Terri's mind turned to practicalities—how could they travel fast with three of the small horses carrying double? What would they do for food, for clothes, for shelter? How would they live?

But the instant the men were settled on their horses, the mob began shouting again, not so much in anger as in celebration—and if anything, the sound was even more terrifying than before. Conaire swung his stallion around and galloped for the gate, shouting for her to follow him. *"Treise Maeve!"* she heard, and saw his frantically waving arm in the torchlight. *"Treise Maeve!"*

As she turned the mare around, she remembered something Conaire had said to her on a fine afternoon a long time ago.

There are some things worse than death. Humiliation. Disgrace. Loss of honor. Making a once-respected man a figure of ridicule.

It was not always necessary to kill a man in order to destroy him.

The company raced through the open gates of the dun, chased by the roaring shouts and laughter of the mob. And in a moment of bitter realization, Terri found that though she could no longer understand their words, she had no trouble understanding their laughter.

Chapter Twenty-one

Into the depths of darkness they galloped, a company of thirteen, outcast and alone. Terri felt as though the night would swallow them and the blackness would never lift. She leaned forward over Firelair's mane and kept her close behind Conaire's red stallion, knowing that the mare's silvery coat would help to guide the others who rode behind her.

She did not know how long they ran. The hypnotic rhythm of the horses' hooves, the swift rocking motion, and the utter lack of anything to see all combined to make her concentrate solely on staying in the saddle and following the tireless red stallion. Her heart pounded with fear and shock. Only pure adrenaline and the cold night air kept her going.

Conaire seemed to know where he was headed. They followed a deliberate path through open country, turning once, then again. There was nothing to do but follow him and trust that he would lead them to some kind of safety.

After a time they eased to a trot, and then to a walk. The world slowed, but darkness still surrounded them, forming a vast wall that kept the little company apart from the rest of the world.

They came to a stream, and paused just long enough to let the horses and their riders drink of the cold rushing water. Terri looked up from the stream and tried to find

Conaire, but he was already back up on his stallion. He sat looking into the sky far ahead of them, and hardly seemed to know that they were there.

The three men helped their wives remount their horses, and spoke quietly to them, though Terri could not tell what they were saying. Then she was back in the saddle and walking through the darkness once again.

She sighed, and breathed deep, trying to force enough energy into her mind and body to stay awake a little while longer. Looking up, she felt heartened to see a tiny gleam in the blackness up ahead—and then another, and another.

Stars. The clouds were moving off and the stars were coming out, as though lighting their way and showing them a place. The southern sky began to open up to them, the only glimmer of light in all of the vast darkened world.

They settled into a steady walk, the weary horses somehow finding strength for one more step, and one more, and one more. They moved in silence, drifting across the open landscape, the footfalls of the horses barely making a sound in the soft thick grass. The only sound was the rushing of the night wind in the grass and distant trees.

It was all so unreal. For a moment, her mind shifted, and it seemed to her that they had always been out here, riding one after another through the night, silent as ghosts and just as invisible. And she recalled, for a moment, something she had heard on her first day in Ireland . . . something old Sean, the stablemaster, had said when she had seen the mysterious bonfire burning out on the highest hill.

The host of the unforgiven dead, he had whispered. *The ghosts of the pagan ancestors who do live yet in these hills and caves.*

His words had been ominous and chilling at the time. But now she looked up at the dark figure of Conaire in front of her, and then glanced back at the silent riders following behind. *Pagan ancestors*.

Now she knew what old Sean had meant. In this time

and place, the days of Saint Patrick had not yet come. Conaire and his people were the ones Sean had been speaking of, though she wished she could somehow tell him that these strong and noble people were nothing for their distant children to fear.

We are the Daoine Sidhe, Terri thought. *We are the Daoine Sidhe*.

They were climbing a hill. She could feel the mare laboring beneath the saddle, stretching out her neck and working her way up the steep slope. Terri could only wonder how the smaller horses, some of them burdened with two riders, would ever make it to the top.

At last they reached level ground. Firelair stood very still, her head down, as though she had taken all the steps she could and was perfectly willing to rest right here in this very spot. Terri looked up, reeling with fatigue, and tried to see where they were. Here the stars were out and the skies were clear, though the light was too faint to see much of the world. She could tell that they were high on a hill, and that there seemed to be a grove of trees near the center of it, but that was all.

She slid down from Firelair's back, her legs sore and trembling from the endless hours in the saddle, and placed her hand against the mare's warm damp shoulder. In a moment she was surrounded by the eight other horses. Their riders, too, dropped wearily to the ground, glad enough for the moment just to feel solid ground beneath their feet.

Only one horse and rider was missing. Terri looked up toward the trees and caught sight of Conaire's black silhouette in the starlight. She led Firelair slowly toward him, but he tied his horse and then walked away as though he were the only one up here on this hill.

She wanted to go to him, but could not leave without caring for the exhausted animal who had carried her so far—and she knew that her own fatigue would not allow her to go on much longer. After Firelair had drunk deeply at the spring, Terri led her to the edge of the trees, pulled off the saddle and bridle, slipped on the halter, and tied her safely to a high solid branch.

Terri started to walk after Conaire, but her legs simply refused to go any further and she sat down beneath a tree at the edge of the grove. She closed her eyes and wrapped the ragged gown close around her knees, telling herself she would sit here for just a moment. Her head buzzed with exhaustion and she leaned back against the rough bark— but looked up quickly at the sound of footfalls.

The other men were leading their horses to the spring and then tying them around the grove. She could hear them walking amongst the trees and speaking an occasional soft word to one another. One by one they walked away from the grove and disappeared into the darkness, following after Conaire. Then there was only silence.

Terri had thought she would sleep the instant she closed her eyes, but now she found that she was so shaky, so tense, so very exhausted, that she was almost too tired to sleep. She could not sit alone beneath this tree another moment with only Firelair and the other horses for company. With a great effort she got to her feet and started into the darkness, where Conaire and the others had gone.

They sat near the edge of the starlit hilltop, twelve shadows against the blackness. The women and their husbands were huddled close together, sheltering each other, while the rest of the men hovered nearby. Conaire sat a little distance away from the others with only two other men for company.

Of course, Terri saw as she walked toward them through the damp grass, at his side were Sivney and Ros—his two most trusted men, always with him even to the end.

She approached them slowly, but they took no notice of her. No one said a word as she went to Conaire and sat down close beside him, leaning her head against his shoulder with a great sigh of relief. He reached up, unfastened the heavy gold brooch high on his chest, and then drew one end of his warm woolen cloak around her.

She closed her eyes. They were outcasts and alone in the darkness, but they still had each other, and for the moment that was all that mattered.

Conaire sat on the hilltop and stared out into the blackness, feeling entirely alone. It made no difference that eight loyal men sat at his feet or that Treise Maeve lay curled against his side, soft and warm beneath his heavy wool cloak. He drew no strength from his men nor comfort from her nearness. He was conscious only of the terrible shock of loss and the overwhelming sense of guilt that filled his heart and mind.

"I have abandoned my people," he whispered.

At the sound of his voice, Treise Maeve stirred slightly. Ros and Sivney glanced at each other and then leaned in closer. "No, *Ri* Conaire," Sivney said quietly. "*They* have abandoned *you*. They allowed themselves to be held hostage by a madman."

Conaire closed his eyes. "No king turns his back on his people. No king would walk away from them while he was yet alive."

"And what good is a king to his people when he is dead?" Ros spoke this time, and shook his head.

"I would be better off dead. This is far worse than death." Conaire looked out into the blackness of the sky, seeing nothing, trying with all his strength to feel nothing. "Any man with the smallest scrap of courage, with the honor of a beast in the field, would have fought to the death for his people—fought for those he loved and had sworn to protect. I have allowed myself to be humiliated and humbled and ridiculed as no living king ever has. I have run away from my own dun."

Ros moved a bit closer. Conaire could hear the urgency

in his low voice. "You had no choice. There were not enough of us! Too many are hiding in fear, the fear of secrecy and lies and the most cowardly of threats—the threat to their children."

Another man approached out of the darkness. "This was no ordinary battle, against an enemy unafraid to make himself known," said Falvy, standing behind Ros. "This was a fight of the worst sort—a fight against a man who is not a man at all, but a coward and a traitor, a coward who fights with lies and deceit instead of with swords and courage. You did not think such an enemy was to be found among your men, the honorable men of Dun Cath, and I will tell you that none of us did either—not until it was too late."

"You are right," Conaire said, and his voice shook with bitterness and self-loathing. "That was my mistake. I thought all of my men were as fine and noble and honorable as the eight who sit with me now, lost in the night. I thought *Ri* Conaire would only have men as great as he himself."

He glanced down at Treise Maeve. "I told her once that everyone has enemies—that the danger lies in not recognizing them. I should have listened to my own advice. Most of all, I should have listened to *her*. She knew Lonan for what he was—she tried to tell me, again and again—but I thought I knew how to handle him."

At that point, Treise Maeve slowly sat up and looked into his face. Her clear gray eyes shone in the faint light of the stars as she reached up and drew one gentle finger down the side of his cheek. At last he had to look away, lowering his head until it rested against his hand and shielded his face from the world.

His men's forgiveness, and Treise Maeve's kindness, only made it harder. His men should despise him for a weakling. She should scorn him as less than a man! Didn't they understand? In their shock and exhaustion, did they not realize what he had done?

"Lonan deceived us all," Ros went on. "We'd grown used to his constant anger and spitefulness—it was simply the way he was. We never expected him to—"

"But I should have expected it! I was the king! I knew how he felt, how he thought he should have been king, and I dismissed it all as petty jealousy!

"I thought I could earn his friendship by showing him kindness, by allowing him his anger. I thought that he would come around in time. But look at the price of choosing that path! I nearly cost Treise Maeve her life, and now I have destroyed the people of Dun Cath!"

At the sound of her name, Treise Maeve tensed against him and sat back slightly. But Conaire found that he could not look at her, could not match that cool gray gaze. He looked out into the night instead, where a faint flicker of light far in the distance caught his eye.

Lightning, he thought. Lightning too far away to be heard, only seen. As he watched, he saw that, one by one, the stars nearest the horizon were disappearing. A storm was moving in, moving toward them slowly but surely.

How he wished he could speak to Treise Maeve . . . how he needed her right now, needed her strong voice and unshakable opinion! It was as if half of his heart had been closed away from him. Though her body stayed pressed up close to his, he was cut off from her mind, her words, her wisdom. Those things had been as important to him as the lusty lovemaking they had shared.

It only added to his grief to think that her voice was one more thing that he had lost tonight. He would have been more than pleased to hear her shout at him and tell him what a fool he had been. But in her towering pride she had thrown away the golden ring, and with it had gone her power to speak to him in the language of Eire—the power he had given her with a bit of magic captured on a singular night.

There would be no recreating that magic. The Summer

Solstice was long past. There was no conjunction of stars in the sky, shining down red and silver and gold, on this black and endless night. He knew something of the ways of the druids . . . enough to know that such a moment would not come again.

Now Treise Maeve was like the distant lightning that he watched. She was brilliant, powerful, crackling with energy and potential, but silent. It was clear that she could follow some of their conversation—her eyes flicked to his face each time the word *ri* was spoken, and she would murmur something in the odd language that must have been the native tongue of Merrica—but there was nothing she could say that any of them could understand.

"You have destroyed nothing, *Ri* Conaire," Ros insisted. "You did the only thing that could be done for the men who stayed behind with their families. You left to save their lives and ours and that of Treise Maeve."

"Treise Maeve . . ." He looked at her, and she smiled gently and relaxed against him once again. He could feel the beating of her heart where she lay pressed close beside him, could smell the musky sweetness of her long dark hair. "Was Lonan right? Did I allow my feelings for her to blind me to the evil he was working within? Did I put my love for her above the good of the people who trusted me to lead them?"

Ros reached out and took his arm. "She is your queen. Your chosen. Lonan tried to take her from you! Now tell me—what kind of man, what kind of *king,* would hand over a woman in exchange for a kingdom, as though she were a slave or a hostage! Not one of your loyal men would have followed you for an instant if you had done any such thing, and Dun Cath truly would have ended then and there.

"You did not run away from your people. We have merely had to retreat for a time, to regroup and ready ourselves for the time when we can take our revenge. When our king can take back the dun!"

"Your king." Conaire looked up at Ros and glared fiercely at him. "Your king is a king no longer. Not when he has deserted his people. Nothing can ever justify that. Nothing can ever make up for that. Nothing will ever make him a king again."

Throwing back his cloak, Conaire pushed himself away from Treise Maeve. He got to his feet and walked off into the darkness of the trees, where no man could see the shame that burned his eyes.

The chill night air washed over Terri as Conaire strode away, leaving his cloak to slide off her shoulders. Quickly she grabbed the heavy cloak, pulled it close, and scrambled to her feet. The damp cold wind chased after her as she followed him. Desperately she tried to keep him in sight, but after only a moment he vanished into the grove.

She could scarcely see anything in the blackness beneath the trees. Feeling her way through the dark, she moved slowly from tree to tree, until something small and faintly white suddenly caught her eye. It bobbed up and down, and with a start she recognized it as the white blaze on the face of one the horses. Carefully she edged around him—she did not want to run into a horse in the dark!

Terri went on stepping cautiously through the grove. "Conaire! Conaire!"

There was no answer. The only sound was the rustling of the trees in the ever-increasing wind. He had simply vanished into the night.

What was she going to do? Wait until the sun came up and hope to find him then? Her heart pounded. At the blackest moment of his life, Conaire had turned and walked away from her and from his men. He could be anywhere, could be planning anything, in the state of mind he was in. She had not needed to understand his language to know how distraught he had been when he'd spoken to Ros and Sivney.

Well, he couldn't have gotten very far. He had to be up on this hill somewhere. She had to find him!

And then she saw it—a gleam of gold within the darkness.

Chapter Twenty-two

Pushing a tree branch out of her way, Terri walked to the place where a small gleam of light shone out of the darkness. She crouched down beside the gleam and slowly, carefully, reached out for it.

Yes, there it was, the heavy golden torque that rested always at his throat. The great piece was hard and cool beneath her fingers. She moved her hand upward over the hot skin of his neck, into the smooth beard, up the side of his face to the thick brows and the smooth skin above them—

He reached up and caught her wrist. Gripping it tightly, he forced her to stop. Then he moved her hand away and released it, letting it fall back to her side.

Terri clenched her fists, her earlier sympathy flaring into anger. "Oh, I see. You want to be alone, so you can sit here and feel sorry for yourself." There was a slight movement of the golden gleam, but the silence and the stillness continued.

She sat down close beside him and clamped her hand on his iron-hard arm. "If you try to leave, you'll have to drag me with you," she began, but he made no move to go. He seemed determined to act as if she were not there at all.

Terri sighed. "Conaire—I know you can't understand what I'm saying anymore, and I can't understand you. I never thought about it before, about how it was that we could speak to each other. It didn't seem any stranger than my being here in the first place. But I know, now, that it must have been the ring . . . the ring you put through the flames on the first night I was here.''

She looked away, though it hardly mattered in the blackness that had swallowed them both. ''I'm so sorry I threw the ring away. I was just so angry at what *he* said. I didn't realize what it would mean to be without it. I'm sorry.''

He made no response, but he made no move to leave, either. And that began to worry her more than if he had merely gotten up and stalked off.

Far above them, the trees made a wild rushing sound as the wind continued to lash them. The first flickers of lightning briefly lit the grove.

She touched his face. He pushed her hand away. She leaned against his chest and tried to pull him close, but he shoved her off and turned his back on her. The golden gleam at his throat disappeared in the darkness as he shifted against the tree.

''Oh, no, you don't. No, I won't let you do this! I won't let you give up!'' Terri got to her feet, letting the wool cloak drop to the ground, and grabbed him by the arm. She wrenched at him with all her strength, but he refused to move.

''You cannot give up!'' she cried. ''You had no choice but to leave the dun. Lonan would have killed you. But you cannot turn your back on us! We need you now! We need the king!''

But her words meant nothing to him.

Terri ground her teeth in frustration. She had to get him up and moving again, had to pull him back from the depths of the despair into which he had fallen. He was consumed by the guilt he felt at leaving Dun Cath, and that guilt would destroy him if something wasn't done to bring him back.

Yet what could she do? She couldn't pick him up and

carry him, she couldn't say anything that he would understand. She didn't know a word of Gaelic!

Or did she?

Terri stood over him and grabbed his arm again, pulling him hard. *"Ri,"* she said to him, as firmly as she could. *"Ri!"*

She waited for his response. For a long moment there was none. Then the gleam of gold moved once more in the darkness, and slowly Conaire stood up, towering over her beneath the windblown trees.

"Ri na folus," she heard him whisper.

Well, she had no idea what that meant. But at least he was standing up. *"Ri!"* she cried again, thumping him on the chest. *"Ri!"* She grabbed his hand and pulled him after her as hard as she could, dragging him toward the edge of the grove. To her relief, he came with her, step after reluctant step.

The wind whipped at her hair as she left the shelter of the trees. "You know what you have to do!" she shouted above the lashing wind. "The old dun is gone—but we are here, now, and we will build another! Another dun! And we'll start right now!"

A flash of lightning showed her the open ground. Terri caught up a long stick and thrust it into the damp earth, working it, tearing at it, at last succeeding in turning over a small clod of soil. "Here's where the trench will be! We'll dig out the earth and build up the walls! Make a new hall, a new barn, new houses for all the men and their families! And we'll start right now, *Ri* Conaire—we'll start right now!"

Frantically she worked the stick again, trying to tear up another small clod—but he walked over and caught her wrist, stopping her. In a glaring flash of lightning she saw him slowly shake his head, his eyes empty, his face a picture of despair.

With all her strength she ripped free of his grasp. "You

can give up if you want to, but I will never give up! I am a part of this land now! It has become a part of me! I will stay here and I will build the new dun, if I have to build every last piece of it all by myself!''

She tried again to dig at the earth with her stick. But Conaire came to her and pulled her close, taking her breath away. Her heart beat wildly as he bent down to take her face in both his hands.

Terri let the stick fall.

The lightning showed her his face, showed her the small glimmer of hope that now gleamed in his eyes. He smoothed her wind-whipped hair, and almost smiled.

"Banrion," he whispered.

She had no time to wonder what it meant. He lifted her up in his arms and carried her back within the shelter of the trees, to the place where his heavy wool cloak still lay on the rippling grass.

The great winds of the storm came howling over the top of the hill, reaching deep within the grove and sending the ancient trees creaking and groaning. Terri turned her face to the winds and breathed deep of their power, reveling in them even as she clung to Conaire with all her strength. He placed her on the woolen cloak and she pulled him down to her, refusing to let go of him even for an instant, craving the weight and warmth of his body as he fell atop her and pinned her to the soft earth.

It only took a moment to pull away the leather and linen that lay between them. Conaire held her close and kissed her neck, and then she heard him speaking softly in her ear, his beard brushing against her cheek. She did not know the words, but she could hear the urgency, the sweetness, the truth that they contained, and she responded with words of her own.

''This land is a part of me now,'' she said to him again, her breath coming in short gasps. ''If you love me, then

257

you must also love the land . . . love it, and claim it, and take it for your own . . . take it, take it . . .''

The lightning flared bright, and now the thunder rolled in straight behind it. But Terri was conscious only of Conaire as he pressed hard against her. She moved to pull him deep within her, welcoming his great strength into her body just as the land itself welcomed the life-giving rays of the hot summer sun.

Again and again the lightning flashed, white hot and glaring, ripping across the stormy night sky with the same sizzling energy that Terri felt racing through her veins. And the last thing she remembered was the trembling roar of the thunder . . . thunder that was a distant echo of the shuddering climax that seized them both, and seemed to race through them, and out of them, into the earth and sky itself.

For long hours, Terri slept. Safe and warm in Conaire's arms, wrapped up close beside him in his heavy cloak, she sank into the bliss of dreamless, formless slumber and closed out the rest of the world.

After a time a soft grayness began to filter through her closed eyelids. She rolled over, stretched, and blinked, and then got slowly to her feet, leaving Conaire undisturbed.

Everything had turned to grayness and dampness and mist. The hilltop was completely covered in fog and silence, as if a soft cloud had settled itself to rest up there along with the sleeping men and women.

Water dripped from the trees onto the horses below, all of whom stood motionless with their heads down. No doubt they still felt the effects of their long journey through the darkness.

Well, even if they didn't, she certainly did. The nervous energy that had carried her through the night was long gone. Now she felt exhausted, burned out, like a bonfire doused by a long soaking rain. She rubbed the chill from her arms and made her way through the trees toward the edge of the grove.

The other men lay wrapped in their cloaks, snoring softly beneath the sheltering trees. The three women slept close to their husbands. No one moved. All was quiet and safe and secure.

Everywhere Terri looked she saw grayness and stillness and fog. All the color seemed to have faded from the world. It was strangely unfinished, like a blank canvas waiting for the artist to fill in the details and colors.

She stepped out of the grove and onto the thick grass of the hilltop. There was indeed a cloud up here; the entire hill was closed in by silvery walls of mist, and she could see nothing of the land around it.

Yet as she watched, the sun rose higher, and gradually the mist began to dissipate. It moved in wisps, parting itself around the nearby hills, unveiling a whole new world even as Terri stood and stared.

She knew this place. She had been here before, had stood right here on this hill, the highest hill, gazing out at the lovely green countryside and the high white cliffs in the distance.

Once she had looked up from this spot to see a conjunction of planets, red and silver and gold, and her life had never been the same.

She stood once again on the hill where the bonfire had burned, where she had found the golden ring, where Firelair had made her great leap into the past. She had come home . . . and this time, she had come with the man she loved.

There was the small sound of a twig breaking. Terri turned to see Conaire emerging from among the trees. He was followed by one of his men, and then another and another, and by the three women, and in a moment the entire company of twelve stood on the hilltop gazing down at her.

They all looked tired and worn, but were smiling none-theless, and even Conaire's expression softened as he walked down to stand beside her. He drew her close with one arm and turned her to face the people. Then, to Terri's amazement, the little group made them a small bow and spoke with one voice.

"Ri Conaire," they said. *"Banrion Treise Maeve."*

She knew that *ri* meant king. *King Conaire,* they had said. But the other word? The one before her name?

Banrion. Conaire had said it to her the night before, had whispered the single word in her ear. And with a cold shock she realized that it could mean only one thing.

Queen.

Conaire had called her queen last night in the darkness. And now these people had called her their queen, Queen Teresa Maeve.

She closed her eyes. "All right then," she began. Though she knew they could not understand her, she had to say it anyway. "If being a queen means helping you to build a new life . . . and standing at the side of the king no matter what . . . and using all the strength I have to do these things, in my own way, according to what my heart tells me as I have always done . . . then I will be your queen."

Terri turned and looked at Conaire, raised her chin and looked him straight in the eye. *"Banrion."*

She would never forget the look on his face. He was very still for a moment, as if not quite believing what he had said—and then a light began to shine in his eyes, fol-lowed by a slow smile of happiness and relief. "Ah, *Treise Maeve,"* he whispered. *"Banrion Treise Maeve."*

He pulled her close, and she held him tight, resting her head on his shoulder. She knew quite well that her life was about to take another strange turn, doubtless the hardest one yet, but she found herself smiling and her heart sang with anticipation. She had a world to build, a whole new world, for herself and for Conaire and for the brave little group that stood with them.

Now, as the last of the mist burned away and the pale gray sky curved over them, the real work would begin.

Conaire raised one hand and beckoned to the group. As they gathered around the little fire he glanced at Terri, his expression almost apologetic, and then he turned to the people and began to speak. To her relief he used almost as many gestures as he did words, and she was able to follow along well enough.

Besides, she thought to herself, there was only one thing any of them would be talking about right now. Survival.

Conaire spoke briefly and then pointed to the trees. The women and four of the men left the fire and went back into the grove, reappearing a moment later with the bundles they had carried from Dun Cath. As they walked back and forth carrying their possessions, Terri studied this little group of people who were now her friends, her neighbors, her family.

The only ones she had in the world.

Ros and Sivney she knew well. They were Conaire's closest friends, his two most trusted men. Both of them were tall and strong as he was, and wore fine-made clothes and a gold ornament or two, and were never without their long swords strapped to their sides. There was no mistaking them as members of the king's court.

But the other six men—she had seen them all many times before at Dun Cath, part of the nameless retinue of warriors that always followed Conaire wherever he went. They, too, were well dressed and outfitted, obviously part of the nobility. But of the whole group of six, the only one she knew by name was Falvy, one of the men who had ridden with Conaire to rescue her—last night? Had it really been only yesterday?

A shiver ran through her. But she closed her eyes and

resolved to put it out of her mind. There were far more important things to worry about now, and would be for a long time to come.

Again Terri looked at the three women, each now carrying a bundle to the fire. As with the men, she knew their faces, had even spoken to them in passing, but drew a blank when it came to their names.

She watched as they set down their bundles. Three young women, fair-skinned and flushed and alike enough to be sisters, and it occurred to her that perhaps they were. All had long, long blond hair done up in various sorts of braids. One had a pair of braids hanging down her back, the second had them done up in a coil at the back of her head, and the third wore just a long loose single braid.

They all wore gowns of lightweight wool, some in bright solid colors, some in plaid, and covered by long mantles pinned across their shoulders like Conaire's cloak. The gowns had been made from fine fabric, and the outfits were accented with gold. Terri saw a gleaming brooch here, a beautiful flat wide bracelet there. But now the gowns were torn and stained from last night's desperate flight; they were not made for riding, and looked almost as bad as her own red-and-white plaid gown. She sighed, and hoped that at least one of the women had a needle and some thread in one of those bundles.

How young the three looked in the pale gray light of the morning! Probably no more than eighteen, twenty at the most, just beginning to build their lives with their husbands. Terri set her jaw. If she had been determined before to rebuild the dun, that determination was even greater now. She wanted nothing more than to see these women in a place where they could live safe and secure, as they had once lived at Dun Cath.

The women looked up and offered shy smiles. Terri grinned back at them, glad to discover that they did seem to be friendly. She had spent so much of her time here by herself, either working or riding out or being alone with Conaire ... there just hadn't been time to make many friends. Especially women friends. But now, it seemed, she would have three.

Under Conaire's direction, everyone began unrolling the bundles and sorting through what they had. Terri stepped closer. Had anyone brought food? she wanted to ask. She couldn't be the only one who was hungry. How much could the people have managed to grab last night while she and Conaire waited hostage for their return? She doubted that they had been thinking about breakfast in the mad dash to get out of Dun Cath.

But as she watched, a fair-sized hoard appeared on the unrolled cloak at the feet of one of the women—the one with the long single braid, in the blue-and-green plaid gown.

Terri crouched down beside her, and smiled into the young face with its shining blue eyes. "Teresa Maeve," she said, first touching her own chest and then pointing toward the other woman. "And you are—"

After only a slight hesitation, the young woman answered. "Sorcha," she said quickly. "Sorcha." And smiled again.

"Sorcha," Terri repeated, nodding. She looked up at the other two women, hovering nearby, and pointed at each of them in turn.

"Clodagh," said the one with the two long braids.

"Orla," said the third, in the yellow-gold dress.

"Sorcha, Clodagh, and Orla," Terri said, nodding at each one in turn, and then she grinned at them all. There was more than one way to communicate, and she was determined not to let a little thing like a language barrier keep her apart from the rest of the people.

She turned her attention back to the food. There was mostly bread—the flat round loaves that had become so familiar—twenty, maybe twenty-five loaves. It seemed like a lot, but would not last long for thirteen very hardworking people.

What else? Several chunks of hard white cheese; a small wooden crock of rich golden butter; two leather bags filled with salt. Terri saw that even in the terrible circumstances of the night before, these people had had the presence of mind to grab the kinds of food that they would not be able to find in the forest. They would have no flour for bread, no cows to milk for butter or cheese. And salt would be more precious than any amount of gold.

Terri had no doubt about the ability of Conaire and his men to bring in meat. They were surrounded by a dense wild forest, filled with deer and all sorts of other game. And certainly there must be all kinds of nuts and berries and things to be gathered in there. City-bred as she was, she would just have to follow everyone else's lead, and she was sure they would know what to do.

Now Clodagh and Orla got on their knees and began sorting out the rest of the things from the bundles. There seemed to be clothes, mostly; hastily folded cloaks, a few tunics, a couple of gowns, a pair or two of breeches. No footwear, no belts. But there was a cooking pot! A small iron pot that looked like a cauldron, rolled up at the very center of the bundled clothes. Terri suddenly realized that this one small thing would make life much easier for them all, and silently blessed whoever had thought to bring it. How would they boil water if they had no pot?

There were a couple of long iron implements, a small knife, and—thankfully—several needles pushed through a large spool of heavy woolen thread. And that was all.

Terri's heart sank as she looked at the colorful stack of fabrics, a stack that now seemed fearfully small. She glanced up at Conaire and saw that he—and all the others—had the same expression. No, they would not starve. But all around were the first signs of fall. It would not be long before winter would be upon them. Shelter and warm clothes would be their biggest and most immediate problem.

But Conaire smiled at her, and spoke a few soft words to the group. The rest of them nodded and sat down on the grass. Clodagh and Orla began picking up the loaves of bread, placing a small lump of the precious butter on top of each one and handing them out, one loaf to each person.

Terri accepted hers from Orla, and sat down beside Conaire to eat it. Now that the immediate desperation of the long night had passed, she found that her apprehension was growing.

How could they hope to survive out here? They might be able to find food, but they must have shelter, they must have cloth to make new clothes—what would they do? How could thirteen people build an entire dun?

But then she looked up at Conaire again, and felt something like hope when she saw the look in his eyes.

The despair of the night before had left him completely. His brown eyes shone fiercely beneath the thick red-brown brows, shone with determination and fearlessness. The dangers they faced out here were nothing to him. He was like a man possessed—driven to do whatever was necessary to build himself another kingdom, preferably within a day or two at most.

She should have known that taking care of his people would be his first priority. He would never let anything happen to them. King Conaire would take care of them all, would do whatever it took to keep them all safe.

Chapter Twenty-three

Conaire finished the last of his buttered bread, brushed the crumbs from his hands, and got to his feet. "Ros! Tully!" he called out, striding to the edge of the small fire. "Help me build this up—as big as we can get it. Dig it out wide. Bring whatever rocks you can find, and as much wood as you can pick up from the ground beneath those trees."

The men started to move toward the grove, but then they hesitated. All the others looked up at him with expressions of uncertainty, though no one said a word. Conaire looked back at them and smiled.

"You're right," he said. "It is a risk. A fire that big, and so high on this hilltop, could be seen from a long way off—from Dun Cath itself—but that is exactly what I have in mind."

He paced across the damp grass, stopping on the other side of the fire. "I must give the loyal men still trapped at the dun every chance to find us if they can. I am betting that Lonan will be so busy trying to hold the remnants of his poisoned kingdom that he will have no time to spare for attacking us—or for chasing down a few escaping families."

He looked steadily at the little group around him. "I possess one great advantage that he will never have. I can be sure of my people. Lonan will never be sure of anyone ever again."

After a moment the men and women glanced at one another, and a few of them nodded—all but Treise Maeve, of course, who stood near the other three women and watched him seriously and intently. He could see the doubt and confusion on her face, and gazed back at her with all the strength of spirit he possessed.

Trust me, I will take of you, I will take care of all of us . . . trust me, Treise Maeve.

She stared into his eyes for a time, and then smiled in resignation. It was just a small smile, but a smile nonetheless, and Conaire felt as though the last of a great weight had been lifted from his shoulders. Last night she had reminded him of who he was and what he owed to his people and his land. The path that he must follow was clear to him now and there would be no turning from it.

Ros and Tully started off for the grove to gather rocks and firewood. Conaire watched them go, and then turned back to the others. "Here is what we will do. First food. Gil and Falvy, go and set traps, bring back whatever meat you can. Shiel and Dowan, go with the women and begin searching the forest for whatever food you can find. The rest of you, stay here with me. We will start the building of a new kingdom."

Some of the weight seemed to lift from his people, too, and their faces brightened as they set about their tasks. He watched as Sorcha took Treise Maeve gently by the arm and urged her to come with them. After only a little hesitation, she went with the other women, glancing back at Conaire just once before disappearing down the side of the hill.

Ros and Tully came back with armloads of wood and rocks, and wasted no time in building up a huge roaring fire. Conaire looked at it with satisfaction. "They'll find us soon," he said.

"And if they don't?"

He glanced at Ros. "Then we will go and get them out."

"We?" Tully asked. "We are only nine men. Lonan still has forty, fifty fighting men back at Dun Cath, fully armed and provisioned. And if even half of those men are still loyal to him—"

"If he had a thousand men, it would not stop me from going back and getting the rest of them out."

Sivney nodded. "That's my feeling, too," he said. "We cannot leave them. By spring, perhaps, we will be ready."

"Aye, spring," Ros concurred. "We'll be stronger then—some of the others will surely have joined us, and we can make short work of Lonan and his band of thugs. I look forward to the fight already!"

"Spring?" Conaire stood very still, and fixed them all with a piercing gaze. "By spring half the old dun could well be dead."

He drew a deep breath. "In twenty days is the Autumn Solstice. I will wait a fortnight after that, two at most. I will wait only long enough to know that the women are safe and sheltered here—and then I will make Lonan regret that he was ever born."

At their stunned expressions, he grinned fiercely. "What's the matter? I thought you said you looked forward to the fight! I'm surprised you can wait so much as a day!"

"I have never turned from a fight, and I'm not about to now," growled Sivney. "Especially against Lonan." He turned and spat on the ground. "But I'd want to take him on when we had at least a chance of defeating him—otherwise, what's the point?"

"The point," Conaire said, pacing again, "is that the people of Dun Cath have been deserted by their king. I only withdrew last night in retreat. I am not defeated. *We* are not defeated! As soon as we have regrouped and made a place of safety for the women, we will go back and finish it. No king could do less. And no matter what else has happened, I am still king of Dun Cath, until I die."

Ros slowly shook his head. "Lonan will stop at nothing

to kill you. He cares nothing for us. It's you he wants. You face certain death if you try to retake the dun without more of us to defend you.''

"Either I will live as a king, or I will die as one. But I will not remain in this half-existence, this exile. If I die in saving my people, then I will have done what a king should do, and I will not regret it.''

He looked closely at his men, and saw them slowly nodding. "We are all trained fighting men, King Conaire," said Lorcan. "We understand. We will go with you wherever you lead, and do whatever you ask of us. But— will everyone understand this the way we do?''

Lorcan turned and looked out into the distance. Conaire followed his gaze. There, just reaching the bottom of the steep hill, walked Treise Maeve with the other three women, all of them smiling and laughing as if they had not a care in the world.

The first day passed, and the second, and the third, and after that Terri no longer kept track. The building of a whole new world had begun, and she had no thought for anything as trivial as timekeeping.

They began by clearing trees. Working from the center of the grove, at the very center of the hilltop, the men shared the single small hatchet and took turns felling tree after tree, all day long.

It hurt Terri to see the trees come crashing down. They were alive, they were beautiful, with their rough gray bark and deep green leaves and shiny blue-black berries. The grove had protected all of them on that first terrible stormy night. But she understood that in order to raise new buildings and paddocks, there must be wood to build them from, and buildings and paddocks must have open space to stand on. So she did as she saw the other women do—she gathered the berries from the fallen trees and spread them out to dry in the sun, and told herself to be grateful that the land had offered them one more source of food and shelter.

Only once did she interfere in the process. When the day came that only a single tree was left standing, and Gil approached it with the hatchet, Terri knew that she could not stand by and watch it be destroyed—not this time. She ran to the tree and placed her hand on Gil's arm. "Please leave just this one," she asked, though she knew he wouldn't understand a word she said. She stood against the tree and gently pushed the hatchet away. "Not this one. Please, leave just this one."

Gil looked curiously at her, and then glanced at Conaire, who stood a short distance away. Conaire laughed and spoke a few words to Gil, who smiled at Terri and then walked away, taking the hatchet with him.

Terri breathed a sigh of relief. When she and Firelair had first come to this place, on that peaceful summer evening so long ago, there had been but a single towering elder tree beside the spring. And now she knew why.

Next came the digging of a large, shallow, rectangular outline at the very center of the hilltop. This, Terri reasoned, would be for the new hall. It did make sense to just put up a single large building that could shelter them all instead of trying to build several individual houses. But it was clear that for a mere thirteen people, working with the crudest of tools and having many other tasks to do as well, building a Great Hall would still be a monumental task.

From the moment the sky showed the faintest light of dawn, Terri was on her feet with everyone else and beginning her long day's work. First the horses must be led from their paddock and driven down the hill to spots where they could graze. She had been greatly concerned about Firelair at first; there was no longer any grain to give her, and Terri could hardly bear to leave her out roaming with the half-wild Celtic ponies. But the mare must graze if she was to survive, and to Terri's relief she stayed with the other horses and none of them strayed too far.

Most of the time it was possible to see the herd from the hilltop. The sight of the beautiful gray mare with her smaller red and gold and brown and black companions always lifted Terri's spirits, though it also put her in mind of the Dun Cath broodmares' fields where she had spent so many happy hours. It hurt to think that she would never see them again . . . but there were people and horses who needed her here, and she could only trust that the horse boys would go on caring for those mares and foals who were now so far away.

The rest of the day was devoted to food and shelter. Terri spent much of her time in the forest collecting berries and nuts and other wild plants that the women pointed out as being edible. It was too early for apples, but each time they returned to the hilltop, their makeshift cloth sacks were filled with acorns and hazelnuts and blackberries. Clover leaves, she learned, made quite a good steamed side dish, and wild plums, purple-black and sweet, were highly prized.

About half of the men spent their days on the hilltop and worked on the new hall. The other half left to set snares and traps for animals and bring in the occasional fish from the forest streams. But while the fish were welcome, it was the animals that were the most valuable, for their furs and hides could substitute for the warm wool cloth that the people no longer had any way of making.

Each day there were more rabbit skins and deer hides stretched out to dry on the hilltop. As with the trees, Terri's feelings were mixed each time she saw them. She had no more wish to destroy animals than she had to cut down trees, but in this time and place there was simply no other way. And so she worked as hard as she could to make certain that nothing was wasted—not a berry from the trees, not a bone from the animals.

When the sun began to set, she would pick up Firelair's black leather halter and walk out to find the horses. The mare was always willing to be caught, often walking right up to Terri as soon as she saw her, as though she never gave up hope of being taken to a warm barn and a bucket full of oats. The other horses would follow as she led the mare in, and then all of them would be safely enclosed in their paddock for the night.

It was important to keep the creatures used to human contact and care, so they would not become completely wild and self-sufficient. There were sometimes tasks for them to do, such as carrying the hunters or packing in game, but for the most part the people of the new dun labored much harder than their horses.

Yet the enormous hard work did not daunt Terri at all. Indeed, she found that as much as she had loved her life at Dun Cath, she loved this even more—if that were possible. She was helping to build a world, her world, Conaire's world, and it was exhilarating to see it take shape beneath her hands. It grew bigger, stronger, and more real with every hour of every day.

She also began learning the Gaelic language in earnest. There was little choice; the other men and women could speak to her in no other way, and so Terri threw herself into the task of learning the words and phrases. The people sometimes looked at her rather oddly as she went about repeating everything they said, but soon seemed to understand what she was doing. Before long they were all making a special effort to speak to her slowly and simply so that she could learn. She managed to pick up a few more words each day, and practiced them on anyone who would listen, even Firelair, who seemed to understand quite well!

But though she was desperate to be able to communicate with the other men and women, she had another, more compelling reason to learn to speak the language.

Conaire.

Though they had no trouble showing their feelings for each other when they lay together at night, safe and warm beneath Conaire's cloak on a fine bed of rushes and furs, Terri often felt a great sense of loss whenever she saw him. At first she did not understand why. He was still so attentive to her, protective, jovial, loving, as he had always been, even in the midst of these desperate circumstances. What was wrong?

It was a bit of a shock to realize that what she missed was his voice—his words—their sparring conversations and fiery discussions. And yet it was a sweetness to discover that they had shared more than just physical love. She knew now that theirs was a love born of friendship, of respect, of a trust that could never be broken. And she would work as hard as any scholar ever had to learn the Gaelic language if it meant that she could talk to him again.

As exhilarating as these times were, a feeling of concern began to grow in the back of Terri's mind. She did not fail to notice a subtle change in Conaire as the days went by. At first she had thought that his great intensity, his boundless energy, his almost obsessive drive had been directed toward the same goal that her own energies were—the rebuilding of the dun. But now she began to suspect there was something more to it than that.

Often she would see him deep in discussion with Ros or Sivney or the other men. She could not catch more than a few words, but the emotions were plain. They were in intense disagreement about something, and she did not believe it was anything to do with the new dun.

Most disconcerting of all, whenever he had a moment to spare Conaire would stand beside the blazing fire and gaze out into the distance. His sharp eyes studied and examined every square inch of the view for as long as there was light to see by. And in those eyes, once so bright with the joy of living, Terri began to see fear, and despair, and guilt.

What are you looking for? she wanted to ask him. But

she did not yet know how to ask; and worse, she already knew the answer.

I am waiting for them to find us, he would have said. *I am waiting for the loyal men of Dun Cath to find us here.* Or he might have added, *I am waiting for Lonan's men to hunt us down and attack us. We cannot be caught unawares.*

But the days passed, and they did not come. No one came, not friend, not foe. And the terrible mystery began to wear on them all.

What was going on at the old dun? What had happened to Conaire's loyal men and their families? What could be keeping them from escaping and finding the hilltop encampment? The arrival of more people, even a few, would have been a great help in building the new kingdom. But there was not a trace of anyone, and the strain on Conaire became more evident by the day.

Terri longed to help him. She knew that he wanted nothing more than to go back to Dun Cath and save his remaining people, but he would not leave the rest of them here unprotected. Such a move would do little good anyway; Conaire's eight men, strong as they were, would hardly be a match for Lonan's many well-armed warriors. Riding into a trap and dying for nothing would not help the people of the old dun or the new.

And as she watched him standing alone beside the fire, she could only hope that he felt the same way.

Now the long warm days of summer were ending. The hours of sunlight were fewer, the air cooler and brisker. The leaves turned gold and brown and brilliant red, spectacular against the clear blue skies, and dropped to the forest floor in rustling masses every time the fresh wind blew.

On the one hand, it was beautiful; on the other, it was frightening. The end of the summer meant the end of warmth and comfort. It meant that winter would soon be upon them, and no one was more aware of it than Terri.

She was alone at the bottom of the hill, in the cold gray shadows of dusk, working among the tall green rushes that always grew along the lowest, wettest spots. Her worn skirts were tucked up into her belt, leaving her bare legs exposed to the cold and damp, but she paid no mind to the working conditions. She had a job to do. And anytime she could do something, no matter how menial, that would make life better for the people, she was more than glad to throw herself into the task.

Clodagh had showed her how the rushes could be harvested for many useful things. The starchy roots were easily dug up with a pointed stick and could be roasted like sweet potatoes in the ashes of the fire. The young shoots and stalks became fresh vegetables with a taste somewhere between cucumbers and asparagus—Terri could never decide which. Any of the flower spikes that were still yellow-green could be boiled like ears of corn, though by now most had turned the familiar deep brown of the cattail and were covered with thick golden pollen ready to be scraped off and used as flour. And the long slender leaves, like soft straps, made very comfortable bedding.

Terri worked diligently in the fading light, trying not to think of how cold her bare feet were. One by one she pulled up the rushes by the roots and tossed them into a pile. At last she stood up, stick still in hand, to catch her breath and push her hair back from her face with a dirt-streaked forearm—and then she saw him.

Conaire stood at the foot of the hill, watching her.

She brightened at the sight of him. They had seen little of each other for the last couple of weeks or so. Terri and the other women had been working every moment of the day to gather and prepare food against the coming winter, while Conaire had seemed to spend all his time doing heaven-knows-what with his two closest friends and advisors, Ros and Sivney.

But now he was here, looking every inch the pagan prince in his deerskin cloak, and they were alone . . . and though she longed to take him in her arms and lose herself in the comfort of his strong embrace, something else pulled at her.

She wanted so much to *talk* to him. Her Gaelic had been getting better by the day, and she could understand even more of it than she could speak, but the language barrier remained. There was still much that was unclear to her. What had happened to the others at Dun Cath? Why had none of them found the hilltop encampment after all this time? Would Conaire and his men wait until spring and then try to spirit out a few at a time? And just how would they get through the winter?

"Hello," she said, and set down the digging stick.

"Good evening to you, Queen Treise Maeve," he answered. As always, her heart quickened at the sight of his gleaming brown eyes and bright smile . . . his teeth so white and even beneath the smooth mustache. How nice it would be to touch his soft curling beard, to run her fingers through it.

"Aren't you cold?" he asked, glancing at her legs. "The sun has gone down, and it's always wet among the rushes." He reached for her hand. "Come up here a little way and tell me how you are. I hear that you can speak Gaelic to perfection now."

She untucked the hems of her skirts and let them drop, and then took his outstretched hand. "Thank you. Work hard, be warm."

He nodded thoughtfully at her response, and she raised her chin, refusing to be embarrassed by her somewhat broken Gaelic. She'd learned a lot in just a few weeks. As long as she could make herself understood, she'd worry about speaking pretty sentences later—much later.

They walked a short way up the hillside and sat down in the soft thick grass, and Terri gazed out at the sunset.

She'd almost missed it this evening, working up until the last moment to gather in the last of the rushes. "Beautiful," she said.

He followed her gaze. "Ah, so it is," he answered. "As are you."

She smiled, and then looked closely at him. "Dun Cath," she said carefully. "The men. The women. Not here. Why?"

His face became very serious. It was clear that he did understand what she was asking. "I hoped that at least a few would find us," he whispered. "The fire burns day and night. It can be seen for miles." His fists clenched. "But I will find them. And I will bring them home."

She frowned. "How?"

"I and my men will go and get them out. We will meet Lonan with all the force we can muster, and we will lead them all home."

"All." A feeling of unease began to creep over her. "Time of spring?"

He paused. "In the spring? You mean, will I bring them home in the spring?" Conaire smiled gently. "No, Treise Maeve. I cannot wait that long. I have waited too long already. That is what I came to tell you—the time has come for me to bring them home. I am going to bring them home now."

She looked up at him in astonishment. "Now!"

"Now. Tomorrow. We'll leave at dawn. Falvy will remain with you and the other women."

A shock ran through Terri. She knew how Conaire had been tormented with thoughts of the people he'd been forced to leave behind. His feelings were plain where they were concerned. But this—this was suicide!

"You *cannot*," she insisted, shaking her head for emphasis. "Not now. Not now! Wait for your men to return! Wait! Then go! Time of spring!"

"I have already waited." His voice was deadly quiet.

"What is happening right now at Dun Cath? I will tell you. Lonan and his criminals are holding everyone hostage there. The children are hostage for the adults. Any man who tries to fight his way out will be killed. If he does manage to escape, his family will be killed after him."

"You do not know!"

"Ah, but I do know, Treise Maeve. Those men are trained warriors. They would not hesitate to battle their way to freedom—unless their wives and children had knives at their throats. They cannot get out with their families, and so they cannot get out at all—unless their king comes for them."

"Fight together," she said, struggling for the words. "The loyal men, fight Lonan together."

He shrugged. "Assuming all the loyal men could even find each other, what do you suppose would happen to their families while they banded together and did their fighting?"

She had no answer. She well remembered how Lonan had managed to divide the entire dun until no one knew who to trust. It could only have gotten worse since Conaire had gone.

"The king," she whispered. "What can the king do?"

Conaire stood up, becoming a tall shadow in the twilight. "The rightful king can face down the pretender. He can give his own men the courage to walk out from among the traitors. The true king can bring his people home."

Terri got to her feet and reached for his hand. "First, tell them! Tell the loyal men! They will be ready. They will be waiting."

But he only shook his head. "How could we get word to anyone? Send Gil or Lorcan riding through the gates of Dun Cath with the message that King Conaire arrives tomorrow? We could have one of our men lie in wait and hope to catch someone out alone, but they could wait for many, many days. It is too great a risk and we have too little time. We are safe and strong here now, while those at Dun Cath grow more desperate every day.''

"Eight men, King Conaire," she said to him. "You have eight men."

But he only laughed, and fear surged through her. His laughter was more frightening than any angry words or threats. "I would rather have eight loyal men than a hundred whom I could not trust—and that is all that Lonan has."

He turned away from her and started up the hillside. "The men of Dun Cath need their king, Treise Maeve. Their king has abandoned them once already. He will not do so again."

She knew he was right about not abandoning his people. But she was also terrified at the thought of him and his handful of men riding into certain death at the hands of Lonan's army.

My head tells me one thing, my heart another!

Terri grabbed his arm and made him turn to face her. "You said *worth living for.*"

She could see him smile gently in the near-dark. "So I did," he answered. "And so you are."

He touched her face, and his words were soft in the darkness. "It is easy to find things to die for, and many men do, fools and kings alike. It is much harder to stay alive and fight the long, exhausting fight, day after day, year after year, for that which is important to you—that which you love.

"But you are also the one who reminded me, on our first night in this place, that I am not just a man. I am a king. And if I wish to remain a king, I cannot abandon my people and hide out here on this hilltop. I cannot be afraid to risk my life for those who gave me their loyalty and are now in desperate need.

"No king runs from a battle. Retreating from certain defeat brings no dishonor; many confuse recklessness with courage. But retreating from the loyalty I owe my people is something I will never do. And I know, Banrion Treise Maeve, that you will never ask it of me.''

He took his hand away from her cheek, and Terri closed her eyes. He was right. It was the one thing she would not ask him to do.

She had been so relieved when he had put down his sword that night at Dun Cath. She had thought, then, that it was over, that they would ride away and live happily for the rest of their lives in a new kingdom that they themselves would build.

How could she have been so wrong? How could she have thought he would simply forget about the people of the old dun?

Had she saved him from one hopeless battle only to see him die in another?

Chapter Twenty-four

She looked up at Conaire, searching for the words. But he must have seen the fear in her expression, the pain in her eyes. "It is difficult to be a queen, Treise Maeve," he said. "In many ways, I think, it is more difficult than being a king. Now you understand why I searched so long for you."

But she only shook her head. "Tell the men of Dun Cath," she said again, her voice trembling now. "Tell them! You have eight men! Not enough! Tell them! They will be waiting!"

His voice hardened. "Eight men is all I have. Seven will go with me tomorrow. And since seven is what I have, then seven will be enough."

At her anguished look, he frowned, and then caught hold of her wrist as though he feared she would run away from him. "Would I take more men if I could? Of course! I would value even one more trained warrior! Just one more could make the difference. A company of nine is always better than a company of eight, just as eight is better than seven. But tell me—how can I hope to gain even one more?"

She had no answer for him. When tomorrow came she would have no choice but to watch him ride into the dawn, and then stand on this hilltop and wait and wonder if he would ever return.

From the top of the hill came the sound of a horse neighing. And then another and another, until it seemed that the whole herd was calling out into the night.

Terri looked quickly at Conaire. Both of them knew that the horses would not just suddenly start neighing for no reason.

From the darkness at the foot of the hill came a rustling in the brush and the snap of a twig. Instantly Conaire drew his sword and pulled Terri behind him. "Who is there?" he demanded. "Who is there?"

The answering voice was faint with exhaustion, yet filled with relief. "A friend, King Conaire. A friend."

A man walked slowly out of the darkness, followed by his silhouetted horse, and stopped a short distance from them. The two creatures stood together with their heads low, as if they were too tired to go a single step further.

Terri moved out from behind Conaire and peered closely at the man's young face in the starlight. Then she ran to him, stumbling over her long skirts, reaching out to him as he dropped to his knees.

"Dary!" she cried, just as he collapsed onto the soft grass. "Oh, Dary!"

In a moment she and Conaire had Dary sitting upright between them. The horse stayed nearby, grazing calmly. "Very happy to see you," Terri said, smoothing the young man's damp hair back from his face. "Where have you been? We were here. Where were you?"

Dary shook his head, gathering the breath to speak. "I hid in the forest for many days," he answered, "not far from the house where you were held. I hid, and I watched, and I waited for any of Conaire's men to come for me—but none ever did."

"Did you see anyone from Dun Cath?" asked Conaire. "Hunters, warriors, anyone?"

Dary shook his head, taking another deep breath. "No

one. I began going in closer and closer until I could see
the walls, but always the gates were closed. I saw no one
but the few servants who came out all too briefly to get
water or work the fields—and the guards who rode out on
patrol each day. The guards are all the worst of Lonan's
men.''

Terri could hear the shame and anger in his voice. ''I
wanted desperately to get inside and get my wife and child
out of there—but each time I thought to try, I feared too
much for their lives. There was just no way for me to get
in without being seen. There were just too many of them.''

''We were here,'' Terri repeated. ''The fire. You saw the
fire?''

He looked up at her, and then stared at Conaire. ''I
thought you were dead,'' Dary told him. ''I never thought
that anything but your death would let Lonan take the kingdom.''

Terri felt Conaire grow very tense, and very still.

''I left the dun and went searching for any of the men
who might have gotten out,'' continued Dary, ''but I began
my search to the north—and you went south. After a very
long time, I did see the fire, and began creeping close
enough to see who it belonged to.''

He looked away and spoke softly, with some combination of relief and wonder. ''I only hoped to find some of
your men. I never thought to find the king . . . surely the
king would have died rather than give up the kingdom. . . .''

Conaire pushed away from both of them and stood up,
a great shadow in the darkness. ''Tomorrow,'' he said. His
voice was deep and almost trembling. ''We will leave tomorrow.''

Terri hastily got to her feet. ''Not tomorrow! You are
not ready!''

She tried to take his arm, but he was as immovable as
the mountain they stood on. ''Now I have eight men. We

will leave at dawn. Falvy will stay with you and the other women.''

Terri closed her eyes. There would be no stopping him this time. She would have to find another way. ''Please,'' she said, searching out his face in the darkness. ''Give Dary one day. One day to rest.''

Conaire glanced at the weary young man, who was only now getting slowly to his feet. ''All right. One day. But one day only.''

He caught her in his arms before she could say any more. ''Courage, Treise Maeve. You have yet to prove your courage to me, the last of my queen's attributes.''

Shocked, she wrenched away from him. ''Courage!'' she cried, and waved her arm toward the hilltop. ''What is the name for all this? A new dun! A new kingdom! Building a world! I have done all this with you! And you tell *me* to have courage?''

But Conaire only shook his head. ''You had little choice but to come here with me. Did you consider remaining behind with Lonan? Did you think of living alone in the forest?''

He reached down and lifted one of her hands. ''Courage is what happens when you have choices. Now you must make a choice. Will you stay here as queen of your people and wait for me until I return? Or will you turn away and think only of yourself?''

Stunned, she searched for words, but he went on before she could find them. ''You have helped me beyond measure. You have reminded me that I am a king. I know what I must do.''

And I know what I must do, too, thought Terri.

The next morning, in the darkness before dawn, Terri placed the saddle on Firelair for the first time in many weeks. She made certain that a couple of the men saw her swing up on the mare and start down the hill with the rest of the horses following. All the people of Dun Cath were well used to the idea of her riding out alone on Firelair and staying out for the best part of the day—and today would be no different.

The journey would be a long one. Terri knew that Firelair, who had done little more than eat grass for six weeks or more, was not in the same hard condition she had been in over the summer. But she kept up a steady pace, and the hours passed slowly but surely as they rode beneath the clearing skies. They reached the broodmares' fields just as the sun was at its height.

Oh, there they were! Far in the distance was the herd of twenty mares, most with their half-grown foals still accompanying them. Her heart leaped at the sight. Firelair raised her head and whinnied, attracting the attention of the distant mares.

And their caretakers.

From beneath the tall trees at the edge of the field, three of the horse boys got to their feet and stood watching her approach. She recognized all three and knew two of them by name. "Donnan! Bercan!" she cried, trotting up to them. "I'm here! I'm so glad to see you! What is—"

But to her amazement, they began to back away. The three young men stood close together beneath the trees and stared at her with suspicion and fear.

"Donnan! What's wrong?" She paused, cursing the language difference. "*Ri* Conaire," she tried. "*Banrion* Treise Maeve. Come with me! Bring the mares! You'll be safe with us! Look—there—about a half day's ride, that way. Where the fire burns! You'll see the fire!"

They only backed farther away from her. Terri reined the mare closer and struggled to remember a few words, any words, of Gaelic, but her hard-won knowledge deserted her. "Please! I must tell you where we are! You must let the others know!"

But to her horror, Donnan pulled the small knife at his

285

belt and held it threateningly. Bercan and the other youth did the same.

She halted Firelair and looked at their faces. There was nothing in their eyes but fear. "Oh, Donnan . . . what is happening here? What is happening at Dun Cath?"

None of them moved. "Look for us at the fire," Terri whispered. "At the fire." She turned the mare away from them and rode on into the pasture.

The fields should have been lush and green, even this far into fall. But the grass was dry and browning, and the bare earth showed through in patches. There was hardly enough grass growing here to feed a single horse, let alone an entire herd.

Now, as she approached the mares and walked Firelair near to them, she felt as though one of the horse boys' knives had pierced her heart. The horses were so thin! All of them, even the young colts and fillies. They should be fat and glossy at this time of year, preparing for the winter to come, the foals running and playing and growing strong.

But all of the horses were rough-coated and thin; a few actually had their ribs showing. The young ones slowly followed their mothers about, or tried to nibble at the browning grass, or simply lay resting on the ground. And this one, lying all alone beneath the trees on the edge . . .

It was dead.

Terri felt tears sting her eyes. Grief and confusion collided within her. What on earth had happened here? The mares and foals dead and dying? The grass brown, the pastures half bare? The horse boys too frightened even to speak to her?

She turned Firelair away and rode her back towards the road to Dun Cath. As bad as this was, she could only imagine what must be happening to the people of the old dun.

Terri longed to go racing at full gallop the entire way to Dun Cath, but the mare had traveled many miles already and had many more to go before this day was out. So she held Firelair to a ground-covering walk, her fear and impatience rising, until finally turning into the forest to stop for water at a stream where it swung near the path.

She crouched down at the bank and splashed a little of the cool water on her face. What should she do now? She had not planned to actually go to the old dun; she'd only hoped to get word to the horse boys, to let them know where King Conaire was. If they knew, they would certainly let some other trusted man know, so that the loyal men would be waiting when the rightful king arrived tomorrow.

Surely the horse boys would have known someone they could tell. Old Sean would never have become one of Lonan's men!

On the long ride over, Terri had almost convinced herself that once they saw her, the boys would simply herd the mares together and follow her home. That had been too much to hope for, but even in her worst fears she had never thought to find the mares and foals starving and the horse boys frightened half to death.

Where should she go from here? Did she dare risk a trip to Dun Cath itself? It was terribly dangerous—but if she did not get word to someone, what would happen when Conaire and his men rode to the gates tomorrow?

She got to her feet, reaching for Firelair's reins, and suddenly realized there was a clamor rising in the distance.

Hoofbeats. Shouting. And then a cloud of dust that she could see through the trees.

Her heart almost stopped. Riders! There were riders on the path! If she had kept going, she would have run straight into them.

Dary had said that Lonan and his men patrolled the roads of Dun Cath every day.

There was no time to hide, no time to wonder who they were or how many. She held tight to the reins and stood very still, pressed up against the mare's shoulder. As the hoofbeats grew louder she reached up and placed one hand over Firelair's nose, hoping to quiet her if she should decide to whinny to the strange horses.

But there weren't any horses on the path. Beneath all the shouting and pounding of hoofbeats came a bellowing sound that sounded an awful lot like "moo."

Terri craned her neck in an effort to see. And there they were—a herd of small black cattle with short heavy horns, cattle that were rough-coated and thin like the mares. They walked slowly down the dusty path, mooing and bellowing and trying their best to avoid their shouting herdsmen.

She let out her breath in relief. Just a herd of cattle being driven somewhere. Even if the men with them had meant her any harm, they were on foot and she had Firelair.

Then the entire herd took a sharp turn and headed into the forest, straight for her.

Apparently she was not the only one who wanted to take advantage of the bend in the stream. She struggled to get her foot up into the stirrup, but the tall mare snorted and shifted as the cattle surged around her. Terri hopped on one foot and tightened the reins, trying to quiet the mare by speaking softly to her, but Firelair continued to dance.

"Whoa, now. We can't stay here, we've got to go, how about standing still, just for a second—"

"Treise Maeve! *Treise Maeve!* Look, *Treise Maeve!*"

She froze on the spot. They were calling her name. The herdsmen were calling her by name!

Terri set her foot back down as the mare swung around. She kept hold of Firelair's mane, determined to stay on her feet and not be separated from her horse as the cattle pushed their way past.

The surging mob of black cattle had her surrounded. Their tossing horns came perilously close as they made their way to the stream. And standing between her and the path were four men who kept repeating her name and looking at each other with great excitement, talking so rapidly in Gaelic that she couldn't understand a single word.

They were four of the biggest, strongest men she'd ever seen. Their well-worn cloaks and tunics were made of plain heavy wool, their folded boots of the thickest possible leather. Except for slings and small daggers at their belts, none of them carried any weapons.

These men were not warriors. She felt certain that they were just what they appeared to be—herdsmen moving their cattle. But they were still strangers, there were still four of them, and they still had her trapped. And if they were moving their herd this close to Dun Cath, they could only be part of Conaire's kingdom—now Lonan's.

And they all knew her name, they knew who she was!

"Hey!" she shouted, cutting off their excited conversation. "You're right. I'm Treise Maeve. But who are you? You?"

They all began talking at once. She could not catch so much as a name. "Stop! I don't understand! Who are you? *You?*"

They fell silent. Terri held on tightly to Firelair as the cattle continued pushing and shoving, but noticed that they were finally starting to get past her. In another moment she would be able to swing back up on the mare and go racing away.

One of the men, the one with the long black hair and soft black mustache, glanced at the others and took a step toward her. He reached beneath his cloak and drew a strange object from his worn leather belt.

The object was heavy and curved and perfectly made, and shone bright like machine-worked steel. As Terri stared at it, blinking, she realized that she was looking at one of Firelair's shoes.

She glanced at the other three men. One by one each pulled a similar object from his belt. Before her stood four shaggy, smiling, wild young Celts, each of them holding one of her mare's modern steel horseshoes.

Instantly her fear gave way to relief. She grinned, and then began to laugh. "Firelair's shoes!" she gasped, laughing out loud. "I know who you are! You're the smith's sons! His sons! And I've found you!"

Terri went with them back to their *rath*. It was a small ring-fort like the place where the horse boys lived, except that these men cared for Dun Cath's cattle instead of its horses. The men herded the cattle into the pens adjoining the *rath* and then led her inside.

From the forge-house came the smith, followed by a dark-haired young man who could only have been another of his sons. From the little white straw-roofed house came a blond woman and yet another man.

"Treise!" The smith came over and clasped her hand. "Where have you been? Where is the king?"

The others began their loud rapid speech again, but the smith shouted to them to be quiet, and then faced her once more. "Now, then. I can see that you are all right, and your mare too—but where is the king?"

Terri took a deep breath. "We are on the hilltop. At the fire. There." She turned to point toward their distant hill, but as she did, she saw only the nearby overhanging cliffs. The herder's *rath* was down in a valley, far enough down so that Conaire's hilltop was blocked from sight.

They would never have seen the fire from here.

"He's alive, then?" asked the smith. He grinned at the others. "I told you he would find a way to live. Most thought he'd been killed when he didn't come back, but I knew he would find a way to live."

Terri smiled at him. "He did find a way. Many would not."

The smith shrugged, and smiled back at her. "Everybody fights for life," he said, "and none harder than King Conaire. Now, then—you say you are on a hilltop? How far?''

''A half day's ride.'' She looked closely at the people who surrounded her. How strange it was to see so many new faces! She'd grown used to seeing only the people of Dun Cath day after day, and then the last several weeks had been spent in the company of just twelve—thirteen, counting Dary. But here were seven she'd never seen before.

The smith saw her looking at his family. ''These are my boys, and my one daughter!'' he said. ''She knows all that anyone could know about medicines and healing. Now my oldest, there in the doorway, is Ailin. He's a builder. My youngest here, Carbry, follows the same trade as I. And the other four—well, they're herders, as you can see, but they can do other things too.

''Piarda is the tallest man in the kingdom and the very best at playing games of skill. Crevan can cook food fit for any king or queen. Finbar knows all you'd care to know about music. And Mahon—well, Mahon is a good man to have at your back in a fight, but mostly he tells the others what to do.''

Terri stared at them all as unexpected hope surged through her. What a difference they would make in building the new dun! Conaire had warriors, but here were herders, craftsmen, builders, healers, the very backbone of daily life in any society. And they had cattle—cattle—there could be butter and cheese and fresh milk once again.

Could she possibly convince them to leave their home for a bare campsite on a faraway hilltop?

''Will you come with me? Be part of the new kingdom? We need you—oh, we need you!''

''Come with you?'' the smith said, taking a step toward her. He glanced at his family. ''I saw the smoke from that distant fire before I left Dun Cath. I knew it must have been the king. I was only waiting for the rest of my sons to come down from the high pastures before searching you out.

"That's why Lonan and his cronies let me come here. I'm supposed to fetch in my sons and the cattle for the winter. Lonan thinks I'm only a servant, that it would never enter my head to leave the kingdom." He shook his head. "When Conaire left, he took the kingdom with him."

Fear crept up on her again. "What happened at Dun Cath? What happened to the people?"

The smith became solemn and still, and he could only shake his head. "Bad. It is very bad. If King Conaire is able, he must go back and put an end to it. He must go back."

Terri wanted to question him further, but as she groped for the right words the smith turned away from her. "What are you waiting for?" he said to his family. "Pack up! Let's go!"

Immediately the *rath* became a whirl of activity. One of the men took Firelair and led her toward a bucket of water, while the rest disappeared into the forge-house and sheds. The woman took Terri into the house, offered her bread and cheese, and began clearing the shelves of food and equipment.

"I don't know what we're going to need, so I'll just take it all," the woman said, stacking up an armload of wooden dishes and iron utensils. "We've men enough here to carry the whole place on their backs if need be."

Terri smiled. "I am Treise," she said. "You?"

The blond woman glanced over her shoulder. "Aine," she said. At Terri's questioning look, she repeated, "*An*-na. Perhaps you've never heard that name before. Anyway," she went on, stuffing things into wooden boxes and leather bags, "my brothers and I will be happy to join you. Though I live here, not within the walls of Dun Cath, I have no wish to live anyplace that Lonan considers his."

"We need you. We need herdsmen, craftsmen. We need you very much!"

"Do you need a midwife?"

Terri stared at her. "A what?

Aine looked puzzled, but went on to explain. "A woman who brings babies and cares for the new mothers."

Midwife! Terri's heart leaped. "You're a midwife?"

Aine smiled. "I am. Spent years learning the art of it. And here," she said, taking down the bundles of dried plants hanging in a corner, "are medicines to ease pain and heal wounds and even bring on sleep when it is needed. I have no doubt we'll be needing these, especially if Conaire plans to go back and fight Lonan for the kingdom. We'll be up to our knees in wounded men if that happens."

Terri's blood suddenly ran cold. So far she had seen no serious injuries in this place, but they had virtually nothing in the way of medical supplies. If Aine was right about the battle—if they found themselves with wounded, dying men—if Conaire—

She forced herself to think of something else. "What is this?" she asked, lifting a small leather pouch. It was filled with soft white powder, almost like flour but with a strange bitter smell.

"Ah, do be careful with that," Aine said, gently taking the pouch from her. "There's enough in there to put all of Dun Cath to sleep for a night and a day."

Terri froze. "Sleep," she said. "Sleep—for a night and a day?"

"Just a pinch in a cup of honey wine. A great help to the wounded, it is, even to the dying. I've used it many times for—"

But Terri barely heard what she was saying. Her mind raced as she looked up at Aine, and as she stared she heard the distant sound of a well-loved voice.

I want a queen who will share her wisdom with me— who will speak to me with the voice of the women of Dun Cath, when all I usually hear is the shouting of the men.

All these weeks, Conaire had talked only of his loyal men. The loyal men of Dun Cath. How to find them, how to get them out. And she had done the same. But now it finally dawned on her as she gingerly lifted the small leather bag.

There were not only men at Dun Cath!

At last Aine had her possessions packed and ready. Terri helped carry the bags and bundles outside—and her jaw dropped at the sight that greeted her in the yard.

She'd expected to find the smith and the rest of the men ready to walk out the gate. But not all of them were walking!

In the center of the yard stood, of all things, a chariot—a two-wheeled chariot with flat, heavy, woven-wicker sides, drawn by a pair of small bay horses. The youngest son, Carbry, was at the reins, while his father stood tall and proud beside him with one hand resting on the chariot's wicker side.

She vaguely recalled seeing a few similar vehicles beneath the sheds at Dun Cath, but had never seen one in use. Conaire and his men, it seemed, preferred to ride their horses instead. But what was such a thing doing here? She felt certain that a well-made chariot and a team to pull it must be meant for a warrior, for a king—it would not normally be found in the possession of an ordinary working-man.

"Where did you get it?" she asked. "Is it yours?"

"Why, of course it's mine," the smith answered.

She paused. "But how? Did you, did you take it from Lonan?"

The smith drew himself up. "You mean, did I steal it? I did no such thing! I won it!"

"Won it?"

He grinned. "Won it at a game of dice. One of Lonan's own fighting men had nothing else to gamble, so he bet his chariot instead. I told him I'd tell his wife how much gold he owed me if the didn't make good the bet. He watched me harness the horses and drive it out the gate the day I left.''

The smith ran his hand along the woven-wicker side as the horses shifted a bit. ''I spent most of my life making the iron pieces for these things. Only seems right somehow, doesn't it?''

''So it does,'' said Terri with a laugh. ''So it does.''

''Well, let's go off and find the king, then!'' he shouted. ''And tell him he can ride in Cormac's chariot when he goes to take back what is his!''

Chapter Twenty-five

They started down the road together, Terri and Cormac the smith and his chariot, along with his daughter, six sons, and herd of cattle. But where the road began to branch, Terri stopped.

"Tell the king I will be back tonight," she said. "Tonight." With that, she set them on the road for the highest hill, and then turned Firelair's head toward Dun Cath.

As the mare cantered along beneath the half-bare trees, Terri tried to hold on to the optimism she had begun to feel. She had found eight people for the new dun, people with desperately needed skills to help build the new kingdom. They even brought with them a herd of cattle and a chariot, a chariot fit for a king to ride in.

But first and foremost, that king must survive. There would be no new kingdom without him. As Terri clutched the small leather bag fastened to her belt, she held on to the hope that she had found a way to ensure that survival.

A half mile from Dun Cath, she tied Firelair deep inside the forest. As she walked the last yards to the familiar stream, Terri tried not to think of all the memories this place held for her, or of how much she had missed it, or how much she feared what she might find.

She hid behind some bushes near the stream, only a short way from the place where she had walked so boldly in front of Conaire and his men such a long time ago.

With a shake of her head she stopped her drifting thoughts and forced her attention to the task at hand. This was also the spot where the servants came out to fetch water. It was mid-afternoon now, but Terri felt sure that someone would be sent out for water at least one more time today.

At first she stayed down behind the bushes. The place was shadowed and damp, and she noticed that the stream was only half as high as it had been before. The banks were all bare mud. She listened closely for the sound of hoofbeats or voices or footsteps, but there was nothing at all.

Nothing.

Her eyes widened as she realized that even the birds were silent. The only sound was the cold breeze rattling in the dry leaves and bare branches of the trees.

Terri peered up over the bushes and crept closer to the edge of the forest. Careful to stay behind a large oak, she peered around it, and finally got a look at what was left of Dun Cath.

One of the gates stood open, crooked and broken and leaning against the outside wall. The earthen walls looked crumbled and decayed in spots, even blackened here and there as though from fire, as did the buildings she could see. And just like the broodmares' pasture, the earth was barren and brown with hardly a blade of anything green.

And then she saw it. The body of a man lay a short distance from the gates. From the cloud of black insects around it she knew the man was dead, lying facedown on the bare ground.

Terri closed her eyes. This place, too, was dead, dying, as though Conaire had taken its spark of life with him when he left.

Quickly she crouched down again. Someone was coming through the gates. Terri moved behind the bushes once again and settled down to wait.

A lone, bent figure made its way slowly down the worn path from the dun with a heavy wooden bucket in each hand. A gray-haired woman, tired and worn, dressed in rags with a brooch of rusted iron.

"Dorren!" The woman froze. "Dorren, it's me! Treise Maeve!" Terri hissed. Dorren's eyes flicked left and right, and finally she saw Terri.

Instantly she moved to the shallow stream and began dragging the buckets through it. "Treise!" she answered without looking up. "Do not come close. It is not safe. Why are you here? Where is the king?"

"The king is safe. We are on the highest hill that way. Where the fire burns. Will you come to us?"

Dorren hesitated, and Terri could see the fear in her eyes. "When Conaire left, he took our courage with him. The body of Sean lies at the gate as a warning to any who might try to follow—and none have dared to try."

Sean! Lonan had dared to kill Sean, the old horsemaster! Terri thought her hatred for Lonan could not have become any more intense, but found that she was wrong . . . she had been wrong.

Terri fought down the impulse to walk straight inside Dun Cath and deal with Lonan herself. "Dorren, listen. The king returns tomorrow. Tomorrow." The woman looked stunned, but stayed crouched beside the stream. Terri unfastened the leather bag at her belt and held it out. "This is for you, Dorren. Here is what you must do—"

In moments, Terri was back on Firelair and riding for home. She would have flown to get back if she could, so eager was she to return, but she had no choice but to let the tired mare remain at a walk. They made their way slowly through the countryside, a step at a time, a step at a time—

And then fear hit Terri like a bolt of lightning. From out

of the forest beside her came horses, riders, the men of Dun Cath, Lonan's men, twenty, thirty of them!

In a moment of blind terror she drove her heels into Firelair's sides and sent her at a headlong gallop up the road toward the highest hill. The mare responded, but Terri could feel her laboring, could feel the exhaustion that was beginning to overtake her.

At any other time the small Celtic horses would not have had a chance of gaining on them. But now the pounding hoofbeats grew closer and the shouting of the men grew louder. She could hear Lonan's voice among them: "Treise Maeve! You have come back to me, Treise Maeve!"

She leaned down over the flying silver mane and spoke softly. "Take us home, Firelair," she whispered. "Take us home."

The great mare pinned back her ears and stretched out her neck. Terri could feel her digging in, reaching down, pulling up reserves of strength that could only have come from the heart. A sling-thrown rock went whizzing past Terri's ear, and a heavy spear bounced off a tree just beside them, but she no longer felt any fear.

No evil can touch the true mare ... and in a race, she will never be bested.

They galloped away into the hills, leaving Lonan and his cursing men and his dead, dying kingdom far behind.

It was long past dark when Terri and Firelair rode slowly up the side of the highest hill. Conaire waited for her, catching her as she slid down from the saddle, and though she braced herself for his disapproval, he only smiled.

"I am so glad you have returned," he said.

"Is Cormac here? Did you see them? They—"

"They're here. It's a fine day's work you've done. But now there are two of you in need of care." He walked with her toward the trees as the tired mare followed.

Terri stopped and looked up at him. "Tomorrow," she

said, placing her hand on his arm. "Tomorrow."

He shook his head gently. "Tomorrow we go," he answered. "Tomorrow the rest of them come home."

Terri knew that there was nothing she could do, nothing she could say, that would stop him. She could only pray that Dorren had understood her halting words, and would agree to do as she had asked.

It was a cold and misty dawn that saw a strange procession assemble itself on the top of the hill. Dary stood at the heads of the team of horses as they were harnessed to the chariot. Eight other fully armed men mounted their horses. And Terri sat waiting on the back of Firelair.

Just as Dary took up the reins and stepped into the chariot, King Conaire came striding out of the mist. Terri caught her breath, and a faint chill ran through her.

Gold gleamed at his wrists and throat. Over his woolen tunic was thrown a deerskin cape. Around his head was a coronet, a narrow band of gold, and attached to the coronet were the two-pronged antlers of a stag.

Terri shivered. Once before she had caught just such an image of him, when he had stood silhouetted before a tree beneath the night sky, and she had thought he resembled the devil of her modern world.

But now she understood. He wore the antlers as a powerful badge of masculinity, as a mark of his lordship of the forest, of his guardianship of all who lived in it. He was a prince of the woods, a king of the land, a horned god.

A king who would return to claim his own.

Somewhere behind the rolling gray clouds, the pale sun reached its height. Terri's heart pounded as the company rode up to the crooked, broken gates of Dun Cath.

"Lonan!"

The horses flinched as Conaire shouted into the silence. For a long moment they all stood waiting, listening, straining to hear the answer which certainly must come.

But there was nothing. Nothing but the banging of a broken window shutter as the wind toyed with it.

Conaire leaped out of the chariot and drew his sword. "Lonan! Come out and face me! I am here to take back what is mine!" And he walked through the gates, striding into Dun Cath until he stood alone on the half-bare lawn. The only sign of his long-repressed rage was the trembling of his upraised sword.

The other men glanced at each other. It seemed to Terri that she could hear their thoughts. *Where are they? Is it a trap? Why are they hiding?* But after a moment the eight riders followed their king through the gates, as did Terri. Only Dary and the chariot remained outside.

She looked around as they rode inside, trying not to show the anguish she felt at the terrible condition of the place. In just a few fortnights the buildings had begun to show damage and disrepair—doors and shutters missing or broken, the straw roofs full of gaps. One house looked as though it had suffered a fire. The few horses and cattle in the pens were thin and shaggy and listless. At least one cow lay unmoving on the filth-covered ground.

Where once there had been life and beauty and vitality, there was now only crumbling and decay. The great dun, the place Terri had grown to love as her own, had become a barren, dying thing, poisoned by a false usurping king.

Conaire glanced over his shoulder at his men. "Begin a search," he told them. "Every house, every shed, the *sou-terrains,* the refuse pits, all of it! Don't stop until—"

Terri caught her breath. The door of one of the houses was slowly moving open.

The rest of the men drew their swords. The door stopped. But as they all stared, and the tension reached its breaking point, a woman appeared in the doorway.

She stood very still and did not say a word. And then

another door creaked open, slowly, cautiously, and a second woman stood watching them.

Conaire lowered his sword. The other men did the same. "Mor!" he cried, to the first woman. "What has happened here? Where are the men? Where are—"

But Mor only glanced toward another of the houses. And from that house, and the one beside it, and the one beside it, and from the sheds and the forge-house and the Great Hall itself, emerged all the women of Dun Cath.

Terri felt that she could almost breathe again. Had they done it? Had they been successful?

"All the men are here, King Conaire," said Mor. She was the wife of one of the warriors, Terri knew, a calm and self-possessed lady. "All of them are safe. But none of them can speak to you right now."

"What do you mean?" demanded Conaire. He walked toward her, his frustration evident. "I must speak to them! I want to see them now!"

In answer, Mor stepped back and held the door open for the king. Conaire disappeared inside the house.

After a long moment, he came back out, with an expression of stunned surprise. He paused, staring up at his men where they sat on their horses, and then turned and dashed into the next house.

"Ros! Sivney!" he shouted, dashing out again. "Search every house until you find Lonan! And when you find him, bring him here to me!"

The two men dismounted and hurried to comply. Terri, unable to contain herself any longer, slid down from Firelair and went into the house where Mor waited.

Blinking in the half-darkness, she glanced quickly about the little house, and then she saw him. Mor's husband, the huge warrior Erevan, lay quietly on the bed against the wall. His head was comfortably pillowed, the heavy linen beneath him smooth and clean; but his hands were tied together behind his back, his ankles were bound together, and a gag of soft leather covered his mouth.

"He is one of Conaire's men, and always has been," Mor said. "But I explained to him what you asked Dorren to do. He agreed. He will not be unbound—nor will any man of Dun Cath—until King Conaire orders it."

Terri closed her eyes. They had done it. She had not dared to hope that Dorren would understand her—would agree to the plan—would convince the other women to do the same. But they had done it all, had followed her instructions to the letter.

She raced back outside and remounted Firelair. Trotting through the dun, she saw a woman standing in every doorway, and through the open doors she caught glimpses of men lying carefully, comfortably, and most efficiently bound and gagged.

"They've done it!" she said to Conaire as the mare swung back into line. "I asked the women to do this—to give the men a dose of Aine's powder in their wine, and keep them tied until the king arrived. I promised them that he would come to them, and they kept the promise they made to me!"

Her spirits soared. The king had returned and no one had died. No one had suffered so much as a scratch. Conaire could get his loyal men, and their families, and they could all ride away to a new life out on the highest hill.

But Conaire only closed his eyes. "You have spared many their lives this day," he said to her, "and for that I thank you. But this is not over yet."

Terri frowned. "What do you mean, it's not over yet? You can free the ones who want to go with us, and leave the rest here with Lonan! No war, no fighting, no death! That was why we did this—so no one would have to die!"

Conaire stared up at her for a long moment before turning away. Ros and Sivney were coming back to the lawn, dragging Lonan between them.

He seemed to have suffered no ill effects from Aine's

powder. He struggled and shouted and almost foamed at the mouth in his rage. Conaire stood and faced him with all the coolness of the conquering hero whose foe is hardly worth his notice.

"I see the weapons you fight with, Conaire!" roared Lonan. "Deceit and sorcery and lies and tricks! You would not come back and fight me the way men fight! You had to let your women do your fighting for you!"

Conaire did not move, but his glare turned to ice. "I have come only to take the men and women who want to go with me. No one will be forced to leave. I want only the ones who want me." He glanced over his shoulder at the rest of his company. "Bring all the men of Dun Cath to the lawn. Remove their bonds except for those on their hands. Hurry."

Terri could only watch as, one by one, the men were herded out of the houses and buildings and onto the lawn. Their eyes flicked left and right, but none of them said a word.

Conaire turned and spoke to them all. "The stranglehold that Lonan has placed upon Dun Cath ends now!" he cried. "All those who wish to come with me, move now to stand beside me. All who wish to stay with Lonan, move to stand beside him. I will take the ones who stand with me, and we will leave this place, and we will not return."

Again Terri dared to hope. This was what she had intended. No fighting, no death, just a simple choice and a rapid departure to—

But no one moved. A voice rang out over their heads. "By what authority do you order such a choice, Conaire?"

Hands bound, Brann pushed forward through the crowd. "You have no authority here. You were king, but you fled your own dun. You abandoned your people. Under the law, you are nothing here."

Brann was a druid, the chief druid, Terri remembered, her hands beginning to shake. He was the one who kept the laws. He kept the laws—and in this place, she knew, no one was above the law.

Not even a king.

Conaire's eyes narrowed. "You are right, Brann the druid," he said coolly. "I have no authority here any longer. But I am a king in my own country, and I return now as one who challenges Lonan."

"You want a fight at last, Conaire?" Lonan shouted. "I welcome it! Unbind my men! They will stand against the few who came here with you, and they will make an end of you at last!"

"I am not asking for a fight," Conaire said, and he almost smiled. "Except with you."

A hush fell over the gathering. Lonan actually turned pale. "First—let all your own men gather round you now!" Conaire declared. "Do it! Order them beside you!" After some hesitation, Lonan's eyes darted over the crowd, and perhaps a third of the men shuffled next to him.

"Now, cut their bonds. Free them." Gil and Falvy turned frowning looks on Conaire, but in a moment they had moved among Lonan's men and cut each one of them loose.

"Now you have your own men back, Lonan!" Conaire shouted. "Now you know the ones who are really yours! But I am not asking for a fight with them. I demand a single combat. A battle of kings!"

Lonan shrank back, but Conaire turned a fierce look on his enemy. "You say you are a king? Then be one! Defend your kingdom! Fight me one on one, man to man, king to king—or have you forgotten how to do that? Look around you! You have twenty free men. Most of mine are still bound! What are you afraid of, Lonan?"

Now Terri understood. This was something Lonan could not refuse, not if he wished to remain a king. This was something that would leave no further doubt. There would be a one-on-one fight between the men who claimed the kingdom—a battle that could only end with the death of one of them.

At any other time, Terri would not have feared for Conaire. He was more than a match for Lonan. But Lonan had twenty men at his back, twenty angry, fanatical men. Men who had already proved they had no honor and played by no rules but their own—and Lonan's.

In an instant, it seemed, both Conaire and Lonan had swords in their hands and were circling each other. Terri expected to see a drawn-out battle, a ritual, almost, leading slowly to the end. But to her shock, Lonan shouted something out and ran straight at Conaire with his sword held high.

All twenty of his men followed him.

Terri thought her heart would stop. "No!" she cried, and set her heels to Firelair's sides. What could she do? They were already upon him! She was too late! It was all for nothing, all for nothing—

But before she could get close, the rush of men stopped. They waited, tense and staring, in a half circle around the fighters, as Conaire dragged Lonan's back against him and held his sword to the other man's throat.

"What shall it be, then?" asked Conaire, his gaze flicking from face to face. "Is this man still your king? In a battle of kings, he struck not a single blow before I subdued him! Do you want him back? Or shall I kill him?"

The mob of men shifted slightly. "Kill him," came one voice.

"Kill him," added another.

Conaire almost laughed. "Do you see, Lonan, the kind of men you chose? They are as loyal to you as they were to me."

Viciously he yanked Lonan's head back. The mob tensed, but made no move to stop him. And then they all went stumbling backwards as Conaire shoved Lonan into their midst and sent him sprawling in the dirt.

"The answer to this does not lie in death," Conaire said, standing over him. "You will live in shame and exile for the rest of your days—you, and your brother Brann, and your twenty *loyal* men." He reached down and picked up the fallen man's sword. "I have learned that such a life is far worse than death. You will not have anyone like Treise Maeve to heal you and give you the strength to be a king. You will be *ri na folus,* the king of emptiness."

He started to walk away, but then he paused. Reaching down again, he caught hold of something on Lonan's belt and jerked it free.

Conaire turned his back on Lonan and his men. Walking over to Terri, he carefully placed the object in her hand and folded her fingers around it. "I believe this is yours, *banrion,*" he said.

Terri opened her hand. On her palm rested her shining golden ring.

Over the next few hours, Conaire and Terri and all of their people stripped Dun Cath bare of its furnishings. The largest pieces, like the weaving looms and the cauldrons and all the iron tools, were loaded into the single wagon and the other two chariots. Anything that had belonged to Lonan and his followers was piled at their feet. The rest was bundled and tied onto horses and oxen and strong men's backs.

When everything was packed and ready to go, and the remaining animals herded outside, Lonan's group was escorted out the gates and set onto the path into the bogland toward the north. They said nothing, and did not look back, but walked slowly away until they vanished into the wood.

"We will not see them again, I think," Conaire said. Then he turned to Terri. "Banrion Treise Maeve—my men and I have one more task left to us. Will you show the rest of your people the way to the highest hill? We will catch up to you in a short time."

She nodded, and rode Firelair just in front of Dary and his chariot. As she started up the path, the whole crowd followed her, a happy mob of creaking chariots and mooing cattle and laughing, shouting people.

Terri kept the pace slow, and was careful to follow the widest and smoothest of the paths. After a time, she heard galloping footsteps, and turned to see Conaire and his men rejoining them.

But there was something else behind them, too—a column of thick black smoke rising into the sky.

Terri did not have to ask what the smoke was from. The old dun was burning. Conaire and his men were returning it to the land from which it had been built, freeing it from the desecration that a wrongful king had visited upon it.

As Conaire rode up beside her, she kept Firelair on the road toward the highest hill, to the place that was now and forever home.

The months passed by. With so many people now taking part in the building, the new dun rose quickly from the top of the hill. A huge circular wall of rocks and logs and earth marked off the boundary. There was a Great Hall, two stories high, which provided shelter while the houses were being built. And as he had once promised, Conaire himself helped raise the tall new barn for Firelair.

The work would continue for months and years to come, but Terri had no doubt that the fortress they were building would last for many centuries.

No doubt at all.

At last, on the evening of the summer solstice, Terri walked outside the walls and stood on the very edge of the hilltop. She moved a bit slower these days, since it would only be another two months or so before her baby arrived. But she sat down and made herself comfortable, watching the sunset as she always liked to do.

Far below in the twilight she could see the white limestone cliffs. She had known a time when those cliffs over-looked a modern inn, but right now horses grazed freely over the acres of lush grass. Firelair's silver coat was visible in the dusk even at this distance. She had taken quite happily to being a part of the broodmare herd, and even more so to the attentions of Conaire's fine red stallion.

"I knew I would find you here," said a voice behind her.

Conaire walked to the edge of the hilltop and extended his hand down to her. "They're waiting for us. It's time."

Terri grasped his wrist and allowed him to help her to her feet. She started to go with him back through the gates, but then paused, looking out at the sunset once again.

"Has it really been a year?" she whispered.

"It has," he answered, gazing out at the magnificent scene with her. "It was a year ago today that we found one another. And allow me to tell you, Treise Maeve, for some-one who insisted that she did not want to be a queen, you have done . . . rather well."

She lifted her chin, and then smiled. "I thought that queens belonged to kings—but I found out that kings also belong to queens."

"And I believe I tried to tell you that all along." He smiled back at her, but then his expression became serious. "You are certain of this now? You are happy, truly, with the thought of being queen?"

Terri paused, and then looked over her shoulder at the massive wall behind them. "When you build a place, when you make it with your own hands, when you help to bring together the people who truly want to be there—that is what makes a queen. Not the whim of a king. And that is what I have learned."

She turned back to him, and he drew her close and held her in his arms. "I am so glad to hear you say it," he answered. "But I have not forgotten your great desire for freedom. Here is what I propose: I will give the days to you, if you will give the nights to me. You will be queen of the sun, while I will be king of the moon.''

Terri took a step back and looked up at him. "Queen of the sun," she said, with a slight frown. Then she grinned. "I do believe I will accept your proposal, King Conaire."

He held her close, and then walked with her back inside the walls.

The people were gathered and waiting near the center of the dun. Beside them was an enormous mound of carefully stacked wood, surrounded by a neat ring of stones. Terri walked to the edge of stones and accepted a torch from one of the men.

"Now, on this the shortest night of the year, we celebrate the building of a new home, a new kingdom," she said. "Now and forever this place shall be known as Dun Solas, the fortress of light, the center of Conaire's kingdom. And every year to come, on this night, I myself will light this fire, now and forever."

And with that she threw the flaming torch high into the air and watched it land on the mountain of wood.

In a few moments, the great bonfire was blazing away. There was only one more thing for her to do.

From a small drawstring bag at her waist she took out her golden ring. How lovely it was, shining like something brand-new, reflecting the light of the great fire before it.

Terri held out the ring and tossed it directly into the center of the bonfire. As it disappeared, she knew that her journey was now finished. The circle was complete, just like the circle of flame carved into the golden ring—an unbroken circle of flame.

PATRICIA GAFFNEY **Fortune's Lady**

"Like moonspun magic...one of the best historical romances I have read in a decade!" —Cassie Edwards

They are natural enemies—traitor's daughter and zealous patriot—yet the moment he sees Cassandra Merlin at her father's graveside, Riordan knows he will never be free of her. She is the key to stopping a heinous plot against the king's life, yet he senses she has her own secret reasons for aiding his cause. Her reputation is in shreds, yet he finds himself believing she is a woman wronged. Her mission is to seduce another man, yet he burns to take her luscious body for himself. She is a ravishing temptress, a woman of mystery, yet he has no choice but to gamble his heart on fortune's lady.

_4153-7 $5.99 US/$6.99 CAN

The Rose of Ravenscrag

Patricia Phillips

Bestselling Author Of *The Constant Flame*

The daughter of a nobleman and a common peasant, Rosamund believes she is doomed to marry a simple swineherd. Then a desperate ruse sweeps the feisty lass from her rustic English village to a faraway castle. And even as Rosamund poses as the betrothed of a wealthy lord, she cannot deny the desire he rouses in her soul. A warrior in battle, and a conqueror in love, Henry of Ravenscrag is all she has ever dreamed of in a husband. But the more Rosamund's passion flares for the gallant who has captured her spirited heart, the more she dreads he will cast her aside if he ever discovers the truth about her.

_3905-2 $4.99 US/$6.99 CAN

DESPERADO

SANDRA HILL

Major Helen Prescott has always played by the rules. That's why Rafe Santiago nicknamed her ''Prissy'' at the military academy years before. Rafe's teasing made her life miserable back then, and with his irresistible good looks, he is the man responsible for her one momentary lapse in self control. When a routine skydive goes awry, the two parachute straight into the 1850 California Gold Rush. Mistaken for a notorious bandit and his infamously sensuous mistress, they find themselves on the wrong side of the law. In a time and place where rules have no meaning, Helen finds Rafe's hard, bronzed body strangely comforting, and his piercing blue eyes leave her all too willing to share his bedroll. Suddenly, his teasing remarks make her feel all woman, and she is ready to throw caution to the wind if she can spend every night in the arms of her very own desperado.

_52182-2 $5.99 US/$6.99 CAN

Lord Byron thinks he's a scream, the fashionable matrons titter behind their fans at a glimpse of his hard form, and nobody knows where he came from. His startling eyes—one gold, one blue—promise a wicked passion, and his voice almost seems to purr. There is only one thing a woman thinks of when looking at a man like that. *Sex.* And there is only one woman he seems to want. *Lilac.* In her wildest dreams she never guesses that bringing a stray cat into her home will soon have her stroking the most wanted man in 1811 London....

_52178-4 $5.99 US/$6.99 CAN

MIRIAM RAFTERY

Taylor James's wrinkled Shar-Pei, Apollo, is always getting into trouble. But the young beauty never expects her mischievous puppy to lead her on the romantic adventure of a lifetime—from a dusty old Victorian attic to the strong arms of Nathaniel Stuart and his turn-of-the-century charm. One minute Taylor and Apollo are in modern-day San Francisco, and the next thing Taylor knows, a shift in the earth's crust, a wrinkle in time, and the lovely historian finds herself facing the terror of California's most infamous earthquake—and a love so monumental it threatens to shake the foundations of her world.

_52084-2 $4.99 US/$6.99 CAN